RAVAGED

A Bicultural Series

Book Two

Kera C. Munnings

2026

Disclaimer

This book is a work of fiction. Unless otherwise indicated, all the names, characters, places, events, and incidents in this book are the product of the author's imagination and used in a fictitious manner. Any resemblance to actual people, living or dead, or actual events is purely coincidental.

Author: Shakera Munnings

www.sommersetwaynovels.com

TAKEN – A Bicultural Series Book One

RAVAGE – A Bicultural Series Book Two

FATE – A Bicultural Series Book Three

Content Advisory

This novel contains themes of violence, abuse, and trauma that may be distressing to some readers.

Dedication

This book is dedicated to Ronel Sands, Carpenter.

Thank you for supporting me and for always believing in me. I cannot recall a single time you dismissed one of my ideas as foolish. Instead, you challenged me to examine them, strengthen them, and see them through.

Thank you for the push.

Prologue

Mischievous Lad

Tantallon, Scotland 1612

*T*he heat of a long summer day clung to the stone walls of

Tantallon as Alex Barton slipped away from the castle grounds with a pack of restless lads trailing behind him. Seventeen summers today, finally old enough, in his mind, to commit every foolish sin he'd been dreaming about.

They had spent a full fortnight planning this escape.

Tonight, they will ride to Dalkeith.

Tonight, they would see the new brothel Rory would not shut his mouth about.

Dalkeith was three hours away, but the promise of forbidden pleasure made the distance feel like nothing.

Rory, barely out of boyhood and already insufferably proud of himself, tipped back a flask. The echo of his swallow drifted across the quiet field.

"Aye, lads, when my father took me through Dalkeith last month, we stopped at that establishment. I dinna lie, one of the wenches pleased me so well I thought my heart would leap from my chest when I came."

Alex barked a laugh.

"A serving girl once tried that with me, but her breath smelled of mutton. I nearly gagged. These ladies ye speak of better be worth the ride."

Rory grinned. "Aye, trust me, they are."

Behind him, Andrew groaned for what felt like the tenth time. "Alex, ye're such a whore. Why must ye ride tae another town? There are a dozen lassies chasing after ye at the keep."

"Aye, and every last one comes with that meddling governess who tattles tae Mother. My ears still ring from her shoutin."

"But Alex," his younger brother Andrew interrupted, "this plan will get us caught."

Alex snapped in annoyance. "If ye're afraid, Andrew, then go home. I'm tired of yer damn whining. Still sucking on Ma's teat, are ye? Go home, crybaby."

The lads erupted into laughter; Andrew's face tightened with embarrassment.

"But Da said…"

"But Da said my arse. Ye always want tae follow but never have the guts tae see anythin through. Go home before ye ruin the night for the rest of us."

The boys howled again until Logan leaned forward on his horse with a smirk. "I think Andrew's afraid tae touch a woman's tits."

Rory added, "The only tit he's ever seen was his mother's!"

That jab landed wrong.

Alex struck Rory hard enough to knock him clean off his horse.

"Mind yer tongue. That's my mother ye insult, and yer laird's wife."

Rory threw up both hands in surrender from the dirt. "Fine, fine. I only jest."

"Aye? Jest about how yer sister tried sneaking into my chamber last winter? Easy lass, that one. I only turned her away because she smelled ripe."

Rory's face darkened to a furious red.

"And yet ye're still a virgin."

"And yet yer sister is still a whore. Ask Haemish, he had his fill."

Haemish stiffened atop his horse, jaw tight. "Dinnae drag me into yer quarrel."

Logan stepped between them before the air could ignite again. "Lads, enough. This journey was supposed tae be fun. We're all mates."

Andrew caught Alex's arm. "Come on, Al. Let's go home. If Ma or Da finds us missing…"

"Leave me be." Alex shook him off without looking back.

Andrew's shoulders sagged. "Fine. I'm going home. But 'tis yer arse if Da finds out. I'm not covering for ye this time.

Chapter One

A- Las Home

*A*ndrew bent low at the edge of the woods, watching the castle guards pace along the ramparts while sweat trickled down his brow.

"How in the devil am I supposed tae get back inside? The gates have extra men on duty this eve."

His eyes swept the grounds. His heart thumped when loud barking split the quiet.

"Did Father release the hounds searching for us? Saints preserve… he'll flog us till dawn."

The fear eased when he caught the familiar sound. Only Una, their family hound, chasing a cat that darted up a tree. The daft beast slipped out most nights, and Andrew was always the poor soul hunting her across the yard.

Tonight, Una might actually save his hide.

He patted his thigh. "Una, here, lass."

She ignored him, too intent on the cat.

"UNA! COME!"

The dog plopped down and panted, tongue lolling. Andrew stomped toward her and caught her by the scruff.

"Ye daft creature… absolutely useless."

But as he led her toward the castle, his nerves tightened with every step. He whispered,
"Still… ye might've saved my arse from a proper thrashin."

A sharp whistle from the rampart made him jump. A guard called out through the night air.

"Who goes there? Andrew or Alex?"

"'Tis me, Andrew, the laird's second son."

One of the senior guards leaned forward into the torchlight.

"What in God's good name are ye doin' outside the keep at this hour?"

"Una's silly behind ran off chasin' a cat. I was in the kitchens when she bolted for the woods."

The guard squinted. "Is that nae your horse tied tae a tree over yonder?"

Andrew froze. "Err… aye. She went deep intae the woods. With wolves about, I figured my horse would keep me safe."

The man snorted. "Aye. Well, get inside before yer father skins ye alive."

"Aye, my thanks."

Andrew slipped through the back entrance, kept low as he took the servants' stairs, and hurried down the dim corridor until he reached his chamber. Relief washed over him when the door clicked shut behind him.

"Saints above…" He let out a breath. "Whew."

He stripped off clothes that reeked of whisky and horse, splashed cold water over his face, then lit the hearth. As the flames flickered, his thoughts drifted straight to his brother.

"Daft. Alex is as pig headed as a wild boar. He'll nae listen tae anyone. When will he ever learn?"

A yawn pulled at him as he crossed the room, the heat from the hearth warming his face.

He stretched, blinked, and scrubbed a hand over his eyes.

Unsure of his surroundings, a shape settled into focus at the edge of his vision. Someone sat quietly in the chair near the hearth.

Andrew froze mid breath. "What the devil… Da?"

His worst nightmare waited there in absolute stillness. It was his father.

Laird Calum Barton sat with his arms folded, leather belt laid across his lap with quiet promise.

The set of his jaw spoke more than any shout ever could.

Andrew swallowed hard and thought, *St Peter, save me… I'm gonna die.*

His father spoke low and steady, danger woven through every word.

"Son. I'll ask ye once. Where in the devil have ye been? And where is yer pig headed brother?"

Andrew swallowed hard. "I… I think he's asleep in his chamber?"

Calum lifted an eyebrow, the kind that stripped every lie bare. Andrew could fool anyone else, but never his father.

Calum rose slowly, rolling up his sleeves as Andrew's back pressed to the wall.

Panic hit first, then instinct. The lie spilled before he could think.

"After the evenin' meal, we went tae the stables with Rory, Logan, and Haemish. I… I saw Una chasin' a cat, so I followed her out."

"Do I have ARSE written across my forehead?"

His voice exploded through the chamber, sharp enough to rattle the hinges.

"I checked the stables hours ago. Ye were nowhere tae be seen. And both horses gone. Ye left Barton lands."

"Da, wait. I can explain…"

"You have less than a breath tae speak the truth before I peel the hide from yer backside."

Andrew trembled. It took one breath, and everything spilled out. "Alex, Logan, Rory, and Haemish talked about visitin' a brothel in Dalkeith. I dinnae want tae go, so I came home."

"WHAT?" Calum roared. "A BROTHEL? Have ye lads lost yer wits entirely? Do ye ken what filth crawls through a place like that?!"

"BUT FATHER, I DIDNAE GO!"

"But father, my ARSE! Ye're fourteen summers! Ye shouldnae have stepped a single foot off these lands! Anything could've happened tae ye!"

The belt came next.

Sharp whistles split the air with every strike.

"Da! Da! Ouch, Da, I'm sorry! I only went tae talk Alex out o' it!"

The door burst open. Lady Andrea rushed in.

"Calum! Cease this instant!"

"This is nae abuse, Andrea. I'm disciplinin' this reckless wee welp before he gets himself killed!"

"If ye dinnae kill him first, Calum!" she snapped back, stepping forward like she meant to snatch the belt from his hand.

Two more lashes cracked through the room before Andrew's body flew, tossed aside like a sack of tatties.

"Da, please!" Andrew winced, fighting tears that burned his eyes and his pride.

At last, Calum stepped back.

Andrew pushed himself off the floor, rubbing his stinging backside, breath shaking.

"I tried tae stop Alex. I told him ye'd be furious. He dinnae listen. He only wanted tae impress his daft friends. I told him tae come home, but he shoved me off and told me tae leave him be."

Calum didn't answer. He stormed from the chamber, boots shaking the floor.

Moments later, shouts echoed through the courtyard.

"OPEN THE GATES!"

Andrew rushed to the window. Fathers of Rory, Logan, and Haemish galloped out of the keep, torches blazing.

He winced. "Da went easy on me. God help Alex."

One Night of Pleasure Turned to Chaos.

Alex drank deep from the flask he'd stolen from his father's solar, coughing as the burn hit his chest. The lads erupted in cheers.

"Tis my birthday celebration!" he declared, lifting the flask again. "Tonight, we make ourselves full men!"

Rory whooped. Logan slapped the side of his horse. Haemish only shook his head, but the corner of his mouth tugged into a smile.

They rode hard through the summer dusk, hooves drumming a reckless rhythm over packed earth. Lanterns flickered in the distance as Dalkeith rose before them, the town restless and bright even at the late hour.

"There she is," Rory breathed, his eyes shining as the lively wooden building came into view. A brothel. Lanterns glowing, music and laughter spilled into the night.

Alex grinned. "Saints above, would ye listen tae that?"

Inside, they were hit by heat and noise all at once.

Laughter, pipe smoke, and the sound of coins. Men hunched over cards. A woman straddled a man in open view, skirts hiked shamelessly, his hands gripping the swell of her hips as she threw her head back and laughed.

Every lad's jaw dropped.

"Sweet merciful Christ," Logan whispered. "We're in heaven."

A stern older woman strode toward them, hands on ample hips, eyes sharp as a hawk's.

"Can I help ye lads?" she demanded. "I've nothin' needin' fixin', and the hour's late."

Before Alex could open his mouth, Logan blurted, "I'd like a lass, please."

The madam barked a laugh. "A lass? Saints preserve us, ye look barely out o' the cradle. The milk's still fresh on yer faces."

Rory bristled. "I've more hair on me chest than half the men in here."

Alex fished out a pouch and let it thump heavy into his palm. The madam's gaze dropped. Her entire demeanor shifted with the speed of a well-practiced woman.

"Well now, if ye've coin, I've rooms. Come along."

She led them down a narrow corridor, candles flickering along the walls, muffled sounds coming from closed doors. Low moans. Laughter. The creak of beds. The lads tried not to stare and failed utterly.

She stopped and pushed open one door, then pointed at Rory and Haemish. "In ya go, lads."

Haemish stalled in the doorway, eyes widening at the sight of a single bed.

"I am no' sharin' a room just tae watch Rory's hairy backside bounce in the dark," he muttered.

Rory shoved his shoulder. "Ye'll be lucky if ye see anything but the pillow, ye great lump."

The madam rolled her eyes. "Ye're not here tae look at each other. Ye're here tae learn how tae use what God gave ye. Get inside."

Grumbling, they went.

She turned back to the others, plucked two young women from the stairs, both in bright chemises and practiced smiles.

"I think every lad here is still a virgin," she announced dryly. "Give them an experience they will not forget."

Logan and Alex each earned their own doors.

Alex stepped into his room, suddenly painfully aware of his own heartbeat. Lantern light softened the small space, a tiny hearth smoldering to the left. The bed looked barely big enough for one person, let alone two.

"Why am I bloody anxious?" he muttered. "I can do this. I can do this."

He inhaled once, deep and steady, and almost choked on the scent, lavender oil and musk, something warm and unfamiliar that curled low in his belly.

The door opened again. The madam guided in a raven-haired girl with quick, careful eyes.

"Do not be shy," the older woman instructed, giving the lass a gentle push before closing the door behind her.

Silence fell.

The girl cleared her throat. "Eh, em… yer… very young."

Alex bowed too quickly, nearly smacking his head on nothing.

"Good eve, miss. I'm Alex."

"I'm Sophie," she replied, a timid smile touching her lips. "Well… shall we begin?"

His mouth went dry.

"Aye… I… suppose we shall."

They undressed in an awkward, fumbling way. There were two people who knew what they were here for but had never done this particular dance together.

For him, it was worse. Every button suddenly stiff, every movement feeling too loud.

Everything about the moment felt painfully transactional.

She took his hand gently, guiding him toward the bed. When he leaned in, desperate just to feel something soft and human, she stopped him with a hand to his chest.

"No kissing."

He froze. "Brilliant… How am I supposed tae get myself ready now?"

Alex sat stiffly on the edge of the bed, feeling young and foolish and far too sober.

Sophie watched him for a long beat.

"Are ye nervous?"

"Nae," he said at once, which only made it more obvious. He scrubbed a hand through his hair. "It's just… I thought my first time would be different. This is… awkward. I cannae even get… I cannae get my body tae cooperate."

She pressed her hands over her mouth, shoulders shaking with a giggle she tried, and failed, to smother.

"This is your first time," she breathed. "I never thought my first client would be a virgin."

Alex shot to his feet, humiliation burning hot.

"Look, am I gettin' my coin back or what?"

The laughter vanished from her eyes. Real fear flashed there. A refund on her first night would earn her more than a scolding.

"Nae, please wait." She stepped toward him quickly. "You must have patience, young pup."

"I am not a young pup," he snapped. "I'm near grown. And you dinnae look that old yourself."

Her grin returned, softer this time, her rosy cheeks dimpling.

"Well, I'm twenty summers."

That made everything worse. She was older. Experienced. And she found him amusing.

His ears went scarlet.

She reached for his hand again, gentler now, and tugged him back toward the bed.

"Come, Alex. There is naught wrong with nerves."

Then she let her chemise slide from her shoulders and fall away.

Alex's breath left him in one sharp, helpless rush.

In all his days, he had never seen a naked woman before. Whether from the drink or the shock, his head spun. Heat shot through him so fast he nearly swayed.

He dropped his gaze, mortified.

Sophie gave a soft, wicked giggle.

"Ye're awful bashful for a lad who came seekin' a woman," she murmured.

"I… aye, well… dinnae judge me. I thought my first time would be less… clumsy. My body's actin' like a daft fool."

Her eyes softened.

"Saints above… a virgin. Who would've thought?"

He made a strangled noise. "If ye say that word one more time, I may throw myself out the window."

She laughed, the sound warm instead of cruel.

"Dinnae worry, Alex. We'll fix that tonight."

She guided him down onto the bed, her touch surprisingly tender, not at all the rough, hurried transaction he'd pictured. Her hands mapped the lines of his shoulders, the tense set of his jaw, the way his chest rose too fast.

"Breathe," she whispered. "Just breathe."

He tried. God help him, he tried.

"This is… truly happenin'?" His voice broke on the last word.

"Aye. It is."

Everything after that unfolded in a blur of heat and discovery. Her body moved over his in a slow, coaxing rhythm, teaching his own what to do. The press of her, the warmth, the slide of skin against skin, it unraveled him. He clutched at the sheets, at her waist, at anything that would keep him tethered to the moment.

He choked on his words. "Ye feel… God… St. Peter… Sophie, I dinnae know what tae say."

"Then dinnae try. Just feel." She rocked her hips slowly.

Courage, wild and new, surged through him. He cupped her face, drawing her down for a kiss, soft and greedy all at once, pouring into it every feeling he had no language for.

She stilled, surprise flickering across her features, then melted into it before pulling back with a breathless laugh.

"Ye're dangerous, lad. Kissin's how a lass loses her heart."

"I dinnae want tae be just a coin in your hand. Not with ye."

Her movements changed. Gentled. Deepened. She rode him in a slow, rolling rhythm, the kind that slipped under his skin and rewrote everything he thought he knew about pleasure. Her soft cries brushed the edge of his hearing, feeding something fierce and protective in him.

She's no' just a girl in a brothel, he realized dimly. She's a woman who's been through hell.

That thought made him bolder.

He gripped her hips, rolling suddenly, turning her beneath him with more enthusiasm than grace.

"My turn…" he breathed against her neck, a boyish grin tugging at his mouth.

She gasped, the sound half laughter, half shock, as he settled above her. The bed creaked beneath them, protesting each new movement, but neither spared it a thought. His body found a rhythm, clumsy at first, then surer as he listened to her sounds, adjusted to the way she arched, the way her fingers dug into his shoulders.

"Oh… saints…" she whispered, his name breaking from her in fractured syllables.

Each sound stoked his confidence. He tried a different angle, a deeper stroke, something one of the old guards had once bragged about by the firepit. Her response was immediate, a sharp inhale, a shudder that ran the length of her.

"So ye liked that?" he managed, voice rough.

Her answer came in the way she clung to him, the way she moved to meet him, the way her breath hitched when he slowed, then quickened again. It was as if her body spoke a language he was suddenly desperate to learn fluently.

"Alex…" she gasped, close to breaking.

He felt the tension coil in him, tight and relentless, every muscle taut. The warnings from the guards flashed through his mind in crude fragments, what to do, what not to do, how not tae land himself in trouble.

At the last moment, he broke the rhythm, fighting his own instincts, and spilled outside, letting out a groan that felt torn from his bones.

"You all right?" she panted, searching his face.

"Aye, I'm going back in."

He let his forehead fall to her shoulder, shaking with effort, then dragged in a ragged breath and found control again. When he moved once more, it was slower, deeper, his hand sliding lower between them, clumsy but reverent.

He remembered another snatch of guard talk, half whisper, half boast.

Mind her pleasure, lad. Mind that, and she'll never forget ye.

He obeyed.

Her reaction was immediate. Sophie's head tipped back, eyes fluttering shut as a choked cry left her throat. Her fingers clawed at his back, not to push him away, but to pull him closer. The bed rocked under them, its frame protesting the fervor.

"Alex… oh, Christ…" she cried, voice breaking.

The sound of it nearly undid him. He pressed his mouth to her neck, her shoulder, swallowing her cries, letting them sink into his skin as if he could keep them.

When she broke, truly broke, her entire body bowed up against him, every muscle drawn taut, a strangled shout tearing from her chest. He felt it, felt the way she shuddered around him, felt the wild, stunned awe, not knowing he could give such a thing.

She collapsed back onto the mattress, trembling.

"And ye say… ye were a virgin."

He managed a breathless laugh, chest heaving.

He grinned. "Aye, I was a virgin. No' a monk."

Something in her face softened at that. A laugh slipped free, genuine and astonished all at once.

"You're the best I've ever had," he blurted, too honest, too proud.

She burst into laughter. "Lad, I'm the only you ever had."

They lay there for a spell, the air thick with spent heat and something quieter. The Lantern light threw soft gold along the curve of her spine. For the first time since entering, Alex's wild thoughts settled long enough to truly see her.

Sophie drew in a slow breath.

"I have worked in other places like this," she said at last. "But never by choice."

He turned his head, watching her profile as she told her life story in broken pieces, her voice steady where it should have broken.

There were fifteen siblings on a crowded farm. Never enough food. The elder children slept in stables.

A stranger with plenty of coin and cold eyes noticed her and forced her into a marriage, not for love, but because her parents needed the money.

During the marriage, there were harsh words. Hard fists that came down. A brutal wedding night she could not forget.

In that home, servants forced themselves on her while her husband was away. When he returned, they reached him before she could. He believed them.

The marriage ended when he beat her until the world went black, leaving her body for the wolves.

She showed Alex the scar on her shoulder. Another at the nape of her neck, hidden by her dark hair.

"My loving husband dumped my body there," she said, her voice flat with remembered pain. "A band of traveling minstrels happened upon me instead. Good folk. They took me in. But they were always moving, always on the road. I feared being taken again, so I slipped away. Came tae Edinburgh. Worked in an alehouse for little more than a roof and a warm meal. When I heard talk of this place and the coin the women made…" She gave a small, bitter shrug. "I kenned at least here I might buy a future for myself. Or so I thought."

Alex's throat tightened.

"That is… awful," he said, the words feeling far too small.

"It was life," she answered. "No' the one I wanted. Just the one I got."

He reached out, almost without thinking, and tucked a strand of hair behind her ear.

"Ye're too bonnie for such a place," he said quietly. "Too good for it. If I come back for ye… would ye go with me? Let me take care of ye. Be the man ye deserve."

Sophie laughed softly, not unkindly.

"You're just a lad," she murmured. "Where could ye possibly take me?"

"My father's keep," he said at once. "We always need chambermaids. I'll talk tae my mother. Ye'd be safe there."

"Alex," she sighed, shaking her head. "I cannot accept. 'Tis too much tae place on your shoulders. You only speak this way because it was your first time. In a few days, you'll forget my name."

Her words stung him. "I willnae… dinnae say that."

She leaned in and kissed his cheek, a soft brush that felt more intimate than anything they'd done on the bed.

"If ye were another six summers older, we might have hit it off. Yer excellent at bed sport."

His pride flared. He slid his hand between her thighs with boldness born of stupid, youthful certainty.

"I'll come back," he said, breathless and sure all at once. "I'll speak tae my mother. I'll get ye work at the keep. Sophie… life can be better.

She faltered. Hope flickered behind her eyes, fragile as blown glass.

Before she could answer.

BOOM. BOOM. BOOM.

The door shook so violently dust fell from the rafters.

Alex and Sophie jolted upright, their hearts slamming against their ribs.

He snatched his dagger from the nightstand on pure instinct, because what else does a half-dressed, terrified young man grab in a brothel?

"Alex, 'tis me, Logan! Yer father, Laird Barton, is downstairs. All o' our fathers are!"

Alex's blood ran cold. "Shite."

Logan mocked him. "Aye, shite. Open the bloody door man! They havenae spotted me yet!"

Alex scrambled into his clothes, hopping on one foot as he tried to jam his heel into a boot. He yanked the door open just long enough for Logan to slip inside like a frightened fox, then slammed it shut.

Logan braced his hands on his knees, gulping air.
"Saints, I nearly ran straight into me Da…"

His fear melted in a heartbeat when he saw Sophie lying naked.

"Well now… hello, bonnie."

"Back off, Logan," Alex snapped, shoving him. "She's my woman."

Logan lifted a brow. "Yer woman? Alex, ye dinnae even ken what she likes for breakfast."

"Doonae question me."

Another round of blows crashed into the door.

From the hall came Mrs. Butler's shrill voice. "Laird, ye cannae go in there! I have employees at work!"

Alex's father roared back, his voice easily cutting through the walls. "I ken my son is in there with one o' yer filthy whores! Now open this door before I break it clean off the hinges!"

Sophie's eyes flew wide.

"He sounds enormous," she whispered.

"He is," Alex hissed. "He's my Da!"

Logan slapped a hand over Alex's mouth. "Dinnae shout, ye daft shite! He'll hear ye!"

The doorframe cracked under the next hit.

Both boys let out the most unmanly squeaks of their lives.

"Window," Logan said, grabbing Alex by the shoulders. "Now. Before yer father skins us alive."

"Aye!"

They bolted. Alex tripped over his own discarded shirt. Logan tripped over Alex. Both slammed into the wall like badly aimed arrows.

Sophie flung a hand toward the latch. "Lift it, you fools! Lift it!"

Alex fumbled it once. Twice. "Shite! It's stuck!"

"Use yer hands, man!" Logan snapped.

On the third try, it flew open. Cool night air blasted in.

"Go!" Logan shoved him.

Alex threw one leg over the sill, lost his balance, and toppled headfirst into the dark.

"SHIIIIITE!"

Logan winced and looked back at Sophie. "If he lives, tell him I jumped gracefully."

"You will not," she replied flatly.

He jumped anyway.

They landed together on a branch that bowed, creaked, and then promptly snapped clean through, sending both lads straight into a hedgerow in a storm of leaves.

Above them, the door to Sophie's chamber burst open.

Alex heard his father's voice boom through the night.
"Where is my son, ye whore?"

Sophie's reply came thin but steady. "I beg your pardon. As ye can see, there is no one here."

"Do not lie tae me, whore!" Calum thundered. "That is my son's dagger on that table!"

Down in the hedge, Logan turned to Alex, eyes round as coins.

Alex mouthed one silent, heartfelt word. *Fuck.*

Logan nodded, whispering back, "Aye. We're in deep shite."

They didn't wait for more.

Both boys tore free of the bushes and ran as if hell itself chased them, sprinting across the yard, dodging a barrel, nearly colliding with a bewildered chicken. They scrambled into their saddles with all the grace of drunken goats.

Behind them, Calum Barton's roar split the night.

"ALEXANDER ROBERT BARTON! YE LITTLE WHELP! GET BACK HERE!"

Alex slapped his horse's flank. "Ride, man! RIDE!"

Logan's laughter was wild, half terror, half exhilaration as they galloped into the darkness, the brothel shrinking behind them and the consequences waiting ahead.

I'm a Man

A few hours later, Alex and Logan trotted across Barton lands, the keep rising pale in the early morning light. Dew clung to the grass, the air cool and sharp, but Logan still looked over his shoulder every few steps, as though expecting his father to thunder into view.

"Alex," he whispered, voice cracking, "what are ye gonnae do when ye get inside?"

"Nothing," Alex answered, lifting his chin as if already victorious. "I'll take my punishment like a man."

Logan swallowed hard.
"Aye, well… my da is gonnae skin me alive."

"Logan, stop greetin' like a scared cat. With great reward comes great responsibility. We kent our fate if we were caught. There's nae use shiverin' in yer boots now."

Logan nodded miserably and pulled his horse toward his family's cottage.
"If we dinnae meet again, ken that last night was worth every second."

Alex laughed and dismounted before the castle gates, striding across the courtyard with the confidence of a lad twice his age. His night with Sophie had puffed him up with a sense of manhood he had no idea how to carry.

A soldier near the gate chuckled.
"Ye best hide, lad. When Laird Calum catches ye, ye'll be good as dead."

Alex ignored him and marched inside.

In the great hall, Lady Andrea sat near the hearth, half dozing after a sleepless night. The instant the doors creaked open, she sprang upright. Fury lit her eyes like sparks leaping from the fire. Alex had not even crossed the threshold before she seized his ear and twisted hard.

"Ow! Mother, that hurts!"

She dragged him across the hall, her small frame fueled with righteous anger. Servants looked up from their morning tasks, whispering as Lady Andrea scolded her eldest son.

"What in God's name possessed ye!" she cried. "Sneakin' off tae some whorehouse in the middle o' nowhere like a runaway stable boy!"

"Ow, Mother… stop!"

She swatted his shoulder, then pinched him twice on the arm for emphasis.

"Ye're supposed tae set an example! Andrew tries his best, but ye have the sense of a stone! And ye come swaggerin' in here reekin' of whisky and a woman's cunt…"

"Mother!" He cut her off.

"Go wash yerself, and ye're no' tae leave that chamber!"

Alex straightened, puffing out his chest as though he still stood in Sophie's room.

"Mother, enough. I'm no' a bairn. I ken what I was doin'. It was my choice. 'Tis my life. Today I'm seventeen summers. If I choose tae spend my coin on a lass…"

Lady Andrea gasped. Servants froze. Even the fire seemed to still.

Alex stepped closer, eyes flashing with the arrogance of false manhood.

"And dinnae speak tae me like I'm some wee stable rat ye can box around. I'm yer eldest. I'll do as I please."

Her hand flew up to strike him, but Alex caught her wrist and pushed it away.

"Do no' lay hands on me again," he said coldly. "I'm no' yours tae command."

For one breathless second, the hall fell silent.

Then a fist came out of nowhere.

Calum Barton's blow landed across Alex's jaw with such force that the crack echoed through the great hall. Alex flew backward, sliding across the polished stone until his shoulder hit a pillar.

Andrew stood at the foot of the stairs, frozen in horror.

He had never heard Alex speak to their mother like that.
No one had.

Calum stormed toward his fallen son, his face a mask of fury and betrayal.

"Ye dare speak tae yer mother with that filthy tongue?" he thundered. "Ye lie with whores one night and ye think ye're a man the next?"

He hauled Alex upright by his tunic and struck him twice more before Lady Andrea threw herself between them.

"Calum, nae! He is just a boy! Enough! Ye'll kill him!"

Calum held his fist suspended midair, trembling with rage. His chest heaved as he stared down at the son who had humiliated his wife, his house, and himself.

"So, ye think ye're a man, aye? Ye think ye're clever? Ye think a night with a lass makes ye fit tae shame yer own mother in her hall?"

Alex stammered, blood on his lip.
"N… nae… Father… I…"

Lady Andrea tended him quickly, her plaid pressed to his mouth, her face streaked with tears.

Calum raked both hands through his dark, salt and pepper hair before letting them fall with a heavy thud at his sides.

"My heir, the idiot. Get yer arse outside. NOW!"

Calum's voice cracked through the hall like a whip. Alex scrambled to his feet, lip bloodied, and followed his father out into the courtyard.

The sun had risen fully, and castle workers were beginning their day. Men carried timber, women swept the stone walkways, and the clang of hammers echoed from the half built tower at the castle's edge.

Calum marched to a row of massive boulders that had been quarried for the new structure. Each one was large, uneven, and heavy as sin.

"Since ye're such a man now, ye'll move every single one o' these boulders yerself. All two hundred o' them. From here tae the front o' the new tower."

He turned to the workers and servants who had paused to watch.

"I dinnae want a single hand liftin' a finger tae help this pup. No servant, no builder, no one."

His gaze shifted to Andrew.

"And I mean no one."

Andrew lowered his head, swallowing hard.

Before Calum left, he faced Alex once more.

"The next time ye disrespect yer mother or pull such trickery, it willnae only be yer face I hit. I'll welt yer arse too."

He strode off, leaving Alex alone with two hundred boulders and a courtyard full of witnesses.

Regret

Alex set to work, each stone heavier than the last. His muscles screamed, his hands blistered, and sweat poured down his back. In the distance, he could see Haemish chopping wood for winter stores, the pile already stacked high as the Highland mountains. Farther off, Logan shoveled waste into a barrel, looking as though life itself had betrayed him.

Alex squinted. "Where the bloody hell is Rory?"

Shouts carried from Rory's home across the green. Someone was getting a thorough thrashing.

"Serves him right. Braggin' that he got his cock sucked. He's the reason we're all in this ."

By evening, the sky glowed gold and violet. Alex staggered beneath the weight of his one hundred ninety-ninth stone. His legs shook. His arms trembled. Dirt streaked his face, and his hands were raw.

Andrew approached with a canteen of water. Just as he lifted it toward Alex, their father's voice boomed from across the yard.

"Andrew, nae."

Andrew froze mid stride.

"I dinnae want tae speak tae ye," Alex ignored him. "Ye traitor."

Andrew frowned. "I got a thrashin' too, ye ken!"

Alex shot him a glare before glancing toward their father. Calum sat beneath a shaded tree, a carving knife in hand, shaping a small wooden figure with steady strokes. A bonnet shaded his face.

The day dragged on, and finally Alex hefted the final stone, dragging it to the tower's base before collapsing to his knees. His breath came in ragged heaves.

Again, his brother brought him water.
"Just apologize, Alex." He shoved it into his hands. "Tell Mother

ye're sorry. Tell Dah ye regret sneakin' out and dishonorin' the family's name. This will pass."

He turned and walked back toward the keep.

Alex sat for a long moment, staring at the ground. Slowly, he pushed himself up and trudged toward his father.

"Father?"

Calum did not answer.

"Dah… I apologize. My behavior was unacceptable. I'll nae do such foolishness again. I swear it."

Calum lifted the bonnet from his face, his eyes tired but sharp.

"Son, look at me."

Alex obeyed.

"Every choice a man makes carries its weight. Ye're my eldest. I raised ye tae be responsible, no' a blockhead. Ye ken right from wrong, and still ye chose wrong."

He pointed the carving knife toward the open yard.

"Ye could have caught the pox and brought it back here. Ye could have died on a strange road. Ye could have gotten the nasty woman's disease and lost yer cock entirely."

Alex's eyes widened. He glanced quickly down at his kilt.

Calum snorted.

"Son, hear me. Choose the wiser path. I willnae be here forever tae steer ye. One day ye'll be a man with sons o' yer own. Make the choices that lead tae honor."

He stood and placed a hand on Alex's shoulder.

"Today is a new day. Ye're seventeen summers now. A new chance tae be better. Now, get inside and take a bath. Ye reek."

"Aye, Da."

Alex turned to go, but paused.

"Dah… I truly am sorry."

Calum's expression softened.

"Son, I love ye. Punishin' ye and yer brother is no' something I enjoy. I dinnae do it out o' anger but out o' love. What ye said tae yer mother was wrong. A man's strength lies in how he treats women. They're delicate creatures, full o' feelin'. Ye honor them by speakin' with respect. Do ye understand me?"

"Aye, Dah. I'll apologize tae Ma."

Night had settled over the keep by the time Alex reached his chambers. His body ached, but his mind would not rest. Every time he closed his eyes, he saw Sophie. Then he saw his father bursting into that brothel. Then he saw Sophie's naked form, exposed and defenseless.

Shame twisted in his gut.

Regret followed.

Unable to sleep, he rose quietly and slipped into Andrew's chamber. He rummaged through the trunk and pulled out a shirt and a pair of britches. Andrew slept soundly, unaware as Alex donned his clothes.

Alex eased the door open and peeked into the corridor. Empty.

He crept down the servants' stairs, passed through the kitchen, and slipped out into the night.

At the stables, the stable hand slept on a pile of hay. Alex saddled his horse in silence and led the animal along the back wall of the castle, keeping to the shadows. He followed a narrow, hidden path toward the woods until it emptied onto the coastline. With dawn still far away, he mounted and urged the horse on.

After several hours, the brothel rose on the horizon.

Alex dismounted and strode inside. The owner's eyes widened with annoyance and disbelief.

"Nae service for ye tonight, laddie. Yer father near tore this place apart lookin' for ye last eve."

"I ken, and I'm sorry," Alex said. "But I'm here tae speak with Sophie. I told her I'd return. Fetch her, please. 'Tis urgent."

The woman raised a brow, glanced at a door on the second floor, then back at Alex.

"Sophie is busy. Now leave."

Alex's chest tightened.

'She didnae wait? She said she would…'

Anger surged. He stormed up the stairs.

"Boy!" the madam shrieked. "Hold it right there. Ye cannae go up. I'll call our man at arms."

Alex did not listen. He rammed his shoulder into the door three times until it flew open. The burst on impact sent him stumbling to the floor.

He looked up.

Sophie lay across the bed, entirely exposed, as a large, hairy man hovered over her.

Her eyes widened in horror when she saw him.

For a heartbeat, neither of them moved.

Alex's stomach twisted, sharp and violent, as though something inside him had torn loose. His hands curled into fists at his sides, nails biting into his palms, but he did not step forward. He did not speak. He turned instead, stumbling down the stairs as if the floor itself had shifted beneath him, bursting out into the open yard where the morning air cut cold against his skin.

He had nearly reached his horse when he heard her.

"Alex."

He froze.

"Please… wait." Her voice broke as she ran after him, skirts gathered in trembling hands. "Alex, ye must understand."

He swung around in the saddle, fury and hurt crashing together in his chest. Sophie stopped short when she saw his face, the swelling along his jaw, the bruise darkening beneath his eye.

"Yer father did that?" she whispered.

Something in her tone undid him.

"Just how many, Sophie?" His voice was rough, barely his own.

She looked down.

His shout tore from him before he could stop it. "HOW MANY TODAY?"

Her shoulders shook. When she spoke again, her voice barely carried.

"Seven."

The word struck him like a blow.

His breath left him in a sickened rush, heat flooding his face, his vision blurring. "Jesus Christ, Sophie," he said hoarsely. "Ye promised me."

She stepped closer, tears spilling freely now. "Listen tae yer father," she cried. "He was right about me. I told ye no' tae place yer trust in me. I am a whore. How could ye come back after what happened? Yer father saw me as I am. He would never accept me as part o' yer family."

Alex stared at her, his chest aching, pride and hope collapsing together into something darker and heavier. He said nothing more. He turned his horse away.

"I accepted ye," he shouted back, the words tearing loose from somewhere raw inside him.

He did not look back.

He rode hard into the fading night, the sky paling toward dawn as his thoughts spiraled, bitter and relentless.

Wrong tae trust her.
Wrong tae think she was mine.
Wrong tae believe a whore could change.

He slipped back into the keep just before first light and climbed the servants' stairs, his body exhausted, his mind hollow. He crossed into Andrew's chamber and slid beneath the blanket without a word.

Andrew stirred. "Where are ye coming from in my clothing?" he whispered. "Did ye go back there?"

Alex drew in a sharp breath. "Aye. But we're done."

Andrew frowned. "Ye should ha' kent better. She took yer virginity, aye, but she's a whore."

"I ken," Alex murmured.

"Dinnae go fallin' in love with another one either. That was stupid."

Alex let out a slow breath. "I said I ken, brother. Now shut yer gob."

As his eyes finally closed, one truth settled deep into his bones.

That night left its mark on Alex Barton. From then on, he trusted lightly, expected little, and guarded much. Whatever softness he once carried toward women cracked there and then, leaving something colder in its place.

Chapter Two

Tafaria, East Africa – 1620

The Arc of Yvonne

*A*s dawn broke over Tafaria, soft golden light began to warm the

thatched roofs of the servants' quarters. Beneath a thin linen sheet in a small hut, Yvonne began to stir, her muscles protesting the night's exertion.

She was left hollowed with pain, the memory of drumming, feasting, and endless movement imprinted on her body, feeling as though the night had depleted her more than just sleep could restore.

Her eyes closed, she held onto the stillness, pleading for a brief extension. The stillness was broken by the pounding on her door.

"Who would dare disturb me now?" she mumbled, rubbing her face as she faced the noise.

The knock sounded once more, louder and more demanding.

She stood up with a groan. "Oh, the deities. Is it too much to ask for a single morning to myself?"

A breathless voice called out to Yvonne through the door. Your presence is requested in the storage hall. King Afonso makes an entrance with his entourage.

Her fatigue vanished immediately upon hearing the words.

"My schedule doesn't include today," she remarked, her hand already moving to her scarf and securing her hair.

"Yes, but, it was the head servant who altered it. You must hurry."

Refusal was not an option. After dressing in a hurry, she stepped out into the mild morning air. The proximity of blooming hibiscus added their scent to the sea spray and the aroma of breakfast fires. On most mornings, the familiar scents steadied her. Today, they only seemed to emphasize the heaviness in her body.

The storage hall greeted her with thick air, heavy with oils and herbs, drying petals, and the sharp musk of cured hippo fat. Yvonne wrinkled her nose and went to work, grinding lotus and hibiscus paste, allowing the rhythm of the task to guide her hands even as her thoughts lagged behind.

Nyema slipped in beside her, bright-eyed and brimming with barely contained excitement.

"You heard, right?" she whispered. "King Oyomo arrived with King Afonso."

Yvonne's hand stilled against the stone.

"I thought…" She swallowed before continuing. "I thought only King Afonso was expected."

Nyema studied her more closely than comfort allowed. "Why does the mention of Oyomo trouble you?"

Yvonne smoothed her expression before answering. "He is not a man I wish to see."

Her voice remained steady, though her body betrayed her, a cold thread tracing its way down her spine.

Nyema nudged a tray toward her. "Take these oils to the bath hall. Afonso's entourage will want their water scented."

Yvonne lifted the tray, drew a careful breath, and stepped into the corridor.

The palace baths lay quiet at that early hour. Steam curled lazily from the pools, and the columns caught the first light of morning.

She approached the attendant's table, intent on setting the oils down and leaving without delay.

Voices drifted from around the corner.

Male voices. Familiar ones.

She stopped.

King Afonso laughed first, the sound deep and indulgent. "You truly thought an eighteen-year-old would remain loyal to a man nearly sixty? Old friend, you tempt fate itself."

Another voice followed, sharp with malice, unmistakable.

Oyomo.

"She was mine. I paid dearly for her. When I catch her, when I close my hands around that ungrateful girl's throat, she will cross over to the gods begging for mercy."

The tray trembled in Yvonne's grip.

Afonso clicked his tongue. "Careful, Oyomo. Her disappearance already shames you. Losing a wife so young..."

"A wife?" Oyomo snarled. "A possession. And one I intend to reclaim."

Yvonne retreated slowly, her pulse roaring in her ears as she went back into the service hall. Her vision blurred, her hands shaking as panic rose swift and merciless, flooding her body with the certainty she had prayed would never return.

He was here. In Tafaria. With Afonso.

She slipped into the laundry storeroom and shut the door behind her. Folded cloths and woven baskets lined the walls, the scent of soap and damp linen filling the air.

She set the tray aside and pressed her fists to her temples.

"He cannot find me," she whispered, her voice thin with fear. "He cannot know I am here."

A footstep sounded beyond the door, close enough to still her breath. Panic rose before thought could catch it, and she moved instinctively, slipping into the woven basket and drawing the lid closed over herself.

Darkness settled around her, thick and enclosing. Her breathing was strained, not relaxed, and her heart pounded rhythmically as voices approached and then receded outside, their brief proximity freezing her with terror before they vanished.

Her mind did not follow them into silence.

Instead, the darkness pulled her under, loosening memories she had spent eight months forcing down. She felt Oyomo's hand at her throat again, the pressure unyielding, his breath hot against her ear as he laughed, his voice slick with triumph.

"You better run, girl. Run as your life depends on it."

The memory of the fall returned without warning; terror stretched across four stories as her body chose the air rather than his hands. The jungle rushed up to meet her, darkness closing in as the ground disappeared beneath her feet.

Salt filled her mouth and burned her lungs as the ocean claimed her, cold and relentless, dragging her under despite her struggle to breathe.

"Please," she whispered, the plea tearing from her chest. "Let me live."

Femi's voice cut through the storm, a calm, steady sound that grounded her as fear threatened to overwhelm her. "We are under the protection of the goddess Yemaya."

Within the basket's darkness, she re-experienced the terror that almost took her and the hands that rescued her, with no escape.

Up until…

The Night I Chose to Live

Eight Months Earlier – Oyomo Kingdom

Yvonne had been eighteen that night, old enough to understand what was happening and young enough to believe she might still change her fate.

Her mother tightened the ceremonial cloth around her waist, tugging until it stole her breath. The dyes were rich, the embroidery heavy, a bride's mantle meant to honor a king. Yvonne felt only its weight, the way it pressed against her ribs.

"Hold still," her mother murmured, smoothing a palm over her daughter's shoulder.
"The first night will hurt, but afterward it becomes easier. Endure it, child. I know it is cruel, but a concubine must please the king if she is to survive."

Yvonne stared at her reflection, painted and adorned, dressed like an offering, and something inside her gave way.

"Mama, please. I beg. Look at me," she said, her voice thin with disbelief.

Her mother hesitated.

It was enough.

Anger rose fast and sharp.

"You know I pleaded with you and Father," Yvonne said. "I begged you not to pawn me off to that old man."

"Mind your tongue," her mother replied. "This marriage will secure our family's place. You will bring honor."

"Honor? You sold me for land, gold, and livestock. Do not speak to me of honor. You care nothing for me. You are horrible."

Her mother flinched, then steadied herself.

"Behave," she said quietly. "Do not let him see you cry. A king deserves dignity."

"No. A daughter does."

Silence settled between them.

Just then, the doors burst open and struck the stone.

King Oyomo filled the threshold, broad and heavy, draped in silks and age, his gaze sweeping the room with a single assessing glance.

"Out!" he demanded.

Every woman startled. Her mother, the senior wives, the attendants all dropped into hurried bows before scrambling for the exit, skirts tangling as they rushed to obey, none of them daring to look back.

The doors closed behind them, and silence settled into the chamber.

Oyomo moved toward her at an unhurried pace, each step deliberate.

The slap came before she could draw breath.

CRACK.

"You embarrassed me," he said. "A bride who cannot behave with dignity shames her king."

He moved closer. His breath struck her face, hot and sharp.

"And the audacity you showed, wailing through our ceremony while my guests laughed at me."

Disgust tightened his mouth.

"Do you know what it is to be mocked because of you? To waste a king's ransom on a bride who behaves like a frightened child?"

Yvonne's stomach hollowed. Her hands shook.

She tried to speak. "I never wanted to..."

His hand closed around her throat and lifted her from the floor.

"Insolence. Did I ask for your counsel?"

Her hands went to his wrist as instinct took over. She clawed at him until blood slicked beneath her nails, his eyes widening not in pain but in anger.

Her vision dimmed. Before she lost consciousness, he released her.

She fell forward, coughing hard, blood sharp on her tongue as her lungs burned. She dragged herself toward the door, each breath tearing at her chest.

"Mama... help... please..."

Her fingers slipped against the latch.

"Mama?"

No answer came.

She tried to rise, but his shadow fell over her before she found her balance. He seized her hair and dragged her back across the floor, her hands useless against his grip.

He threw her onto the bed.

"Pathetic," he said, wiping the blood from his wrist.

He turned away from her and crossed the room, poured water, and drank slowly, allowing the quiet to stretch until it pressed against her skin.

Then he snapped his fingers.

The doors opened, and three guards entered.

"Restrain this feral cat," he demanded. "She needs taming before I take her to my bed."

They advanced with ropes already in hand.

Something inside her broke.

Before they could reach her, Yvonne bolted for the balcony. She did not think. She moved.

She threw herself out the window.

Cold air struck her face, and the world fell away.

Pain tore through her arm. She rolled onto her back, gasping, fighting the dark at the edges of her vision.

Above her, the shutters opened.

Oyomo leaned out into the firelight, his mouth curling as he looked down at her.

"I see you live."

His voice carried across the courtyard.

"Run. If I catch you, I will take what I paid for. Then I will kill you."

He raised his hand.

"Fetch her."

Torches flared. Sandals hit the pavement.

And wounded, shaking, barely able to stand, Yvonne ran into the night.

Into the Dark Jungle

Sharp prickles pierced the soles of her feet, each step sending pain up her legs, but she did not slow. She could not. The jungle swallowed her so quickly it felt as though the earth itself had opened to hide her, leaves whipping at her cheeks and vines brushing her arms as the world narrowed into a maze of shadows and clawing branches.

She tried to see, to make sense of the twisting paths ahead, but the canopy smothered nearly all the light. Only thin threads of moonlight slipped through the tangled leaves, glimmering faintly on the ground, enough to keep her moving, never enough to feel safe.

Behind her, the sounds of pursuit faded into the heavy hush of the wilderness. There were no torches, no shouts, only the pounding of her own heartbeat and the rasp of breath tearing through her throat.

The deeper she ran, the darker the jungle became. The air thickened, heavy and humid, clinging to her like a second skin. Her broken arm throbbed with every movement, each pulse sharp enough to steal her breath, but she forced her legs forward all the same.

Her foot caught on a root, and she lurched, catching herself against a tree. She had no sense of direction, only the certainty that she had to keep moving, because stopping meant death, and moving, even blindly, still held the promise of escape.

Her legs betrayed her at last. She stumbled to a halt beside a thick tree trunk and braced her hand against the bark as her lungs dragged in ragged breaths. Sweat stung her eyes, and for a brief moment she rested her forehead against the rough surface, trying to steady the trembling that had taken hold of her body.

A low sound rolled through the darkness, deep and resonant, sliding beneath her skin like cold water.

She lifted her head slowly and peered into the shadows.

Two golden eyes watched her from the underbrush, steady and unblinking.

A black jaguar stepped forward, its body a ripple of shadow and moonlight, moving with deliberate grace as its sleek tail cut the air behind it.

Yvonne's breath caught as the animal advanced another step. She pressed herself back against the tree, afraid to run, and acted on instinct instead, pushing upward with her good arm.

Bark scraped her palms as she climbed, hauling herself up the trunk with raw desperation. Pain burned through her broken arm, but she did not stop until she reached a thick branch and clung to it.

Below her, the jaguar prowled once, then again, circling the base of the tree. It reared up, claws scraping bark, then slid back down. It tried once more and failed.

At last, it settled beneath her, tail curling neatly around its paws, patient and unhurried.

Yvonne clung to the branch, her chest rising and falling in shallow breaths as the night pressed close and the jungle hummed around her. Exhaustion seeped into her bones, heavy and unavoidable.

Her eyes drifted shut, though her mind refused to follow.

Where could she run? How far could she go with a broken arm and no food? Was there anywhere in this vast, merciless jungle that would not hunt her as surely as the king's men?

The questions churned through her, losing shape as her strength ebbed away. Time stretched and distorted, minutes blurring into something larger, heavier, until her body sagged against the branch and the last edge of fear dissolved into exhaustion.

Sleep came quietly, uninvited.

And high above the waiting predator, Yvonne surrendered to the darkness.

The Prince That Found Me

The hours crawled.

Yvonne clung to the tree until her limbs ached and her fingers went numb. Her broken arm throbbed with a slow, brutal pulse that left her lightheaded, each breath shallow and careful. Below, the jaguar lay coiled at the base of the trunk, a dark shape in the grass, its tail flicking now and then, as if to remind her it was still there.

She drifted in and out.

Sometimes she heard nothing but the heavy breath of the beast and the hum of insects. Sometimes she thought she heard men shouting in the far distance, torches cracking, boots pounding stone. Each time she tensed, the pain in her arm sharpened until black spots danced across her vision.

At some point, the jungle began to pale. The dark bled into gray, then into the first thin wash of dawn. Her body sagged against the branch, too tired to tremble, too sore to move.

A rustle came from the undergrowth. Not the sleek, silent glide of the jaguar, but something heavier, marked by the low creak of leather and the soft jangle of metal.

A horse.

Yvonne blinked, forcing her eyes to focus. Through the tangle of leaves, she saw a figure leading a stallion between the trees, moving with the unhurried confidence of a man who feared neither dark nor jungle.

He stopped directly beneath her tree.

For a moment, he simply hummed under his breath, set his belt aside, and relieved himself against the roots, as casually as if he stood in a private courtyard, not a forest where kings sent men to kill.

A small shower of dry leaves slipped loose from her branch and drifted down. They landed on his shoulder.

He paused. Slowly, he lifted his head and looked up.

Their eyes met.

Recognition flashed across his face, wiping away the relaxed ease he carried like a second skin.

"Yvonne Efengo. What are you doing up there? Hiding in a tree when you should be at your wedding feast? I was just at the celebrations yesterday." The absurdity of it nearly undid him.

Her throat tightened, not from fear this time, but from the terrible relief of seeing a familiar face that did not belong to a man who owned her.

"That man is not my husband," she said, her voice raw. "And I will never go back to him."

Prince Femi stared up at her, his mouth parting on a short, disbelieving breath. Even shaken, his wit surfaced out of habit.

"So, you have chosen a tree instead? Do you plan to eat fruit until you grow roots? That is not a very clever survival strategy, Yvonne."

She did not laugh. She could not.

When he saw her properly, the humor faded from his eyes.

He stepped closer to the trunk, fingers brushing the rough bark as he peered up through the branches. In the pale morning light, the damage told its own story: the swollen cheek, the dark bruises ringing her throat like the ghost of a hand, the torn ceremonial cloth, the arm hanging wrong, as if the bone itself had abandoned its place.

His jaw set. Without another word, he began to climb.

He moved with a wiry, unhurried grace, finding holds as if the tree had always known him. When he reached her branch, he eased himself into a crouch, bracing one hand against the trunk as he took her in fully.

"By all the gods," he murmured.

Anger burned through his expression, deep and steady, not wild. Not for her. For the man who had left these marks.

"What happened?" he asked. "Tell me, Yvonne. Did he do this?"

She whispered, her lips trembling. "He... he hurt me. Because I cried. Because I begged. Because I called for my mother. He said I was property. I jumped from his window to escape being tied to his bed."

Femi closed his eyes for a moment, as if steadying himself against the trunk.

"That man is no king. He is a monster who sits on a chair of gold."

Hoofbeats rolled faintly through the trees.

Yvonne flinched, fingers digging into the bark. The sound came and went on the wind, but the panic it stirred in her would not settle. Every muscle tightened as if she expected Oyomo's hand to close around her throat again.

Femi listened as well, head tilted. He spoke quietly. "They are close. Too close."

Her eyes went frantic.

"Yvonne, look at me."

One eye swollen shut, the effort came.

Femi kept his tone even, as if guiding a frightened child away from a cliff's edge.

"I'm going to take you down from this tree. You don't need to be brave. You only have to do one thing. Stay with me and I promise I will keep you safe. Do you understand?"

His hand lifted, not touching her, just close enough to anchor her.

She nodded, though the motion made her dizzy.

He slid an arm carefully around her waist, testing how much weight she could bear, then shifted to support her broken arm as best he could. Even with his care, the movement drew a sharp breath from her lips.

"I know. Breathe. We are going down."

He guided her inch by inch along the trunk, choosing each foothold before she moved, letting her rest when her legs threatened to give out. By the time they reached the lower branches, her whole body was shaking, her eyes glazed with pain. She did not resist his help.

When her bare feet touched the leaf-littered ground, he did not release her immediately.
He shrugged off his outer robe and wrapped it around her shoulders, drawing the edges together to cover the torn wedding cloth and most of the bruising at her throat.

"There," he said. "You are not a spectacle for any man's eyes."

The hoofbeats grew louder, then began to fade; riders cutting across the jungle in search of her.

Femi murmured, "We wait. If we step into the open now, they may see us through the trees. Stand behind me. Breathe slowly."

He shifted, placing himself between her and the sound, broad shoulders blocking her from view. Yvonne pressed her forehead lightly against his back, drawing in the faint scent of jasmine oil and leather. It steadied her in a way she did not yet understand, pulling her out of memories that tried to drag her under.

Only when the last distant echo of hooves vanished did he move.

"Come. We are finished with this place. Can you walk?"

"I can try," she whispered.

"That is more than enough."

He helped her mount, careful of her splinted arm, then swung up behind her. His arm locked around her waist as he turned the horse toward the thinning trees.

"You have my protection now," he said into her hair. "No other hand will touch you while I still draw breath."

The jungle thinned and opened toward the coast, the salt wind threading through the trees ahead of them. The sea rose into sound before it came into view, waves breaking hard against black rock. Beyond a low ridge of stone, half hidden from the beach, waited a small wooden rowboat.

Femi set her down first, steadying her only long enough to be sure she would not fall, then shoved the boat into the surf. A swell broke across the bow, spraying them both. Salt struck her exposed arm like fire.

Yvonne gasped, her body jerking.

He held her, one arm braced behind her. "I know," he murmured. "Hold on. We're almost clear."

He lifted her without hesitation and set her in the center of the boat, padding her broken arm with folds torn from his robe. Only when she was secured did he climb in and take the oars.

The sea fought them. Each wave lifted the boat and dropped it hard. Water leapt over the sides, cold and biting. Yvonne clenched her jaw as salt soaked her bandages again and again, her gaze fixed ahead.

Thunder rolled.

"Do not fear the water," Femi said, strokes steady. "It tests us. That is all."

A larger swell struck the bow, shoving the boat sideways. Femi shifted his weight and hauled on the oars until the vessel answered him.

Through the mist, his ship took shape. Shouts carried across the water as ropes dropped and a ladder slapped against the hull.

One of the guards reached for Yvonne too quickly.

"Slowly now," Femi snapped. "She is gravely injured."

The man froze.

As they lifted her, another guard stared. "By the gods… my prince, is that not King Oyomo's bride, Yvonne Efengo?"

Silence rippled across the deck.

Femi's voice cut low and absolute. "You will not speak that name again. Not here. Not anywhere."

The guard swallowed. "Will not her presence cause a rift between our tribes if King Oyomo receives word that she hides in Tafaria?"

Femi's gaze hardened. "That concern is not yours. Her identity is sealed. Now obey."

They carried her into his cabin and laid her beside the prince's bed. The door shut. Warmth replaced wind.

Yvonne began to shake, the soaked ceremonial cloth clinging to every wound.

Femi knelt and drew a small dagger. "Hold still. You cannot remain in wet clothing."

He slid the blade beneath the fabric and cut it away with measured care, never tugging, never jarring her arm. When the cloth fell aside, he stopped.

A deep bruise spread across her shoulder. Not from a fall.

His jaw tightened. Control returned just as quickly.

She whimpered at the cold. Her body leaned toward him without thought.

"Easy," he breathed.

He wrapped her in his dry robe, lifting carefully from her uninjured side. When his fingers brushed the bruised shoulder, she flinched, a sharp, broken gasp. Her hand trembled against his chest, seeking something solid.

Femi softened everything, his touch, his breath, his posture. He tucked the robe securely around her and drew warm furs up over her trembling form. Each shallow breath she took cut at him more than he let show.

He brushed a damp curl from her forehead with the back of his knuckles. She didn't fully wake, but her lips parted in a faint sigh, her body recognizing gentleness even if her mind could not yet hold on to consciousness.

Femi exhaled slowly, steadying himself, then stood.

He opened the cabin door.

"Go, Fetch the healer. Bring blankets, and boil water. Quickly.

The guards rushed to obey.

"A storm is forming," one of the crew muttered, eyes on the darkening sky.

"Then move faster," Femi replied.

The healer arrived in a flurry of herbs and sharp eyes, dropping to a crouch beside the pallet where Yvonne lay wrapped in Femi's robe and furs. He examined her arm with practiced fingers, his mouth tightening at the sight of the swelling.

"This limb, It has suffered greatly."

Femi kneeled close to her, examining the break. "Can you mend it?"

"I can, but bone returns to its place only through pain."

He pressed a strip of dried root to Yvonne's lips. "Chew. It will soften the edge."
Then he handed her a smooth carved stick. "Bite down when the pain comes."

Her jaw trembled, but she obeyed, working the bitter root slowly as the numbness began to seep through her limbs.

Femi took her uninjured hand in both of his, anchoring her.

"Begin," he said quietly.

A Servant's Life

Eight Months After the Rescue

The early weeks in Tafaria moved in careful rhythms, slow, deliberate, shaped around healing.

Yvonne healed by degrees. Some days she woke steady enough to rise before the sun; others she lay beneath the thin blanket until the dizziness eased and her breath found its pace again. Her arm remained bound in splints. Her steps were small. Her spirit refused to bend.

Femi visited often in those days. Not as a prince come to inspect, but as a man determined to ease her world without startling her. He knocked before entering every time, even when she was too tired to answer.

One morning she tried standing on her own. Her knees wobbled, the room tilting for a breath. She caught the wall with her good hand just as the door creaked.

"Are you challenging the floor to a duel?" Femi asked, his voice warm with laughter.

Despite herself, she smiled. "The floor is winning."

"That is concerning. The floor is not known for its courage," he replied, crossing the room to offer his arm.

She accepted his help with a reluctant sigh.

"I am fine."

"No, you are not." he said gently." But you will be."

He guided her back to her mat, poured fresh water into a carved cup, and handed it to her. Their fingers brushed, barely a touch, but enough to send a quiet warmth up her arm.

Femi pretended not to notice.

Yvonne pretended not to feel it.

✕

By the end of her first month, she knew nearly every task in the handmaids' quarters: washing linens until they smelled of lavender, sorting herbs, stirring fragrant oils, heating stones for the bath halls. She worked with quiet focus, always eager to learn.

The handmaids liked her immediately. They noticed her soft laugh, the murmured apologies when she bumped a basin with her splinted arm, the steadiness she brought even to the most tedious chores.

One afternoon, while grinding hibiscus into paste, she felt a familiar gaze.

Femi leaned in the doorway, arms folded, amusement tugging at his mouth.

Yvonne sensed his presence.

"You observe too quietly. It is unsettling."

"I thought your hearing had improved," he teased.

"It has. I hear your bracelets before you step into a room."

He lifted his wrist and gave it a light shake; the faint chime echoed.

"Ah, so that is why you always stand straighter when I arrive."

"I do not," she muttered, cheeks warming.

"You do. I find it endearing."

Yvonne tried and failed. She could not hold back her smile.

He stepped closer, close enough that she felt his presence but not so near as to crowd her.

"You are settling well. The handmaids speak highly of you."

"They tease me, but it is kind."

"That means they have accepted you."

She hesitated. "Do you think I belong here?"

"You belong wherever you choose to stand. But until the world is safer, I am grateful you stand here."

Something warm unfurled in her chest, gentle, unfamiliar.

Their bond grew in small, unexpected moments: a shared look across the hall, brief conversations between chores, the slow realization that she did not fear his closeness anymore.

One evening she struggled to lift a basin of water with one hand. It tilted dangerously before Femi stepped in, relieving her of the weight as though it were nothing.

"This task requires two hands," he said.

"It requires two hands," she answered. "I have one. It will do."

He eased the weight from her grasp, anyway.

"But you also have me."

The words settled slowly, deeper than she expected.

Her heart answered before her mind could.

He noticed.

He always did.

Rain whispered against the windows one afternoon as she crushed lotus petals into oil. Femi sat nearby, sharpening one of his small knives, a quiet rhythm that somehow steadied her.

"May I ask something?" she said.

"You may ask me anything."

"Why do you come here so often?"

He paused mid-stroke. "Does it trouble you?"

"No," she said quickly. "I only want to understand."

He considered the blade, then her.

"When someone arrives in your life wounded and afraid," he said quietly, "you do not leave their healing to chance."

Her breath caught.

"So you watch over me."

"I look after what the gods place in my path," he said. "That is all."

But she saw it, warmth beneath the restraint.

"I… feel safer when you are near," she whispered.

His breath left him in a slow exhale.

"And that," he murmured, "is all I could hope for."

She didn't hide from that truth anymore.

Weeks passed.
Her strength returned.
The servants praised her diligence, her steady hands, her kindness.

And though she told herself not to look for Femi, she always sensed when he entered a room, before he spoke, before he reached the doorway.

But today was different.

He entered with purpose in his stride, a lightness beneath it she had never seen. She was polishing carved jars when his shadow fell across her work.

"Yvonne," he said, and the softness in his voice made her look up. "I have come to steal some of your time."

She blinked. "Steal?"

"Yes. Borrow. Claim. Choose whichever word offends you least."

She laughed quietly. "What is it?"

"It is nearly sunset. And tomorrow is your nineteenth birthday."

She went still. "How… how do you know that?"

"You told me once," he said. "On a night you barely remember. I remember everything."

Her throat tightened. "You remembered for me."

"Of course."

He stepped closer, never too close, but enough that she felt his warmth wrap gently around her.

"I would like to show you something," he said. "A surprise. If you will come."

Her heart lifted in a way she had not felt in years.

"Where?"

He answered with a quiet smile. "Now that… is a surprise."

She found herself smiling back.

"When?"

"After sunset," he replied. "I will come for you myself."

Her pulse fluttered like a bird's wings.

"I will be ready."

He gave a slow, almost reverent nod before stepping away.

When the door closed behind him, the handmaids exchanged grins.

"Yvonne," one whispered, "your heart is showing."

She pressed a hand to her chest, warm, startled, alive.

For the first time in her life, she did not deny what she felt.

A Surprise by the Ocean

The sun had long set, leaving the evening warm and softly perfumed with salt and jasmine. Yvonne waited outside her small servant home, smoothing the simple green wrap dress she had chosen for the night. Her palms were damp. Her heartbeat would not calm.

For reasons she could not explain, she had braided her hair twice… and unbraided it twice… before settling on a loose coil at her nape.

Why was she nervous?

It was only Femi.

Her friend.

Her protector.

Her Lo....?

She shook her head and swallowed the thought before it finished forming.

The sound of approaching footsteps made her straighten. Femi stepped into view, carrying two buckets of fresh water and wearing deep blue garments trimmed in gold. He looked almost ceremonial, almost princely, far too elegant to be walking toward her.

His gaze warmed when it found her.

"You look beautiful," he said quietly.

Heat flooded her cheeks. "You exaggerate."

"I do not," he replied, offering her his arm. "Come. Your surprise awaits."

She placed her hand on his forearm, the gesture innocent, but her pulse fluttered like a trapped bird. Femi noticed, but he only smiled and guided her toward the coast.

They rode by horse until the forest thinned and moonlight spilled across the sand in silver sheets. The ocean shimmered, alive and restless.

A tent stood near the waterline, enormous and glowing red beneath hundreds of candles inside. It looked like a lantern shaped by the night itself.

Yvonne slowed. Her breath caught.

"Oh my, Femi… what is this?"

"A birthday deserves celebration," he said. "Nineteen is a milestone."

"I am still surprised," she grinned. "You remembered."

"Yes," He ushered her in. "I will always remember."

Her heart tightened.

Inside, woven mats were layered with cushions in rich earth tones. Garlands of woven flowers arched above platters of roasted plantain, coconut rice, spiced okra soup, mango slices dusted with cinnamon, and sweet dates arranged in a bowl of carved ebony.

Candles flickered everywhere, throwing warm light across her face.

Yvonne pressed a hand to her lips. "Femi… this is too much."

"I disagree," he said, taking her hand to guide her to the cushions. "You deserve far more than this."

His thumb lingered at the back of her hand before releasing it. The touch felt warm enough to travel up her arm.

They ate slowly, laughing between bites. He told her stories of slipping from war elephants as a boy, of his brother's terrible singing voice, and of his niece Nzingha, the most outrageously spoiled child ever born in Tafaria. He said her father once let her keep a lion cub inside the palace.

"I could not believe it," he said, shaking his head. "A lion cub, simply because she cried when the guards tried to take it away."

Yvonne laughed, the sound spilling out of her before she could stop it.

Femi seized the moment, reenacting the scene with dramatic flair, mimicking the cub's tiny growl and Nzingha's loud, hiccupping sobs until Yvonne nearly choked on her drink from laughing so hard.

She wiped her mouth, still smiling. "Do princes often fall into fountains while rescuing lion cubs?"

"Only the handsome ones," he replied smoothly.

She shook her head, but her smile lingered. Something about being with him felt easy. Lighter than anything she remembered. As if she had stepped briefly into a life untouched by fear.

While reaching for a mango slice, her fingers brushed his.

The contact was accidental. The stillness was not.

She felt it immediately, the quiet awareness passing between them. He did not move away. Neither did she.

Femi watched her for a moment, as though weighing something he had held back too long. When he spoke again, his voice was low, careful.

"May I hold your hand?"

She nodded before she had time to think.

His fingers laced with hers, warm and steady, not possessive, just present. Her pulse leapt, loud in her ears. Suddenly the tent felt smaller, the air thicker.

She drew in a breath and pressed her free hand to her chest. "I need some air."

He released her at once and stood, offering his hand instead of taking it. "Come."

Outside, the night opened around them. Moonlight stretched across the sand, the ocean breathing softly in the distance. She smiled without meaning to, the tension easing just enough to let wonder slip in.

"Do you wish to walk?" he asked.

"Yes," she said, surprised by the tremor in her voice.

They walked along the water's edge, close but not touching. Every so often she glanced at him and found his attention already on her, his expression unreadable, thoughtful.

"You are quiet tonight," he said gently. "From a woman who can out talk a crow, this concerns me."

She huffed a soft laugh. "I am trying to decide whether I am brave or foolish."

"And which are you leaning toward?"

"I do not know," she admitted. "But I feel… different."

He nodded slowly. "I feel it too."

The admission lingered between them, fragile and unguarded, neither of them moving to break it. The sea breathed nearby, steady and patient, as if giving them space to decide what came next.

"I don't know what to say," she admitted.

He studied her for a moment, then nodded, as if that answer was enough.

"Then don't say anything," he said quietly. "Just stay beside me."

Something in her chest loosened at the permission.

They walked together, unhurried, the sound of the waves filling the space where words no longer felt necessary.

The simplicity of it loosened something in her chest.

A wave curled forward and broke against her ankles. She gasped at the chill and stepped back quickly.

He laughed under his breath, amused. "It is only water."

"It is cold," she protested, hugging her arms. "How are you enjoying this madness?"

"It wakes the spirit." He reached for her hand, palm open in invitation. "Come. Let us swim."

"Swim?" she repeated. "At night? Do you have a death wish?"

He tilted his head. "Do you fear the ocean?"

"No,"

He studied her face. "Well, do you trust me?"

The question slipped between them with unexpected weight, soft as a whisper yet heavy enough to still the world around them.

She lifted her gaze to him. In the moonlight, the gold in his eyes flickered like candle fire.

"I do," she whispered. "It is only that…"

He stepped back slowly, untying the sash at his waist. "Then come."

The fabric slid from him. Beneath it, his body emerged in lean lines and quiet power, the moonlight glazing every curve of muscle across his chest. She tried not to stare, but her breath betrayed her, rising unsteadily.

"You expect me to go in looking like this?" she murmured, plucking at her dress as if it might shield her from his gaze.

He stepped close enough that she felt the heat of him, his tone lowering with reverence.

"Yes, your dress is beautiful," he said, a smile curving at his mouth. "But I think you would look better in whatever is underneath."

Her stomach fluttered so sharply she nearly lost her footing.

With careful hands, she loosened the ties of her wrap dress. The fabric slipped from her shoulders and fell to her waist, revealing the simple shift beneath. When she looked up, she caught Femi's breath hitch, the smallest, startled sound of a man who had not expected to be moved.

The tension changed, gentler, warmer, and charged with something new.

They walked into the waves together.

The sea rose around them in warm, steady pulses, the water wrapping her body like silk heated by the sun. Yvonne closed her eyes and lifted her face to the sky, letting the breeze cool her cheeks while the ocean lifted and swayed her hips.

For the first time in months, she felt weightless.
Unburdened.
Alive.

When she opened her eyes again, Femi was near. Carved in moonlight, his gaze tender, inviting her into a world where her body was hers again. There was an edge to him, a quiet question lingering in his eyes.

"Yvonne… may I kiss you?"

Her breath trembled.
She nodded.

He cupped her face and kissed her softly, tender at first, as if asking her heart to open in its own time. She melted against him. He deepened the kiss, slow and hungry. She parted her lips instinctively.

Pleasure bloomed through her like warmth spreading from the center of her chest.

He murmured against her mouth, "Your kisses are sweet."

The low base in his voice, sent butterflies to her stomach

He kissed her again.
Deeper.
Hotter.

He lifted her slightly as the waves rose, her legs instinctively circling his waist for balance. They gasped into each other, gripping, holding, discovering.

Her fingers slid into his wet hair.
His lips traced her jaw, her throat, the curve of her shoulder.
She arched into him with a soft, startled moan, her first sound of desire in her life.

He groaned quietly, forehead pressing to hers. "Yvonne… you undo me."

He walked with her as her legs stayed secured around his waist.

They stumbled back onto the sandy tent floor, dripping and breathless.

He lowered her onto the cushions, his mouth still claiming hers with a slow, hungry certainty.

Heat curled through her belly.

Her shift clung to her wet skin, revealing the soft curve of her breasts and the peaks of her nipples that strained through the thin fabric. Femi's hands traced reverent paths along her waist, her hips, the delicate lines of her ribs, as if learning her by touch alone.

"Are you comfortable with my touches?" he murmured against her lips.

She answered in a heavy breath. "Yes...Femi... I am."

He kissed her again, lowering himself partly across her body, guiding her down with gentle insistence. His weight settled over her thighs and hips, warm and anchoring. Her body responded before her mind could catch up, arching into him, grinding softly as something fierce and new ignited inside her.

His mouth trailed along the length of her throat.

His hand braced on the cushion beside her neck.

And the world snapped.

Oyomo's face above her.

His fingers locking around her throat.

Breath crushed. Voice stolen.

Yvonne's lungs seized.

Her body stiffened beneath Femi, every muscle locking as panic poured through her veins. Femi didn't notice at first, still kissing her deeply, still lost in the heat of the moment.

"Femi…" she whispered, barely audible.

"Stop…"

Her voice broke against the weight of memory. He shifted to kiss her again, unaware.

Her hands pushed weakly.

Then harder.

He was still in the swell of desire, still caught in the pull of her body against his, until she shoved him with sudden force. He jolted back, breath unsteady.

"I said stop," she gasped, voice cracking open.

Femi froze.

His eyes widened with instant horror. He lifted his hands in surrender, not retreating from her presence, but removing his weight from her body with careful, measured restraint.

"Yvonne…" His voice was raw. "I'm sorry. I didn't hear you. I swear I never meant to hurt you."

She curled into herself at once, knees tucked to her chest, arms wrapped tightly around her body, trembling as though the very air had turned against her. Sharp, broken breaths tore through her throat.

Femi sank to the ground beside her, not touching her, not crowding the fragile space she had created.

"Breathe. Yvonne. Steady. Take your time." he whispered. "I will not touch you unless you allow it."

Her shoulders shook.

Tears fell silently, tracing hot paths down her cheeks. She pressed her forehead to her knees, trying to breathe through the storm ravaging her chest.

"You did nothing wrong," he said, voice low and aching.

Slowly, her sobs softened to shivers. She wiped her face with trembling fingers, refusing to look at him.

"I cannot… I cannot do this," she whispered. "I thought I could. I wanted to… but when you touched my neck, it felt like I was back there."

Femi's jaw tightened, fury rising, not at her, but at the ghost who still haunted her skin.

"You never need to explain trauma to me," he said. "Your body remembers what cruelty stole from you. I will never judge you for surviving."

She gave a weak shake of her head.
"The last thing I would ever want is to fear you...I… like you."
His breath caught; his voice carried a crack she wasn't meant to hear, a quiet wound laid bare. "And I would give anything to take that fear from your heart."

Her eyes lifted to his at last, swollen from crying, but still searching.

"Femi… why do all this? Why care so much?"

He hesitated.
Then truth left him in a quiet exhale.

"Because I wanted you to feel cherished. Because you matter to me more than you know. I want you beside me… not as a servant, but as my sixth wife."

The news hit like a gut punch.

Sixth wife?

She hadn't even known he had *one*. Her mind flashed to Oyomo… to her mother bartering her away as a concubine. A fake smile tugged at her lips,

not from flattery,

but from shock.

"I… cannot," she breathed.

"Yvonne,"

"No! Why ask me this? My mother sold me. A king nearly killed me," she said, her voice thinning. "I will never be a man's concubine. Not now. Not ever."

Pain flickered through him, but he accepted her answer with a slow nod.

"Then, I will never ask again," he said softly. "But the desire to protect you… that will stay. I cannot change that."

She turned her face away.

"Please… I want to go home."

He stood immediately and extended his arm, gentle, cautious, offering, not demanding.

"I will take you."

She didn't take his hand.

She stood on her own.

They walked back to Tafaria in silence, the surf whispering behind them, both of them changed by a night that began with promise and ended in a chasm neither of them knew how to cross.

And somewhere deep within Yvonne, a truth settled quietly, painfully:

Desire is powerful.
But trauma speaks louder.
And feelings, once awakened, do not die cleanly.

Yvonne awoke with a gasp, her heart pounding against the tight weave of the basket walls. Warm air clung beneath the lid, thick with the mingled scents of hibiscus paste and drying cloths. For a moment, her mind was still trapped in the dream she had fled from, the ocean, the tent, the weight of a body she once trusted, the voice she once longed to hear.

She swallowed hard and pressed her palms against the woven slats until her breathing steadied.

Silence surrounded her.

No footsteps.

No voices.

No deep royal command echoing down the corridor.

She lifted the lid just enough to let in a sliver of light and peered into the empty hall.

Now.

This was her chance.

Present Day – Tafaria Kingdom

Yvonne awoke with a gasp, her heart pounding against the tight weave of the basket walls. Warm air clung beneath the lid, thick with the mingled scents of hibiscus paste and drying cloths. For a moment, her mind was still trapped in the dream she had fled from the ocean, the tent, the weight of a body she once trusted, the voice she once longed to hear.

She swallowed hard and pressed her palms against the woven slats until her breathing steadied.

Silence surrounded her.

No footsteps.

No voices.

No deep royal command echoing down the corridor.

She lifted the lid just enough to let in a **sliver** of light and peered into the empty hall.

Now. This was her chance.

Yvonne eased her body upward and stepped quietly from the basket. Her knees were stiff from crouching, her pulse still fragile from the dream, **a** memory she could not fully shake. She brushed dust from her dress, steadied her breath, and turned toward the exit.

She took two steps outside the storage room.

"Yvonne!"

She stopped cold.

Femi was there, standing in the archway, chest rising hard as if he had been searching every corner of the castle for her. Relief washed over his face so openly she felt it strike her in the ribs.

"I searched everywhere for you," he said, striding toward her. "When they said you were missing, I feared for the worst."

He stopped himself, but she saw it.

His fear.

His protectiveness.

The ghost of what happened between them.

Her heart pinched.

Since the night by the ocean, she had kept her distance, unsure of what to do with the feelings he awakened, unsure what to do with the fear that followed. Yet he still came. He still checked on her. He still looked at her as though she mattered.

"I hid," she said simply. "The moment I heard King Oyomo arrived, I…" She shook her head, unable to finish.

His expression softened with understanding. "You did the right thing."

For a moment, neither moved.

Then the softness inside him shifted, replaced with something far heavier.

"I must travel," he said quietly.

She stared at him, blood draining from her face. "Now? While he is here? While that monster sits under the same roof as me?"

"My brother has ordered me to the coast. Portuguese ships were spotted in the outer tides. They intend another raid. The villages must be evacuated. We ride within the hour."

The words dropped between them like stones.

"But the king is here," she whispered. "How can you leave now? What if… what if he…"

She stopped, her throat tightening.

He knew exactly what she feared.

Femi stepped closer, his voice low and unwavering. "Oyomo will not come near you. I spoke with the head servant myself. You are excused from all duties until he leaves the palace. No one will summon you. No one will call your name for any task. If he requests additional servants, others will attend him."

He held her gaze, letting the weight of his promise settle gently between them.

"You will stay inside these inner halls," he continued. "And if you must move, you move with an escort. You are not to be anywhere near the royal chambers."

His reassurance steadied her… yet something else churned in her chest, sharp and unsteady.

A question she had tried to bury since dawn.

Her eyes lifted to his. "Speaking of… things said and done… Nyema told me something this morning."

Femi's brow lifted. "What did she say?"

"She said you asked her to be your sixth wife."

His face froze.

Then a slow, incredulous breath left him.

"She lied."

Yvonne's chest squeezed. "Why would she lie?"

"Because she is infatuated," he said, not unkindly. "And because long before you came, we had a very short… foolish entanglement. Nothing lasting. Nothing meaningful. It ended before it even began."

Her heart throbbed painfully.

"She said it with such certainty," Yvonne whispered.

"Yes," Femi replied. "Because she wants you uncertain. She hears people talk. They see the way I look at you. The way I check on you.

The way I protect you. They assume I must want you as a wife." He exhaled slowly. "Perhaps it made her jealous."

Yvonne lowered her gaze, unsure what burned in her chest, embarrassment, disappointment, confusion, or a mixture of all three.

"I do not want to be entangled in rumors," she said softly. "Not with you. Not after everything."

He stepped closer, stopping just before he touched her.

"Yvonne," he said gently, "whatever happened between us… whatever feelings rose and whatever fears followed… none of it was a lie. I do not chase every woman. And I certainly did not propose to Nyema."

Her breath shivered.

"But you did propose to me."

His jaw tightened for a heartbeat. "Yes. And I meant it. Not for ownership. For protection."

She shook her head gently, a sad, fragile smile touching her lips. "That is why we cannot. You do not love me. You see marriage as a shield. You describe it as a cage."

Pain flickered through his eyes, but he nodded with quiet acceptance. He wished to confess, but his title and thoughts of his other wives blocked it.

He stretched a hand, then withdrew quickly.

His actions became those of the reserved prince again.

"I leave in moments," he said softly. "And when I return… I will ask for nothing. Not trust. Not closeness. Only that you stay safe."

Her throat tightened.

She wanted to tell him to be careful… that she cared for him more than she dared admit.

Yvonne wished this moment could end in gentleness, not fear. She wished to give him words that didn't leave bitterness sitting heavy on her tongue.

Instead, she stepped back.

"When will you return?"

"When the coast is secured. A few days, perhaps more."

He hesitated, as if he wanted to touch her cheek, then remembered the boundary between them and let his hand fall.

"Do not wander alone," he told her. "Keep to the inner halls. And if anything frightens you, call for the guard I assigned."

Yvonne nodded.

Femi held her gaze another moment, something unspoken straining between them.

Then he turned and left her beneath the archway, the pounding of his footsteps fading until the hall fell silent again.

Yvonne pressed a hand to her chest, feeling the tremor still there.

Chapter Three

Alex's Old Wounds

Alex Barton had just turned twenty-fourth, yet the weight of the

hall pressed on him like a stone across his chest. He tried to slip

through the crowd quietly, shoulders angled, gaze lowered, but every

few steps another hand caught his arm, another body drifted neatly

into his path, another voice rose with condolences he did not know

what to do with anymore.

Cousin Catherine touched his sleeve, eyes shining.
"I'm sorry for yer loss, Alex."

An elder clasped his hand next, solemn and heavy.
"Yer father was a great man."

A distant cousin hugged him without warning and declared, loudly,
"Ye show strength today, lad."

Alex nodded where required. Murmured thanks where expected. Each exchange felt like a toll paid to move a single step closer to the door.

He angled himself left, then right, threading between mourners, only for the hall to rearrange itself around him. Every clear path vanished just as he reached it.

By the time Rory and Logan stepped into his way, blocking the last open stretch before the doors, Alex was holding himself together by nothing but habit.

Rory laid a hand on his arm, grip firm and familiar.
"Our condolences, brother. Laird Calum was like a Da tae us."

Logan nodded beside him.
"Aye. He raised us as if we were his own."

Alex stared at them for a heartbeat too long, the words landing heavier than the others because they were true.

Something in him gave way.

"Christ above," he said, voice rough, "could the two o' ye move out o' my way? I'm tryin' tae leave."

They blinked, caught off guard.

Rory searched his face. "What's the matter with ye?"

Alex dragged a hand down his face and let out a breath that might have been a laugh if he'd the strength for it.

"I've nodded so much today my neck's about to give out," he said. "I just need tae get out of here before someone else tells me how well I'm holdin' up."

Understanding flickered across Logan's expression first.

"Go, then," he said, already stepping aside. "We'll keep folk off ye."

Rory followed suit, squeezing Alex's arm once before letting go.

Alex gave them a grateful, weary look and didn't wait for another word. He slipped past them and headed straight for the doors before the hall could change its mind again.

Without another word, he slipped past them, stepped out into the courtyard, and breathed in the cold air as though it were the first full breath he'd taken all day.

Within minutes, his horse was saddled, and he rode away from the suffocating hall and the endless condolences he could no longer endure.

The ride to Mr. Amos's alehouse did little to settle Alex's thoughts. The farther he traveled from the castle, the more the tightness in his chest eased, yet the grief sat stubbornly at the back of his throat.

When he pushed open the alehouse door, the noise and warmth washed over him. Men argued over cards at one table while others leaned into their meals, grateful for a hot supper. Life moved on without hesitation, and for a moment, Alex felt like a ghost drifting through it.

He sat in a quiet corner, away from the hearth light, and ordered ale without looking up. By the time his fifth cup arrived, followed by a third whisky, the sharp burn of the drink was the only thing grounding him.

How am I meant to do any of this without Da?

First Mother… now him.

four and twenty, and I've lost everything that mattered.

He tipped back two shots in quick succession, letting the fire numb the raw edge in his chest. He winced as the liquor hit him hard.

"Ugh," he muttered, scrubbing his hand across his face. "At least Andrew's holdin' himself together."

But the thoughts that followed dragged heavier. Barton ships, clan duties, taxes, tenants, elders, trade, leadership. His father's voice echoing expectations he wasn't ready to face.

"I'm goin' tae ruin the whole damned legacy," he whispered under his breath. "My daft arse is no' fit for any o' this."

He tossed back another whisky and let the cup hit the table with more force than intended.

Just as he lifted it again, the door opened. Alex didn't look up at first, but when he did, he swore under his breath and sank lower in his seat.

Andrew spotted him instantly.

"Nice of ye tae leave Da's repast," Andrew said as he walked over.

Alex drank again. "How'd ye find me?"

"I followed the scent o' whisky." He sat with a straight face and raised a hand to draw the server's attention.

Alex gave a humorless huff. "Aye, well… ye found me."

Andrew studied him for a long moment. "Ye've been runnin' from folk all day. What's truly the matter?"

"I told ye. I needed tae get out. Everyone whisperin' condolences, lookin' at me like I should give them answers I dinnae have… it's too much."

"Aye," Andrew said quietly. "Grief makes the world heavier."

Alex looked away. "I just need a moment where no one expects somethin' from me."

His brother didn't argue. He knew better.

"We have a meetin' with the elders tomorrow." Andrew finished his ale in one gulp.. "Try no' tae drown yerself before then."

Alex snorted softly but didn't reply.

"I'll see ye at home." Andrew stood. "Dinnae stay too long."

When his brother left, Alex exhaled slowly, thinking the pressure might ease now that he was alone.

But then a server walked by.

Thin. Exhausted. Dark hair pulled loosely back.

Something in her profile tugged at a memory he hadn't touched in years.

He squinted.

"…Sophie?"

He blinked, focusing past the haze of whisky until the shape in front of him settled.

"Sophie."

She moved between tables with practiced ease, balancing bowls of stew as she worked her way through the crowded alehouse. She hadn't seen him yet.

Before he could call her name, one of the men she served caught her wrist, tugging her toward him with a grin.

"I ken ye," he said loudly. "Ye're from Miss Butler's house. Come upstairs with me. I'll pay extra."

His friends erupted in laughter.

Alex didn't hesitate. He pushed away from the table and reached them in moments.

"Let go o' her hand."

The man turned, ready to argue, but the words died in his throat as soon as he recognized who stood before him.

"Chief, my apologies. I meant nae disrespect."

"It makes nae difference," Alex said sharply. "Ye dinnae grab a woman like that."

The man tossed a coin onto the table as a tip and hurried to retreat. "A crown. My mistake."
He and his friends left, leaving Sophie standing where she was, her face warm with embarrassment.

Alex's expression softened.

"Sophie… it truly is you."

"Aye." She nodded, barely lifting her gaze. "It's been some time."

He smiled. "I didnae expect tae find ye here."

"Tis my place o' work now," she said simply, rubbing her hands on her apron. "We're short-staffed tonight. Forgive the state I'm in."

"There's nothing tae forgive," Alex said. "I've not seen ye in nearly nine years. I'd no idea ye were anywhere near Barton lands."

"A lot changes in nine years," she murmured. "Folk go where they must."

Her voice carried exhaustion, not self-pity, just the quiet truth of someone who had learned to endure.
Alex studied her face more closely now.

"How've ye been keepin'?"

"I manage... it's long days, but it keeps a roof over my head."

Before Alex could respond, a harsh voice barked from the kitchen:

"Sophie! Move yerself!"

She flinched, not dramatically, just enough for Alex to see the strain behind her eyes.

"You must excuse me, my husband needs me." she said quickly, slipping away toward the shouting.

Alex watched her disappear toward the kitchen, a tightness settling in his chest he hadn't expected. Something in the man's voice, and the way Sophie stiffened at the sound of it, stirred an unease he couldn't ignore. The faint shadow along her jaw only deepened the feeling that all was not well behind that door.

He pushed back from the table and followed after her.

Raised voices carried through the kitchen even before Alex reached the doorway. Pots rattled, something metal struck the floor, and Sophie's voice trembled through the noise as she tried to explain herself.

"I was only thankin' the son of Laird Calum Barton," she said quickly. "He stopped two men from harassin' me. That's all it was."

Her husband's reply came sharp and venomous.

"Ye think I'm a fool? Showin' yer teeth at him like that? I warned ye already. Next time I catch ye flirtin', I'll break yer jaw myself."

A harsh crack split the air, followed by Sophie's cry.

Alex's jaw clenched. He stepped inside without hesitation.

Her husband loomed over her, arm raised again, fury blotching his face. Before the man could strike, Alex caught his wrist and yanked him backward, sending him stumbling across the room.

The man barely hit the ground before Alex was on him.

"This is what ye call bein' a husband?" Alex snapped, landing a hard strike that knocked the wind from him.

"Beat a woman who cannae defend herself? Is that the measure o' yer strength?"

The man tried to shield his face, sputtering curses, but Alex drove him back with two more sharp blows.

Sophie's voice trembled behind him.

"Alex, please… stop…"

He froze long enough to steady his breath, the anger still burning hot behind his ribs. Her husband groaned on the floor, clutching his side.

Alex stood over him.

"Touch her again, and I'll be the one tae break yer jaw. This is Barton land. Yer tavern stays open only if I allow it."

Sophie pressed a shaking hand to her cheek, eyes wide as she looked between them.

Alex turned to her, his voice gentler.

"Come. Ye're no stayin' here another moment."

Sophie pulled against his hold the moment they stepped into the main room, her breath uneven and eyes darting toward the kitchen.

"Alex, what are ye doin'? Let me go."

"I'm takin' ye out o' here," he said, not slowing. "Ye're no' spendin' another night under that man's hand."

"But my husband, my work," she shook her head, panic rising. "Ye cannae just drag me off."

"Aye, I can." His voice was steady, but the anger had not cooled. "Being married doesnae give him the right to knock ye senseless. Ye're leavin'."

Sophie glanced back at the tavern, her voice cracking.

"What will become of him? And the business? This is his livelihood, Alex."

"If he wishes it to stay open," Alex said, "he'll keep his fists to himself." His tone left no room for argument.

She swallowed, torn between fear and the faint, bewildered relief that someone, anyone, was standing for her.

"Where are ye takin' me?" she asked as he helped her onto the horse.

"Tae my father's huntin' lodge."

She stiffened. "I cannae go there. What if he finds out?"

Alex paused only a breath, his expression softening as he met her eyes.

"Sophie… my Da is gone."

Her face fell, all color draining. "Alex… I'm sorry. Truly."

He nodded once. The grief sat heavy behind his eyes, but he didn't linger on it.

"Come. It's safe. Ye'll rest tonight without worry."

He mounted behind her and turned the horse toward the trail leading into the forest. The tavern lights fell away behind them as they rode deeper into Barton lands, neither speaking for a long while.

The forest grew darker as they rode, moonlight slipping through the trees in thin silver traces. By the time the hunting lodge appeared between the pines, Sophie's trembling had eased, though she still held herself tightly, unsure of what waited ahead.

Alex dismounted first and reached up to steady her as she slid down from the horse. When she stepped into the open light from the lodge window, the extent of her injuries became clear. Fading bruises along her jaw. A deeper mark near her eye. A split in her lip she had tried to hide.

Alex felt his chest tighten.

"How long has he been beatin' on ye?" he asked, his voice low.

Sophie looked away. "It started six months after we wed."

He waited, giving her space to continue if she chose to.

"My husband says I'm worthless because I cannae give him a child."
Her hand brushed her stomach unconsciously. "I lost four before
they ever had a chance. Each time, he blamed me for it."

"That doesnae give him leave to lay a hand on ye."

"Before him, I belonged to Miss Butler's establishment. When the
madam began takin' more of my wages, I feared I'd never be free of
that life." She gave a small, tired laugh. "He offered marriage, a
home, respectable work… I thought it was a blessing."

"And now?" Alex asked.

"Now it feels like another place I'm locked inside." She wrapped
her arms around herself. "A great reward, aye… but great sacrifice."

Alex stepped closer, not touching her, but offering the steadiness she
had been denied for years.

"Ye're safe here, no one will come tae harm ye. Not while I have
breath."

Her eyes lifted to his, weary but grateful.

"What am I meant to do now?"

"For tonight, ye'll rest. Tomorrow… we'll figure the rest out."

Sophie smiled faintly and rested a hand on Alex's shoulder before entering.

"I was such a fool for not keeping my promise," she said quietly. "Instead, I let money and fear get in the way of something that could have been wonderful."

Alex eased her hand off his shoulder, fingers gentle but firm.

"Well, that was in the past, think of this as a friend helpin' a friend."

He pushed the door open and stepped aside for her to enter.

The cabin's interior was small but well-kept, the air warm with the scent of peat smoke and old timber. A box bed was built snugly into the far wall, its wooden frame polished by years of use. Opposite it sat a deep wooden tub, waiting to be filled. A narrow table with two chairs stood near the hearth, and beyond that a modest kitchen nook held shelves of preserved goods, jars of fruit, vegetables, and whatever his parents had left from their last visit.

The cabin was simple, but it felt solid. It was safe.

Alex motioned around the room.

"There's a tub in the corner. Make yourself comfortable while I fetch water for your bath. Ye can light the hearth with the dried peat, and there's firewood stacked just there. And if you're hungry, my parents left enough jars to feed a small army."

"This is all too kind; how can I ever repay you?"

"No need." He shrugged, avoiding her eyes. "You can stay here as long as you like. I'll speak tae the cook at the keep, and see about the kitchens or scullery. Maybe find you a bed in the servants' quarters. We'll figure it out, aye? New life. New start."

"But what about my…" She played with the hem of her apron. "Never mind." Something weighed on her, but she was too afraid to speak. Alex figured she would mention it when she was ready.

"Very well," he said.

He glanced to the window, noting how fast the light was dying. "I'll fetch your water before the sun drops."

She caught his sleeve lightly. "Why would you do that yourself? You're dressed so nicely. Were you at a wedding?"

His jaw tightened. "Nae. My father's funeral."

He pulled his arm free. "Besides, why would I have a woman carry heavy buckets?"

He grabbed two empty pails and stepped outside, letting the door thud shut behind him.

The air near the loch felt cooler, but the work still drew a sweat. Before he reached the bank, he stripped off his coat, shirt, and cravat, tossing them over a low branch.

The late sun glinted off the water and the damp reeds, and he crouched at the edge, filling each bucket.

The prickling at the back of his neck made him glance over his shoulder.

Sure enough, Sophie's pale face hovered at the cabin window, half-hidden, watching him.

He snorted softly to himself and bent back to the task.

When both buckets were full and sloshing, he hefted them and trudged back. By the time he reached the cabin door, sweat was running down his spine, and the heat had him swearing under his breath.

He shouldered the door open, boots scuffing across the floor.

"Jesus Christ," he muttered. "It's hotter than hell's blue fire out there."

He set the buckets down beside the tub.

"There's your water. I'll leave ye be."
"Leavin' again?" she asked.
"Aye. I need a wash myself." He raked a hand through his damp hair. "It's bloody hot. And ye need privacy. I'll be back with supper."

He didn't wait for a reply. The door closed behind him with a solid thud.

Outside, the forest felt quieter. He walked deeper into the trees, trying not to think about the fragile woman now standing in his childhood refuge. Eight years ago, she'd been radiant, so sure of herself. Tonight, he'd seen the bruises, the hollows under her eyes, the way she flinched when her husband raised his voice.

'Life has wrung her dry,' he thought bleakly. 'The lass is used and broken.'

He tried to remember the girl who had laughed in his arms, but memory refused him. What rose instead was the woman who had endured too much and learned to stand afterward.

Da was right, he thought bitterly. I was a fool.

A stir in the underbrush cut through him. Instinct answered before thought, muscle and breath aligning as the musket came up and the shot cracked through the trees.

The rabbit dropped where it had hidden, still warm, still whole.

A breath left him, sharp with satisfaction. "Ha. Yer a juicy one."

He took the carcass down toward the loch, the familiar work settling into his hands as his mind wandered elsewhere. Each motion was practiced, unremarkable, carried out without care, while his thoughts curved back toward the keep and the body laid beneath white cloth. Even finished, even washed clean at the water's edge, that image would not leave him.

He reached for the flask in his satchel, the one meant for emergencies, though he no longer bothered to define the word. He drank, choked on the burn, then drank again.

By the time he lowered it, grief no longer cut so sharply, but it had not loosened its grip.

He sank down by the loch, elbows braced on his knees, watching his reflection shatter and gather again with every small ripple.

His father's voice rose clear in his mind, as if the man still drew breath. "

My block heided son, I'm so proud o' the man ye've become. It's time for the good laird tae take me home. I ken you and Andrew will do a fine job keepin' the Barton name strong."

Alex had choked on the air. "But Da, I'm nae ready tae take over. I'll make a mess of everything. I'm the daft son. Ye must get better and keep guidin' me."

Calum's cough had rattled through his chest. "Wheesht. Yer more than ready, Yer not a laddy, yer four and twenty. Leave those daft lassies alone and focus on the keep and the ships. Ye have Andrew at your back. Bein' a leader will come. It always does."

"Aye, Da."
"And son?"
"Aye?"
"Promise me ye'll never touch that Atlantic trade. We're Christians. We ken right from sin, and we dinnae do evil and call it God's will. Not for coin. Not for power. Never. "The memory burned. Alex clutched the flask tighter, knuckles white.

"Aye, Da," he whispered tae the empty shoreline.
"Son. I love ye."

His throat closed, eyes stinging.
"I love ye too, Da."

He'd folded himself over his father, arms locked tight as tears streamed unchecked down his face. Pressing close, he felt the old man's chest fight for air, one shallow rise, one broken fall.

Then came the soft, final exhale, a breath that seemed tae empty the whole world with it.

His father was gone.

By the water now, the grief hit him fresh. Alex bowed his head, shoulders shaking. Tears fell silently into the loch, breaking the smooth surface into trembling circles.

He stripped and plunged into the shallows, letting the cold close over his skin, washing away sweat and some of the ache. When he climbed out, the air bit at him, grounding him enough tae move again.

By the time he returned tae the cabin, rabbit cleaned and roasted over a quick fire, the whisky had loosened his limbs and sharpened his tongue.

He slammed the door open without thought.

Sophie, stepping out of the tub, turned with a soft gasp, bare as the night he first met her.

Alex spun around so fast his damp hair whipped his neck. "Saints!" He stared hard at the door.

She stiffened, unsure of what to do. She asked faintly, "Do ye have any extra clothing? My garments are filthy," her voice small behind him.

"There's an extra shirt in my satchel," he said roughly. "Use that."

He kept his back firmly turned and strode tae his satchel. Without daring a glance in her direction, he rummaged through the contents until his hand closed around a fresh linen shirt. Holding it out behind him, eyes locked stubbornly on the far wall, he offered it tae her. "Here. Take this."

Her fingers brushed his knuckles as she took it, light and accidental, enough to send a sharp shiver down his spine.

"My thanks," she murmured. "So… what now? Did ye find meat?"

"Aye. Roasted a rabbit." He lifted the satchel. "Oat cakes and bread as well. I meant tae stay here a few days, afore I met you at the ale house. My brother thinks I've gone home, but I needed space. The keep's crawlin' with kin and guests, all sayin' the same cursed words. My condolences. Every turn. Same phrase. Feels like a dream I cannae wake from."

"Understood," she said softly. "And I am… truly sorry for your loss."

He flinched. "And there ye go again." He shook his head. "Ye dinnae need tae say it."

She bit her lip. "My apologies. I wasnae thinkin'. Ye may turn around now. I'm dressed."

He did, and the sight of her in his shirt stopped him short. The hem skimmed her thighs, bare legs pale in the firelight. Something twisted in his chest, sharp and unwelcome.

He crossed to the shelf and took a long swallow of whisky before stepping outside. When he returned, the roasted rabbit swung from his hand.

Sophie hovered near the hearth, hands clasped, eyes darting.

"Stop hoverin'," he muttered, dropping the meat on the table. "Grab two plates. I've nae the patience tonight."

The edge in his voice wasn't cruelty. Just weariness, stretched thin.

She moved at once, setting down the dishes as he carved the rabbit, giving her the larger portion without comment. He added pickled cabbage and oat cakes.

She ate quickly, with quiet focus, like someone afraid the food might vanish if she slowed.

He watched her for a moment. "Is that enough?" he asked. "Want more?"

She swallowed, colouring. "Nae. Forgive my manners. My husband allows me one meal a day, in the mornin'. The ale house is always busy. There's never time after."

His jaw tightened. "What kind o' man lets his wife starve while he fills his pockets?"

Her shoulders drew inward. "The kind I married."

Silence settled between them, broken only by the hearth.

After a moment, she tried again. "And… how has life been for ye?"

He wiped his hands on his kilt, reached for the whisky, and set it down harder than needed.

"Shitty."

Her brows lifted. "Why do ye say that?"

He leaned back. "Mother died three months ago. Father followed her. I'm laird in all but name, with a keep full o' expectations and a dozen ships I'm meant tae command. Every man thinks I'm ready. I'm nae. I can barely breathe in that castle with all their pityin' faces."

She opened her mouth, caught herself, then faltered anyway. "I am… truly sorry."

"For Christ's sake, Sophie." His voice snapped. "Would ye stop with the condolences?"

Heat rose in her cheeks. She fixed her gaze on the carved lines of the table, tracing them as if they mattered.

To distract herself, she blurted, "Have ye married?"

He barked a laugh, the sound sharp and humourless. "Me? Married? It'll be a cold day in hell before I tie myself tae a woman."

"Why would ye say such a thing? Marriage is beautiful."

"Beautiful," he echoed, the word sour on his tongue. "Lass, women see me as a walkin' bag o' coin. Firstborn heir to Laird Calum Barton. Captain o' Barton and Sons. Every ambitious mother in Scotland wants her daughter tae trap me. They tell lies about bairns, claim they're with child when I've been at sea six months." He took another drink. "I've no time for that shite."

He looked at her, eyes glassy, words loosened by whisky. "And how do you ken marriage is beautiful? Yours sounds like hell on earth."

Her eyes shone, but she blinked the tears back, tilting her chin.

"So you're sayin' everyone you meet wants to trap ye?" she asked.

"Aye. Marriage is a trap. You said yourself, you married tae escape and ended in worse. I'm a sailor. What kind of husband would I be, beddin' women in foreign ports and comin' home tae a wife pretendin' I was faithful? That's not a life I want. Let Andrew have it. He's better for marriage than me."

He hesitated, his gaze locking onto hers, the room suddenly too small.

"I've had my share of disappointment," he added, voice low. "Once was plenty. I've no wish tae feel that again."

She knew exactly who he meant.

The shame settled like a stone in her stomach. Their meal ended in heavy silence, broken only by the quiet clink of plates and the occasional swallow of whisky.

When they were done, Alex stood, the room tilting slightly under his feet. He grabbed the bottle and stumbled to the trunk by the hearth, pulling out a spare blanket and pillow.

"Well, I'm for sleep," he muttered. "I've an early morn at the keep. You take the box bed. I'll take the floor."

He tossed the blanket toward the hearth, dropped down heavily, and turned onto his side, giving her his back. Firelight flickered across his shoulders, the bottle resting close to his hand.

Sophie climbed into the box bed, pulling the covers to her chin. In the quiet, she could hear his rough, uneven breaths settle into a heavy snore.

Sleep did not come.

She stared at the ceiling boards, at the shadows swinging across them. Memories slipped in. The boy of ten, and seven summers later, who had looked at her like she was the only woman in the world. The way he had touched her back then, not as a man buying time, but as a lad overwhelmed by wanting.

No man had ever made her feel like that before or since.

Her fingers drifted absentmindedly to her own skin, the ache of loneliness rising sharp between her legs. She thought of how he had stood up to her husband, how he had risked a scene at the tavern, how he had brought her here, offered food, shelter, a path out.

No one has ever done that for me, she realized.

And yet he had hardly looked at her since.

Perhaps he grieves, she thought. *Perhaps that is why he keeps his distance?*

She lay awake for a long time, as his snores rose and fell. At last, with her heart beating too loud to ignore, she slipped out of the box bed and padded softly across the floor.

She paused over him in the dim light. His lashes cast faint shadows on his cheeks, his brow furrowed even in sleep. The boy she had known had grown into a man, and despite his harsh words, he had saved her life tonight.

She let the shirt slip from her shoulders and flow to the floor, feeling the cool air kissed her skin. She slid beneath the blanket beside him, pressing her bare body lightly against his side. Leaning in, she brushed her lips over his chest, then his neck, then his mouth.

In his dream, Alex was kissing a younger Sophie. The girl who had laughed in his arms. The girl who had promised to wait.

He groaned softly, his hands moving on instinct. His palm slid up to cup her breast, his thumb brushing across sensitive skin.

The dream shattered.

His eyes flew open.

The cabin came into blurry focus. The hearth. The ceiling beams. The weight against him. He jerked back as if scalded.

"What the devil are you doin'?" he rasped, scrubbing a hand across his mouth.

Sophie swallowed. "Alex, it's me. I only… I wanted to make up for the hurt I caused you. Ye've been so good to me. I thought, perhaps..."

"Nae!" He shoved himself upright, the blanket sliding to his waist. His eyes were bright in the firelight, hard with drink and something sharper. "Are ye mad?"

She froze.

"It's nine years past," he went on, each word clipped. "Nine years since ye chose to sell yourself. Ye didnae choose me. Ye chose the brothel. Ye chose that life. I didnae force it on ye. I tried tae get ye out o' it."

He laughed, short and ugly. "I walked in on ye with a man old enough tae be yer grandsire. An old fart pawin' at ye like he owned ye."

His eyes burned. "Aye, I was young. But ye looked me in the eye and said ye would wait."

Her breath caught.

"And now? Now, ye're married. A wife. And here I am, tryin' tae keep ye safe, and ye come crawlin' into my bed like nothin's changed."

She flinched as if struck.

"I'm no' your savior," he said coldly. "And I'm no' the lad ye once knew. That girl who laughed in my arms is gone. Ye buried her the day ye chose coin over honour."

Tears welled, spilling over her lashes.

"I brought ye here not tae have ye throw yourself at me like a whore hopin' it'll buy forgiveness."

Her face burned. "Alex, enough."

"Nae." He cut her off, sharp as a blade. "Do not touch me again. Do not pretend this is love, or longing, or regret. It's shame. And I willnae carry it for ye."

She shook, hands curling into the blanket.

"I've had enough o' bein' your mistake," he said hoarsely. "The past near broke me once. Ye dinnae get tae do it again."

He jabbed a finger toward the box bed. "Go. Sleep. In the mornin',
I'll see ye handed to the cook and sent on your way. After that, you
and I are naught but strangers who once shared a foolish memory."

Sophie snatched up his shirt, dragging it over her shoulders with
trembling hands. She stumbled back to the bed, humiliation
wrapping tight around her chest, her heart pounding so hard it hurt.

She lay awake for a long time. Silence whistled through the room,
broken only by the low crackle of the hearth.

Below her, on the floor, Alex stared at the ceiling, eyes open despite
the heaviness of drink. He could still feel the warmth of her skin
against his, the ghost of the girl she used to be, and the ache of the
boy he had once been.

His chest tightened.

"I'm only helpin' you," he thought fiercely, as if repeating it enough
would steady him.
"That's all.."

He took one last swallow from the bottle and closed his eyes, letting
grief, anger, and whisky drag him under, while outside the cabin the
night pressed close, holding them both in a silence neither knew how
to break.

Alex's Discovery

Morning bled into the cabin in a thin wash of pale light, and Alex woke with a skull-splitting ache. His tongue felt thick, his throat raw, and the moment he blinked toward the shuttered window, he froze.

"Shit," he muttered. "Andrew will skin me alive."

Alex jerked upright, his skull pounding like a drum.

"Sophie, I must leave. I'm late..."

He turned, expecting to see her still curled beneath the blanket, but the bed was empty.

Neatly made.
Too neatly.

His shirt lay folded across the mattress, as though she had set it there with trembling hands.

A cold ripple slid down his spine.

"Sophie?"

He stepped outside, squinting into the morning light, and froze.

His horse was nowhere in sight.

"What in God's name…?"

He hurried back inside, searching the room out of instinct, and only then noticed the rest.

His boots were missing from the hearth.
His sword was not by the door where he had left it.
The hook where his dirk should have hung stood empty.
His musket was gone as well.

Not in a neat list.
Gone in a way that struck him all at once, as though the room itself had been hollowed out.

He pressed both hands to his head.

"She took all of it?"

A breath punched out of him.

"Bloody hell, Sophie… what have you done? You have *got* to be jesting." He threw his hands into the air.

"She took everything. Even my fucking boots?"

A slip of parchment lay on the table.

He snatched it up.

Alex,

By the time you read this, I will be gone. Forgive me for taking your horse and belongings. I know what it cost you.

Everything you said last night was true. I have thought on it, and I cannot remain here. Nor can I return home. If I go back to my husband, the harm will be worse than before, and I will not survive it.

So I am leaving Scotland.

I have no money of my own. Selling what I took is the only way I can secure passage to France. I swear to you, I would not have done this if there were any other path left to me.

If God allows it, I will repay you one day, when I can earn my bread without selling myself.

Last eve, the way you looked at me made everything clear. I cannot live in the past or pretend I am still the girl you once knew. When you turned away from me, I finally understood what I have become. Your father was right.

Forgive me for the wrong I have done you, and for the shame I brought upon your kindness.

Sophie

Alex crushed the letter in his fist and flung it across the room. Fury burned through him, but beneath it, shame. A hollow, cutting shame.

Hoofbeats thundered outside.

Andrew's horse barely stopped before Andrew began shouting.

"Dammit, Alex! Why in God's name did you miss the council meeting? Because of you, every elder and distant cousin is stayin' another night."

Andrew's eyes swept the clearing. "Where the hell is your horse?"

"Will you shut up a moment and come inside."

Alex stepped through the doorway and instantly sobered.

Andrew, on the other hand, was taken aback by the look on his brother's face. "What ails you? Yer face is pale, like ye've seen a spirit."

Alex paced, rubbing the back of his neck until the skin went red.

"Do you remember my seventeenth birthday? When I lost my virginity to the lass from the brothel?"

Andrew blinked. "Aye… pray tell."

"Well, yesterday, after you left, I saw her at the tavern. She's married now, to Mr. Amos."

Andrew frowned. "Uh-huh. And?"

"He grew jealous when I merely greeted her. Dragged her into the kitchens and beat her senseless. Everyone heard the commotion. So I stepped in and returned the favour. I brought her here afterward, tryin' to get her safe. Then I drank far too much…"

He rubbed the back of his neck, shame tightening his voice.

"…and I fell asleep."

Andrew stared at him. "Did ye bed her?"

"Nae. I was piss-poor drunk yesterday, could barely see the damned floor. She tried to kiss me and… aye, I shouted at her." His voice cracked. "Made her feel shame. She left. And took, well… everything."

"Brilliant," Andrew grumbled. "First she's a whore, now a thief. And Da told ye plain as day. Yet here ye stand, head still thick as a peat log."

"She said she needed the money to flee to France." Alex's voice broke. "Andrew… I need to find her. Da gave me that dirk. And my horse, Bruce, Da gave him to me for my twenty-first birthday."

Andrew exhaled sharply, then nodded. "Come. Let's track her. The prints should still be fresh."

Andrew pushed his horse into a hard ride through dense woodland, Alex riding double behind him, weaving between pines and low brush. After nearly two miles, the trees opened to a narrow path, and there stood Bruce, calm as if nothing in the world were amiss, lazily grazing.

Andrew lifted a hand. "There. Is that not your belongings?"

Scattered across the grass lay Alex's sword, his musket, the dirk his father had gifted him, and both boots, one upright, the other toppled on its side, as though tossed in haste.

Alex slid from his saddle, brow furrowed. "Where the devil did she go? If highwaymen took her, they'd have taken Bruce as well."

"Think she stopped to relieve herself?" Andrew offered.

"Perhaps," Alex muttered, though dread twisted low in his gut.

They split off in opposite directions, pushing deeper into the underbrush. Only a few breaths passed before Andrew's voice cracked through the trees, raw and strangled.

"Mother of God!"

Alex's heart seized. "Andrew?" He broke into a run. "Andrew! What do you see?"

He burst through a line of brambles and skidded to a halt beside his brother, and the world lurched sideways.

The sight hit him so violently he bent over and vomited uncontrollably.

A severed leg lay half-hidden in the brush, torn brutally at the thigh. A small hand rested nearby, fingers scattered like snapped twigs. The earth itself looked gouged and wounded, some patches of blood dried dark, others still fresh.

And Sophie, or what was left of her body, lay scattered in the clearing. An arm was missing, her throat torn open so savagely the wound widened into her chest, her gown shredded into ribbons.

Alex wiped his mouth with a shaking hand, his entire body trembling. "Oh God, Sophie…" His voice cracked, breaking into a sob. "This is my fault. All of it. I'm so… so sorry."

Andrew knelt, forcing his attention to the ground instead of the body. "These prints…" He traced a paw mark with his fingertips, jaw tightening. "Wolves. Mackenzie wolves. Big ones. A full pack, by the look of it. More than five."

He shifted, gesturing toward the broken branches and churned earth. "Bruce must've panicked. Threw her when they came on him. She tried to run... see here?" He traced the disturbed ground with his hand. "She tripped. They dragged her from that point."

His voice dropped. "The attack was quick. She never had a chance. If she left before dawn alone, they'd have taken her easy."

Alex squeezed his eyes shut, grief ripping through him. He crouched and touched the side of Sophie's face, what little had been spared, then gently closed her eyes with trembling fingers.

Andrew pulled off his plaid and held it out. Wordlessly, Alex took it and wrapped what remained of her body, his hands shaking as he tucked the cloth around her as carefully as if she might still feel pain.

"She only sought comfort," he whispered. "I pushed her away. If I had spoken gently… if I had listened… she might still be alive."

Andrew rested a hand on his shoulder. "Stop, Alex. She made a reckless choice. She stole your things and ran into the woods alone. Wolves or slavers, someone would've found her. This wasnae your doing."

Alex lifted a hand, cutting him off. His grief was a solid, impenetrable wall.

With Sophie wrapped in the plaid, he lifted her into his arms, mounted Bruce, and turned toward home.

He rode ahead in silence, alone, with nothing but the weight of her death pressing against his spine.

The Only Commitment Requested

Alex made it back to the entrance of Tantallon's road just as Father McPherson crossed the cemetery path ahead of him.

"Father," Alex called. "May I have a word?"

The priest stopped, smiling at first, until he took Alex in properly.

Barefoot. Shirtless. Blood-streaked.
A body wrapped behind him on the horse.

"Oh, dear God," the priest breathed. "What has come tae pass?"

Alex bowed his head. "My heart is sore, Father."

The priest swallowed. "And who is that ye carry?"

"A friend," Alex said quietly. "I meant tae help her rebuild her life. Instead…" His voice faltered. "My words sent her runnin' into the woods. The wolves found her before I did."

"Poor lass." The priest crossed himself. "Does she have kin?"

"Her husband owns the town tavern. Her folk live in Edinburgh, but she'd nae ties left to them." His voice cracked. "I would see her laid tae rest. Under the old tree I loved as a boy." He looked up then. "Father… will ye commit her body?"

"Aye, Chieftain," the priest said gently. "I will see it done."

Alex handed Sophie's remains over for cleansing. A single tear traced down his cheek as he stepped away.

Now a Widower

Alex bathed, dressed, and rode into town. The tavern was shuttered, a crooked sign reading **CLOSED** hanging from a single hinge.

He entered through the back. The silence pressed in on him.

"Mr. Amos?" he called.

The man sat alone at a table, a whisky bottle clenched in his fist. His face was bruised, his nose crooked, his eyes hollowed out by drink and sleeplessness.

Alex took a step closer. "Is all well? I've never known this place tae close."

Mr. Amos didn't answer the question. He didn't bother with pleasantries.

"What is my dear wife?" he said flatly. "Did she not ride off into the sunset with ye?"

Alex stiffened. "I was trying tae save her from your abuse."

Mr. Amos let out a short, broken laugh.
"Abuse?" He shook his head. "After all I did for her? Raisin' a child that isnae mine?"

Alex went still.

Mr. Amos looked up sharply. "Did she tell ye that?"

Something cold settled in Alex's chest. Sophie's voice came back to him, the hesitation, the words she had almost said and then swallowed.

What about... Never mind. She meant to mention a child.

Mr. Amos wiped at his nose with the back of his hand, his voice cracking despite himself.
"She lied. Tricked me. Lost the ability tae bear more children because she got rid of many before she ever gave me my lad."

Alex said nothing. Sophie had never told him. Not once.

"I loved her," Mr. Amos said hoarsely. "I treated the boy as my own." His shoulders sagged. "Chieftain… bring her home. I swear I'll never lay a hand on her again."

Alex drew a slow breath, pain tightening behind his ribs.

"Mr. Amos… I met Sophie when I was seventeen summers. I wished tae marry her. My da forbade it. Yesterday, I only meant tae help her leave ye." His voice wavered. "She wanted tae bed me. I refused her, so she fled before sunrise."

Mr. Amos burst into laughter. "The shameless rake Alex Barton?" He scoffed. "Please, tell me a shorter tale."

"Mr. Amos, I'm tellin' ye the truth," Alex said tightly. "She took everything and left."

Mr. Amos's jaw clenched.

"So, she stole from ye," he said. "She tried that once with me." His eyes narrowed. "Where is she now? France?"

Alex swallowed.

"Nae, Mr. Amos."

His voice dropped, heavy as stone.

"Sophie is dead."

Mr. Amos lurched to his feet. "What did ye say?"

"She went through the woods. Wolves took her. My brother and I found what remained. She rests with the Kirk now. Ye may go and see her."

The man collapsed back into his chair, sobbing into his hands.

"Sophie… ye foolish girl."

Alex placed a hand on his shoulder. "If ye'll allow it, I would hold a small service for her. Bury her on Barton land."

Grief

The next day, Alex, Andrew, Mr. Amos, and young Amos Jr. stood beneath the great ash tree overlooking Barton lands. Sophie's grave lay before them, the small wooden casket lowered gently into the earth. Morning wind stirred the leaves above, carrying the scent of damp soil and heather.

Father McPherson closed his Bible softly.
"And the Lord saw a young lass's pain," he said, voice low. "So He called her home. Earth to earth, ashes to ashes, dust to dust."

Soil scattered across the lid. Andrew and Alex finished lowering the casket, their movements slow and reverent. Mr. Amos clutched his son's shoulders, shaking.

Alex could bear no more. Grief tightened his chest until breath failed him. He excused himself quietly and walked away before anyone saw the tears gather.

He made it only as far as his chambers before whisky drowned the world.

For the rest of the week, Alex missed every council meeting.

Andrew watched helplessly as his brother unraveled. Three deaths weighed on him. Mother. Father. Sophie.

One night, Andrew forced open the chamber door and followed the sound of low groans.

He found Alex collapsed in the privy closet, half-conscious, covered in his own vomit and urine.

"Christ, Alex…" Andrew whispered, the sight cracking something inside him.

Without hesitation, he hauled his brother up, cleaned him, washed the floor before the maids could gossip, and carried Alex to bed. He tucked the blankets around him like he had when they were boys.

Andrew fussed, brushing damp hair from his brother's forehead,

"For God's sake Alex, I ken ye loved Da… and I ken ye cared for the lass. But this, this is killing ye. Ye're laird now. Da trusted ye. Ye must find yer feet again."

Alex said nothing. But even drunk, the words pierced him.

By morning, Alex looked less like a man and more like a ghost wearing his face.

Still, something inside him had shifted. It was Andrew's voice

find yer feet again

He stood, and drag himself toward the basin..

A knock sounded at his chamber door.

"Who goes there?" he called, irritation sharp in his voice.

"Tis me, Sarah… the chambermaid."

He grunted. "Come."

The door creaked open, and a young woman stepped inside with a basket of linens hugged to her waist. Her eyes widened the moment she took in the state of his room, and him, but she curtseyed softly.

"Good morn, my laird. Andrew asked me tae tidy yer chambers and see tae the linens ye left out."

Alex barely spared her a glance, too focused on the careful art of shaving.

The razor slipped, slicing across his cheek.

"Damnation… bloody hell," he muttered, more irritated by his own carelessness than the sting.

Sarah gasped when she saw the blood. "My laird, ye're cut."

Before he could dismiss her, she rushed into the privy for a cloth. He pressed a finger to the warm trickle, exhaling sharply.

"Lass, a cloth. Quickly."

She returned at once, breathless, placing a folded rag into his hand, though her fingers trembled as they brushed his.

"Oh my… ye've cut yerself deeper than ye think. Please, allow me."

Alex did not care enough to protest, yet when she stepped close to dab the wound, the scent of her hair and the softness of her touch stole the breath straight from his lungs.

Delicate features.
Wide, earnest eyes.
Breasts the size of melons.

And her dress, saints preserve him, fit in ways God Himself surely intended for the torment of men.

He whispered, "Christ above… when did this one appear?"

She looked up at him. "What was that, my laird?"

"Oh, ah… nothin'." He averted his gaze.

Grief had not loosened its hold, but something warm threaded through the cold edges of it.

"Lass, it's just a scratch," he muttered. "Do yer chores and be gone."

But she dabbed gently at his cheek anyway, her touch feather-light.

Her scent, wildflowers and clean linens, slipped beneath his guard.

Her innocence was unmistakable.

And Alex Barton was a man who, in his darkest moments, sought distraction the way drowning men sought air.

He watched her beneath lowered lashes, already measuring her.

"Are ye new here?" he asked, as though the thought had only just occurred to him.

"Nae, my laird. I came just afore yer father took ill."

"I must have been away then."

"Aye. You and yer brother were gone near ten months."

That explained it. Too long for him to have noticed her before.

His gaze lingered now, openly, tracing the shy curve of her smile, the careful way she held herself, as though afraid of taking up more space than she was allowed.

"What's yer name, lass?"

"Sarah McDonald."

"McDonald," he repeated, tasting it, lips tilting into a slow, practiced smile. "And is there some poor lad courtin' ye?"

Her blush bloomed instantly, honest and unguarded. "Nae, my laird. I… I hope tae find the right one."

Of course she did.

Alex shifted slightly, easing back against the mattress and propping himself on one elbow. His voice softened, warming as it drew her in. He patted the mattress for a friendly chat.

"Come then. Sit a moment," he said gently. "Ye look like ye're about tae bolt."

She hesitated, fingers twisting in her apron, then perched beside him, smoothing her skirts with nervous care.

He leaned closer, just enough for her to notice.

"With beauty like yours, ye shouldna be hid away changin' sheets and scrubbin' floors. Ye deserve someone of station."

"A title means nothing," she said quietly. "Not if it comes without happiness."

That struck him harder than he expected.
Simple words. Too honest.
It made him look at her, not as a distraction, but as a girl who still believed the world might offer her something kind.

"Oh?" He turned her hand over in his thumb brushing her palm as though absentmindedly. "Then tell me, Sarah McDonald. What makes ye happy?"

Her lips parted, her smile small and hopeful, as if no one had ever asked her that before.

And that was all the permission he needed.

He leaned in and brushed his mouth against hers, light as breath.

A test.

If she pulled away, he would laugh it off, call it a mistake.

She did not.

Her hand rose, uncertain, resting against his shoulder as though she feared being sent away. She leaned in instead, trusting, clumsy with it.

Alex deepened the kiss slowly, expertly, giving her time to follow, to believe she was choosing this.

"Lass," he breathed, knuckles brushing her cheek, "has any man kissed ye before?"

"Nae," she whispered, breathless. "I'm two and twenty. I meant tae wait for marriage."

Of course she had.

Alex exhaled slowly.
It won't be me.
But perhaps he could gift her one moment that felt like something more than chores and stone corridors.

"Ye're special, Sarah," he said quietly, the words delivered with the ease of long practice. "Far more than ye ken."

Her breath hitched. "Ye think me special?"

"Aye," he said, smiling as though it were the simplest truth in the world. "And I want tae show ye."

He kissed her again, slower now, guiding rather than taking, letting her feel as though every step was her own choice.

"My laird," she whispered, unsteady but not afraid. "What are ye doin'?"

"Shh…" he whispered against her throat. "Trust me."

His fingers stroked her womanhood softly in circular motions, she moaned softly, clutching the sheets.

"I… I feel like I'm falling," she whispered, overwhelmed.

Moments later, pleasure broke through her like a wave she never saw coming, her body trembling as tears shimmered at the corners of her eyes.

When she finally sagged back against him, stunned and breathless, Alex allowed himself a slow, wicked smile, one that masked grief with ego, guilt with charm, loneliness with indulgence.

Aye, he thought smugly.
This could be the start of a very lovely friendship.

Rock Bottom

Two years had passed since the death of Alex's father.

The grief no longer crushed him outright; instead, it lingered, a shadow that followed him from dawn to dusk, whispering failure with every breath.

Andrew had taken charge of the estate and Clan matters as requested, stepping into the role Alex should have filled. But Alex… he could not pull himself into any shape that resembled a laird.

Home felt like judgment.

Tantallon felt like a mirror he refused to look into.

So he hid.

And the tavern became the place where he drowned himself, quietly, privately, disgracefully.

He spent his nights in Mr. Amos's alehouse, watching over Sophie's young son as if the boy were the last flicker of goodness he still possessed. But the rest of the night… whisky, cards, flesh, and anything else that dulled the ache behind his ribs.

The tiny back room had turned into his sanctuary of ruin.

Whispers circled of the laird who indulged in acts he'd never dare commit beneath the stone towers of Tantallon. Anonymous bodies, shared pleasures, nights tangled with strangers whose names he never asked. Ménage-à-trois, gambling until dawn, whisky poured like water, every sin was simply a way to quiet his ghosts.

Mr. Amos, once only an acquaintance, now reluctantly claimed him as a friend. And friends, eventually, reached their limit.

That night, Amos stood at the kitchen entry, arms folded, watching Alex slumped over a card table. Drunk beyond sense. Cheating openly. Slurring insults. His very presence poisoning the room.

One of the card players slammed his palms onto the table.

"Not because ye're the chieftain's son and newly named laird must I stomach yer insults," the man barked. "How dare ye call me a cheatin' bastard. Look at ye. Ye're drunk, a menace, and an embarrassment to this place. I admired yer father all my life, Laird Calum. He'd roll in his grave if he saw ye cheatin' through life like yer uncle Graham."

A hush fell around the room.

Alex rose, or tried to. His fist swung wide, missing the mark entirely.

"Keep my Da's name out yer filthy mouth, ye daft Highlander!"

He missed again.

The other man didn't.

One clean punch sent Alex crashing backward, scattering cards and mugs across the floor. Patrons slipped out the door, wanting no part of the laird's downfall.

Alex staggered, swaying as he lurched to follow his opponent. His legs gave out. He collapsed in the entryway, dead weight on the planks.

Mr. Amos rushed forward and knelt beside him.

"Laird Alex, enough is enough. I'm sendin' word tae yer brother. Ye're goin' home."

Alex didn't stir.

He woke only when the wagon wheels rattled beneath him.

His head swam. His stomach rolled. Andrew's silhouette sat stiff at the front of the wagon. Haemish steered the reins. But the world blurred before Alex could make sense of it.

He drifted again.

And the dream swept him back.

He stood carrying heavy stones, the same punishment his father set upon him for sneakin' off tae a brothel as a lad. The weight bowed his shoulders. His arms trembled. But he trudged on because he'd been told a Barton man endured.

His father appeared ahead.

Alex's heart leapt. "Da!"

But he slowed.

Calum Barton's face carried a deep scowl.

"Da… what is the matter? Do I upset ye?"

"Son," Calum's voice thundered, "ye're a disgrace tae the Barton name. After all I taught ye, this is what ye become? A drunk. A cheat. And what of yer mother? Andrew? Poor Mr. Amos who must endure yer misery? What was the point of raisin' ye into a man, only for ye tae act an arse now that I am gone?"

"Da… I…"

Calum pointed to the younger Alex, still staggering beneath the stones.

"Do ye see them? Each stone is the burden ye lay on others. Yer brother… the Clan. All who care for ye. We all leave this earth, lad. Grieve me, aye, but donnae drown yerself tryin' tae join me."

Alex broke. He dropped the stones and fell into his father's arms, sobbing.

"I miss ye so much, Da…"

"Oh, enough, ye block heided fool." Calum muttered, annoyed. "I dinna raise a lass. Ye're Highland strong. Cease yer cryin' and be the elder brother Andrew needs. Can I depend on ye?"

Alex nodded helplessly.

Then Calum's voice softened, shifted, becoming someone else's.

"Laird Alex… Laird…"

He jolted awake in his chambers, breath ragged.

Sarah stood beside the bed, worry etched across her features.

"Laird Alex, is all well with ye? I came tae gather yer linens, and… ye were tossin' terribly. Cryin'."

He sat up, scrubbing his face. "Is it mornin' already?"

"Aye. Several hours past."

He swallowed hard. "I dreamt of my Da."

Concern softened her small features. She sat beside him, too close, but he had no strength to push her away. She rubbed his back gently.

"I see ye still grieve, my laird. Is that why ye've been gone so long?"

The words loosened something inside him.

Alex had no strength left to hold anything together, not pride, not dignity, not the image of the laird he was meant to be. He bowed his head, unable to hide the tears that spilled freely down his cheeks.

"My father… he… he's disappointed in me. He said so in my dream. God, I've been such an arse these past few years…"

"Oh, there now, Laird Alex," she soothed, handing him a cloth. "I lost my mother too. Sometimes all ye need is kindness."

But when he realized how exposed he was,
how vulnerable,
his voice wavered.

"It hurts," he whispered. "Knowin' he sees my actions."

Sarah cupped his face.

"I dinna think yer father sees yer actions. He rests peacefully. But ye see them, my laird. And because ye ken he would never approve… ye believe he's disappointed. That means ye care. That means ye're still good."

Her words pierced deeper than she knew.

Alex nodded slowly, unsure whether he agreed with Sarah or simply lacked the strength to contradict her. Before he could find his footing, she leaned forward and pressed her lips to his, soft, trembling, and full of a hope he had never promised her. She remembered the passion he had shown her once before, misunderstanding it as something meaningful. In her young, unguarded heart, she believed he could be the man she dreamed of.

The kiss startled him, and he froze beneath it. A frown tugged at his brow as he gently pulled back.

"It's no' the right time, lass," he murmured, but the disappointment in her eyes barely had a moment to settle before she acted again.

His name still lingered in the air,
"Laird Alex… Please, allow me."

She swung a leg over his waist and settled atop him. Her fingers trembled as she worked at the ties of her chemise, letting the garment slip from her shoulders with hesitant bravery. Her breath came quick and uneven, a blend of nerves and yearning.

Alex reached for her shoulders, steadying her. "Sarah… are ye certain ye want tae do this?"

"I'm nae certain," she admitted, "but I feel drawn tae ye. Like I can trust ye."

Her words struck him in a way he wished they didn't.

"Lass… donnae place all yer trust in me. I'm no' the man ye think I am."

But she cupped his cheek with tender fingers, refusing to hear the warning. "Today… we trust each other."

Before he could gather the right words to stop her, she kissed him again, this time with a desperate hunger she mistook for affection. She pressed herself against him, seeking comfort, validation, something to fill the emptiness she believed he shared. The soft grind of her hips forced a sound from his throat he never meant to give, and in his hollow, exhausted state, he lacked the strength to push her away.

She took his stillness as permission.

He knew it the moment she lay back, opening herself in full trust.

But what she expected from him, a gentle joining, a moment of shared warmth, was not what he delivered. Whatever tenderness he possessed had long been drowned beneath grief and shame. Something inside him shut down the moment he moved over her.

He did not kiss her.

He did not whisper comfort.

He did not take her hand or guide her gently.

He simply entered her, quick and unthinking, never pausing to understand what her sharp gasp truly meant. Her fingers twisted into the bedding as pain flashed across her face, but Alex's mind, clouded and numb, saw none of it.

The encounter was over almost as soon as it began, five or six hurried thrusts followed by a hollow shudder that left him colder than before. Shame crept over him the instant he rolled away, staring at the canopy above as if it might hold an answer to the question tormenting him.

He placed a hand over his face. "What in God's name is wrong with me?"

He lay for a moment, thinking of a way to tell her his sins.

When he finally spoke, his voice was rough.

"Sarah… I'm no' a good man. And I donnae love ye. Please… leave my chambers. And dinna return."

She stiffened as the truth cut through her, the hopeful glow in her eyes extinguished in an instant. Tears spilled silently as she gathered her garments and his laundry, clinging to whatever dignity she could salvage.

At the doorway, he called her once more. "Sarah… forgive me. And… this must remain between us."

Her voice trembled, but she stood tall.

"Ye have my word, Laird Alex. This was my foolishness. I thought we shared somethin'. But ye're my superior, and I'm only a chambermaid. I'll take my leave now. Good day, Chieftain."

"Sarah, wait…"

But the door closed before he could finish.

He struck the mattress in frustration, but his hand landed in something wet and warm. He looked down and saw the smear of blood.

"Shite…" he whispered, horror rising in his throat. "She was a virgin."

Dragging a hand down his face, he forced himself out of bed and hurried to dress. Shame clung to him as he walked the corridor toward the great hall.

At the bottom of the stair, he heard Andrew's sharp voice carrying across the room. Alex grabbed an apple from a passing servant, taking a large bite before stepping forward.

"Mornin', Andrew," he said, forcing calm. "What is it I'll no' like?"

Andrew turned, the strain of responsibility etched plainly on his face. In that moment, Alex remembered his father's words, *each stone ye carry is the burden ye place upon others.*

Andrew set down the cloth in his hands. "We leave at dawn. We must sail tae receive a seal of voyage from King James."

Alex nearly choked. "Andrew, we just returned. Apologies, but I'm nae goin'."

Irritation flickered across Andrew's features, though he held his tongue.

"Listen," Alex continued, "it's time I step up as Da's heir. I ken I've disappointed ye. But I've been grievin'."

"I know," Andrew admitted quietly.

"Then allow me this," Alex said. "Let me stay. Taxes must be collected, and the villagers think we've forgotten them. Da trained me for this since I could stand and piss. Let me prove myself now. And I swear, I'll never touch another bottle of spirit again."

Andrew studied him long and hard before stepping forward and pressing his forehead to Alex's.

"I trust ye," he murmured. "And I ken ye'll do what's right."

He turned to leave, tossing one final remark over his shoulder.

"Let yer cock rest… and let yer mind think."

Andrew had been lost at sea for nearly two years, and Alex had not let the fear of that absence drag him back into foolishness. He had worked as his father taught him, handling what needed tending, trusting his brother would return.

And he had.

Andrew came home with a bairn on the way and handfasted to a princess of a foreign land. Their next voyage together would not be for trade, but for rescue.

Chapter Four

Part I – The Foreigners

Yvonne wiped the stone floor in slow circles, dipping the cloth

back into the warm water as steam rose around her. The scent of soap and crushed herbs filled the room, but it did nothing to calm the tightness in her chest. Every sound outside the bath hall caught her attention, guards shifting in the courtyard, footsteps climbing the outer stairs, a distant shout carried on the wind.

She hated how jumpy she had become. Always listening, watching, and waiting for the wrong face to appear.

King Oyomo's men could be anywhere. His name traveled farther than his feet ever would. As long as no one recognized her, she could pretend she was safe. But she knew the truth. Her safety was borrowed, and one day he would come to collect.

She drew in a slow breath and forced her hand to keep moving.

Nyema walked in carrying a basket of drying cloths. Her arms were full, but her spirit looked empty. The usual softness in her eyes was gone. Her mouth formed a small, miserable pout.

Yvonne's shoulders dropped. "Nyema, your lips are pouted up at the sky… what is the matter?"

Nyema set the basket on the table a little too hard. "Prince Femi has been gone three months," she said, voice already shaking. "Three. And he left without even saying goodbye."

Yvonne sat back on her heels and studied her. "Ah, Nyema…"

"I miss him," Nyema whispered. "More than I want to admit."

Yvonne dipped the cloth again, more out of habit than need. "Missing a man like him is dangerous business."

Nyema blinked quickly, trying to hold back tears. "I think I am in love."

Yvonne's mouth tightened, though she kept her tone gentle. "You are infatuated. There is a difference."

"He once admitted that he loved me." Nyema studied Yvonne's reaction to her words. She knew of their closeness. "I still await to be his concubine."

Yvonne's hand stilled. For a breath, the bath hall tilted, and she saw not walls and steam, but memories. Femi's easy smile, his warm words, the way he seemed to see only her.

She swallowed and steadied herself. "Nyema, Prince Femi speaks very sweetly when it pleases him. That does not mean he intends to keep those words. His position requires charm. It does not promise loyalty."

Nyema stared at her. "You sound jealous."

A soft, tired laugh slipped from Yvonne. "No. I care about you. That is why I am warning you. Femi's kindness feels special, I know that. But it can be mistaken for something deeper than it truly is."

Nyema's expression softened. "He hurt you."

Yvonne looked down at the wet stone beneath her. "No. Another man did." Her voice dropped to a whisper. "And I would spare you anything that feels close to that."

Before Nyema could answer, a ceremonial horn sounded across the courtyard. Deep. Heavy. A sound that made Yvonne's bones vibrate.

Nyema gasped. "That is not the morning patrol."

"No," Yvonne said, rising slowly. "Someone important has arrived."

The lead servant burst through the doorway, cheeks flushed, breathing fast. "Ladies, quickly. Prince Femi has returned, and he brings Princess Nzingha with him."

Yvonne's heart stumbled. "Princess Nzingha? She has been missing nearly three years."

"Yes," the woman said as she hurried to the windows and threw open the curtains, letting bright sunlight spill into the hall. "And she is accompanied by three special guests from across the sea. We must have everything prepared at once."

The room moved in a flurry after that. By midday, the bath hall shone like a jewel. Warm pools steamed beneath floating petals. Copper basins of herbs simmered along the walls. Polished trays of oils, combs, razors, and neat cloths lined every bench and shelf.

Yvonne stood at her station, arranging her grooming tools, grateful for the distraction of straight lines and clean steel.

Then she heard them.

Footsteps on the stone staircase. It was heavy. Confident.

Their voices followed, low and deep, the syllables thick and unfamiliar.

Laughter rolled into the chamber in a sound that did not belong to Tafaria.

She turned her head and peeked from behind a curtain.

Three men were descending the stair.

They were enormous by Tafarian measure, broad shoulders, strong arms, thick chests that made the air around them feel smaller. Their clothing was unlike anything she had ever seen, pleated cloth wrapped at their waists and draped over one shoulder, fastened with silver brooches that glinted in the light. Their skin was pale as smooth stone, their features sharp, noses and jaws carved in angles.

Two of them had dark hair, wet from the heat of the room, falling past their necks.

The third carried hair the color of sunlight poured over grain. Gold, bright and startling.

Yvonne could not look away.

The golden haired man's gaze swept the hall with practiced ease, taking in everything. Then his eyes found hers. His gaze held her. For a heartbeat, the world shrank to the space between them.

Her breath hitched.

She ducked back at once, pretending to fuss with soaps that were already perfectly aligned on a tray.

Prince Femi entered moments later. His stride was composed as always, his eyes less so. Yvonne lowered her gaze out of habit, but he was already looking her way.

"Prince Femi," she said softly, "does your brother know of these men from across the sea?"

"Yes," he answered a little too quickly. "He invited them."

"There is no need to bite," she murmured. "I only asked a question."

His shoulders eased. "These men returned my niece safely. Their presence honors our land. That is all you need to know."

Yvonne nodded once. "And King Oyomo. Where is he today?"

Femi hesitated, then took a step closer to her. "Traveling through nearby villages."

Something troubled lingered in his gaze.

"Yvonne," he said quietly, "there is something I must tell you."

The fear inside her lifted its head. "What is it?"

He looked at her for a long moment, as if weighing whether to say the words at all. "Oyomo is searching for you. If he does not find you, he intends to execute your parents. He believes they helped you escape."

Yvonne's knees weakened. "No. No, that cannot be true."

"I would not lie about this," Femi replied. "Not to you."

She gripped the edge of the nearby table until her fingers ached. "What am I supposed to do?"

"There is one way I know to protect you. But you will likely hate it." He reached for her hand. His touch was gentle, thumb brushing lightly over the back of her wrist.

"Well, what is it?"

"Become my sixth wife. If you belong to my household, Oyomo cannot claim you without starting a war he cannot win."

Her heart twisted so sharply she almost winced. "Femi, that is not a solution. You are already warming the bed of my friend. And whether we like it or not, I am still married to Oyomo in the eyes of the tribes. This would only bring more trouble."

"Then give me another answer," he snapped, just for a second, before his tone softened. "Tell me how to keep you safe, Yvonne."

"Bring my parents here," she said. "Keep them close. If he wishes to punish someone, let him meet you instead of them."

Femi pulled his hand back, frustration tightening his jaw. "No. They caused this when they gave you to him."

Yvonne straightened. "Then understand this. I will not marry you out of fear. Not for protection. Not for duty. Not like that."

Before he could reply, Nyema stepped between them, her brows lifting. "This looks… intimate."

Femi straightened immediately, his tone shifting to something cool and princely.

"We were discussing who these men are," he said. "Nothing more."

Nyema's expression tightened anyway, reading far more into the moment than was actually spoken.

Yvonne released a small, exhausted breath.

"By the ancestors, this day grows worse with every minute."

The foreign men began to undress, their movements easy and unashamed. Linen fell from broad shoulders, muscles shifting beneath pale skin as though carved from stone. Nyema stole a look and nearly dropped the cloth she was holding.

"Yvonne," she hissed, clutching her wrist. "Do you see them? These men are huge; their bodies look like they were sculpted by the gods themselves."

"I have eyes," Yvonne muttered, though she kept hers pointed firmly at her tray.

The lead servant clapped sharply. "Enough gawking. Nyema, attend to Prince Femi. Yvonne, take your grooming tray and serve the honored guests."

Yvonne groaned under her breath. "Why must it be me who tends to the giants…"

"Go."

"Yes, miss."

She lifted her tray and approached the nearest foreigner, one of the dark-haired men. His expression was calm, polite even. No arrogance. No ogling. Just quiet curiosity, which she appreciated more than she expected.

"Excuse me, honored guest," she said softly. "May I offer a shave or a trim?"

"Aye," he answered.

She blinked, unsure of his answer. "I am sorry… what does that mean?"

His lips curved, the corners of his eyes crinkling with amusement. "It means yes, lass."

"Then say yes."

"Aye sounds better." He winked.

She tried to keep her face stern, but a reluctant smile tugged at the corner of her mouth. He settled himself, and she stepped behind him, working with steady hands. He sat so still, so cooperative, that she silently thanked him as she shaved the edges of his beard and smoothed the damp hair at his neck.

When she finished and stepped back, she felt it at once. Another gaze. She turned.
The golden-haired foreigner sat at the edge of the pool, arms resting along the stone rim, water lapping quietly against his skin. He was watching her without apology, and when their eyes met, he did not look away.

"Well," he said slowly, his voice warm, "that's a dangerous way tae look at a man. Especially with beauty like yers."

Yvonne blinked once.

"Apologies, honored guest," she said, steadying her tone. "May I offer you a service? Shaving, perhaps, waxing?"

His mouth curved, half smile, half curiosity. "Aye, though I dinnae ken what a wax is."

She paused, listening to the shape of his words. Familiar, but thickened. The syllables rolled from his tongue in a way she was not used to hearing. She let the silence stretch before answering.

"It removes the hair instead of shaving," she said. "Even from the most intimate areas. For cleanliness."

His brows lifted. "That sounds… thorough."

"Will you be needing a full service this day?"

"Aye. Yer finest."

She gestured toward the pallet. He stood, reached for a drying cloth, and fastened it around his waist, glancing at her as though waiting to see if she would object.
She did not.
He followed her with an easy stride, confidence worn loosely, like a habit.

"What is your name, honored guest?" she asked once he lay back.

"Alex. Laird Alex Barton."

"Laird," the word rolled from her tongue. "Very well, Laird Alex. Please remove your drying cloth."

He blinked, then laughed under his breath. "Straight tae business, I see. Why must I remove my cloth?"

"Because this is grooming. Not seduction."

"A pity. I was hopin' I'd misread the room."

She shot him a look.

"I'm teasin'," he added, grin widening. "Well… mostly."

"I will begin with your face," she said firmly, reaching for her blade. "Then finish with your intimate area."

"Right. Aye. Of course. I ken I'm in good hands."

She stepped closer to shave his beard, careful and precise. As she leaned in, her breast brushed his arm.
Alex went still.
Color rushed into his cheeks, deep and unmistakable. He swallowed and fixed his eyes on the ceiling.

Yvonne noticed.

She withdrew at once, rinsing the blade longer than necessary. "Hold still. I wish not to slip and harm you."

"Aye, I'm tryin'." He pushed out a breath as she leaned in again, his skin growing hot as her closeness lingered.

It had been years since his confidence had dwindled. Her beauty made him nervous. He could see she was not interested in conversing, but he was Alex. What lass could not resist his charm?

"You do this often?"

"It is my work," she replied, her head tilted in concentration.

"Must be difficult, standin' so close tae strangers. Touchin' them in the most ungodly areas."

"It keeps them clean."

"That's no' what I meant," he said softly.

She did not answer.

As she worked, she noticed the fine gold in the hair beneath his arms, the softer strands across his chest, the contrast of his pale skin against the darker cloth.

"Fascinating," she murmured.

He tilted his head slightly. "What's so fascinatin'?"

"Nothing. Hold still."

When she applied the wax, her hand brushed him again. He hardened instantly.
She froze.

"Oh, my."

He glanced down, then back at her, clearly mortified. "I… it does that. Apologies."

She kept her eyes firmly on her task. "I can see that."

"So ye're no' impressed."

"No, I am working."

His smile softened, embarrassment giving way to something gentler. "You do yer work very well, lass. Ye've got gentle hands."

She finally looked up. "Please do not call me that. I do not know what it means."

"What should I call ye, then?"

She looked at him coolly. "Woman."

He studied her a moment, heat still coloring his face. "Lass sounds softer," he said quietly. "And it suits ye."

Her pulse stumbled. She turned away, suddenly very invested in her tools.

After a moment, he spoke again, slower now. "Why does yer skin catch the light that way? Ye have small gold hair, matching the hair on yer head. And yer eyes… I've never seen them like. Ye are breath taking.."

She hesitated.

"I descend from a tribe that carries golden features. in the north. When my mother was young, she was taken," she said quietly. "Because of her beauty, she was forced to become a concubine. I have her features." "And yer father?"

"He is from the west, but I do not wish to speak of them."

He nodded.

She stepped back. "The trimming is finished. Now for the waxing. There may be discomfort."

"Discomfort," he repeated. "That word carries many meanings."

"It means pain."

"Well, that would have been good tae ken earlier."

She pressed the wax cloth into place with practiced ease. "Hold still."

He exhaled slowly through his nose.

"You will be fine," she said. "You may even appreciate it later."

"That's what men always say afore somethin' terrible happens."

She positioned her hand at the edge of the cloth and began to count.
"One."
He tensed beneath her fingers.
"Two."

His jaw tightened. "Ye take pleasure in this part, don't ye?"

"Three."

She ripped the wax away in one swift motion.
Alex shouted, loud and unrestrained, the sound echoing off the stone walls. Nearby, a servant startled and nearly dropped a basin. His whole body went rigid, then sagged back against the pallet.

"God above," he groaned. "That was barbaric."

Yvonne hid her smile as she cleaned the strip. "There. Much better."

"That was the work of a tormentor, no' a healer."

"It builds character."

"I had enough character afore I arrived," he muttered.

She reached for another strip. He eyed it warily. "We're no' done?"

"You asked for a full service."

"Aye, I did."

She applied the next strip. His breath hitched, and she paused just long enough to notice.

"You're very quiet now," she observed.

"I'm considerin' my life choices. This was a daft idea."

She pulled. He swore under his breath, fingers curling into the linen.

"Now, all clean."

He glanced down, wincing. "Tell me honestly. Does it look bigger?"

She finally glanced, expression unreadable, then pressed her fingers together, leaving the smallest bit of space. "Barely."

"Ye are cruel."

"No," she corrected, "but, efficient."

She began cleaning her tools, methodically and focused, already moving away from him. Before she could step back fully, his hand closed gently around her wrist.

She stilled.

"Will ye meet me this evenin'? I'd love tae speak with ye more. Perhaps ye can show me yer lands."

She looked at his hand on her wrist, then at his face. He was well out of line.

"My apologies, no. Servants are not allowed to mingle with honored guests."

"What if I ask someone who can change that?"

"Please. Do not."

But he was already lifting his head, his grin returning as his voice carried easily across the bath hall. "Prince Femi, may Yvonne escort me around the grounds this evenin'?"

The room froze. Nyema nearly dropped her sponge. The lead servant stopped mid-step.
Femi turned.

His gaze landed first on Alex, then on Alex's hand around Yvonne's wrist. A muscle in his jaw ticked.

"No!"

"Aw, come on, Prince," Alex said lightly. "We leave in a few days. If no' the grounds, then perhaps the castle?"

"Does the servant agree?" Femi asked coolly.

Servant.

Yvonne almost laughed. Since when had he remembered what she was paid to be?

She drew her hand free and straightened. "Yes," she said, her voice tight. "I agree."

Alex smiled, entirely too pleased with himself.

Rage beamed across Femi's face. Before he could say another word, Yvonne turned on her heel and left the bath hall.

Out in the corridor, the air felt cooler, but it did not soothe her. She walked too fast, trying to outpace her own thoughts, and nearly collided with two of King Oyomo's guards as they turned the corner.

Her heart stopped.

One of them squinted at her, his gaze raking over her face, as if he were trying to pull her from a memory.

Recognition flickered in his eyes.

Yvonne knew him. He was one of the men who had been summoned to tie her to the bed when Oyomo prepared to claim her.

She dropped her head at once and clutched the tray closer to her, forcing her feet to move. One step. Then another. She did not breathe until she was past them.

By the time she reached her small room, her hands trembled so badly she had to set the tray down before she dropped it. Memories crashed through her, the rough ropes, the weight on her chest, the sound of Oyomo's breathing.

"I will not go back," she whispered.

A light knock sounded.

"Yvonne," Nyema's voice came through the door. "It is me."

Yvonne wiped her face quickly and opened it. Nyema slipped inside, brows knitted with concern.

"What happened?" Nyema asked. "You looked frightened when you left."

"I cannot do this," Yvonne said, pacing the small room. "The yellow-haired man expects a tour this evening. I cannot go alone."

She looked at Nyema with desperation.

In turn, Nyema wrinkled her nose. "Do you think the two of us can manage that giant? He looks strong enough to lift a cow."

Despite everything, a short laugh broke out of Yvonne.

"That is exactly the problem. Who knows what tricks he has."

She paused, then an idea sparked. "We will not go alone. We will bring Zara."

"The king's favorite?" Nyema's eyes went wide, "Yvonne, she is too…"

"Expensive, I know. But she is also useful."

Nyema's lips curled into a grin. "Then let us go."

They walked down the narrow paths toward Zara's village. The air outside was thick with dust and the smell of cooking food. Children ran toward Yvonne as they always did, wrapping their arms around her waist.

"Hujambo, Bi Yvonne," one of the girls chirped. "Do you have sweets today?"

"Not today," Yvonne answered with a soft smile in their tongue. "But tomorrow, I will bring some only for you."

The child beamed and ran off.

Nyema nudged her. "They love you."

"They are easier to please than most grown adults," Yvonne replied.

They reached Zara's small home. Yvonne pulled a small bag of coins from her sash and clutched it against her palm before knocking.

"Yes. Who is it?" Zara called from inside.

"It is Yvonne and Nyema. We would speak with you."

Zara opened the door and smiled. "Come in."

They exchanged quick hugs before Yvonne got to the point.

"I have a proposition for you," Yvonne said. "It involves no heavy work. I promise it will be… entertaining."

Zara folded her arms. "I am listening."

"One of Prince Femi's honored guests has requested a tour this evening," Yvonne explained. "I cannot go alone. I need someone charming to distract him."

"You mean the pale foreigner with golden hair," Zara said, amused. "I heard about him already."

Yvonne's eyes turned wide. "Great Deity, Eyo… I step away for one turn of the sand-glass, and somehow you already know?"

The women laughed at how fast news traveled.

Yvonne held out the bag of coins. "Take. You would be there as company. Nothing more. Just talk. Laugh. Keep him entertained."

Zara arched a brow. "How much?"

"Three months' wages," Yvonne said.

"Make it four," Zara answered without blinking.

Yvonne sighed. "Fine."

She handed over the coins. Zara's expression grew more serious.

"No trickery," Zara warned. "Do not send me, then disappear. Meet me at the castle after the king's supper."

"We will be there," Yvonne said.

She stepped back out into the light with Nyema at her side. The sun was beginning to lower, painting the path in warm gold. The beauty of it did not comfort her.

Somewhere beyond the horizon, King Oyomo continued his search.

Yvonne could feel the world slowly closing its hand around her.

Part II – The Foreigners

Alex strode out of the bath hall with his chin high and his pride dragging behind him like a wounded hound.

The courtyard air hit his freshly shaved skin, cool, sharp, insulting. Every step reminded him of what had just happened: stripped, scrubbed, shaven, and savaged by wax while a woman smiled at his suffering.

Haemish stopped dead, blinked once, then burst into such violent laughter he had to clutch his ribs.

"Saints above, Alex," he wheezed, circling him. "Look at ye. Smooth as a bairn's backside. Did the lass wash ye… or prepare ye for roastin'?"

Alex shot him a glare. "Mock me once more and I'll drown ye in that basin."

"Not a hair left. Not one," Haemish went on, inspecting him like a rare and suspicious creature. "Ye went in a warrior and came out a polished statue."

"Keep talkin', Haemish," Alex muttered, "and I'll polish ye against that pillar."

Andrew arrived then, hair still damp, a drying cloth draped over his shoulder. One look at Alex sent his lips twitching.

"I heard a scream," he said mildly. "Thought someone met their end."

"Aye," Alex said flatly. "I nearly did. Hot wax."

That set Haemish off again.
"Och, the mighty Alex Barton, defender of Clan Barton, felled by hot honey. I cannae wait tae share this with Rory and Logan."

"Try it and I'll gut ye, ye daft goat." Alex jabbed a finger at him. "She didnae warn me she meant tae rip half my soul out."

"Aye, she did," Andrew said, brows lifting. "Ye just were nae listenin'."

Alex shut his mouth and looked away. Damn them both.

Haemish elbowed Andrew. "Go on. Ask him."

Andrew folded his arms. "Tell us about the lass."

"There's naught tae tell," Alex said too quickly.

Haemish snorted. "Aye? Then why did ye shout across the whole hall at Prince Femi, beggin' him tae let her walk ye round the grounds?"

Alex froze. "Ye heard that?"

Andrew didn't blink. "Alex… the goats outside heard that."

Haemish slapped him on the back. "Bold, aye. Foolish. But bold."

Alex dragged a hand down his face. "I needed a guide. That's all."

"A guide," Haemish echoed, leaning in. "With eyes shaped like that? Curvy hips and a stare that near put ye on yer knees?"

"I never said—"

"Aye, ye did," Andrew cut in. "With yer face. All my life I never ken ye to be smitten."

Haemish's grin widened. "So? Was it her hands? Her voice? Or the way she near made ye weep over wax?"

Alex breathed out hard, the truth slipping free before he could stop it.

"Her eyes," he muttered. "They carry somethin'. Pain, maybe. Things she doesnae say. She sees folk clear."

Silence fell.

Then Haemish smirked. "Och. Saints preserve us. Alex, the rake, is smitten by a lass. Ye and yer brother are one in the same. Takes a foreign lass tae catch yer eye."

"Shut yer gob, Haemish. It doesnae," Alex snapped

"Look at em'," Andrew nodded once. "he's beamin.."

"Aye," Haemish agreed. "Bright as a beacon."

Alex threw his hands up. "I need new companions."

"What ye need," Andrew said mildly, "is trousers. Before the lass returns and finishes the job."

Haemish slung an arm over Alex's shoulders. "Come on then, smooth lad. Let's get ye covered before she comes back with another pot. I doubt ye'd survive round two."

"I hate you both," Alex muttered.

"No, ye don't," Haemish said easily. "Ye're rattled. Not used tae wantin' somethin' ye cannae charm, drink, or gamble yer way into."

Alex stopped walking, that truth prickling beneath his skin.

Andrew's voice dropped. "Femi was watchin' ye."

"Watchin'?" Alex frowned.

"Aye. His jaw went tight the moment ye touched her wrist. He didnae care for it."

Haemish whistled low. "So the lass brings danger. Prince Femi's temper."

Alex glanced back toward the bath hall, steam curling beneath the closed door. He had not meant to shout like a lovesick fool. Had not meant to reach for her wrist.

Something had simply pulled.

Tonight, when she walked him through her world, he meant to listen. Truly listen.

And the first thing he would ask was her name.

Chapter Five

Defiance-forward

*N*ervousness curled in Yvonne's stomach as she paced her tiny

house, chewing at the edge of her fingernail. When her hand brushed the faint scar along her arm, she flinched and covered it, as if hiding it might erase the memory.

Her history with men had never been kind.

She had been forced into a marriage she did not want, beaten for refusing to open her legs to a tyrant who called himself husband. The only man she had dared to trust was Prince Femi, and he offered his protection only if she would take a place as one of his wives, a bargain that felt no different from another cage.

"I need to calm my nerves," she muttered.

She crossed to the low stand, uncorked a bottle of palm wine, and drank deep. The first swallow burned. The second numbed. By the fourth, her thoughts blurred around the edges, but no amount of sweet, fermented fruit could wash away the memory of King Oyomo's weight atop her, his hands around her neck.

She sank onto her pallet and let the tears fall quietly.

"This misery will not leave me," she whispered. "I cannot escape it. Not in my waking hours… not even in my dreams."

She took another swallow, then lay back, letting the wine drag her under.

Sleep came as a tumble into another life. She was eight summers again, running in the dust with the village children, bare feet pounding, laughter echoing between the huts. She leaped, misjudged, and caught her foot on a broken tree branch. The world tilted, and she crashed into a puddle of mud.

Brown water splashed her face and dress. She stared at herself, filthy and shocked, and the tears came fast.

One of the boys laughed loud enough to carry. "Ah-ha! You are too slow. You cannot play with us. We are the hunters and warriors. Go home and play with your needle and thread, little girl. Make the mud your rag doll."

Yvonne shot him a glare through muddy lashes.

"Shut your mouth. I do not need to be a stupid hunter or warrior. My father is Chieftain of these lands and bigger than you, you nasty mandrill. When I am grown, I will marry someone royal. You will see."

He sauntered closer and kicked mud into her face. The other children laughed as she sobbed.

Somewhere behind the noise, she heard her mother's voice.

"Yvonne. Yvonne, come inside."

The call pulled at her, tugging her from the scene, from the mud, from the taunts.

"Yvonne."

She pitched awake, blinking against the dark. Her lashes were sticky with dried tears. Her head swam. Her vision swayed before settling on a shadowed figure at the door, lantern held high.

"Nyema?" she croaked. "Is that you?"

"Nae. It is I. Femi."

She tried to stand too quickly, and the room spun. Her foot slipped, and she toppled forward, landing hard on her hands and knees.

"Ouch," she mumbled, then squinted up at him. "What are you doing here? You never come by anymore."

He set the lantern down, jaw tight. "What is the matter with you? Are you in your cups? Do you intend to meet this foreigner like this?"

She pointed a wobbly finger at him. "That is none… hic… none of your concern, Prince."

His brow furrowed. "I thought you would be more sensible than this."

She snorted. "You thought wrong."

He exhaled slowly, anger and something like worry warring in his eyes. "Listen. I know you have no respect for me after… what happened between us. I have apologized. I am still sorry. Truly. But whether you believe me or not, I do not wish to see harm come to you. He is a stranger."

"If he is such a stranger," she shot back, squinting against the lantern light, "why did you give him permission? After all I am just a servant."

"I did not call you a servant out of disrespect, it is to shield your identity.," Femi replied. "After all, you are the one who agreed. I asked, and you said yes.."

She scowled. "He brought the princess home. How dangerous can he be?"

"He did not bring Nzingha back to Tafaria."

She stared, the room gently tilting. "What do you mean? I do not understand. Did she not arrive today?"

"Yes, she did." His mouth thinned. "But I cannot explain how. Not yet. Just hear me. I listened to that man speak in the bath today. He has no wife, no children, and very little respect for women in his lands. Be careful."

She wanted him jealous. Wanted him stung. The same man who now warned her had bedded her best friend.

"You should be the last to speak of respect, "Her voice grew louder, "I will not be alone. There will be others with me this evening. An entourage, as you men like to say. Worry about your second wife, who is with child. Worry about the other four waiting for you in Mbemba. And worry about your outside lover, Nyema."

She wobbled to her feet and swayed toward the door, pulling it open as a clear dismissal.

"So you are telling the man who saved your life to leave," he asked quietly. "If something happens tonight, I will not be your savior."

"You do not have to be," she shut the door in his face.

The Wrong Kind of Bargain

Sometime later, the night air had cooled, but Yvonne's head still felt thick as she met Nyema at the path, with Zara and another woman, Meka, joining them.

Nyema eyed the small jug in Yvonne's hand and grinned. "A bottle of palm wine for this evening's audience with the foreigner?"

Yvonne grimaced. The word *wine* made her stomach twist. "I have had enough to last three lifetimes."

Zara laughed, the sound low and smooth. "Are you planning to get him drunk and ravish him? It would certainly make for an interesting tale."

Nyema nudged Yvonne. "You must admit, for a foreigner, he is handsome. I am not usually drawn to men who are not of our people, but this one… he is striking. I have never seen a man with a face like his."

Yvonne shifted, the ground feeling unsteady beneath her feet. "He is pleasant to look at, perhaps. But what does he want with me?"

Nyema's voice softened. "For a start? He might help you escape."

Yvonne snapped her head toward her. "What? What are you talking about?"

The other two women wandered ahead, chattering, while Nyema tugged Yvonne's hand gently and slowed their pace.

"I know who you are," Nyema whispered. "You are Chieftain Baako Efango's daughter. Born of nobility."

Yvonne stopped walking. "Who told you that?"

"Everyone knows," Nyema said. "We have been protecting you."

Anger and betrayal flared in Yvonne's chest. "Femi!"

"Yes," Nyema admitted. "He told me in confidence. But I told the servants when King Oyomo first came to Tafaria. If I had not, the lead servant would have assigned you to attend him in the upper chambers. I swore I would not tell anyone else outside of them."

"I cannot believe he lied," Yvonne muttered. "He said only the lead servant knew."

Nyema squeezed her hand and pressed a kiss to her knuckles.

Nyema squeezed her hand and pressed a kiss to her knuckles.

"Never mind who knows. You need to live. Speak with the foreigner. He could be your way out, Yvonne. I overheard one of the bathers, and the king still speaks of you. There is hatred there, and he said that when he finds you, he will kill you."

Yvonne's gaze flicked to the shadows between buildings. "One of his guards recognized me today," she whispered. "I saw it in his eyes. He remembered I was the woman he was ordered to restrain. I must leave."

"Tonight, might be your only chance to get into that foreigner's mind," Nyema insisted. "Listen. There is more. Femi told me in private. The dark-haired foreigner, the one you shaved in the bath? He is married to Princess Nzingha."

Yvonne gasped. "Married to the princess? Do not jest."

"It is true." Nyema drew closer. "You cannot run to another part of Africa. His men are everywhere, west, north, south. Did you know he trades across the great waters? If you want to live free, you must go beyond his reach. Let the foreigner want you enough to take you back with him."

Yvonne stared at her, horrified. "Excuse me? I am not a whore. I am untouched. You expect me to give the only thing I own, my innocence, as payment? What kind of friend are you to suggest such a thing?"

"No," Nyema protested. "I am trying to help you escape. Do you not wish for a better life?"

"I do," Yvonne said, lowering her voice, "but it sounds more like you are pushing me away."

The thought slithered in. *Is she saying this because she thinks I am in love with Femi? Because she wants me gone?*

Yvonne studied her friend's face. There was a scowl there now, buried beneath the concern. *She hates me. Oh, Great Eyo… she does.*

"Listen, Nyema," Yvonne said carefully. "From the day I came here, you have been kind. I trust you. But you must understand… I will never stand between you and whatever you have with Femi. I do not love him. In truth, the sight of him often angers me."

Nyema's eyes narrowed. "How can you not care for the man who saved your life?"

Yvonne's temper cracked. "He offered marriage for my protection. That is why. You do not need to push me toward a stranger just to get me to leave. What would I gain from a man with five wives? As I told you before, get your head out of the clouds. You cannot live in his wives' quarters. What do you intend to do? Follow him from house to house while he is stationed in Tafaria? People will look at you as an outsider. A plaything. He told me himself, Nyema. You two had ended before it even started. He will not wed you."

"Shut your mouth," Nyema snapped. "You know nothing about what we share." She hesitated, then blurted, "I am with child."

Yvonne's stomach plunged. "What did you say? You carry his child?"

Nyema lifted her chin, eyes bright with pride and fear. "Yes."

"Oh, Nyema," Yvonne breathed. "If the lead servant finds out, she will dismiss you from the castle. You could be exiled from the Tafaria."

Yvonne reached for her, but Nyema jerked away.

"Leave me alone," she cried. "Go and entertain your foreigner."

She turned and ran, leaving Yvonne standing on the path, heart pounding.

"Nyema, wait. I am sorry. I did not mean…" Her voice faded. Nyema did not look back.

Yvonne sighed. "Wonderful. Completely wonderful. If they learn she is with child, she will lose everything."

Before the Night Turns

King Afonso held a private supper to honor the foreign men who had brought his daughter home. It should have been a night of celebration, but the tension at the high table could be felt down to the servants' benches.

There had been sharp words between father and daughter. Voices raised. Chairs scraping back. Princess Nzingha left the table with fury in her eyes and tears just behind them.

After she stormed out, King Afonso requested a private audience with Andrew. Alex watched as he stood from the table; he and Haemish were escorted back to their guest quarters. A knot formed in his gut. He knew his brother all too well. Andrew was honest, too honest, and sometimes that honesty had gotten them into trouble, both as lads and as grown men.

Later, Alex and Haemish waited in the guest corridor, sitting on low benches, listening to the muffled roar of the ocean beyond the stone walls. Alex could not shake the feeling that something had shifted at that table. He paced, hands at his waist.

Footsteps sounded on the stairs. He glanced up and saw Andrew returning, the five guards still at his back. His brother's face was tight with anger.

Alex hurried to meet him.
"Where is Prince Femi? And why do these men look as though they'd haul ye off at any moment? What happened?"

Andrew shook his head.
"The king knows I'm wed tae his daughter. He knows of our child."

"Christ," Alex muttered. "How?"

"I told him."

"You great big oaf," Alex groaned. "Why would ye go blabberin'? What'll happen now?"

Andrew opened his mouth to answer, but his gaze shifted over Alex's shoulder.

Yvonne approached, walking at the head of the small group of women. Zara followed with an easy sway to her hips, Meka just behind her. Yvonne's steps were steadier than they had been earlier, though Alex could see the faint fog of wine still in her eyes.

She stopped at a polite distance and dipped her head. "Good evening, Laird Chieftain. Are you ready to see Tafaria's castle?"

Andrew hesitated.

"I'm sorry, Alex. The king's ordered us tae remain above the stairs until the princess is found. They're searchin' for her."

"How can she be lost?" Alex asked. "We just found her."

Yvonne heard the exchange, and for a heartbeat, relief flickered. Perhaps the night will be canceled. Perhaps she would not have to go through with any of it.

Just then, Femi came up the stairs, his eyes reaching Alex first. He made a gesture toward Andrew's guest chamber and mouthed the word *Princess.*

Alex nodded with relief.

Yvonne stood in view. "Shall we come back another time, Chieftain?"

Alex turned toward her, a slow grin tugging at his mouth.
"Nae, please. Stay. I'm sure Nzingha's fine."
He clapped a hand on Andrew's shoulder.
"She'll return tae ye, and we'll leave this place when she does."

Andrew eyed the women, his gaze lingering on Yvonne when he caught the way Alex kept glancing at her.

"Alex," he murmured under his breath, "be careful. This isnae Scotland. We've different customs here. Try tae mind yerself."

"It's an innocent introduction," Alex said. "Nothin' more. Go tae yer room and enjoy yer night." He winked.

He turned back to the women, charm sliding neatly into place. "Come, ladies. I look forward to hearing about your beautiful country."

As Yvonne stepped into the guest chamber, she caught sight of movement at the far end of the corridor. Prince Femi stood in the shadows, watching. As Alex passed, Femi brushed his shoulder hard against Alex's arm.

Alex glanced back. "What is his problem?" he muttered.

Yvonne pretended not to notice. Her heart did.

The Heat of The Night

Inside, the royal guest chamber had been prepared in the style of Tafaria. Brightly woven pillows ringed a wide rug on the floor. The walls were draped in cloth of rich reds and deep gold. Lantern light softened the edges of everything it touched.

Zara and Meka stepped inside with open curiosity, eyes roaming over Alex's massive sword and the foreign clothing displayed, freshly washed and laid out for him.

One of them bit her lip in a flirtatious smile. The other clasped her hands and giggled nervously.

Yvonne stood with her arms folded, her expression guarded and carrying the faintest scowl. Alex saw it and nearly laughed. She clearly did not wish to be here., that much was clear. Still, he was glad she had come.

"Is everythin' well?" Alex asked quietly. He studied her a moment longer. "Ye look troubled."

Yvonne did not answer at once. Her gaze drifted past him, toward the lantern-lit wall, before returning.

"I was thinking about a friend who decided not to come after all."

"Did she fall ill?" he asked.

"I hope not." She drew a slow breath. "I think she will manage."

"That's good tae hear." He tipped his head toward the cushions. "Come. Sit."

He settled onto one of the lower cushions, stretching his legs as the others gathered loosely around the low table. Yvonne lingered where she was, then stepped forward and placed a jug before him.

"This is the wine we brought, our healer prepared it himself. Palm wine."

Alex turned the jug slowly in his hands, studying the painted clay. "I've heard o' this drink. It's Princess Nzingha's favorite."

Her brows knit. "How do you know that?"

He paused, then looked up. "I beg yer pardon?"

"You said it as though you were certain," Yvonne said. "How do you know it is her favorite?"

For a heartbeat, he considered Andrew's secret; he was already up to his neck with issues concerning the princess.

Alex answered evenly, "She ah... She mentioned it on our journey here."

Yvonne folded her arms tighter. "I see."

He poured himself a generous cup, lifted it, and inhaled. It smelled sweet, yes, but there was something sharper beneath it. He shrugged and drank anyway.

Warmth slid down his throat and spread through his chest.

Zara lifted her own cup, sniffed, and laughed.

"There is more than simple palm wine in here."

Yvonne stiffened. "Nyema asked the healer to add a small medicinal herb."

"Did she now," Zara murmured. "There is nothing subtle about what I am smelling." She continued drinking.

Alex took another swallow. The warmth flared hotter this time, settling deeper in his blood. "That is… quite good," he said, even as the room tipped just slightly. He poured for the women, then set the jug aside. "Would ye like tae play a game o' cards?"

Yvonne frowned. "Cards?"

"It's a set o' small sheets," he explained, reaching for the deck in his satchel. "Each has numbers and signs. Some beat others. It's a game o' chance and a wee bit o' wit. This one's called Captain's Plunder."

Zara's eyes gleamed. "Plunder you say? Well now, that sounds entertaining. Show us."

"Gladly." He shuffled the cards with an easy, practiced motion. "We play in partners. The highest card each round takes the trick. Yvonne, you and I'll partner."

He glanced at the others. "And what are yer names?"

"I am Zara," the bold one replied. "This is Meka."

Alex smiled. "Well then, Zara and Meka, prepare tae lose."

Soon they were laughing at Zara's dramatic sighs when she lost a hand, at Meka's delighted squeals when she won one, at Yvonne's dry comments every time Alex bragged too soon and lost a round.

I've no laughed like this in ages, he thought.

The night thickened. The heat in the room climbed. His vision sharpened and then blurred at the edges, as though the lantern flames were smearing slowly across the walls.

"Is it always this bloody hot?" he asked, tugging at the cloth of his borrowed shirt.

Meka giggled. "This is nothing. After the next moon, we pray for rain."

Alex muttered under his breath and pulled the shirt over his head. Sweat glistened along his chest and shoulders. Zara and Meka exchanged a look, trying not to stare and failing completely.

Yvonne shifted a little farther away, crossing one leg beneath the other. The movement drew his gaze without permission. Her skirt pulled just enough to bare the smooth length of one thigh. Her bodice was modest by local standards, but the gentle swell of her breasts pressed against the fabric each time she breathed.

The warmth inside him coiled tighter.

What in God's name is in this wine? he wondered.

The laughter in the room turned slow and echoing. The lantern light blurred. Every breath felt thick.

Alex wiped sweat from his brow, blinking hard as the room tilted a little.

"Blast, it's too hot," he muttered, pushing himself to his feet. "I need a breeze. If I dinnae get one soon, I'll melt clean intae the floor."

Zara watched him go, then nudged Yvonne with her foot. "Go," she whispered. "Join him."

Yvonne pointed at herself. "Me? Why must I be the one?"

"Oh, Yvonne," Zara sighed. "You are not that foolish. The man has done nothing but look at you all night. The least you can do is be pleasant. We have been here half an evening, and you have barely spoken to him."

"I am here," Yvonne protested. "I played his game. How much more entertaining does he need?"

Zara rolled her eyes, stepped behind Yvonne, and before Yvonne could even gasp, she shoved her straight onto the balcony.

The door slammed shut a heartbeat later.

Click.

The latch locked.

Yvonne grabbed the handle. It did not budge.

"Of course," Yvonne muttered. "Of course you would do this. You have no sense. Open the door."

Alex turned at the noise. "Is somethin' the matter with the door?"

Through the small lattice opening, Zara's face flashed for half a second.

She stuck out her tongue, wiggled her fingers, and sang, "Smile pretty!"

She disappeared before Yvonne could lunge at her reflection.

Yvonne exhaled sharply. "Unbelievable."

She forced a tight smile. "I believe Zara has had too much to drink. She has locked us out."

He huffed a laugh, then turned back to the view. From the balcony, the sea stretched out into the deep velvet of the night, the moon laying a silver path over the waves. Palm trees swayed, their leaves whispering.

"This place is bonnie," he said quietly. "I've traveled tae many lands, but I've never seen anythin' like this. The trees. The animals. The food. It's all… different. Fiercer. Alive."

Yvonne stepped closer to the rail, resting her hands along the cool stone. The night breeze kissed her face, but the heat in her body would not lower.

"It is beautiful, yet I cannot seem to enjoy it. The world beyond the castle feels out of reach."

"Why can ye not go beyond the castle?"

"Because Prince Femi brought me here," she said, staring out at the horizon. "And I must remain in hiding as long as I stay."

He glanced at her.

"Hidin'? From what… or should I say, who?"

She hesitated before speaking. "Someone who believes he owns me. If I remain unseen, I am safe enough. But, if found, I am good as dead."

He went quiet at that.

"I have never seen anyone like you before," she said softly. "Your eyes… they are as blue as a clear sky. Your hair is the color of the sun before it disappears. It feels as though there is another world beyond the sea."

He smiled at the wonder in her voice. "Aye, there is. I'm a sailor. I've seen most places my ship can carry me."

The thought made her smile. As the daughter of a chieftain, she had never left her homeland.
Not until she was forced into Oyomo's lands.

Her gaze drifted toward the roaring sea. "Your home," she asked quietly, "what is it called?"

"Scotland," he said. "'Tis far away. Four… maybe eight moons by sea."

She tasted the word. "Scot… land."

More curiosity came. "Do all your people speak as you do? Do they all carry such features? Your brother has the same eyes, but his hair is black, like a crow's feather."

"We come in all ways," Alex replied. "I've a cousin whose hair is as red as fire."

Her eyes widened. "Truly? Fire? Fascinating." She smiled faintly. "You complimented me earlier, and you have been kind. People in the villages say men from across the sea are cruel. They say you take and leave nothing behind. But you are… different. I heard you risked much to help Princess Nzingha."

"There are cruel men everywhere," Alex said. "No' only in my lands." He paused when he saw her sway ever so slightly where she stood. "Ye do no' look well, lass. Sit, please."

He guided her gently toward the cushioned lounge in the corner of the balcony. Her steps faltered. He caught her when she stumbled, and she giggled, the sound breathy, unlike her usual brisk tone.

"Something is wrong with my body," she murmured. "I am hot. Too hot. My thoughts are… slow."

He helped her settle, then knocked on the balcony door. Zara opened it, smiling as though nothing at all was out of place.

"Could ye bring her some water?" Alex asked. "She needs tae cool her head."

"Of course," Zara said lightly.

Within moments, she reappeared with a cup, passing it to Alex before drifting back inside.

"Drink," Alex said, holding it to Yvonne's lips. "Ye're sorted."

She blinked at him. "What.... Sorted?"

"Aye. Drunk. In yer cups."

"Oh." She took a long swallow.

Alex lifted his own cup of palm wine again and sniffed, more cautious this time. There it was, that sharp, smoky note beneath the sweetness. He knew that smell from taverns and dark corners of ports. Not just wine. Something stronger. Something meant to loosen more than tongues.

He drank some of the water himself, but the strange heat had already sunk its claws into him. Every breath drew in more of her scent; it was soap, oil, and something unmistakably female. He dragged his gaze away.

"I promised Andrew I would behave," he murmured. "One night. That is all I need tae survive without foolishness."

She let out a soft moan, her eyes fluttering before rolling back.

"Did you say something?"

"Nothing," he said, tilting the cup back to her mouth. "Have some more water."

She took a small sip, then sank back, her body slackening, almost limp.

Behind them, a soft murmur rose. Zara's laughter drifted through the chamber, warm and lilting. Meka answered with a shy giggle. When Alex glanced back toward the room, he caught a startling sight.

Zara held a slender smoking pipe between her fingers, lifted it to her lips, breathed in deeply, then leaned toward Meka and shared the smoke in a gentle, lingering kiss.

His brows shot up.

"That is certainly… different from a Highland feast," he muttered.

Zara glided back toward them, eyes bright with mischief, pipe in hand.

"You look tense, Chieftain," she purred. "Our herbs can help you breathe easier."

Before he could protest, she lifted the stem to his mouth.

"Inhale."

He did, instinct, not intent.

The smoke burned at first, then sank warmth into his limbs. He coughed, eyes watering. Zara only laughed softly and took another draw.

Then she turned to Yvonne.

Her touch was surprisingly gentle. With the back of her fingers, she brushed Yvonne's cheek, whispering,

"Such a frightened little lion cub… all that strength curled in on itself. Just a little courage, yes?"

Yvonne's lashes fluttered. When her eyes lifted again, they were darker, unfocused yet fixed on Alex.

She rose slowly, almost cautiously, and slid her arms around his neck.

"You are warm," she whispered, voice soft and drifting. "Like the sun." A soft moan escaped.

He cursed. "Shit." His shaft turned hard. Heat and sin flooded him from head to toe.

"Yvonne, nae..." he tried to remove her arms. "Ye're no' in yer right..."

Her lips brushed him.

A shy peck, then a second, a deeper one. Hungrier. Longing filled the space between them as their breath mingled.

His eyes widened when she slid her tongue into his mouth.

And for a moment, just a moment, Alex forgot himself and kissed her back.

Every part of him leaned into her, her softness, her scent, the tremble of her fingers. She tasted like wine and herbs and something purely, painfully honest.

Then guilt slammed through him, sharp as steel.

He broke the kiss, breath ragged.

"No, lass. No' like this."

She blinked up at him, confused and swaying.

Behind them, Zara's coaxing voice drifted closer.

"She wants you. Can you not see it?" A hand slid along Yvonne's shoulder, a feather-light touch. "She deserves tenderness tonight."

Yvonne's breath shivered. Her hands still rested at Alex's neck, trembling.

Alex closed his eyes for one hard second.

He wanted her. God, he wanted her more fiercely than he'd expected. But he could not take advantage of a woman longing for escape, for safety, for anything gentle in a brutal life.

"This is no' consent," he murmured under his breath.

He cupped her face and eased her down onto the cushions. Her lashes dipped, heavy with wine and exhaustion. She whispered something he could not hear before slipping into a soft, uneven sleep.

Zara's attention drifted away. She lifted the pipe again, sharing another curling breath of smoke with Meka. Their laughter softened into murmured affection as they pressed close.

Alex's world blurred at the edges.

There were hands on his shoulders.

A soft breast brushed his back.

Warm breath ghosted along his neck.

He did not know how he had moved, only that he suddenly found himself on a large woven pallet layered with cushions and shadows. Zara straddled him, allowing his shaft to enter her. She turned and kissed Meka. Alex felt a surge of pleasure humming throughout his body.

The night pressed around them, thick with heat and smoke. The herbs hummed in his blood, blurring edges, loosening restraint, dragging him under.

Another realization crept through his intoxication, though his vision blurred. Meka was on all fours; he powered into her from behind. Zara lay beneath Meka, tasting her.

The sight drove him mad. He could not get enough.

Soft moans drifted through the room, rising and falling like the pull of the tide.

Women moved in the half-light, bodies arching in silhouette, shadows rippling across the walls as if the fire itself breathed with them.

None of these sinful touches,
none of this hungry, fevered noise,
belonged to the woman sleeping on the balcony.

Somewhere beyond the adjoining wall, another cry carried faintly.

Nzingha's.

Andrew's voice followed, low, rough, unmistakable.

Alex let out a strangled laugh.

"Is that Andrew? By Christ… what manner o' night is this?"

Something in him cracked then.

Old habits, old hungers rose like ghosts. The man he used to be, before grief carved hollows in his chest, clawed forward. Heat and sound blurred his thoughts until the edges of the world dissolved.

The Sight Before Her

Yvonne did not know how she reached the balcony's cushions.

One moment, warmth cradled her like a heavy cloud.

The next, the night air struck her skin sharp and cold as she clung to the railing, trying to steady herself.

Her head throbbed.

Her vision swayed.

From inside the chamber came sounds, breathy, rhythmic, unmistakable.

Her stomach twisted.

"What am I doing here?" she whispered, arms wrapped tight around herself. "This is not me. I am not this woman."

Shaking, she crept toward the open doorway and peered in.

The lanterns burned low.

Shadows shifted.

Bodies tangled in a slow, fevered knot of limbs and murmurs. She could not see faces clearly, only fragments caught the dim light:

A pale shoulder, his strong arms moving in a rhythm as he rode Meka. Zara giving kisses to the foreign man.

Her chest caved in on itself.

She turned away sharply, pressing a hand over her mouth as nausea surged. She stumbled to the far edge of the balcony and retched until there was nothing left in her but bitterness and air. When she finally sank to her knees, she wiped her mouth with trembling fingers.

"What did I walk into?" she breathed.

"What did they make us drink? Who am I becoming?"

She slid down against the wall, pulling her knees to her chest as the sea whispered below. The night wrapped cold around her, but inside the chambers, the heat continued, soft gasps, the rustle of sheets, the sound of pleasure that should never have touched her ears.

Somewhere in the distance, a woman cried out.

Somewhere closer, a man answered her.

Yvonne closed her eyes, tears slipping free.

For the first time since arriving in Tafaria, she realized danger did not only come wearing a crown and holding a whip.

Sometimes, it came with blue eyes, a gentle smile…

and friends that will lead you to wrong.

Chapter Six

Walk of Shame

A sharp tapping at the chamber door tugged Yvonne up from the depths of sleep.

For a breath, she lay very still, staring at a ceiling she did not recognize. The air smelled of wine, spice and something foul. She pressed a hand covering her nose and mouth. Her skull throbbed dully. Her tongue felt thick and dry.

Where am I?

She shifted, and her breath lodged in her throat.

Bare skin slid over cool linen.

She jerked upright, dragging the sheet to her chin. Naked. She was naked in a bed that was not hers.

Panic swept through her so fast she had to squeeze her eyes shut against it. The last clear memory she possessed was of the balcony, the wine, the bitter-sweet herbs in the pipe, the way the world had begun to tilt beneath her feet. She recalled the ocean glittering beyond the rail. Zara's laughter. The weight of exhaustion pulling her down as she lay along the stone.

I fell asleep on the balcony. This is not the balcony. Why am I in his bed?

The knocking came again, sharper now.

"Alex," a man's voice called, muffled by the heavy door. "Alex, get up."

Yvonne forced herself to look.

The foreigner lay beside her.

Alex slept sprawled on his back, one arm flung over his head, blond hair tousled and wild, chest rising and falling in an easy, unbothered rhythm. On his other side, Zara was tucked against him, dark hair spilling across the pillow, lips curved in a sleepy, satisfied smile.

The tapping persisted.

Meka shuffled across the room with a sleepy grumble and pulled the door open.

Yvonne's eyes flew wide. She slid deeper beneath the covers, heart kicking against her ribs. *Blast. Is that Femi? Oh, gods, he cannot see me like this.* Her stomach turned; she bit hard on her fingernail to keep from making a sound.

Footsteps crossed the threshold, steady and familiar. Alex did not stir. If anything, his snoring grew louder.

The voice came again, clearer now, the Highland cadence unmistakable. "Alex. Alex, get up. 'Tis me. Andrew."

Relief broke over her in a dizzy rush. Andrew. Not Femi.

Seeing his brother lying insensible, Andrew gave his leg a sound kick. "Wake, ye great lump. Haste now. Gather your belongings. We are leaving."

Alex yawned and blinked, eyes squinting against the light. His gaze swept the chamber, the women, the tangle of limbs and linen, his own nakedness, and a strangled little sound escaped him.

"Ah… eh-hem." He cleared his throat. "Ladies, it was… a lovely time last eve. However, my brother and I must have privacy."

Yvonne pushed herself upright, keeping one fist locked around the sheet at her chest, head carefully bowed. If she moved quickly, if she did not meet Andrew's eyes, perhaps he would never know she had been here at all.

One foot found the floor, then the other. She eased herself off the bed, edging sideways, breath held, gaze fixed on the door.

She was nearly there when fingers closed gently but firmly around her wrist.

"Yvonne, wait," Alex murmured. "Will I see you before I depart?"

Sarcasm was all she had left to armor herself with. "Oh, uh," she said, not quite looking at him. "I do not know. Perhaps next time."

His brows rose, but she did not give him time to answer.

She fled his chamber like prey loosed from a snare, not daring to look back.

The corridor felt cooler than the chamber, yet no easier to breathe in. Her pulse still raced as she hurried after Zara, bare feet whispering over the stone.

They had nearly reached the turn in the passage when her steps faltered.

Femi stood further down, speaking quietly with one of his warriors. At the sound of the chamber door closing, he glanced over his shoulder.

His gaze found her at once.

For the briefest heartbeat, he simply looked, taking in her loosened hair, the hastily belted robe, the bare strip of ankle showing beneath the hem. The smile that had been resting easily on his mouth flattened. Warmth drained from his eyes, leaving them hard and shuttered.

Yvonne's throat closed. Shame burned from her chest to the tips of her fingers. No words came. No excuse formed.

She straightened her spine on instinct, lifting her chin as if she did not care who had seen her slip from a foreigner's room at dawn.

By the time she dared look again, he was gone.

Silence swallowed the corridor, broken only by the distant murmur of servants beginning their morning's work. She stood alone, heart pounding so loudly she was certain the walls could hear it.

What was I thinking? How could I have listened to Nyema and her foolish suggestion? Now Femi will never look at me the same. After all I have done to stay hidden… I cannot keep living like this. I must leave.

She ran all the way back to her tiny house at the edge of the village.

The moment the door slammed behind her, she moved. There was no time to sit and drown in humiliation; movement was the only thing keeping her from falling apart. She reached for her satchel, for the small clay pot where she kept her coins, for the bundle of dried provisions on the shelf. Food and linens went into the bag first. Clothing could be replaced. Her life could not.

She would be gone before nightfall. Gone from Tafaria. She would hire a fishing boat, sail north, and keep sailing until she reached a place where no one knew her name or her father's, where no king claimed her body as his property.

She had just closed her fingers around a strip of dried meat when a heavy pounding shook the door on its hinges.

She went still.

Another blow rattled the wood.

"Who comes this early?" she whispered. "Femi? He must be…"

Her mouth dried. She stepped closer, pulse thundering in her ears.

"Yes?" she called, barely above a murmur.

No answer.

The silence that followed felt worse than any shouted threat.

She took two small steps back, dread crawling cold along her spine.

The door burst inward, wood splintering and flying across the room. Yvonne screamed as three large men surged through the opening, armor painted in Oyomo's colors, eyes flat and merciless.

She spun and lunged for the window.

Fingers like iron clamped around her ankle, yanking her off her feet. She crashed sideways into a row of clay pots stacked along the wall. They shattered beneath her with a deafening crack. Shards cut into her arms and back. Pain flared white-hot up her neck.

The room tilted. Warmth slid down her temple, blurring her vision in red streaks.

Somewhere above her, the shouting dimmed beneath the hammering in her skull. Boots thudded against the floor. Then another step sounded, a slow, unhurried tread that made the tiny hairs at the back of her neck stand on end.

Yvonne kept her head down, too afraid to lift it, too afraid to see the face she knew must be there.

"Well now," a calm, sinister voice emerged. "And to think I have searched high and low, from Oyomo to Mbemba… and here you are. Clever little rabbit. Running east. To my dear friend's lands, no less. Tafaria."

Her whole body shook.

She scrubbed at her face with shaking fingers, clearing blood and tears enough to look up.

King Oyomo loomed over her.

He smiled as if greeting a guest at a banquet, not a wife he had hunted like prey.

In that moment, he looked every inch like *Ogbunabali*, the god of death her mother had warned her about, wrapped in flesh and silk.

He knelt, still smiling, and closed one large hand around her throat.

"Do you remember," he asked lightly, as if recalling some shared jest, "I told you if I ever had you again, I would strangle you with my bare hands? But I find I cannot quite bring myself to do it. You cost me too much to kill. I will sell you instead. Like the whore you are. Your family took too much of my gold. You must pay somehow."

Yvonne clawed at his fingers, lungs burning. "Please… husband…" she rasped. "I will yield. I will be the wife you wished. I will do whatever you want. I beg you."

"Oh?" His head tilted, eyes glittering. "You yield?"

His smile widened. "My dear wife, what I have planned for you will make you wish you had died when you leapt from my window. But look on the bright side." His voice softened into mockery. "Your family will live. On the other hand?" He leaned closer. "I visited your village and burned it. Many of your people are dead. Those who live have no homes. No crops. No livestock. All because you ran."

His laughter boomed through the tiny house, echoed by the men behind him.

Something inside her snapped.

Rage surged up through the terror.

She gathered what little strength she had left and spat full in his face.

"Curse you," she hissed. "I would rather die a thousand deaths than be bound to a tyrant like you. You are old, ugly, and cruel. I hate you."

His eyes turned cold as stone.

He wiped her spit from his cheek with slow, deliberate care. Then he drew back his fist and struck.

The blow cracked across her face with such force that her world shattered into darkness.

Newly Crowned King

Alex strode into Andrew and Nzingha's guest chamber with his temper frayed and his head pounding, still feeling the ghosts of the night before and the sting of shame at his own weakness.

"I see you found your wife," he said, forcing levity as he shut the door. "What is the plan now?"

Andrew stood by the window, shoulders tight, eyes distant. "We must find Haemish and get the hell away from these lands."

Yvonne's face ghosted across Alex's mind.
What must she think of me now? A lust-driven fool. She had fled in the middle of that cursed display. She must think me a disgusting pig.

The wine, the heat, the drugged desire that had clawed through his veins, he wished he could rip the memory out by the roots.

Haemish stepped into the chamber, jaw set.

"Chieftain, how in God's name do you intend we leave? Men are guarding the stairs."

Andrew looked to his wife. "My love. What say you? I am out of ideas."

Nzingha's dark eyes flashed. She pointed upward. "The rooftop. I tied the bed linens together. We can use them as ropes to climb down from the high arches."

In one smooth motion, Andrew lifted his tiny wife. She scrambled up to a narrow ledge, worked free a hidden panel in the ceiling, and pushed it aside. Fresh air spilled down into the room.

Within minutes, the three Scots and Nzingha were sliding through the opening and onto the palace roof. They moved like shadows along the tiles, dropping down from one level to the next until at last they slipped beyond the palace walls and made their way toward the beach where Femi had told them to meet at first light.

Earlier, the Prince had laid out the plan with cold precision; Nzingha would appear to have run from her father yet again, hiding in Andrew's chambers. They would feed the king heavy herbs, let him sleep, and flee at dawn.

They had not counted on King Afonso waiting at the shore.

"Shit," Alex muttered as they crested a dune and saw the line of men ahead. "Nzingha, we have been discovered."

Down on the hard-packed sand, the king sat atop his horse, ringed by warriors. Spears and swords glinted in the rising sun.

Another horse thundered toward them. Femi dismounted before it fully stopped and strode into the circle, sword at his hip.

"Brother," he began.

Afonso's hand lifted, halting him. "Enough," he said, voice low and dangerous. "I trusted you. Where did we go wrong, eh?"

Nzingha stepped forward, eyes bright with desperation. "Father, please hear me. I cannot stay. I cannot." Her voice broke. "My daughter, Destiny, needs me. She is only eight months old. How can I abandon my child?"

"Silence." His shout cracked across the shore like a whip. "You will come with me. Your pretend husband will go home. If you resist, your husband dies."

"Then I shall die with him," she cried. "Please, Father, do not make me resent you more than I already do. When will you see you do not own me?"

Something flickered behind his eyes. It vanished as quickly as it came.

He raised his arm.

All his guards drew their swords in one long, hissing sound.

"Seize the princess," he commanded.

Alex edged closer to Andrew. "Bloody hell, we are surrounded."

Femi stepped between the king's line and the Scots, lifting his own hand. His men unsheathed their blades, forming a second ring.

"Brother," he called, voice ringing, "if she does not leave with her husband this morning, we go to war."

Afonso laughed. "You and what army?"

"The army I built while your lazy ass sat on the throne," Femi snapped. "They are loyal to me. You gave me Tafaria to lead after these people were attacked, and you sent no one from Mbemba to fight. I built an army from Tafaria's men, women, and boys."

The king's smile was thin as a knife. "Very touching. I will still be taking my daughter."

One of his soldiers strode forward and grabbed Nzingha's arm.

Andrew moved like lightning, his fist crashing into the man's jaw. The soldier dropped boneless into the sand.

"Take your bloody hands off my wife," Andrew snarled.

Afonso's brow knotted. A vein pulsed at his temple. "You are a stubborn foreigner. Do you wish to die in this country? We had a deal. You could still walk away and return to your daughter. Or you can challenge me and die. Your choice."

Andrew took Nzingha's hand and held it tight. "Nae, King. Ye made a deal. I disagreed. I am taking my wife home."

The king's lips peeled back in something too sharp to be a smile. He lifted his arm high and clenched his fist.

A mounted warrior spurred her horse, charging with sword raised, aiming for Andrew's neck.

The princess screamed. "ANDREW, nae!"

Time slowed.

Alex saw his brother reach for his own blade, saw the terrible realization as Andrew understood he would not clear it in time. The rider's sword arced down.

Steel met steel, not Andrew.

Femi's sword punched through the attacker's side.

The woman toppled from her saddle, dead before she hit the ground.

Femi dragged his blade free, chest heaving. He turned toward the Scots, fury and something like grief blazing in his eyes. By saving Andrew, he had just raised his hand against his own king.

"If you do not wish to die," he roared, "take your wife and leave this place. NOW!"

"FEMI!" Afonso bellowed, rage and disbelief tangled in his voice.

The beach erupted.

Steel rang. Men shouted. Femi's soldiers closed ranks around the Scots and Nzingha, cutting down anyone who tried to reach them. Together they ran for the waiting ship, sand flying under their boots.

Behind them, the king threw himself from his horse and lunged after his daughter.

"NZINGHA!" he roared. "NZINGHA! HOW COULD YOU LEAVE YOUR FATHER? YOUR KING? YOUR HOME? TRAITOR!"

Nzingha had never heard him sound so broken. Her heart squeezed even as she ran faster, knowing if she faltered, they were finished.

She glanced back.

Femi fought four men at once, sword flashing, his arm streaked with blood. Beyond him, Afonso snatched a fallen blade and charged straight for his brother's exposed back.

"UNCLE FEMI!" Nzingha screamed. "LOOK BEHIND YOU!"

Femi turned at the last instant and swung.

His blade slashed across the king's throat.

The world stopped.

Men froze mid-strike. Swords hung in the air.

Afonso staggered, eyes wide. His hand flew to his neck as blood spilled between his fingers. He sank to his knees, then crumpled face-first into the sand.

Femi stared at his brother's body, horror carving hard lines into his face. "Afonso…" he choked. "Brotha… Brotha… No…"

The sea breeze carried the copper scent of blood. For one suspended heartbeat, everything held still.

A new King was to be Crowned.

The Cost of the Night

Zara walked toward the village as the sun climbed higher, a heavy pouch of coins bumping against her hip.

"I must say, she thought, lips curving, that was my best performance yet."

The memory of the foreigner's stunned expression, the wild tangle of limbs and heat on the balcony, made her chuckle under her breath. But beneath the amusement, worry pricked sharp.

"Poor Yvonne," she murmured. "To put herself in such a predicament… running off in the middle of the bedding? She must still be untouched."

Her legs ached with fatigue as she rounded the bend toward her cluster of houses.

She slowed.

A line of men in Oyomo's colors marched past, leaving Yvonne's doorway. The door hung crooked on its hinges, splintered nearly in half.

"What is going on?" she breathed. "Oh, the God's. No."

She ducked behind a broad tree, hand clamped over her mouth.

A warrior stepped from the ruined house with a limp figure slung over his shoulder.

Yvonne.

Her arms were bound, a gag cut cruelly into her cheeks. Blood dripped from her hair, spotting the man's back with dark red.

Zara pressed her fist against her lips to keep from crying out. "No… Yvonne…"

She waited, heart pounding, until the last of Oyomo's men vanished from sight. Then she ran.

The bath hall was empty; the morning was still young. The east wing stairwell was deserted, no guards at their posts, no familiar warrior faces.

"Hh… hh…" She leaned on the rail for half a breath, chest heaving. "Where is everyone?"

She sprinted to Femi's door and slammed her fist against it.

At last, the door cracked open.

Nyema peered out, eyes narrowed. "Oh, the gods, Zara. What is the matter?"

"Please," Zara gasped. "Prince Femi. I need Prince Femi. Hurry."

Nyema crossed her arms, expression cooling. "And what is it you need from him?"

"Please, it is Yvonne," Zara said, voice breaking. "She… she is in trouble."

"Oh, well." Nyema's gaze flicked over her. "The Prince is not here."

She closed the door in Zara's face.

Zara stared, stunned for a heartbeat, then resumed pounding. "Nyema! Open the door. Your friend is in danger. Please!"

Silence.

No answer.

She spun and flew down the stairwell. Her foot caught the last step; she pitched forward with a small cry.

Strong hands caught her before she hit the floor.

She collided with a solid chest. Blinking up, she found herself staring at Alex.

"Honored guest, please," she gasped, tears in her eyes, as she gripped his shirt in both fists. "You must help her. Come, I beg you."

Alex's body ached from the battle on the shore. Every bruise screamed. But the fear in Zara's eyes cut through the haze at once.

"Steady, lass," he said. "What is wrong? Slow down."

"Where is the prince?" she blurted. "Prince Femi, have you seen him?"

"Aye," Alex replied. "He is with his niece, the princess. There were casualties this morning. They are dealing with it."

"Please, honored guest. It is Yvonne." Her voice shook. "She is in grave danger. King Oyomo took her. I saw him leave her home with his warriors. She was bound and bloodied. I do not know if she still lives. She looked unconscious."

"WHAT?" The word ripped from him. "Are ye certain? Why would he take her?"

"I do not know." Her voice dropped. "They walked toward his guest quarters." She swallowed hard. "Before today, it was said she was married to the king of the Oyomo tribe, but escaped him and fled here, hiding in Tafaria. Please. You must haste."

She tugged his arm, already turning. He followed without another question.

What Coin Cannot Claim.

They reached the west wing to find one warrior posted outside King Oyomo's chamber. Alex and Zara ducked behind a carved stone pillar, peering out.

"Perhaps we should fetch the Prince," Alex murmured. "We could use his help."

"No..." Zara whispered. "There is no time. I can distract the guard while you slip inside and see if she is there."

Alex studied her quickly, then nodded.

She tugged her skirts higher, baring more of her leg, then adjusted the bodice of her gown until her breasts pressed plump against the cloth. She smoothed her hair, drew in a steadying breath, and stepped out with a practiced sway.

Alex watched as she approached the guard, her voice turning liquid in her own tongue.

"I see the others left you alone," she purred. "Shall I whisper something lovely in your ear?"

She lifted her skirts a fraction more, crooking her finger.

The guard's stern face softened into a grin. He stepped away from the door.

Alex slid along the wall while their attention was fixed on each other and slipped into the chamber.

Inside, the room was dim, lit by a few smoky lamps. The air stank of sweat and something rotten. Alex hugged the shadows, eyes adjusting.

King Oyomo stood near the bed, bare-chested, clad only in loose breeches. His voice flowed low and cruel in his own tongue, but Alex did not need the words to feel the malice.

His gaze shifted, and his hands curled into fists.

Yvonne lay tied to the bed, arms and legs bound wide to the posts. Angry welts and bruises marred her skin. One eye was swollen nearly shut; blood crusted at her lip. Each shallow breath seemed to hurt.

He whispered. "Bastard, I should run you through where you stand."

Oyomo continued to taunt her. "Now it is time we enjoy marital bliss," he crooned. "I will take you as long as I wish, however I wish. When I am finished, I will trade you for a single goat."

Tears slipped from Yvonne's eyes. She shook her head frantically; muffled pleas lost behind the gag.

He gripped her face, squeezing until her cheeks bulged. "Cry all you like. Your claws are bound this time. You cannot rake me as you did before."

He climbed atop her, laughing, and Yvonne squeezed her eyes shut, wishing for death.

Then, in the middle of her muffled screams, the laughter cut off. A loud crack sounded once, before collapsing heavily across hers.

For a heartbeat, she wondered if madness had finally claimed her.

Another voice broke through, rough and urgent. "Easy now."

Her lashes fluttered.

Alex leaned over her, jaw clenched so tight the muscle jumped in his cheek. He cut and tugged at the knots with swift, sure movements.

When the last bond fell away, he shoved Oyomo's dead weight aside and hauled Yvonne into his arms.

"Shhh," he murmured, holding her tight against his chest as she cried. "I need you to be strong, lass. Can ye do that for me?"

She clung to his shirt, still shaking. "I… owe you my life," she whispered.

He managed to smile a crooked smile. "I'll think of a payment once we're away. A bottle of whisky should do."

Despite everything, a broken little laugh escaped her.

"Do ye have clothing?" he asked, scanning the wreckage of the room.

"The bastard tore everything to shreds," she whispered.

Alex spotted a heavy robe draped across a chair and grabbed it. "Here. Put this on. We must hurry."

When she was covered as best as she could be, he took her hand and guided her to the balcony. The doors opened onto a stone ledge high above the churning sea. Waves smashed against the rocks far below.

Yvonne balked. "What are you doing?" Her voice rose in panic. "Alex, what are you…"

"Listen to me," he said, turning to face her. "We must jump. Zara is outside distractin' the guard. This is the only way out."

"But I am afraid."

He cupped her face gently in both hands. "Fear is nae an option, Yvonne. I will be at your side every step of the way. Do ye trust me?"

Her throat worked. "No," she admitted in a small voice. "I cannot swim; I am afraid. Please… stay close to me."

He gathered her in his arms and stepped up onto the ledge.

"On the count of three," he said quietly. "We jump. One… two… three."

They leapt.

The cold hit like a blade. The sea roared up to swallow them whole. Water closed over Yvonne's head, tearing her from Alex's grip. She tumbled end over end, ears full of rushing sound.

Alex burst to the surface with a gasp. "Shit, where did she go?"

He dove under, lungs burning, eyes straining in the dark water, searching for a human form.

He came up for air once more, dragging in a gasp as the waves shoved him sideways. Salt stung his eyes. His lungs burned. Then, far off, a splash, followed by a thin, desperate cry.

"Help… please…"

He cut through the water toward the sound, every kick weighted by his sword, dirk, musket, and scabbard dragging him down. His muscles screamed, the bruises from the morning's fight flaring with every stroke.

"Yvonne!" he bellowed into the wind.

Something struck his arm, her hand. She clung to him in blind panic, nails digging into his skin.

"Yvonne, listen," he panted, fighting for breath. "Ye must relax. Can ye do that for me?"

She nodded, barely, and loosened her grip.

He swept one arm firmly around her waist, keeping her head above water, and powered forward with the other. Each stroke was agony, fire tearing through his ribs and shoulders, but he didn't stop. Not until his feet slammed into sand.

They staggered up the slope of the shallows and collapsed where the surf met the shore. Yvonne dragged herself onto the dry sand and rolled onto her back, chest heaving. Alex fell beside her, too spent to do anything but breathe.

The sun had climbed higher; the sky was streaked with soft gold. For a long moment, they simply breathed.

At last, Alex forced himself upright. "Where is the fishing village yer friend Zara mentioned?" he asked, still panting. "We must gain distance. He'll be hell-bent on huntin' ye down."

"If we walk to the right," she said, pointing along the curve of the shore, "we should reach it by mid-morning."

They rose and began to walk.

Alex studied her injuries quietly, his gaze skimming the marks at her throat and wrists. "Tell me, why is he so cruel to ye? Ye're covered in welts and bruises."

"There are many reasons," she said softly. "I never wanted him. I refused his hand until refusal became punishment. He is old enough to be my grand-elder. I fought him, spoke against him, and shamed him. King Oyomo does not forgive denial. My parents traded me for wealth. I begged them not to. I ran. My father always brought me back."

Alex frowned. "If yer family knows he is such a bastard, why offer ye at all?"

"For wealth," she said simply. "All for wealth. I would rather feed myself to a pride of hungry lions than be married to him. Alex, I need to get away from here. No matter where I run, he finds me. Each time, the beatings and torture grow worse. This time, he threatened to sell me. Thank the gods you and Zara found me first."

His heart twisted. She looked so small against the stretch of sand and sea, face bruised and swollen, both eyes darkening, lip split.

He stopped. "Here," he said gently. "Let me have a look."

He tore a strip from his shirt and dabbed carefully at her lip, careful not to press too hard.

"I have never been to these lands," he admitted. "I am not sure how much use I can be findin' ye safety. I heard ye are from King Oyomo's kingdom. Do ye have family here in Tafaria?"

She stared at the shoreline. "No. I am tired of running. Sometimes… I wish to die."

"Och, dinnae say such things," he said quickly. "Can Princess Nzingha or Prince Femi help?"

"Nae. The law says I belong to him. I was forced to make a union before the gods with him, husband and wife. No one can interfere."

Alex began walking again, matching his steps to hers. After a few paces, he slowed and reached for her hand when he noticed she lagged behind.

"Perhaps I can take you back with us," he said. "Yer presence aboard must stay a secret from my brother and his wife. He will think differently if he sees you."

Suspicion flickered. "And why is that?"

He glanced away. "Well… ah… my brother kens I've never been a careful man where women are concerned," he admitted. "He might think I brought ye aboard for my own reasons. We both ken that's no' so. I dinnae want him gettin' the wrong idea… that we're courtin'."

Her eyes narrowed. Gratitude curdled in an instant.

She yanked her hand away. "What is the matter with you?"

"Me?" he asked, startled. "What did I say?"

"Yes, you," she snapped. "Do not speak to me as if I am hoping to gain something from you. Do not treat me like some sick dog you dragged in off the trenches to feed and shelter. After all I have endured, do you truly think I wish to open my legs to you? Are you mad?"

"What?" His brows shot up. "Now haud a moment, lass. I'm the one riskin' my life tae save yers. I only meant ye should ken the circumstances if ye board my ship. 'Tisnae me I worry for, but my younger brother. This is the thanks I get for tryin' tae help ye? Christ above, women."

She scoffed. "You obnoxious ass of a man."

Yvonne stormed ahead, muttering in her language, "Why are men so awful?"

Alex glowered at her back. "Why in God's name is she all riled up? I am only tryin' tae help."

They reached the fishing village near mid-morning, the sun burning higher in the sky.

They spoke barely two words along the way.

Alex brooded far behind. "This is why I will never take a wife. No matter where ye travel, women twist yer words and flay ye for them. For Christ's sake, I only told her the truth. I cannae disappoint Andrew. Would she get over it already?"

Yvonne spotted an older fisherman perched on a rock jutting into the shallows, coiling his net. She approached with her head bowed slightly.

"Good morning, Uncle," she greeted in her native tongue. "My friend is stranded and wishes to trade something of his for your small boat."

The old man's gaze slid to Alex's waist, lingering on the sword and the dagger with the ruby in its hilt. He pointed and replied, *"Ningependa kisu chake kilicho na rubi."*

Yvonne chewed her lip.

Irritated by her silence, Alex asked, "Well? What the hell did he say?"

"He wants your knife," she said. "The one with the ruby."

"Nae!" Alex answered at once. "My father gave me this dagger. I shan't trade it for a busted old boat. Ask if he will take coin."

Yvonne turned back to the fisherman and knelt, pressing her palms together in respect. "Would you take gold instead?" she asked.

He gestured to the pouch at her waist and shook his head.

"Gold means little here. We trade what we can use." His gaze dropped to Alex's boots, and a slow smile spread across his face.

"Those," he said. "Those are good."

Yvonne looked over her shoulder. "He says he will trade his boat for your boots."

Alex stared at the weathered little craft, then at his boots. "These were made in Venice," he grumbled. "Venice leather, for Christ's sake." He huffed. "Fine. I have another pair aboard."

Yvonne could not help the small laugh that slipped free as he peeled off the boots with bad grace and handed them over. The fisherman sniffed them, nodded once in approval, and gestured toward the boat.

She bowed again. *"Asante,"* she said softly. "Thank you."

They clambered into the small vessel. Alex took the oars, setting his shoulders and rowing them out into deeper water. With each stroke, the shore grew smaller behind them, and his own ship grew larger ahead, tall masts spearing the sky, sails furled and ready.

Yvonne stared, wide-eyed. Prince Femi's ship had once seemed grand. Compared to this, it was a toy.

They reached the hull; ropes were thrown down. Alex climbed first, then turned and hauled Yvonne up after him.

She stepped onto the deck and turned slowly, taking it all in. Men moved about with practiced ease, checking rigging, coiling ropes. The upper deck held a massive wheel, and just behind it, a sturdy timbered structure with glass windows.

"Oh my," she breathed. "You have a cottage on your ship. How is that possible?"

Alex snorted. "Nae cottage. 'Tis the captain's quarters. That is where Andrew and Nzingha sleep."

Yvonne's eyes narrowed. "Now you finally tell the truth. You warned me your brother, and his wife should not know I was aboard, yet now you say Andrew and Nzingha both sleep in there. Nyema was right. They are wed."

"Well, there is no use trying to hide it now," he admitted. "They are. Her uncle is helping her return home with us."

"Oh? Is that so?" she answered, as though she had just been handed a piece of gossip.

"Aye, I'm nae feedin' ye anything else. Enough about them." He jerked his chin toward stairs. "Come."

"Where do you sleep?" she asked.

"In the quartermaster's cabin below deck. Since he didnae join us, it stands empty. Now that you are aboard, you may stay there. I will sleep in a hammock with the crew."

"But I do not wish to stay, Alex."

He snapped, patience fraying. "Woman, dinnae be ridiculous. If ye stay, that bastard will kill ye. Is that what ye want?"

"No," she whispered.

"Good. Then stop yer whinin and come on."

Voices carried from the far side of the deck. He caught her hand and tugged her toward the stairway, moving quickly. They slipped down into the cooler shadows below deck, their steps hushed by the planks. He opened a narrow door and guided her inside.

His breath came heavy as he whispered, "Shh. Stay put. I will be but a moment."

He slipped from the room, closing the door softly behind him.

Yvonne sank onto the narrow bunk, no longer caring that her clothes were damp, every muscle trembling now that the danger had passed. The morning's horrors finally caught up with her, exhaustion dragging at her limbs. She curled onto her side and pulled the thin blanket over herself.

Outside, voices carried faintly through the ship's timbers.

Above deck, a crewman called, "Ah, Captain. Ye made it back then. Are we castin' off soon?"

Alex's reply drifted down, calm and steady. "No' yet. Andrew's tendin' a few matters ashore. Once he's back, we sail. Should be within the sennight."

Groans of disappointment followed.

"Come now, lads," Alex called. "Dinnae sour on me. The princess brings a fine dowry. Yer pay'll be one block of gold apiece, on top o' what ye're owed."

A roar went up at once. "What? Ye're jestin', Captain! Two blocks o' gold for every man?"

"Aye," Alex said easily. "Ye heard me right."

Laughter and cheers rolled across the deck.

Another voice spoke, Euan's, more measured. "Beggin' yer pardon, Captain. Will Laird Andrew be returnin' afore we cast off?"

"Aye," Alex replied. "He stayed behind tae secure escort for the gold. He'll join us soon enough. Now enough blether." He clapped his hands. "This ship's in need of a good scrubbin. Bale seawater, grab a rag. Come on, the lot of ye. Move."

"Aye, Captain!" came the chorus.

Moments later, the cabin door creaked open.

"Yvonne," Alex said softly.

She did not stir.

He stepped inside and found her curled on the bunk, already asleep, lashes still damp, one hand tucked beneath her bruised cheek, as though she were once again the frightened girl hiding in a basket to save her own life.

Something unfamiliar turned over in his chest.

He stood there a long moment, watching her breathe.

Then he closed the door quietly and left her to her dreams.

Chapter Seven

Trial To Exile

*A*lex took his time rowing back toward the seashore near the

entrance of Tafaria lands. His shoulders burned, his head throbbed with exhaustion, but he forced his strokes steadily. The moment he stepped onto the sand, Femi's warriors stopped him. One lowered a carved staff across Alex's chest.

"Laird Chieftain," the warrior said in a measured, regal tone, "His Majesty King Femi and Princess Nzingha request your presence."

Alex frowned. "Aye? And where is my brother?"

"He sits with the King and the Princess. They await your arrival in the throne room."

"And the other Scot who traveled with us, Haemish?"

"He remains in his quarters until summoned."

Alex gave a tight nod and followed the guard through the palace corridors. When he entered the throne room, he found Femi seated upon the high seat, Nzingha standing with quiet dignity beside her uncle.

Then his gaze shifted, and there stood Andrew beside the tyrant himself, King Oyomo. Alex's lip curled when he noticed the king's head wrapped in linen.

"Serves the bastard right," he muttered under his breath.

King Femi inclined his head. "Good morning, Laird Chieftain. Before you stands King Oyomo of the Oyomo tribe. He arrived to reclaim his wife, who was discovered hidden within our lands this morning."

Alex folded his arms, unimpressed.

Femi continued, his tone sharpening with controlled frustration. "One of our castle workers was seen speaking with a palace warrior outside King Oyomo's chambers shortly before the King was struck unconscious. Someone opened the lion's den, and I intend to know who."

Alex raised a brow. "And what has that to do with me?"

Femi replied, "Your absence was noted. You were not seen within the castle grounds after Yvonne, the king's wife, went missing from his guest quarters."

Alex blinked innocently. "Sorry, Femi. I've nae idea what you're goin' on about."

King Femi's voice lowered. "King Oyomo has informed us that an informant saw Yvonne entering your guest chambers last eve. This occurred before the incident with my brother."

Alex shrugged. "Aye, she was there. But she left. My brother can attest to that. Andrew came to my chambers to say we were departin'."

He met Andrew's eyes briefly. They both knew Femi was putting on a performance for Oyomo's sake.

Femi clapped sharply.

Zara and Nyema were escorted in, wrists bound.

He addressed Zara first. "Did you assist Yvonne in leaving her husband's chambers this morning?"

Zara bowed her head. "No, my King. I only approached one of the warriors outside the King's door. That is all. Forgive me, but I have no wish to discuss the rest."

Nyema snapped immediately, her voice sharp and defensive. "This is absurd! She came to Femi.... Sorry, King Femi's chambers this morning begging aid for Yvonne!"

Femi's glare silenced her at once. "Nyema. Why were you at my chamber?"

Nyema's mouth opened; nothing came out. Her face blanched.

Femi watched her coolly. *So she believes herself my wife now...?* he thought. *The woman has lost her senses.*

He pressed, voice slow and dangerous. "So. You were aware of Yvonne's presence here. You knew what she was. Is that correct?"

Nyema trembled.

King Femi slammed his palm down on the armrest. "ANSWER, Nyema!"

She stood frozen, lips quivering, unable to betray Femi further.

Femi turned to Zara. "Zara. Only a yes or no. Did you assist Yvonne in escaping?"

Zara answered at once, steady and respectful. "No, King Femi."

Nyema spat out suddenly, "It was the foreigner! He must have helped her. Why else would he have left the castle? Search his ship!"

Jealousy twisted her voice. Femi had heard enough.

King Oyomo's rage burst forth. "I do not care for these delays! The foreigner likely hides my wife even now. Nyema said as much!"

Alex barked a laugh. "Ha! Listen here, King o' whatever land ye come from, ye're welcome to search my ship. There's nae Yvonne aboard. Go on then, have a look."

He turned to Femi, who gave the smallest nod.

A warrior slipped out to relay the order, and King Oyomo stormed from the throne room with his men.

As soon as Oyomo departed, Femi faced Nyema, hands clasped behind his back in a rigid, regal stance.

"I know it was you who informed King Oyomo of Yvonne's presence. You were seen conspiring with his men." His voice was low, stripped of warmth. "You confuse a night of lust with comfort, with obligation. You will leave these lands," he said quietly, voice like steel wrapped in velvet. "Never return. Should you be found here again, your life will be forfeit."

Nyema gasped. "My love, you cannot! I carry your child!"

Femi's expression twisted with disgust. "Must I repeat myself? Last time I checked, I had five wives. You are a servant who once warmed my bed. We have no child, and never shall."

He left her presence and nodded to a guard, who removed her.

She was dragged away screaming.

Tiny Dark Box..

Boom. Boom. Boom.

With a jolt, Yvonne awoke, holding her pained face.

Once more, the sound of pounding echoed.

Her heart raced. Is there a reason for such a knock? The Scotsman would barge in…

She spoke with a trembling voice. "Who goes there?"

"It is Idi," came the answer, smooth, dignified, a warrior's calm. "I serve as King Femi's trusted warrior. I have news. You must hide at once. King Oyomo approaches the ship. He rides in a rowboat with King Femi and the Foreigner."

Yvonne flung the cabin door open. "King? You said King Femi? What has happened to King Afonso Mbemba?"

Idi stepped inside. "There was battle. Princess Nzingha attempted to flee with her husband. Femi defended her. King Afonso fell."

Yvonne pressed a hand to her mouth. "So Femi is King now…? Nyema must be rejoicing."

Idi frowned. "Your friend? Nyema was the one who informed King Oyomo of your presence. She betrayed you."

He swept the room with a soldier's quick efficiency, found a trunk of clothing, and dumped its contents onto the floor.

He pointed firmly. "Inside. Quickly."

Yvonne climbed into the trunk, curling tight.

Idi piled clothing over her until she was smothered in linen.

"Hold on.." she whispered, "Idi, I cannot breathe."

"You must endure," Idi answered, lowering his voice. "The foreigner will retrieve you when the danger passes."

The door shut.

Yvonne lay still, wrapped in darkness and cloth, listening.

Idi's voice carried faintly through the wood, low and controlled. He received answers from others. The hull and distance interfered with the words, causing them to fade in and out. "Captain. Documents. Trunk."

After that, there was silence.

Time grew longer, its nature becoming less defined and more precarious.

There were footsteps on the stairs. It was Heavy. Having a clear purpose.

Cutting through the cabin was Alex's voice. "Aye, look about if ye must. But mind yerselves, there's valuable documents on my desk an' trunk."

Holding her breath, Yvonne pressed her lips together.

Boots made their way across the floor. The bed made a creaking sound. Cabinets opened, slammed shut.

"Nothing, sire. All clear."

Her pulse thudded once. Twice.

Then King Oyomo spoke. Calm. Certain.

"The trunk. Open it."

The lid shifted.

Light seeped through the linen above her face, faint and shifting. Cloth stirred, slow, deliberate, and hands moved close enough that she felt the air change. Fingers passed inches from her cheek. Something scraped softly. The sound of parchment crumpled.

Alex's voice cut in sharp and sudden. "Careful with my bloody documents! They're for port clearances!"

The trunk jolted as he pulled them free. For a breathless instant, the lid hovered.

Then it shut.

"My King," a guard said, unsettled, "the trunk is clear."

Alex did not bother hiding his impatience. "What now? Shall I fetch ye wine an' cheese? Get the hell off my ship."

Boots moved away. Voices followed. The sounds thinned, then vanished, until only the creak of timber and the low groan of the hull remained.

Inside the trunk, the air grew close.

Heat settled over Yvonne's chest, heavy and pressing. She tried to swallow, but her throat refused. Each breath came smaller than the last, as though the space itself were drawing tight around her.

She pushed at the lid. It did not yield.

The air grew stale, offering less than it took.

"Alex…?" The whisper barely stirred the cloth. "Chieftain… are you there…?"

Nothing answered.

Only the ship, shifting above her. Only footsteps, distant now, fading away.

She struck the lid again, but the sound vanished at once, swallowed by linen and wood.

"Please…" The word thinned on her tongue. "Someone…"

Darkness gathered behind her eyes, slow and inevitable, rising like water in a sealed space.

Her hand slipped from the lid.

And she drifted quietly into blackness.

Chapter Eight

Leaving It Behind

Yvonne opened her eyes and winced, one hand flying to the back of her head. A hard lump throbbed there, sharp and relentless. As her thoughts slowly settled, memories returned in fragments.

The trunk. The darkness. The heat.

She blinked and realized she lay in a narrow bed, soft linen beneath her cheek, the gentle sway of the ship rocking her from side to side.

Laird Alex's vessel.

"Alex?" She tried to sit up, only to be met with pain. She winced. "Ouch... Chieftain, are you back?" she called, her voice hoarse.

"I wouldnae do that if I were you."

She turned toward the sound. Alex sat at a small desk in the corner, back half-turned to her, shoulders relaxed but gaze sharp. He pivoted in the chair.

"Good. Ye're awake," he said. "I was worried after findin' ye half dead in my trunk."

Her throat felt dry as sand. "Water… please?"

"Aye. Of course."

He rose, crossed the room, poured from a clay pitcher into a cup, and placed it in her hands. She drank greedily, the cool liquid easing the fire in her throat. Only then did she notice how fiercely the ship rolled beneath them.

"Is it raining outside?" she asked, frowning. "The ship is rocking harshly."

"Nae," he replied. "We're out tae sea."

Yvonne froze. "Out to sea?" she repeated, voice rising. "Where to?"

Alex lifted a finger to his lips. "Shh. Keep yer voice low. We're on our way tae my lands."

"What?" Her heart lurched. "No. Please, you must take me back."

He arched a brow. "I thought that's what ye wanted."

"No… well… yes." She faltered over the words. "I mean, I do not know. I wished to leave, but not with you."

He gave a short huff of disbelief. "Ye said ye were tired o' runnin'. So I did yer biddin' and took you away. Femi said it was best for your safety."

"He did?"

"Aye. O' course he did. Looked about ready tae cry, the poor bastard."

The room seemed to tilt again, this time from more than the sea. She sank back onto the pillow as the pain in her skull flared, turning everything hazy around the edges.

"I heard you say to your men you were to leave in a sennight," she murmured.

"Aye, we were," Alex said. "But Oyomo's no leavin' Tafaria's castle any time soon. I convinced Andrew we needed tae quit the place earlier."

Everything was happening too fast. The course of her life had shifted in a single day, and she no longer knew what waited ahead.

"I am grateful for all you have done," she said quietly. "But what of my family? You must understand, Africa is all I know. I never left my village until Femi rescued me. I do not know what is written in the stars for me, but this cannot be it. Please. At the very least, you must take me back to my village."

"Yvonne." His tone softened, though it held an edge of stubbornness. "I had nae intention of oversteppin' your decisions. But that husband of yers is hell-bent on makin' yer life a misery. I need ye tae have faith in me. Under my protection, nae one will ever lay a finger on ye again. With me, there is only safety."

He leaned forward, elbows on his knees.

"When we arrive, I'll see ye settled in a cottage," he continued. "Ye'll have privacy and, more importantly, peace. Mayhap, in a year or two, we can see you safely back tae your home. Anything ye need, I'll see it done. But for now, Femi and I cannae risk ye bein' harmed. We spoke of it, and weighed the cost. He could only protect ye so much before he'd be forced into war with Oyomo's tribe."

She swallowed hard.

She knew how deeply Femi cared. He had risked his life more than once to shield her. And Alex, though brash, shameless, and far too fond of women, had done the same this day. All her life, the men around her had wanted something from her, her body, her status, her obedience. Kings and suitors had treated women like toys, vessels for desire or broodmares to trade for power.

But Femi and Alex were different. They had no need of her wealth or name. They had more women than they could count, yet when danger came, their actions had been fierce and strangely pure.

She closed her eyes, feeling a tear slip free. "It all sounds kind and generous," she whispered. "Truly it does. But I am afraid. How will I find my way in this new world? What of Princess Nzingha? Does she know I am here? What will she think of me?"

A single tear slid down her cheek. Alex reached out and gently brushed it away with his thumb.

"Lass, you'll be fine," he said. "I've no' told a soul. We'll cross that bridge when we come tae it. Right now, ye need tae heal. Ye could be at risk o' fever."

He gave her a playful wink. She only winced, fingers seeking the back of her head.

"Ouch," she hissed. "The pain is unbearable. I felt a lump there."

"Hm." His mouth tilted as his gaze flicked to her head. "I've somethin' that'll set ye tae rights."

He crossed back to the desk and rummaged through a drawer.

She watched him, wary. "What is it? Herbs?"

He laughed outright, pulled out a small flask, and took a long swallow before offering it. "Nae. Somethin' better. Whisky."

Yvonne eyed the flask as if it might bite her, then lifted it, trusting him more than trusting the word. She took a bold gulp.

Fire tore down her tongue and throat.

She spluttered, choking, and sprayed half of it straight back at him. Alex jerked away, blinking, whisky dripping from his cheek.

He stared at her, horrified. "Ye just wasted a perfect tot o' whisky."

"It burns." She clutched her throat. "Oh, the gods…it burns...what sort o' medicine is that?"

"Scottish whisky," he said proudly. "Best cure I ken."

"It is like drinking fire," she croaked.

"Aye, that's how ye ken it's workin'. It's my version o' yer palm wine. Here. Try again. Smaller sips, unless ye fancy drownin' me."

She shook her head, but he tipped the flask gently until she relented and took a cautious sip.

"Fine," she said grudgingly as the burn softened into warmth. "It is a hot drink. It makes my insides warm."

"Good. Hold onto that feelin'. In a few more sips, ye'll be numb enough."

She drank a little more and handed it back. He took several quick gulps, clearly satisfied.

"Are you hungry?" he asked. "You shouldnae be drinkin' on an empty stomach."

"I am famished," she admitted. "I have not eaten since the night I went to your chambers."

"God's bones," he muttered. "That was ages ago. I'll fetch ye something. Yer princess was generous with the livestock for the voyage. Our cook's made goat stew."

"Mmm," her mouth watered at the thought. "I can almost taste it."

He shifted abruptly from the sound she made. and for a moment his expression went oddly tight.

Christ's bones, what is wrong with me, he thought. *The woman is injured, for the love o' God.*

He passed the flask back to her with an awkward smile. "Good. I'll be but a moment. I've an audience with my brother. When we're done, I'll bring yer meal."

The idea of a beautiful half-dressed woman in his cabin, wrapped in his linen, made his thoughts darken in ways he refused to entertain. He turned away quickly and left, slamming the door a little harder than he meant to.

She frowned as the cabin shuddered with the impact. "What has gotten into him?" she murmured. "He looked as though he saw a demon."

She took another careful sip of whisky and lay back, stretching as stiffness protested every movement. After a moment, curiosity tugged her gaze toward the desk.

The book.

He had been writing in it when she woke.

She slid from the bed, the ship rocking beneath her bare feet. Crossing to the desk, she hesitated, then opened the leather journal.

A smile touched her lips.

The first page held a sketch of his brother, Andrew. The lines were strong and sure, the likeness so true he looked ready to step from the page.

She turned the leaf.

A woman's face met her, beautiful, but with eyes weighted by sorrow. Beneath the drawing, written in careful script, was a name and a short apology. Yvonne sounded it out.

"Soo… phey," she whispered. "Sophie."

Her gaze moved lower.

My apologies for not understanding the pain you felt. Instead of helping, I pushed you away. Forgive me for not providing you with a better life.
Alex.

Yvonne's heart tightened. "May the gods protect her," she whispered.

She lingered on Sophie's face, tracing the edge of the jaw with her eyes, then turned the page again,

and choked.

"Great goddess, Oshun."

This sketch was no sorrowful portrait. A naked woman lounged with her legs indecently parted, head thrown back, eyes closed in open pleasure. The next page showed a woman touching herself, another a couple entwined in a position that made Yvonne's cheeks burn.

"Alex, what is the matter with you?" she muttered, scandalized. "First you lie with two women at once, now you sketch such things. How can you be so vile?"

She kept turning pages, each drawing more brazen than the last. The whisky no longer burned; instead, it warmed her veins and fed a strange, reluctant fascination she hated herself for feeling.

By the time the door burst open, her face was aflame.

Ledgers and Lies

Alex strode into Haemish's cabin without knocking. Both Andrew and Haemish looked up from the desk where they were bent over parchments.

"Good eve, Captain," Haemish greeted.

"Aye," Alex replied curtly.

Andrew arched a brow. "Well, it took ye long enough. What in God's name were ye doin'?"

"My bloody head hurts," Alex dropped into a chair and flung his feet up on the table with less grace than usual. "Let's get on with it. Andrew walked over and handed him a parchment, the seal pressed in gold. "Here is the discussion we had with Nzingha's uncle earlier today. Do ye recall her father speakin' of recompense?"

"Aye," Alex said, the corner of his mouth quirking. "I recall nearly chokin' on my wine. Thought the old king meant tae drown us in it. Twenty thousand gold coins, aye?"

"Nae, that's changed," Andrew said.

Alex took the parchment, squinting hard at the foreign script. He turned it slightly, then scowled. "Ah. That explains nothin'. I cannae read this."

Andrew took it back and pointed at the lines. "That was her father's word, spoken before his death. But with him gone, Femi now stands as her acting guardian. He went through the deeds himself."

Alex leaned back in his chair. "And?"

"And the account was corrected," Andrew said evenly. "Not twenty thousand coins. That was removed, now it's One thousand gold bars, weighed and drawn from Tafaria's treasury. Femi wished tae grant her more, God ken he did, but even he saw sense. Our ship couldnae carry the weight without puttin' her at risk again."

Alex let out a low breath. "Still enough tae make a man forget his prayers."

Andrew continued. "Before all this, Nzingha was meant tae wed King Oyomo's eldest son. 'Twas nae a love match, but an alliance. He would rule as king, she as queen, their kingdoms bound together. As part o' that bargain, her father agreed tae pay King Oyomo ten thousand gold bars as bride price, set aside in this very treasury."

Alex shook his head. "Ten thousand. No wonder the man's fit tae spit nails."

"But she chose me instead," Andrew said simply, "and that agreement was broken. The gold didnae go tae Oyomo. It stayed tied tae Nzingha's name, here in Tafaria's lands and coffers."

He handed Alex another parchment. "Her uncle has settled matters this way. One thousand bars for bringin' her home alive. Fifty thousand in gold coins for Tafaria's keep, and jewels and diamonds listed in her father's will. This sits in trust for our bairns. When they're grown, they can travel tae their mother's land and claim what's theirs."

Alex stared at the page for a long moment.

"…Bairns," he said quietly. "Saints preserve us."

Andrew slid the final parchment across the table. "Here is what we intend tae pay the crew. And this," he tapped the second line, "is what Nzingha and I wish tae gift you and Haemish for your loyalty and aid."

Alex read the figures once.

Then again.

Then he shot to his feet so fast his chair toppled behind him.

"Holy shite!" he blurted. "We're richer than the king himself. Christ alive… we'll nae have tae sail ever again. I cannae believe my eyes."

He stared at Andrew. "This kind o' coin gives us the means tae stand as counts. Do you ken the land we can buy in the New World? The number o' galleys we could command, with overseers tae do our biddin'? Ha! We are filthy rich."

Andrew smiled, pleased to see his brother's joy. "Aye, but we must be careful. We do not shout this from the castle walls. That is how wars begin."

"So, what say you, brother?" Alex asked.

"We will gift the crown one hundred blocks and tae the Kirk ten," Andrew replied. "When we do, I will bring Nzingha before the king as my wife. His coffers will be fat with gold; that should soften his differences with Nzingha if any."

"I agree." Alex's grin broadened. "Tell me, where is your wealthy wife now?"

"She is resting in the captain's cabin."

A knock sounded. As if summoned, Nzingha stepped inside.

"Well," she teased, "look who crawled out of his cave. You've been in your cabin all afternoon. Did you have your meal?"

"Nae yet," Alex answered. "But I'm starvin'. I was headin' tae the kitchens this very moment."

He started toward the door, but Nzingha laid a hand on his shoulder.

"The young noblewoman, Yvonne," she asked softly. "Were you able to see her safely away?"

Alex hesitated. "I… took her tae a friend in another village," he said.

Without waiting for a reply, he slipped past and left, closing the door sharply behind him.

Nzingha turned to her husband. "What is his problem?"

Andrew shrugged. "Nae inkling, wife. Alex can be a wee bit daft."

She laughed. "I agree."

Sketches and Stew

The smell of fresh bread and rich stew greeted Alex the moment he stepped into the ship's kitchen. His stomach growled loudly enough to make him curse under his breath.

"Christ, I'm bloody starvin'."

A loaf of bread cooled on the table. He tore off a huge chunk and bit in, leaning over the table as he devoured it.

"Captain?" The ship's cook eyed him with amusement. "Shall I fix you a bowl o' stew? I was worried ye were ill. You refused tae eat earlier. But seein' you tackle that loaf, I'd say ye're fine."

"My thanks," Alex said around another bite. "I took a much-needed nap. This trip has me spent."

"Aye, I ken the feelin'," the cook replied. "I'm tired myself. I'm still thinkin' on what your uncle did tae Andrew's wife. If it were my wee wife, I'd have run him through."

The cook ladled a bowl of goat stew and passed it to him. Alex ate as if it were the last meal he'd ever see.

"Can you pour me some ale?" he asked after several mouthfuls.

"Aye, Captain. Right away."

"And another bowl," Alex added. "I'm hungrier than a wolf in winter. I'll be takin' one back tae my cabin."

"Of course, sir. Ye're hungry this night, that's for certain."

"Aye. We've had a long day on the continent, layin' Nzingha's father tae rest. I lost most o' my strength."

When he'd finished, he wiped his mouth. "My thanks. That was excellent. Have a good night."

He took the second bowl and a tankard and headed back above deck, then down toward his cabin. He paused outside the door, glanced up and down the corridor, and slipped inside.

The moment he entered, Yvonne jerked away from his desk like a guilty child caught stealing sweets. His gaze snapped from her to the open sketchbook, and heat rushed to his face.

The drawing in plain view was of her, Yvonne, nude, captured with far too much care.

She moved quickly back to the bed and sat, clutching the linen to her chest, saying nothing.

Perfect, Alex thought miserably. *Now she thinks I'm a bloody pervert.*

He held the bowl out. "I… ah… brought you stew."

She nodded stiffly. "My thanks, Laird Chieftain."

Silence settled over the room. They stared at one another, tension thick between them.

"Well?" he said at last. "Will you just sit there, or are you goin' tae eat?"

Yvonne bit her lip. Every word she wished to hurl at him burned on her tongue.

"I have lost my appetite," she said.

"What? I thought you were starvin'."

"I was. Then I saw your sketchbook."

"Listen, I..."

"No need for explanation, Chieftain," she cut in sharply. "I can see the sort of man you are. Please. I cannot travel to your home. I do not feel safe with you. May we return? I will escape to another village if I must. I would rather face wild animals on the savannah than be locked in a room with you."

"Have ye lost your wits?" he snapped. "There's nae way I'm turnin' this ship around. And I dinnae recall givin' ye leave tae rummage through my things."

"I knew I should never have trusted you after seeing you with those two women at our little gathering," she fired back. "Both women, Alex? And you tried to pull me into such a vile act."

She paused, then frowned sharply.

"And how did I end up naked next to you? I do not recall lying with you."

Alex huffed, running a hand over his face. "For the love o' God… listen."

He leaned forward, voice tight with irritation and something else, hurt pride.

"When I found you, you were on the balcony shiverin' like a drowned pup, your gown soaked in vomit. You could barely stand. I had tae undress you, lass, unless ye wished tae sleep in filth."

Her eyes widened, but he pressed on.

"And before ye accuse me o' more wickedness, I put ye under the covers and kept my bloody distance. I didnae touch a hair on yer head."

She crossed her arms. "You could not dress me in something else?"

He stared at her as if she'd lost her senses.

"In what? My boots? My cloak? I had nae spare gown lyin' about, Yvonne. Dinnae be daft."

She opened her mouth, but he cut her off, temper flickering.

"And while we're on the matter, dinnae pretend you were some saint that night. The opium in my wine? Do ye recall that, Miss Nobility? So do not stand there lookin' ready tae faint and tell me you came tae my chambers for polite conversation."

Yvonne strode to the desk, grabbed the sketchbook, and threw it at him. It hit his chest with a dull thud.

"I am not a whore," she shouted. "Just because I came to your chambers does not mean I came to lie with you. You… pig."

She flung herself onto the bed and yanked the covers over her head, ending the conversation. Alex stood there, chest heaving, then let out a long breath and rolled his eyes.

"Why are women so bloody nosy?" he muttered. Guilt pricked at him. After all, Yvonne was aboard his ship to escape men like Oyomo. For all his urges, he had not touched her. She was innocent.

"Listen, lass," he said more softly. "Forgive me. Please. Dinnae think I'm some depraved beast."

Yvonne said nothing, only tightened the blankets around her.

He exhaled sharply. "Fine. Suit yerself. I've already apologized."

He made himself a pallet on the floor, stretched out with a yawn, and, with a full belly and a head full of chaos, fell asleep.

When Hunger Won

Hours slipped by.

Yvonne lay stiff beneath the covers, listening to Alex snore on the floor. Her stomach growled so loudly she pressed a hand to it. The smell of the cooled stew haunted her.

At last, she sat up, peeking over the edge of the bed.

Alex lay on his side, mouth open, snoring like a bear in winter. She rolled her eyes.

"You truly are insufferable," she whispered.

She slid carefully to the floor, stepping over him, and tiptoed to the desk. She picked up the wooden spoon and tasted the now-cold stew.

Her eyes closed. It was still delicious, cold but rich and comforting. She finished the bowl in minutes, then laid her head on the desk. Her head still ached, but less sharply now.

A scent reached her nose.

She sniffed. "What is that?"

She lifted her arm and sniffed again. "Oh my. It is me."

Captured by Oyomo, dragged through dirt, salt, and fear, she could not remember the last time she had bathed.

"I cannot return to bed like this," she whispered. "What if he notices?"

Her gaze swept the cabin. In the corner, a barrel stood near the wall. She crept to it, lifted the lid, and smiled when she saw it filled with water. Nearby sat a basin, a bar of soap, and a washcloth.

She filled a bucket and carried it to the far corner, glancing over her shoulder. Alex still slept, curled on his side, snoring louder than ever.

Satisfied he was truly asleep, she stripped and began to wash, ears straining for any change in his breathing.

Careful Hands

Alex woke to the sound of water trickling.

For a moment he thought he was dreaming, visions of streams and river stones. Then he opened his eyes.

And saw Yvonne.

She stood in the cabin's dim glow, bare as the day she was born. Moonlight spilled through the small window, mingling with the candle's soft flame, caressing every line of her.

He stayed very still.

His gaze followed the slow, careful path of the cloth as she washed, down over her chest, circling her breasts, along the smooth line of her stomach. She lifted an arm to scrub beneath it, then braced one foot on a chair and washed between her thighs.

Desire punched through him, swift and brutal. *Why in God's name did I bring her aboard? Now I've tae fight the urge tae bed her every bloody night.*

When she shifted in the candlelight, the truth revealed itself. His eyes widened in shock. Her skin was mapped with bruises, dark lesions along her ribs, stomach, and thighs.

The sight hit him like a fist. *How can I be lustin' after a woman in such a state?* he thought. *Her life's been naught but hell.*

She finished washing and carried the basin to the window, standing on a chair to toss the water out into the dark sea. She refilled a smaller bowl, bathed her face, and sighed.

"Ah," she murmured. "I feel much better."

Her eyes brightened when she saw a small bundle of mint leaves. She plucked two, sniffed them, and began to chew, savoring the clean taste.

Then she looked down at herself and stilled.

Of course she could not continue wearing Oyomo's robe. The memory of him haunted her nights, his voice, his hands, the knotted rope, the pain he delighted in. Even awake, she heard his threat:

"By the time I am done teaching you a lesson, you will know the true meaning of obey. If you run again, I will kill you. You are my wife. Do you understand? Mine."

Her teeth clenched. In a sudden burst of fury, she snatched up the robe and threw it out the window, watching it drift away across the water.

She dropped to her knees as the weight of it all crashed over her.

"I hate my life," she whispered. "A future chosen for me waits ahead. Home feels farther with every step. I miss my friends. Most of all, Femi."

She tried to cry quietly so as not to wake Alex, but the sobs tore out of her, anyway. Her shoulders shook.

A shadow fell over her. A shirt slipped over her shoulders, the fabric warm from his hands.

"Shh," Alex said softly. "There now, lass. Ye can wear this."

She turned, pressed her face into his chest, and gave muffled wails. He wrapped his arms around her, careful of her bruises. Remorse twisted in his chest. He had found her tied to a bed, naked and broken. Her face had been swollen with pain, her lips cracked and bloody.

"I'm here, Yvonne," he murmured. "All will be right. I cannae imagine what that bastard did tae ye."

She pulled back and wiped her cheeks. "My thanks, Chieftain. I felt unclean. I needed privacy. Forgive me for bathing while you slept, but I had nowhere else to go."

"Och, dinnae fash yourself," he said gently. "I heard you cryin'. Are ye hale enough? Ye shouldnae trouble yerself about that brute findin' you. Ye're safe here."

"Sometimes... I slip into a daze," she confessed. "I think about the pain. It was unbearable. He found such pleasure in tormenting me. If you had not arrived when you did, I would not be a virgin. The gods were merciful."

Alex held her tighter at that. "When my grandsire died," he said quietly, "I was gutted. My mother told me this: the hurt o' today will be a memory for tomorrow. All the pain we've suffered will make us stronger."

He looked straight into her eyes. "I'll be yer friend, Yvonne. I give ye my word. When ye're ready tae go home, I'll help. Gladly. For now, rest. In the mornin', I'll see what I can pilfer from Nzingha's wardrobe. I'm sure she'll no' miss a gown or two. Until then, ye can wear my extra clothes."

She lowered her gaze, the fight draining from her. He could see how defeated she felt.

"Listen," he added, forcing a crooked smile. "I'm no pervert. Whatever happened with the two women the other night was thanks tae that cursed drug in my wine. I'd never take advantage o' ye. If I meant ye harm, I'd have lift yer skirts long before now That's no the man I am."

She studied him. "Then why do you draw such vulgar scenes?"

Alex sat beside her, shoulders relaxing. "Honestly? Women are the most beautiful, mysterious creatures God ever made. A woman's body is… perfect. She deserves tae be cherished. I love the intimacy between a man and a woman. I dinnae ken how tae say it without soundin' crude. Sometimes my urges are… difficult tae control. I'm a man. So I sketch instead o' bedding every lass who catches my eye. I put the vision on paper. I draw what I find beautiful."

"So that is why you sketched me?" she asked quietly. "Because you think I am beautiful? That I ought to be cherished?"

She gave a small laugh. "I do not know whether to be offended or flattered."

"I thought ye were beautiful from the first moment I saw ye," he admitted. "That night on the balcony, when we kissed, even drunk as I was, I remember every heartbeat of it. I was the one who carried ye back inside. But Zara… she wanted tae wake you and see if ye'd participate. I told her tae leave ye be."

Yvonne frowned. "Zara can be overly bold," she said. "She was the king's special servant."

She looked down at her hands. "I have never been with a man. The thought frightens me. I thank the gods you came when you did, for he was about to force himself upon me. My virginity is the only thing I consider sacred. I wish to share that only with a man I love, and who loves me in return."

Alex watched her carefully, his voice dropping low.

"I ken… ye've never been touched."

Color touched her cheeks. "Why does that matter?"

"It doesnae," he said softly. "No' tae me. I only… worry for ye, lass. Ye flinch every time someone gets too close. Even when I'm no' layin' a hand on ye."

She looked away, breathing shallow.

Alex leaned forward, elbows on his knees.

"Yvonne… I need tae ken something. No' out o' curiosity, out o' concern."

His tone softened further. "What is it that truly frightens ye?"

Her throat bobbed.

Slowly, she lifted her hand to her neck, the place just under her ear, and her fingers hovered there without touching.

"When a man's hand touches here," she whispered, "my body remembers. I am back in that room. His hand closing… pressing. His breath on me. His voice. I see nothing but him."

Alex's jaw clenched, eyes dark with fury, but not at her.

She curled into herself. "It has ruined any closeness. Any thought of being touched. My mind screams before I can think. Even kindness feels dangerous."

"Yvonne…" His voice cracked, then steadied. "No woman should carry that weight."

"I tried once…" She forced a breath. "To push past it. Not wickedly. With trust. A man who had shown me nothing but respect. We kissed. He touched my cheek. My arm. Nothing more. But then…"

Her hand trembled over her neck. "His fingers brushed here, and I fell apart. I could not breathe. I begged him to stop."

Alex swallowed hard.

"Did he stop?"

"Yes," she said quietly. "But the shame remained."

Alex exhaled, rubbing the back of his neck.

"Listen tae me well," he said, voice rough with sincerity. "If ever ye flinch around me, I'll step back. If ye say stop, I'll stop. If ye cannae bear a touch, I'll keep my hands tae myself. Ye have my word."

Her eyes widened, not in fear, but surprise.

"I've kenned plenty o' women," he muttered. "But none that made me want tae be… careful. Ye make me want tae watch my tongue, hold my temper, and no' scare ye worse than ye already are."

Her lips parted in a soft breath.

"And for God's sake," he added gruffly, ears reddening, "I'm tryin' no' tae be a damned bastard."

She let out a small, shaky laugh.

"Alex," she murmured, "I did not expect gentleness from you."

"Aye, well," he grumbled, "keep that tae yerself. Ruin my reputation and I'll never forgive ye."

A silence settled, warm, not wounded.

He finally stood and held out his hand.

"Come, lass. I want tae show ye somethin'."

"Where?" she asked softly. "Here in your cabin?"

"Nae. Above deck."

"What if your crew sees me?"

"Dinnae fret. They're either sleepin' or gamblin' away their wages. Come on, now."

She placed her hand in his.

For the first time in a long while, the world felt a little less terrifying.

Above Deck

They slipped out of the cabin and climbed the narrow stairwell. Alex paused at the top, scanning left and right with a practiced sailor's eye. Spotting two crewmen leaning against the railing, he gently placed Yvonne behind him.

He strode forward with calm authority. "Evening, men. 'Tis a fine night."

"Aye, Captain," One tipped his cap. "I see ye're taking the air, enjoying the breeze?"

"Indeed," Alex said lightly. "The cabin felt a bit stuffy."

He cast a quick look over his shoulder; Yvonne stayed cloaked behind him.

The crewmen smiled knowingly.

"Tell ye what," Alex said, lowering his voice. "Take a break. I'll call for ye when ye're needed."

"Captain, are ye sure?"

"Aye. Go on. Down to the kitchen, tell the cook I sent ye. Hurry before I change my mind."

"Aye, chief. Our thanks."

They bolted below deck, grinning like thieves who'd stolen a holiday.

Alex led Yvonne toward the starboard side, where the sea opened beneath the moon. They stopped beside a post, the soft slap of waves rising to meet them.

She looked around. "Is there anyone else here other than us?"

He pointed upward. "Aye. Men in the crow's nest. But look at them."

Two dark shapes slumped motionless above. "Lazy bastards are asleep."

He turned his gaze outward. The ocean shimmered with moonlight, vast and silver.

"The sea is calm this time o' night," he murmured. "We're safe enough."

Yvonne lifted her face to the sky, stars spilled across it like powdered diamonds.

"This is lovely," she whispered. "I've never had the chance to stand beneath stars like these… not even at the castle. Thank you. It makes me feel… better."

Alex's voice softened. "Yvonne… if I offended ye with my drawing, I truly am sorry."

She shook her head. "No, do not apologize. All is well. You told me why you drew it. And I had no right to pry through your things."

Her fingers brushed the rail. "You've seen me naked, weak… but never once have you taken advantage of me. I… feel safe with you."

He exhaled, something easing in his chest. Slowly, he placed a warm hand on her shoulder.

"I promise ye this, lass, whatever storms come, I'll protect ye. Though I'm a man with urges, I'll do my damnedest to keep them under control."

They stood quietly, the wind tugging at their hair. Yvonne caught herself studying him, broad shoulders, wind-tossed hair, the fierce yet gentle expression she was only beginning to understand. Five hands taller than she, built like a warrior carved from the earth itself.

"Do you have a special lady back home?" she asked, voice soft.

His answer was immediate. "Nae!"

Then he cleared his throat. "I mean… I havenae time for courting. The sea keeps me busy. As do my father's lands."

"I see…" She hesitated. "Will you ever seek a wife? Children?"

He held back a sigh. "I told ye, lass, I appreciate all women. But I cannae imagine myself with only one. I respect women, aye, but if a lass fancies raising her skirts, I'm not the man to deny her."

She elbowed him. "Alex, you are insufferable. Why stay unwed? Do you not want children?"

He smirked. "I'd no' say I'm insufferable. I'd say I'm honest. And aye, I do want bairns someday. But I love the sea. I love to travel. 'Twould break my heart no' being there for them."

His voice dropped. "But… who kens. After this voyage, life may change."

The topic unsettled him, marriage always had, so he straightened abruptly.

"Come now. Enough talk o' wives and bairns. Let's head back before my men think I gave them the whole night off."

But as they rounded the corner,
they stopped dead.

Standing alone in the moonlit passage was Nzingha.

The sight struck Alex like a memory, like seeing his mother on the night he'd been caught sneaking out of the brothel.

Immediately, Yvonne dropped to one knee. "My princess."

Nzingha lifted her chin, her expression unreadable. "Come now, Yvonne. Stand. We are not in Tafaria."

Then she turned her eyes, sharp as drawn steel, on Alex.

"A fine night for a walk, Alex? You did not tell me we had a guest from my kingdom aboard."

Alex folded his arms, bracing for the inevitable barrage. Their relationship had always been a tug-of-war between snark and reluctant respect.

Nzingha smiled, though it did not reach her eyes.

"Well… at least you were somewhat honest. She is safe. But why is she aboard this vessel? I thought you left her in a nearby village for protection."

Alex exhaled through his nose. She made him feel twelve again.

"Nzingha… I can explain."

She arched a brow. "Tell me? Or shall I fetch Andrew so he may hear as well?"

"Please, no' Andrew," he said quickly. "If he finds out… he'll be furious. And the elders at home, God knows what they'll say about bringin' in another outsider."

Yvonne froze.

Outsider? Elders?

Pain and humiliation pricked her eyes.

"Forgive me," she whispered. "I am tired. I must take my leave."

She hurried away before Alex could call after her.

Alex rounded on his sister-in-law. "Nzingha, why? She's terrified."

"Why?" Nzingha shot back. "Because you look like a man caught with his hand in the wrong basket. Did you bring that girl aboard for your own pleasure? How much of a pig can you be?"

"Nae!" he growled. "She needed help. Femi and I agreed."

"Femi?" Nzingha demanded. "What part does he play in this?"

"Och... he wrote the bloody play," Alex snapped.

"Why did you not tell Andrew?"

"And ye think that thick head would believe me?" Alex planted his hands on his waist. "He's just like our father. Besides, she had nowhere tae go. When I found her, she was bound tae that man's bed. He'd beaten her senseless. Her body's still covered in bruises. He meant tae force himself on her, then sell her."

Nzingha's hand flew to her mouth, horror flickering in her eyes.

"That monster... I had no idea."

Alex rubbed his forehead. "When we reach Scotland... the elders will object. I ken it. I planned tae hide her at my father's old hunting cabin. She'd be safe if no one kenned she was there. Or..."

He hesitated. "She could stay with ye and Andrew in Leith. Help with Destiny?"

Nzingha exhaled slowly. "Give me time to speak with Andrew."

"Nae. I'll tell him. Just pretend ye know nothing."

"I cannot hide things from my husband, Alex."

He stepped closer, voice low. "Please. I have always respected you. Kept your secrets. Never spoke out of turn when it came to your arrival in our lands. I have never asked you for anything. This lass… she has been through hell."

Nzingha's gaze softened.

"Very well," she said at last. "But you must tell Andrew before we reach Scotland."

"I will. We've four months yet."

Footsteps approached. Andrew appeared at the end of the passage, worry etched across his face.

"There ye are," he said to Nzingha. "I grew frantic when I didn't see ye in our chambers."

"My love," she said smoothly, "I wanted to check on your brother. He left Haemish's cabin looking unwell."

Alex forced a smile. "Nae, I'm fine. Just tired. Have a good evening. I'm off tae bed."

As Andrew escorted Nzingha away, she glanced back and gave Alex a firm, meaningful nod.

Thank You.

Alex opened the door quietly.
Yvonne lay in the bunk, wrapped from head to toe beneath the covers like a frightened child.

"Yvonne," he whispered. "Are ye asleep?"

Silence.

He sighed, removed his boots and shirt, and poured himself a generous glass of whisky. When the burn slid down his throat, he lay back on his pallet and stared at the low wooden ceiling.

A small voice broke the quiet.

"Why did you not give me the option to stay in another town on my own continent?"

Her voice trembled. "Why must you take me somewhere I will suffer?"

Alex swallowed, the guilt heavy in his chest.

"Yvonne… please trust me. Ye'll be safe. Ye have my word."

After a small pause, she asked, "Will I live with Princess Nzingha?"

"'Tis possible," he answered gently. "She can protect ye. She's a warrior unlike any I've seen. Ye'll be loved, respected. No one will harm ye."

His voice darkened. "And if anyone even tries… ye tell me. I'll personally carve them a new arsehole."

Yvonne let out a tiny breath, half laugh, half sob.

"Alex?"

"Hmm?"

"…Thank you."

He closed his eyes, letting the words warm him more than the whisky ever could.

Chapter Nine

The Breaking Point

*F*our moons had passed since Andrew, Haemish, Alex, and

Nzingha fled Tafaria with Yvonne hidden deep below deck.
Four long months in which the sea revealed every face she
possessed.

Some days she was gentle, her swells rocking the ship like a cradle.
Other days she roared with a fury fit to break kingdoms. Winds
screamed across the masts like banshees, waves rose taller than the
ship's hull, and even the most seasoned sailors whispered prayers
into the storm.

By November, the voyage had turned brutal.

The colder waters churned beneath them like living beasts, dark and
hungry. The crew barely slept, always running, always bracing,
always fighting to keep the vessel alive. At each crack of thunder,
men flew across the deck, fists burning as they hauled rope, boots

slipping on rain slick planks, voices hoarse from shouting warnings into the wind.

Andrew and Haemish were the ship's spine.

Hour after hour, day after day, they drove themselves harder than any man aboard. Andrew's voice cut through storms like steel. Haemish's strength held the sails firm when waves threatened to tear them apart. Together they reminded the men,

Too much was at stake.
One block of gold each.

They could not fail.

But despite the storm's rage, despite the danger in every wave, Alex was nowhere to be found.

Not for days.
Not even during the worst surges.

Andrew's patience snapped like a frayed rope.

He stood at the bow, rain pouring down his face, fingers numbed from gripping a waterlogged line. The storm had quieted for only a moment, giving him breath enough to realize,
his brother had vanished again.

His jaw flexed. Heat ignited behind his ribs.

"Where the hell is he?" Andrew hissed under his breath, shaking out the rope before looping it around a cleat. The wind whipped against his back, but it was nothing compared to the storm boiling inside him.

He glanced up at Haemish, who stood balancing on the slick railing above, tightening a pulley.

"Haemish!" Andrew shouted over the wind. "D'ye see my brother anywhere? It's near dawn and we're short-handed again!"

Haemish braced his boots. "I spoke tae him this morning! He said he was no' feelin' well!"

Andrew barked a humorless laugh.

"No' feelin' well? That's rich. He hasnae been himself since we left Tafaria. Four months, Haemish. Four months of hiding in that blasted cabin!"

A wave crashed over the deck, drenching them. Andrew wiped his face, fury simmering hotter than the cold sea.

"We're a week from Scotland," he growled, grabbing another rope. "A week. And still the bastard refuses tae lift a hand!"

Haemish shouted down, "Looks like he's returnin' tae his old habits, laziness!"

That did it.

"Not on my watch," Andrew hurled the rope to the deck with a thud. he spat, rain dripping from his chin.

He stormed across the soaked boards, boots slamming with purpose, fury carrying him below deck. The wooden stairs rattled under his weight as he descended, water pooling beneath each step.

In the narrow hall, lanterns flickered with the ship's violent sway. Andrew slowed only when he reached Alex's cabin, his ear pressed to the door.

Whispers.
Low and unmistakable.

Andrew's eyes widened.

"Alex!" He pounded the door so hard it shook on its hinges. "Open the bloody door!"

Silence.

He struck again, harder, louder.

"'Tis Andrew! Open up!"

Inside, fabric rustled. Feet thumped. A muffled curse.

"Uh, give me a moment!"

Andrew folded his arms, breath steaming in the cold air, jaw ticking as the seconds crawled.

"Come now," he growled. "What in God's name is takin' ye so long?"

A latch clacked.

The door flew open.

Alex appeared, sweat beading at his temples, hair sticking in damp strands to his forehead. His chest rose and fell too quickly.

Andrew stepped forward, eyes narrowing.

"What. Why are ye knockin' like Lucifer himself?" Alex demanded, trying for nonchalance, failing miserably.

"Why are ye abed?" Andrew shot back. "Are ye ill? Do ye have a fever? Yer sweatin'."

"Uh… aye. I was asleep."

"Who were ye talkin' to?" Andrew leaned sideways, peering into the cabin. "I heard voices."

"Nae, I was reading aloud."

His story did not make sense.

"Thought ye was asleep." Andrew folded his arms. "Now yer readin'. Which is it."

"What de ye want?" Alex let out a breath. "I nae feel well."

Andrew pushed half his body into the doorway. "D'ye want Nzingha tae make ye tea?"

"Och, nae. I'll be fine."

"Very well," Andrew said tightly. "If ye feel better, come above deck and pull yer weight. We're short-handed after losin' men in Tafaria."

"Of course," Alex said quickly.

Andrew nodded and began to step back.

For a heartbeat, the ship seemed to hesitate with him, suspended between breaths.

Then the sea struck.

The hull shuddered with a bone-deep crack, wood screaming as a monstrous wave slammed broadside. The deck pitched violently, lanterns swinging wild as chairs skidded and books slid free, scattering across the floor.

Andrew lurched, fingers clawing for purchase, while Alex caught the doorframe at the same moment, boots scraping as the room tilted hard to starboard. Another surge hit, and the cabin groaned under the strain.

Something heavy shifted.

Alex's eyes snapped to the corner, dread flaring just a heartbeat too late.

A deep, hollow thud split the air as the trunk broke loose and toppled forward, slamming into the floor. The lid burst open, and Yvonne flew out with a shriek.

Andrew froze. The roar of the storm seemed to vanish, sound dropping away as his mind struggled to catch up to what his eyes were seeing.

Alex's blood drained from his face.

Yvonne sprawled across the floor, disheveled and shaking, hair tangled from sleep as she scrambled upright. Her wide, terrified eyes met Andrew's.

For one terrible second, no one moved.

Then Andrew's fury detonated like cannon fire.

"ALEX, NAE!"

Wait." Alex lifted his hands, his words rushing out. "Hold on. I can explain."

"EXPLAIN WHAT?!" Andrew roared. "We're out there fightin' for our lives, and you're hidin' away bedding some castle wench?"

Yvonne flinched hard, trembling.

Alex's temper snapped, protective and immediate. "Dinnae call her that!" he barked. "She is NOT a whore. I was helpin' her. Ye've no idea."

 "Ever since we were lads, I've cleaned up after ye!" Andrew slammed a fist against the doorframe. "And now this? Bringing her aboard? Hidin' her in a trunk?!"

He jabbed a finger toward her, his voice breaking with rage. "Did she no' warm yer bed at Tafaria's castle with two other women? And now ye drag her tae Scotland? When ye tire o' her, ye'll toss her aside, just like all the rest, and I'll be left tae fix yer disaster!"

Yvonne's breath hitched painfully.

Alex's eyes darkened. "Andrew," he warned, "take that back."

But Andrew was already turning away.

Alex caught his arm. "Brother, wait."

Andrew spun and punched him square in the jaw.

Alex stumbled, caught himself, and answered with a blow of his own.

All of hell broke loose.

Yvonne screamed, "STOP! PLEASE, YOU MUST STOP!"

She ran past them, heart slamming against her ribs as she tore up the stairs.

"Princess Nzingha! Princess!" she cried, her voice breaking as she fled into the rain

Yvonne burst above deck into a wall of rain. The storm had returned with a vengeance. Sheets of water hammered the planks, turning the world into a blur of gray and silver. The mast groaned under the strain, sails snapping violently overhead.

She ran, breath breaking, skirts plastered to her legs, hair whipping across her face.

"Princess Nzingha!" she cried again. "Princess, please!"

Crewmen looked up in shock as she flew past.

One sailor grabbed Haemish's arm. "Who the devil is that lass?"

"What?" Haemish blinked at her, stunned. "The waxing lass?"

The deck pitched. Haemish tried to chase her, but his boot slid across the slick boards, sending him crashing onto his backside.

"Son of a...!" he shouted as rain pelted his face.

Yvonne didn't see him fall. She had already reached the captain's quarters. She flung the door open with trembling hands.

Nzingha spun around. "Yvonne? What is...?"

"My Princess..." Yvonne gasped, chest heaving. "The brothers… they fight with fists. Andrew, he is choking him. Please, come, quickly!"

Nzingha's book hit the floor.

Without a word, she ran.

As she darted past Haemish, she snapped, "Get up, ye big oaf! Yer lairds are fighting!"

He scrambled to his feet, cursing as he went, and tore after her.

Below deck, the storm's deep groans echoed through the wooden ribs of the ship. The brothers were a thunderstorm of their own.

Andrew had Alex pinned against the wall, his forearm locked across his throat, breath roaring in his ears. Alex drove a desperate punch into Andrew's ribs, making his brother grunt and loosen his hold. They collided again, fists flying, boots sliding across the tilting floorboards as the ship pitched beneath them.

"STOP THIS!" Yvonne cried, trying to force herself between them.

She was too small, her hands useless against their strength.

Too shaken, fear stealing the air from her lungs.

Too frightened to stop what had already broken loose.

Nzingha rushed in, grabbing Andrew's arm and pulling with all her strength. "Andrew, stop! This is yer brother!"

But Andrew was too far gone in fury.

Haemish barreled in, hooked his arms under Andrew's shoulders, and wrenched him backward with brute force. Andrew struggled, breath roaring, jaw clenched.

Alex sagged to one knee, blood running from the corner of his mouth.

Yvonne fell beside him, grabbing a cloth and wiping the crimson from his lip with shaking hands.

He jerked away, not from her, but from humiliation, and pushed himself upright, storming out of the cabin without a word.

Yvonne stared after him, stunned.

"What is the matter with you?" Nzingha rounded on Andrew, eyes blazing. "That is yer elder brother! How dare you strike him!"

"Nzingha, I am exhausted," he snapped, rubbing his aching jaw. "We've been breakin' our backs for weeks, tryin' tae keep this ship afloat. And he, he hides in that cabin pleasurin' himself!"

He waved sharply toward Yvonne.

He did not see her flinch.

"You idiot." Nzingha smacked him hard, upside the head.

"Do you even know who this is?"

Andrew paused, breath heaving. "Aye. I know exactly who she is."

"Nae, ye do not," Nzingha shot back. "Did it ever occur tae ye that Alex helped this lass escape death? That he risked everything? That she took my place when my father demanded I wed into their tribe?"

Andrew blinked.

Nzingha stepped between him and Yvonne, protective as a lioness.

"She suffered for it. She bears bruises that should have been mine. And you accuse her as though she is some harlot? Andrew Barton, I expected better."

Andrew's shoulders fell. The fight bled out of him.

"My apologies," Nzingha murmured softly to Yvonne. "Come, husband. We shall talk."

She tugged Andrew's hand and led him away.

Yvonne curtsied deeply, showing respect even through trembling limbs.

When they were gone, the cabin felt cavernous and empty. Alex had vanished like smoke. Haemish glanced at Yvonne helplessly before heading after Andrew, leaving her alone in the quiet.

What Was Owed

Alex lay stretched on Haemish's cot, his arm flung over his eyes. His head throbbed. His ribs ached. He could still feel his brother's fist cracking against his jaw.

It had been years since they last fought, real fighting, not childhood scraps.

He hated how easily they slipped back into it.

"What possessed him…" he muttered.

A knock sounded.

"Aye?" he called.

The door opened.

Andrew stood there, one eye already darkening with a bruise, jaw tight, expression uncertain.

"Alex…" His voice was rough. "I came tae say I'm sorry."

Alex sat up slowly.

Andrew continued, his voice cracking. "Nzingha told me everything. About Yvonne. About the king. About how ye found her." He swallowed hard. "I acted the fool. I let the storm and exhaustion blind me."

He rubbed the back of his neck. "But why keep her a secret? Why no' tell me?"

"I wished tae wait for the right time," Alex said quietly. "I planned tae tell ye before we reached Tantallon."

Andrew nodded, though guilt still shadowed his face.

"Alex… be honest with me. Have ye been bedding her these past months? Ye ken I must ask. I know ye."

Alex jolted upright. "Andrew, nae! I swear on our parents' graves, I havenae touched her. Back in Tafaria, when ye walked in… aye, she was naked, but we were drunk, and she passed out. One of the women tried somethin', but I stopped her. Yvonne is still a virgin. Her husband never touched her. He beat her instead."

Andrew shut his eyes, shame twisting his features.

"Aye… I ken. Ye've always had a soft heart for the mistreated. Mama would've done the same."

Alex looked down, something tender passing over his face.

"I plan tae take her back in a year or so," he said. "Once she's healed."

"As long as 'tis what she wants…" Andrew nodded. "she may stay with Nzingha and me. Destiny could use the help."

Alex's shoulders eased. "Thank ye."

He rose, steadying himself as the ship rocked.

"Och, ye're lucky my wife is aboard." Andrew smiled faintly. "Else I'd toss ye in the brig."

Alex snorted. "Aye? Or we could settle it with a tussle. Winner takes all."

Andrew laughed, despite the bruise swelling along his cheek.

Held Against the Sea

The ship groaned as another wave slammed against the bow. Rain drummed against the small window near Yvonne. She sat curled on the cot beside Nzingha, hands clasped tight.

"Princess," Yvonne whispered, her voice trembling, "this is my fault. If I had woken sooner, if I had told Alex I did not wish to travel… your husband would not have been angered."

"Hush," Nzingha said warmly, rubbing her back. "Alex wished to protect you. You did nothing wrong."

Yvonne lowered her gaze. "I fear being a wedge between brothers."

"You are not," Nzingha said gently. "Alex has his flaws, but he would never endanger you intentionally."

A knock sounded, and Alex stepped in.

Yvonne gasped softly. His face was bloodied, his lip split, one eye darkened.

"Alex, your face. Nzingha stood in shock. "Did Andrew apologize?"

"Och, it's nothing," Alex said with a smirk. "Ye should've seen him when we were lads. I had him beat most days."

Yvonne rose instinctively, dipped a cloth in water, and stepped toward him. Standing on her toes, she dabbed the dried blood away with trembling care.

His breath caught, but he said nothing.

"Nzingha," he murmured, "may I have a word with her alone?"

Nzingha nodded, but paused at the door. "Will you be moving her to another cabin now?"

"Aye," Alex replied quietly. "She'll have her privacy."

When the door closed, Yvonne turned to him, her voice fragile.

"You wish to leave me alone? There are men aboard."

"I thought ye wanted privacy," he said gently. "Besides, my back aches. I've slept on the floor for four months."

 "Would you… stay with me?" Yvonne swallowed. "If I allowed you to sleep in the same bed?"

Alex froze.

Blood rushed south so fast he nearly took a step back.

"Yvonne," he said carefully, "as much as I'd enjoy lyin' beside ye in a small bed… 'tis best we stay apart."

Before she could answer, the ship lurched violently.

She pitched into the wall, then staggered forward and dropped to her knees as a wave of nausea ripped through her.

"Yvonne!" Alex knelt quickly as she retched into the chamber pot.

He rubbed her back in slow circles. "Classic case o' sea sickness. Come, lie down."

He tucked her into the bed, then, without asking, slid in behind her.

She twisted. "What are you doing?"

"If ye dinnae lie against me, the motion will make it worse. Wrappin' ye in stillness helps."

"Fine," she muttered weakly, "but I do not wish to be touched."

"Aye," he smirked. "I'll keep my hands tae myself."

He pulled the blanket around them both. The warmth of his chest steadied her.

"When Andrew and I were lads," he whispered, "during storms he'd crawl into my bed, askin' if I was afraid. I lied every time. Told him I'd protect him."

Yvonne gave the faintest laugh.

"The secret tae survivin' a storm, ear, is sleep." He murmured, breath warm at her ear

Her breathing softened as she drifted off.

Alex waited until she slept, pressed a kiss to her hair, and slipped out of the bed.

He sat at the desk, charcoal in hand, sketching her curled form with reverence.

The last line, her name, was when sleep finally claimed him.

Sleep Betrays Her

"Obey me," the king's voice snarled in her dream.
A lash cracked.
She screamed.

"Someone, please, help me..."

She thrashed her arms wildly, kicking the sheets away from her. "NO!" she cried out until strong arms wrapped around her.

"Yvonne, wake up. Shh...'tis just a dream."

Alex held her tight as her sobs soaked through his shirt. She clung to him with desperate fingers.

"You're safe," he whispered. "I swear it. Yer safe with me."

A knock sounded.

"Alex? Open the door." Nzingha's voice carried urgency.

Alex opened it just enough for her to slip inside.

"I brought tea for you, Yvonne." She smiled without looking up. Then she frowned when she saw Alex standing shirtless and Yvonne crying. "Alex, what the hell? Why is your skin showing, and why is Yvonne crying? What the hell is going on?"

Alex glared. "What the hell are ye on about? She had a bad dream. I'm shirtless because it got wet, and I nae have a clean one. That's all."

Yvonne nodded quickly in confirmation.

Nzingha relaxed, relieved. "Forgive me, Alex. My misjudgment."

"Aye, a bad one." He folded his arms.

She peered around the small room, her eyes going from Yvonne to Alex. Guilt tickled the back of her neck. She asked, "May I speak with Yvonne alone?"

Alex brushed Yvonne's knuckles before stepping out. "I'll be right outside."

Yvonne smiled faintly.

Setting the tea aside, Nzingha gave Yvonne a comforting smile and sat extremely close to her, as she observed her up close and personal.

"You are even more beautiful in person," Yvonne whispered to Nzingha.

Nzingha squeezed her hand. "You are stunning as well. I see why King Oyomo would not leave you be."

She glanced toward the desk, spotted the sketchbook.

"Ah… Alex's old hobby," she teased.

Yvonne's cheeks warmed. "I saw more than I should have. Alex is talented, yes, but he is a bit demented."

Nzingha flipped through the sketches, pausing on Andrew, landscapes, and women, until she reached the final page.

Her breath softened.

A portrait of Yvonne sleeping, drawn with care so tender it was almost sacred. Staring at the drawing, she gave a warning.

"Be careful with your heart," Nzingha warned gently. "He means well, but he does not keep loyalty to one woman. Let his actions for you be kindness, not promise."

Yvonne nodded, eyes on the drawing.

A BOOM cracked above them. Shouts erupted on deck.

Nzingha stood abruptly. "Come. Something's happening."

Chapter Ten

Surviving The Plunder

*T*he first cannon blast struck like the hand of God, jolting the ship

so hard the wheel nearly tore free from Andrew's grip.

He dug his boots into the slick planks, muscles burning as he fought
the pull of the sea and the screaming wind. Salt spray lashed his face.
Smoke rolled across the deck, stinging his eyes and choking the air.

Alex grabbed the rail beside him, shouting through the chaos.
"Bloody hell, grandsire could spin a wheel faster than ye. Put yer
back into it and steer north, man. Those bastards are upon us."

Andrew wrenched the wheel, teeth clenched.
"Nae. Their cannons nearly split us in two already. Why in God's
name would I draw closer? Look at their sails, black as sin. That's
nae Portuguese."

High above, in the crow's nest, Haemish braced himself against the mast and lifted the spyglass, the ship bucking beneath him like a living thing.

Alex craned his neck.

"Haemish. How far off are those damned pirates?"

Haemish squinted into the distance. The enemy vessel cut through the waves like a dark predator, closing fast.

"Close," he called. "No more than a few miles. They're gainin'."

"Shit," Alex hissed. "If they close that gap, we can kiss our gold goodbye."

Another blast thundered, closer this time. A cannonball slammed into the water off their bow, throwing up a wall of spray that crashed across the deck and sent men staggering.

Andrew spun the wheel in a brutal arc, pitching the ship into a violent turn that knocked half the crew off balance. His eyes burned.

"Nae. It'll be a cold day in hell before our ship is plundered. We fire back."

He snapped his head toward the men.

"Ready the floor cannons."

"Aye, Captain," the crew roared.

Boots thundered below. Moments later the shout came up from the lower deck.

"Floor cannons ready."

"Fire," Andrew bellowed.

The ship shuddered as their cannons answered. Smoke belched from the lower ports, the roar of the volley rattling bone and teeth alike.

Alex seized Andrew's arm.

"I'll see tae Nzingha and Yvonne. Keep us afloat. We're about tae dance."

He didn't wait for a reply.

Alex tore down the steps, the ship pitching hard beneath his feet, he burst into the cabin below deck just as both women were moving toward the door.

"Nzingha. Yvonne," he barked, breathless. "Stay below, we're under attack by pirates."

Nzingha's eyes flew wide. She caught herself on the bed as another blast rattled the beams.

"We survive a storm only to be hunted?"

BOOM. BOOM. BOOM.

The deck lurched under the force of another salvo. Dust rained down from the ceiling. Yvonne clapped her hands over her ears and cried out, "Princess Nzingha."

Alex shoved his sword through his belt, strapped on his dirk, then slung three muskets over his shoulder, moving with the practiced ease of a man long accustomed to blood and battle. His jaw was set, expression carved from stone.

"Yer husband ordered ye tae stay put," he told Nzingha. "Bolt the door and dinnae open it for Jesus Christ himself."

He slammed the door behind him.

Alex charged up the stairs and onto the main deck, straight into chaos.

Ropes swung loose. Smoke rolled thick across the boards. Men clashed steel to steel as the enemy poured in, filthy, scarred raiders with rotten teeth and hunger burning in their eyes.

One pirate came at Alex from the side, sword raised high.

Alex leapt back, the blade narrowly missing his throat. He twisted, arm whipping in a deadly arc, and his sword sliced clean across the raider's neck. Blood sprayed. The man dropped bonelessly to the deck.

Two more rushed him.

Alex cocked both muskets and fired without hesitation.

CRACK. CRACK.

Both men pitched forward, dead before they struck the planks.

All around him the fight raged, steel ringing, men shouting, the ship groaning beneath it all.

Alex scanned the deck, heart hammering. "Andrew," he shouted, voice raw.

He spotted his brother slumped near the starboard rail, one hand clamped to his stomach, fingers slick with blood. Two of their men stood over him, barely holding attackers at bay.

Alex lunged toward him, but another pirate burst from the smoke, sword already arcing down toward Alex's neck.

He barely had time to raise his blade.

An arrow whistled past his ear and buried itself in the pirate's forehead. The man toppled backward with a grunt.

Alex spun toward the source.

Nzingha stood on the raised deck near the captain's quarters, longbow in hand, hair whipping wild in the wind. She nocked another arrow in one fluid motion and loosed it. Another raider crumpled where he stood.

She moved with a hunter's calm, each shot precise. Men began dropping like game at a hunt.

"Sweet merciful Christ, she's a murderin' wee goddess with a bow,"

Nzingha knocked quickly.

Loose.

Whistles flew three consecutive times.

Alex cut through another man and glimce Nzingha once more Giving a grin.

"The lass sends arrows like she's deliverin' debts tae Hell."

Nzingha spotted Andrew.

Her gaze locked on her husband sprawled on the deck, blood soaking his shirt, and something inside her snapped.

She flung the bow aside, drew her long blade, and charged down the steps with a wordless scream, cutting through pirates as though they were nothing but shadows between her and the man she loved.

Haemish seized the moment. He leapt behind the wheel, shoving the helmsman aside, and wrenched the ship hard. Their vessel veered just enough to avoid another direct hit. The pirate ship, already burning from their volley, caught faster, flames licking up her black sails.

Alex fought his way toward Andrew, cutting down anyone who crossed his path. The raiders began to fall back, their own ship crippled and ablaze. Some scrambled for the rail and leapt screaming into the sea.

Of the thirty men who'd boarded, only three remained standing when the smoke finally began to clear.

Alex's crew closed in around them, muskets raised, swords at their throats. The pirates' bravado drained away, replaced by raw fear.

Alex ignored them.

He dropped to his knees beside Andrew and Nzingha. His heart twisted at the sight. Nzingha sat with Andrew's head in her lap, rocking him gently, her face streaked with blood and tears.

"Nzingha," Alex said hoarsely. "Is my brother alive?"

She looked up, eyes blazing and wet. "Yes. He lives. But he is badly injured."

Andrew's lips were pale. His eyes fluttered, struggling to open.

Alex stood slowly and turned to the remaining pirates.

"Ye sons of whores, made a grave mistake layin' a hand on my ship."

He was about to give the order when steel flashed at the edge of his vision.

Nzingha strode past him.

Without a word, she drew her blade across the first man's throat. He fell.

She moved to the second, the cut clean and efficient.

The third tried to back away, eyes wild with terror. Her sword found him just as surely.

All three bodies hit the deck in a line.

Men stared, some swallowing hard. The only sound was Nzingha's harsh breathing as she dropped back to her knees beside Andrew.

Her scream tore across the deck when his eyes slid shut. She shook him, sobbing. "Andrew. No. You cannot leave me. Not now. Not yet."

Alex knelt and pulled her into his arms. "Zing, he still breathes," he said, forcing calm into his voice. "He's losin' blood, aye, but he's still with us. We'll no' lose him. D'ye hear me."

He lifted his head. "Haemish."

"Aye, Captain," Haemish answered, already moving.

"Help me get him below," Alex ordered. "Now."

Frayed Nerves

They burst into Nzingha's cabin moments later, Alex and Haemish half carrying, half dragging Andrew to the bed.
Nzingha was at his side before they even laid him down, ripping open his shirt with shaking hands.
The sight stole the air from her lungs.

A long, savage gash ran across his abdomen. Skin hung loose, and blood poured in a steady, sickening sheet.

"My husband has lost too much blood," she whispered, her voice cracking. "Please. Help him."

Alex pressed a cloth hard against the wound. Blood soaked through instantly. He did not let up.

"Haemish," he snapped, "alert the ship's physician and fetch a bucket of hot water. Move."

"Aye!" Haemish thundered out of the room.

Andrew's head lolled. His breathing was shallow, his lips tinged blue.

Alex grabbed the whisky from the bedside table. "Come on, brother. Stay with me." He forced the bottle to Andrew's mouth and tipped it.

Andrew coughed and sputtered, his eyes flying open in shock. "Alex," he rasped. "Where… where is my wife?"

"I am right here," Nzingha said, leaning close so he could see her through the haze. "I am not leaving you."

He tried to smile, but it twisted with pain. "Those bastards…" He winced as his hand drifted toward his stomach. "They caught us off guard. They swam aboard… we had no idea…"

"Shh," Alex murmured. "Save yer strength. Let me see the wound properly."

He lifted the soaked cloth.

"Saint Christopher's cross," he muttered under his breath. The cut was deep, but angled. "Ye stepped back at the last moment. Any deeper and we'd be pickin' yer guts up off the floor. Thank the heavens ye moved when ye did."

Haemish burst through the door with a steaming bucket of water. "Alex, water. How's Andrew holdin'?"

"Place it on the stand here, next tae the bed." A look of worry crossed Alex's face. "Did we lose men?"

"Aye. Seven dead. Five badly wounded." Haemish's jaw tightened. "The physician is on his way. Yvonne is out there helpin' him patch the men up."

Nzingha dipped a cloth into the hot water, wrung it out, and pressed it gently around the edges of Andrew's wound, clearing the blood so the physician could see the damage.

"My love," she whispered, her voice ragged. "You must endure it. Destiny needs her father. I need you."

Her tears fell freely now, splashing onto his chest. Andrew lifted a hand, heavy and shaking, and brushed her wrist with the tips of his fingers.

"I'm no' goin' anywhere," he slurred. "Not yet."

Alex watched them for half a heartbeat, worry tightening his chest. Then another thought punched through him.

Yvonne.

She was out there. On a deck that had just been swimming in blood, among wounded and dead men.

"Brother," Alex said abruptly, "I'll be back shortly. Keep pressure on the wound. Haemish, stay with them till the physician comes."

He tossed the bloody cloth into the bucket and strode out.

On the main deck, the scene changed from battle to aftermath.

The pirate ship burned in the distance, a dying ember on the horizon. On their own deck, wounded men lay propped against the rails or stretched on blankets, groaning softly. The dead were already covered with cloth, lined near the side in grim silence.

The ship's physician, Mr. McMillan, moved briskly between them, sleeves rolled, spectacles perched on the end of his nose. Beside him, Yvonne knelt, hands stained red, carefully binding a sailor's arm.

Alex's jaw tightened.

He walked over, boots thudding on the wet planks. "Lass, what are ye doin' out of the cabin?" he demanded. "I ordered ye tae stay put."

Yvonne did not flinch. She finished tying the bandage, then stood slowly, her chin lifting as she faced him.

"You did not see fit to return after the noise stopped. Nzingha left to find her husband. I heard nothing from anyone. I thought you were all dead." Her eyes flashed. "How was I to know if anyone survived?"

"So ye left anyway," Alex shot back. "Suppose we had all been dead. Ye'd have been easy pickings for any man left standin'. Ye should have remained hidden, as ordered."

"When I give an order, I expect ye tae heed it. 'Tis for yer safety, no' because I wish tae control ye." He flung his arms up. "Christ, why are women so damned dramatic?"

She stared at him, outrage simmering, then turned deliberately away.

Alex's jaw dropped at her dismissal.

"Is there anything more I can help with?" she asked the physician, ignoring Alex as thoroughly as if he were mist.

Mr. McMillan paused in his stitching and peered at her over his glasses. His stern features softened into a smile. "You are very capable," he said, his voice tinged with a refined English lilt. "And quite a remarkable young lady. Would you be a dear and gather more rags and a bucket of fresh water? And fetch my medicine basket from below?"

Alex's temper snapped. "Nae."

Both of them looked at him.

"Excuse me, Mr. McMillan," Alex said tightly. "Go and see to my brother. He's bleedin' out."

The physician nodded and stepped away.

Before she could protest, he caught her lightly, but firmly, by the arm and guided her away from the wounded, toward the corridor that led back to the cabins.

She jerked in fear. He could feel it even through her sleeve.

The moment they reached the door of their cabin, he turned her to face him. "Tell me," he said low and irritated, "did I hire ye as the ship's healer?"

She snatched her arm free. "Let go of me," she snapped.

She stepped inside and slammed the door in his face.

"Yvonne!" he called.

The only answer was the click of the lock.

Alex dragged a hand through his hair and blew out a hard breath. "Bloody perfect," he muttered. "I save her hide and she slams the door on me."

He stood there for a long moment, his fists clenching and unclenching, then shook his head and turned away.

My brother needs me more than this bloody argument, he thought, and stalked back toward Andrew's cabin.

Bruised Pride Softer Hearts

Night settled heavily over the sea.

By then, the worst of the chaos had ended. The dead had been wrapped and slid over the rail into the dark water, given a brief prayer and the only burial a sailor could expect. The wounded lay resting, watched in turns by uninjured men. The pirate ship was little more than a smoldering ghost on the horizon.

Alex lay in a different cabin now, away from Yvonne's door, staring up at the black curve of the ceiling. The ship creaked around him, wood settling after the violence of the day. His body ached, bruises blooming beneath his shirt.

He turned onto his side, exhaling.

Images returned unbidden. Andrew's blood. Nzingha's blade. Yvonne's furious eyes above blood streaked hands.

He thought of Nzingha first. Tiny, fierce Nzingha, who had stepped between death and Andrew more than once. He had never seen someone move with such deadly grace, bow in hand one moment, blade carving through their enemies the next.

She is everything tae my brother, he thought. And important tae me as well.

He could have lost them both.

Then his thoughts snagged on Yvonne.

Sassy as Nzingha. Brave, in her own way. Hopeless at following orders. Infuriating. Exhausting. Vulnerable. Strong.

He rolled his eyes into the dark. "This was a terrible idea," he muttered.

Restless, he swung his legs over the side of the bunk and stood, joints protesting. He grabbed his flask from the small table and took a long swallow.

"Ahh... I have got tae stop drinkin'." He took another swig. "Well. Not tonight."

Boredom and agitation twined in his chest. He pulled a piece of coal and a scrap of parchment from the desk and sat, letting his hand move without much thought.

At first, the lines came clumsy, his vision blurred from the whisky. "Christ," he grumbled. "I can barely see."

Still, he drew.

The curve of almond shaped eyes.
The small, rounded bubble of a nose.
Full, plump lips.

When he blinked and the image cleared, his gut tightened.

Another likeness of Yvonne.

He stared at it for a long second, then snorted harshly. "I should have killed her bastard of a husband and left her with her family," he muttered. "Would've saved me the trouble."

He crumpled the parchment in his fist and tossed it aside.

"I'll never fall for another lass," he told the empty room.

The walls did not argue.

He grabbed the flask again, took one last mouthful, and left the cabin, climbing up toward the main deck.

Voices drifted on the cool night air. At first, he assumed it was Nzingha speaking with Haemish or one of the watchmen. But then he listened more closely.

That laugh.

Yvonne.

Alex moved quietly into the shadows near one of the masts, leaning against a beam, letting the darkness swallow him as he listened.

Euan, one of the younger crewmen, sat on a coil of rope near the rail, relaxed, a faint grin on his face. Yvonne stood close by, her cloak wrapped around her shoulders, her hair stirring in the breeze.

"I had no idea I would be traveling to some strange land." Her voice was filled with amusement. "Yes, the captain somehow abducted me, but he was concerned for my safety. At first, I was grateful. Your captain is caring."

Alex's brows rose. He hadn't expected that.

Then she added, "But after the skirmish today... he has been an overbearing, stubborn ass."

"What?" Alex mouthed the word silently.

Euan laughed. "Och, he is no' all bad, miss. He's a fine leader in our homeland. Ye must give him time. His brother is badly injured, he's likely more tense than usual. The captain is normally free spirited. He never stays in one place long, no' even at home. Ye needn't worry. The laird just gets cranky if he's trapped for too long."

"I am sure he is very free," Yvonne said dryly.

Euan grinned. "Ye speak with sarcasm. What did he do now?"

She sighed. "He is just... a pervert."

Euan choked. "What?"

"I am sorry to speak of your chief in such a manner," Yvonne added quickly. "He saved my life, and I am grateful. But his behavior angers me. Did you know he mated two women at once in my homeland? I saw it from the balcony. From what I observed, your captain is quite a stallion. What saddens me is... he does not deny it."

Alex closed his eyes briefly and pinched the bridge of his nose. "Perfect," he muttered. "Gossip now. Why no'? I am a sailor, after all."

Euan laughed again. "Aye, I've heard enough tales of the captain. There's no shock in that. But I'd rather hear more about ye."

His tone shifted lower, more intentionally. "Are ye seekin' a man on yer journey? Ye're a bonnie lass. Ye've a sweet face, beautiful lips, and a body carved by God himself. I find ye very attractive."

Alex's frown deepened. He watched as Euan took Yvonne's hand and pressed a kiss lightly to her knuckles.

She stiffened, clearly startled.

Alex leaned forward, arms folding. If she slapped Euan, he'd let the boy learn his lesson. If Euan pushed, then Alex would intervene.

"What are you doing?" She snatched her hand back. "No. I am quite fine. I intend to aid the princess and do not wish to be courted. Excuse me. I shall return to my cabin."

"My apologies." Euan stood quickly, blocking her path, still grinning. "Dinnae leave yet. I only meant tae ask if ye'd consider bein' my woman?"

Alex stepped from the shadows.

"Nae, arseling. She does not wish tae be yer woman, ye horny bastard. Off with ye."

"Captain!" Euan jumped so hard he nearly fell over the coil of rope.. "Good eve. Yvonne and I were only havin' a conversation. I was... admiring her beauty."

"Aye, I heard enough." Alex's brows shot up. "Leave my presence and find somethin' useful tae do."

"But I'm off duty, sir,"

"Then go tae bed!" Alex replied, his hand on his hip.

"Right away, sir." He scuttled off toward the hatch.

Yvonne turned as well, intending to slip away, but Alex caught her wrist gently.

"Not you. You, I need tae speak with."

She faced him, eyes narrowed.

He frowned.

"Just what d'ye think ye're doin', out here alone with that scoundrel, talkin' about me as if I'm Satan himself?"

"I was tired of being locked away like a caged animal," she shot back. "I wanted fresh air. Did I commit a crime, Chieftain?"

Her voice sharpened. "There is no king hunting me here, no whips, no shackles. You said your people were kind, yet you keep me hidden. Am I your prisoner?"

His anger deflated, replaced by something heavier.

"My behavior today was unacceptable," he said after a moment, his jaw working. "I'll grant ye that. But ye must understand, my frustration comes from almost losing my brother. Some of my men died today. That's a heavy cross I'll carry when I face their families. I lashed out, aye. But no' because I enjoy caging ye. I do not wish tae see ye harmed. Ye cannae trust a sailor, lass. That's why I asked ye tae stay in the cabin."

She folded her arms, weighing his words. "If grabbing my arm and speaking to me like a child is what you call concern, then I prefer to stay out of your way," she said coolly. "Have a good evening, Captain."

She turned again, but he stepped in front of her.

"Oh, for Christ's sake. Can ye hear me out first?"

She exhaled sharply, then clasped her hands in front of her, her chin lifting. "Very well. You have my attention."

"Thank ye." He offered his arm. "Come have a walk with me."

He tucked her hand around his biceps and led her up toward the high deck near the ship's wheel, where the air was fresher and the sea spread out like black glass beneath the stars.

He took a breath, choosing his words with care.

"My father raised us with an iron fist," he said quietly. "My brother and I learned tae give orders the same way. That's how we lead our clan. When I care for someone, my voice gets rougher, no' softer. I shout, I bark, I demand. No' because I wish tae own them, but because I ken how easily the world can rip them away. When I sound harsh, it is no' from cruelty. It's because... I care."

He met her gaze straight on. "So, I ask yer forgiveness. I am no' a horrible man. A bit of a cloth head at times, aye, but no' a monster."

A reluctant smile tugged at her lips.

"I know you are not a bad person," she said slowly. "You are rough. And I hear what you are saying." She hesitated, fingers curling against her palm. "But when you grabbed me… it frightened me. Not because of you. Because it reminded me how quickly my body forgets that I am safe."

His expression shifted at once, the humor draining from it. "I should never have touched ye like that," he said quietly. "I swear it to ye. I didnae think past my temper, and for that, I am sorry."

She studied him a moment, then nodded.

Silence stretched as the gaze between them grew. They could not look away. It was a pull of the eyes, then the heart.

Yvonne exhaled and looked up at the stars.

"The day my father sold me to King Oyomo for a bride price, I could not understand. I loved him. I hated him. It is… a difficult thing to live with."

"'Tis a strange cruelty," Alex murmured. "Those we love can wound us deepest. That's how we ended up in Tafaria. Our own uncle, a man we admired, who watched us grow into men, betrayed us for greed. Took Nzingha without Andrew's knowledge. Tried selling her future for gold and jewels. In the end, he died for it."

"Very much like my father, who sold me for cattle, coin, and status," she said softly. "I do not know if I can ever look at him again when I return home. I love him because he is my father. I hate him for what he has done. When I go back, Tafaria's keep will be my home, not my father's compound."

"My lady, ye're breakin' my wee heart. So ye do plan tae leave me," Alex said, one hand pressed theatrically over his chest. "

"Oh, do be silent," a faint smile curved her mouth. "As soon as we dock, you will disappear, like a spirit from another world."

"Nae," he countered. "Ye'll still see me. My brother and I are close. Ye'll no' be rid of me so easily."

"Good," she said. "Then perhaps you will show me how beautiful your land is. I never had the chance to show you Tafaria's landscapes. King Oyomo ruined that for you."

Alex's expression softened. He reached for her hand and lifted it gently. "I saw enough," he said. "What I needed was no' more scenery… but an audience with ye."

He winked.

She pushed him lightly in the chest, her lips twitching. He laughed.

"Come," he said at last. "The hour's late. I'll see ye back tae yer cabin."

She placed her hand into his without hesitation this time. They walked in silence, boots thudding softly on the planks, the sea murmuring below.

At her door, she hesitated.

"Do you think… you can stay until I fall asleep?" she asked quietly. "It is one of the reasons I left the cabin earlier. My dreams haunt me. If you cannot stay, I understand. But… may I have some of your harsh drink? It helps me sleep."

He grinned. "I'll do ye one better. I'll give ye the drink and watch ye fall asleep. Then I'll leave. Agreed?"

She nodded.

Inside, she curled on the bunk while he handed her his flask. She took a long gulp, then winced as the burn hit her chest.

A loud burp escaped her. "Oh my, apologies." She slapped a hand over her mouth. "That drink is so strong. It burns all the way down."

"This?" Alex chuckled. "This is light. Surely ye can handle it."

He tipped the flask back toward her lips. "Here. Have some more."

She pushed it away with a laugh. "I think I've had my fill."

"Ye dinnae wish tae drink?" he said. "I've another remedy for sleep."

"I do not trust you when you say things like that." She eyed him warily, tilting her head.

"Och, come now." He laughed outright. "Ye can trust me for this at least. Nothing vulgar, I swear it. May I?"

At her small nod, he sat on the floor at the foot of the bunk, gently lifted one of her feet into his hands, and slipped off her slipper. His fingers kneaded the arch slowly, working out the tension.

"Most lassies love a good foot rub," he said with a wink.

She said nothing at first, just studied him, trying to decide what game he played now.

"So, you are charming, a protector, and gifted with your hands. You do all this… yet refuse to take a wife. Do you know what I think, Captain?"

"Nae," he murmured, "Tell me what fills that clever head."

"You are selfish," she said simply. "What are you afraid of?"

He scoffed with a straight face.

"A nagging woman."

"I am not nagging" She frowned. "I asked a question. Truly, you can be an ass."

Her annoyance softened as the massage spread warmth through her limbs. The whisky hummed in her veins. She leaned back against the headboard, her eyes slowly drifting shut.

He watched as she took another sip of whisky, closed her eyes, and licked her lips. Warmth hit him below the waist. He needed to release her. Quickly.

He patted her foot.

"There. My work here is done."

As he stood, she cracked one eye open. "Where are you going so soon?"

"I cannae stay here all night," he said. "I'm exhausted myself. I need tae check on my brother before I sleep. We've an early mornin'. We're docking at a small island tae take on fresh water. There's barely any left after tending tae the injured. Many of the men are runnin' fevers."

Her face fell. "May I ask another question?"

"Of course."

"Will you come back after you see your brother? At least until I sleep?"

He hesitated only a heartbeat.

"If ye wish me tae return," he said softly, "I will. But it'll be a moment."

She nodded.

He left, closing the door gently behind him.

The cabin felt smaller the moment he was gone. The sliver of moonlight that had crept across the floor earlier shifted behind a cloud, leaving the room steeped in shadow.

Yvonne shivered.

"I need more light," she whispered.

She moved to the small desk, her hands patting over the surface. No candle. No lantern. She frowned. "I could have sworn there was a candle here…"

Her fingers brushed nothing but wood.

"Well, there is nothing I can do about it," she murmured. "I shall wait in bed until Alex returns."

She turned toward the bunk and froze.

A presence stood behind her. She could feel it in the air, the way the tiny hairs on her arms rose, the subtle shift of breath.

"Alex?" she asked quietly. "Did you forget something?"

Silence.

"Chieftain?" she tried again.

"Nae," a male voice answered. "'Tis me… Euan."

Yvonne jumped, her hand flying to her chest. "What? Why are you here? If your captain sees you, he will be furious. Please, you must leave."

"I ken," Euan said from the shadows. "I only wanted tae apologize. I came on too strong earlier. It was wrong of me. Will ye forgive me?"

Her shoulders relaxed a fraction. "Of course," she said. "I told you I harbor no grudge. Now, you should go before…"

"And… if ye will no' be my woman," he cut in gently, "would ye consider bein' my friend?"

She hesitated.

"I could surely use one," she admitted at last. "You were kind to me when I arrived."

She stepped forward and hugged him quickly, a brief squeeze in the low lighted room.

"Now go," she urged. "Before the captain comes back."

Euan shifted, but his boots did not move. "Wait," he said. "One more thing. When we dock tomorrow… meet me on shore. Perhaps we can explore a bit. Just the two of us."

She paused, her fingers still on the door latch.

Alex's face flashed in her mind. His protectiveness. His rough apologies. His promise to return.

Euan's hand hovered near hers in the dark, not touching, but close enough that she could feel his warmth.

"Yes," she said slowly. "I will meet you. Now… go."

He eased the door open a crack, peered out, then slipped away into the corridor.

Yvonne closed the door softly behind him.

Alone once more, she leaned her forehead against the wood, torn between unease and a foolish, fragile hope that tomorrow, on solid land, under open sky, it might finally feel like a step toward a new life.

She only hoped she was not walking toward a different kind of danger.

Chapter Eleven

The Opening

Yvonne woke slowly, her body heavy, as if she were surfacing from deep water.

For a moment she lay still, blinking up at a ceiling she did not recognize. The pallet beneath her felt too soft; the air too warm. This was not the narrow bunk below deck. No creaking timbers. No roll of the sea.

Tafaria.

She pushed herself up slowly. She was in the guest chamber she had once shared with Zara and Meka, the carved beams and painted walls exactly as she remembered them. Her heart stuttered.

"We left this place ages ago," she whispered. "Did he bring me back?"

Bare feet whispering against the floor, Yvonne crossed to the balcony and stepped outside. The once-familiar shoreline lay before her, the sea glazed in rose and gold. The air smelled of salt and jasmine and something sweet she could not name.

Behind her, the familiar sound of his voice rolled smoothly from his tongue, and her body answered before her mind could stop it.

"Are ye ready fer me tae take ye tae a special place?"

She turned. Alex stood in the archway, shirt open at the throat, hair stirred by the same breeze that tugged at her gown. He looked impossably at ease, hands hooked at his belt, blue eyes intent on her alone.

"Special?" she repeated. "What do you mean? What place do you speak of, Alex? You always jest."

"Nae jest this time." He came a step closer. "This place is special, because 'tis where I found ye."

She frowned. "You did not find me. I was already here."

He closed the distance between them until his shadow mingled with hers.

"Shh," he murmured. "Dinnae speak. Just feel. Then ye'll ken what's special."

"Alex, I do not understand what you are saying. Cease your games."

He cupped her face in both hands, his touch unexpectedly gentle, thumbs brushing the corners of her mouth. The mischief left his gaze, leaving only something deep and unnervingly earnest.

"I want tae show ye what ye are tae me," he said quietly. "Special."

Before she could pull back, his mouth covered hers.

Her eyes flew wide at the first brush of his lips, then fluttered closed as he deepened the kiss, coaxing rather than claiming. His tongue slid softly against hers, tasting, teasing. A sigh escaped her throat, low and traitorous. She parted for him, heat curling through her belly.

Her fingers clutched at his shirt as he angled his head, drawing her closer. One hand slid into her hair, tugging just enough to tilt her head back, baring the line of her throat. His lips left her mouth and traced a slow path along her jaw, down to the hollow beneath her ear.

She shivered.

"Alex..." she breathed.

His mouth warmed her skin, his voice a whisper against her neck. "Yvonne..."

"Yes." Her answer came as a sigh, all soft edges and surrender.

"Yvonne." He whispered more, the low rumble in his voice, forcing an ache between her legs. Her knees grew weak.

"Oh, Yes, yes Alex..."

"Yvonne!"

His tone shifted, rougher now. "Yvonne, wake up, lass."

The balcony vanished.

She jerked upright with a gasp, heart thudding, the low ceiling of the ship's cabin swimming into focus. The cramped timber walls. The faint sway of the hammock hooks. The single candle flickering on the desk.

Alex's face hovered over her, brows drawn tight.

"Captain," she blurted, cheeks blazing, "you are back. And you found candles. My, I must have fallen asleep."

"Aye, ye did," he said, still watching her carefully. "Ye were tossin' and turnin', givin' wee moans like ye were in pain. Were ye havin' another bad dream? Did that bastard haunt ye again?" His jaw tightened. "Nae worries. I'm here now."

She stared at him, flustered.

Did I just dream Alex seduced me? And it felt… right. As if I wanted more.

Heat crept up her throat, soft and startling.

Alex's voice was there; she saw his mouth moving, but the sound blurred, muted by the rush in her ears. She could not seem to look away from his lips, the way he licked them before taking a slow pull from his flask. A warm ache unfurled between her legs, her breath fluttering in and out.

"Did ye hear me, lass?" he asked.

"No, I mean, yes." She fumbled. "I am fine. Truly. My thanks for coming back to stay with me this eve. Today's events left me a bit… shaky. How is your brother?"

Alex leaned back on his heels, some of the strain easing from his features. "Och, Andrew's strong as an ox. With a wife like Nzingha, he's in excellent hands."

He glanced around the small cabin, eyeing the narrow bed and the pallet of blankets on the floor. He looked for a heartbeat as if he'd like nothing more than to flee back to his own quarters, but he had given his word.

"So," he said at last, scratching the back of his neck, "what now?"

She offered a small, tentative smile. "Do you have a book? Perhaps you could read to me. Or I to you."

"Nae," he said with a low chuckle. "I leave the books tae my brother. I'm more interested in usin' me hands." He flashed her a wicked grin.

She scowled. "I meant reading."

"I ken, I ken." He lifted a bit of charcoal from the desk and twirled it between his fingers. "I meant sketchin', lass. Ye've seen worse in my book already."

The devil's curve of his smile made her stomach flutter. Yvonne dropped her gaze to her hands, steadying herself. With Femi, she had learned the hard way that letting feelings bloom only made the betrayal cut deeper. Fondness had soured into fear, on the night she shared a kiss with him.

She would not let that happen again. Not with Alex. Not when their fragile friendship meant more than she dared admit.

They snuffed two of the three candles, leaving only a warm pool of light near the bed. Together they climbed into the narrow frame, bodies aligned but not quite touching. Yvonne shifted, nestling into the curve of his body as he lay behind her.

When she pressed back for comfort, she felt him tense and edge away, leaving a breath of cool air between them.

"Alex?" she asked softly.

"Hm?"

"When you lie next to me…" She hesitated, then pushed on. "Do you not have the urge to touch me?"

His body reacted before his tongue; she could feel the sudden tightness in him like a bowstring. He eased another inch back.

"Ugh… of course I do," he muttered. "Ye're beautiful. I'm no' blind. But every man ye've trusted has either beaten ye or tried tae force ye. I'll no' add my name tae that list because I cannae keep my hands tae meself." He huffed. "Besides, yer constant whinin' makes my headache."

"I do not whine," she protested, giving him a little shove with her elbow.

He chuckled into her hair. "Och, I'm only pokin' at ye. But I'm serious. I'm a Barton. A man o' honor. I dinnae lay a hand on a woman who hasna' asked me tae. Now, sleep, lass, before I change my mind and go curl up in a hammock with the lads."

Yvonne fell quiet. The creak of the ship, the distant murmur of waves against the hull, and the warmth of his body at her back wrapped around her like another blanket.

"Alex?" she whispered again.

"Aye?"

"The sketches in your book…You seemed to have an obsession. But… I understand why. And… I know you can control your urges. I feel that I can trust you with my life."

She leaned in, brushed a shy kiss against his cheek, then turned away quickly, as if terrified of what she'd just done.

This time, Alex did not move.

He exhaled slowly, letting his chin rest near the crown of her head. "Sleep, Yvonne." His voice and breath rumbled through her hair. "Ye're safe. I give ye my word."

For the first time since Tafaria, her dreams were quiet.

That's An Order

Morning light slipped through the tiny cabin window, spearing straight into Alex's eyes. He squinted, then glanced down.
Yvonne lay curled in front of him, breathing slow and even, lips parted slightly in sleep. No clenched jaw. No tears on her cheeks. No muffled cries for help.
He eased himself from beneath the blanket, careful not to wake her, tugged on his boots, and slipped out the door.

On the upper deck, the air bit with a sharper chill. Haemish stood by the rail, staring ahead.

"Chief, over here," he called.

Alex joined him, following his gaze. A dark, green-topped shape sat on the horizon. "What is it?"

"We're comin' upon Madeira," Haemish said. "Do ye think it wise tae make this our stop for fresh water? If we do, I strongly suggest yer new friend stays aboard. The place is said tae be crawlin' with savages and worse."

Alex watched the island for a long moment, jaw working.

"We move on," he said.

"Why? She can stay on board."

"Aye, she can." He slid Haemish a look. "But did ye forget we've enough gold in that hold tae start a new kingdom? Dinnae be daft. If they smell coin, we're done for."

"So what say ye, Captain?"

"We sail where there are no towns," Alex decided. "If I recall, there's a small isle north of here. We can hunt pheasants, refill our barrels from a stream. Fewer eyes, fewer questions."

"Aye. I'll relay it tae the men."

Alex left the rail and headed back toward the cabins. On the way, he nearly collided with Euan, who straightened in a hurry.

"Good morning, Captain," Euan said, too bright. "I trust ye got some rest? I came to ask about our next stop, but ye were not in yer cabin last eve. Did ye stay the night with the other laird?"

"Nae," Alex said shortly. "He's got a wife fer that. Now excuse me."

Euan shifted subtly, blocking his path. "Oh, I see, Captain. So… where did ye sleep?"

Alex stared at him, a muscle ticking in his jaw. *Is he snoopin' tae ken if I stayed with Yvonne?*

"Euan," he said in a low voice, "I am the captain of this ship. Where I decide tae sleep is none o' yer concern. Now get back tae yer duties."

He brushed past him, then paused, not looking back.

"And Euan," his tone turned to steel. "Stay the hell away from Yvonne. That's an order."

"Aye, Captain," the man answered, but Alex did not like the gleam in his eye.

Before returning to his own quarters, Alex rapped his knuckles on the captain's door. Nzingha's voice answered, "Come."

He stepped inside. Andrew sat propped against pillows, pale but alert; Nzingha perched at his side, one hand on his arm.

"Good morrow," Alex said, suddenly lighter. "How's my brother?"

"Better than before," Andrew replied. "My, ye're in high spirits."

"I came with news." Alex lifted both hands. "We may have another threat on our hands."

Andrew groaned. "Ye call that good news?"

"For starters," Alex went on, ignoring him, "we're passin' Madeira. I'd wager the pirates that attacked us hail from there. I told Haemish tae keep the men sharp. We're also low on fresh water. We'll disembark on a smaller isle once we're past that hell-hole."

Nzingha frowned. "Did you not store enough water from my homeland?"

"We did," Alex said. "But many o' the men have fevers from their wounds. We upped their rations tae keep them alive."

Andrew exhaled. "So what say ye? How do we sail past and no' be seen?"

"We steer center o' the North Atlantic," Alex replied. "Keep tae open sea, away from trade routes. The north-western waters have the worst pirates, aye, but fewer eyes."

Andrew coughed. "Eh-hem. We'll stay in the center. We are almost home. 'Tis only a few days or so till we arrive."

"Aye. I'll see it done." Alex clapped the doorframe. "Hurry and mend, brother. We need ye above deck."

They both nodded as he left.

Poking The Bear

By the time Alex returned to the main deck, the fires of hell were
already licking up his spine.

Yvonne stood beside Euan near a coil of rope, laughing as she
practiced tying knots, the morning sun gilding her hair. Euan's head
was bent toward hers, grin wide.

That son of a bitch is testin' me.

Alex forced his shoulders to loosen. The last thing he wanted was to
frighten Yvonne by showing her exactly how violent a Barton
temper could be.

He walked over at an easy pace and mustered a smile. "Yvonne. This
is a surprise. What are ye doin'?"

She turned to him, eyes bright, proud as a child. "I was becoming
bored within my cabin, so I decided to provide a helping hand. Alex,
look," she held up the rope. "I learned how to tie a midshipman's
hitch."

He took in the knot, the eagerness on her face, the way Euan watched her like she was some rare prize.

"Well done," Alex said, keeping his voice smooth. "I'm proud o' ye. But truly, lass, ye shouldna' be haulin' rope with all these men about. Let these lazy buggers earn their pay. That's what I keep 'em for. Isn't that right… Euan?"

He turned the full heat of his gaze on the younger man.

"Captain, sir." Euan straightened. "I'm doin' me duties as ordered. She insisted on helpin'. I told her she didna' need tae lift a finger."

Yvonne's smile faltered into a frown. "What is the matter? Alex, I can tell you are upset with Euan. He is my friend. There is nothing to worry about. If you must know, he visited me last eve after you went to see your brother. He apologized and assured me being my friend was only his intention. I should be allowed to have friends if your lands are to be my new home."

"Oh, is that so," Alex said softly. "He came tae visit ye. And ye wish tae be his friend."

"Yes," she said, chin lifting.

"Very well, Yvonne." He smiled, all teeth. "Euan, ye have my blessing."

He turned as if to leave, then stepped close to Euan's ear, voice dropping to a growl only the other man could hear.

"If ye try anything with her," he murmured, "if ye hurt one strand o' hair on her head, I'll hang ye upside down from yer cock and let the gulls do the rest."

He straightened, face easy again. "Enjoy the rest o' yer day," he said to Yvonne, and strode off, fingers brushing the hilt of his sword as he went.

There was something wrong about Euan. Alex did not know his clan, his blood, his past, only that Haemish had vouched for him when the voyage began. Now, every instinct Alex possessed bristled.

A Short Stay

Three days later, they dropped anchor off a small green island not far from Ireland. They hunted pheasants in the scrub, felled trees for repairs, and found a narrow river to fill the water barrels. Andrew, still mending, walked the shore to stretch his legs and regain his strength. Haemish and Alex oversaw repairs at the stern while the rest of the men patched damage along the bow.

Nzingha and Yvonne took the chance to escape the noise of hammers and shouted orders, slipping away into the trees.

"Um, Nzingha," Yvonne ventured as they walked, skirts brushing the ferns, "may I ask you something?"

"Of course," Nzingha said. "Ask anything you wish."

"What is it like in Scotland?"

"Cold." Nzingha's lips curved; it was the very first question she herself had asked Andrew. "Sometimes unbearably cold, but the summers are nice. The rain comes often. I will have to make sure you have proper clothing. But the people…" She lifted a shoulder. "They can be very kind. Some are skeptical, but I learned to ignore the stares. Many have never left the village. Some have never even left Scotland. Curiosity can look like hostility when one is afraid. When you arrive, you must be careful whom you trust."

"Did you trust Alex and Andrew's uncle?" Yvonne asked quietly. "The one who captured you? Is that how you found yourself in Tafaria's keep?"

"Yes," Nzingha said. "I let him into my home because I trusted him. I did not know he was a dangerous man."

Yvonne fell silent, turning that over.

"May I ask something else?" she said softly. "How did the Princess of Mbemba come to trust Andrew? If he is anything like his brother… how did you endure his stubbornness, his temper?"

"Oh, that is a long story." Nzingha smiled faintly. "Where do I begin? Back in Mbemba, I had a secret relationship with one of my father's warriors for many years. My father discovered us and had him brought in for treason. I thought his punishment would be exile or slavery. I believed I might find him and rescue him before anything so terrible happened, so I escaped from my chambers to search for him. Instead, the same night of my search for my lover, pirates invaded Mbemba's shores and abducted me. My guard, Iney, was taken as well. We ended up shackled on the same ship."

Pain flickered in her eyes, but she went on. "I learned from Iney that my father had executed Mikel, that was my lover's name. Rage gave me strength. I fought, crashed us overboard, and we drifted to a strange island. That is where I crossed paths with Andrew."

Yvonne pressed a hand to her chest. "Oh, my princess, that must have been frightening. I am so sorry, you endured plenty."

"Yes, I grieved," Nzingha said simply. "But I was not alone. Andrew was there. He let me cry on his shoulder. He honored my pain. Somewhere in that, I began to heal."

Yvonne's cheeks warmed as thoughts of Alex crept in, how he had pulled her from the sea, how he held her when nightmares clawed her awake, how he'd kissed her forehead on deck as if the gesture meant nothing and everything at once.

"Princess," Yvonne said, "when you first met Andrew, was he deviant like Alex? What was he like? How did you come to fall in love with him?"

"Nae." Nzingha laughed, genuine and bright. "Andrew was very respectful. On the island, he was my savior. He opened himself to me, shared his own grief, protected me. He took my brokenness and gave me something in return, laughter, shelter, purpose. Love followed."

"What a beautiful story," Yvonne murmured. "Again, my condolences."

"Thank you," Nzingha said softly. "I believe my mother and Mikel and Iney were watching. They knew Andrew's fate was to protect me."

Yvonne swallowed, then blurted, "When you first met his brother, Alex… what did you think of him?"

"When I first met him?" Nzingha snorted. "He was a goat in heat. Women would brawl over him. Truly. He did not care for any of them." A fondness tugged at her features. "But the more I watched, the more I saw he cared for his family. He has been trying, very hard, to be a good chieftain."

She slanted Yvonne a look. "Have you developed feelings for Alex? If so, I am telling you as a friend, be careful. He has had so many women. It may be dangerous for you to get involved."

"Me? Ah-ha-ha… No, Princess." Yvonne's laugh came out too high. "I think Alex is a very nice person. A man of honor. He has never forced or persuaded me to lie with him. He has seen me at my lowest. During this entire voyage, he has consoled me, in secret. Lately he has been overprotective whenever I am near his crew, and he told me what his uncle did. Though what his uncle did was horrible, I would never have met Alex if you had not come to Tafaria's shores."

"The gods have smiled on us both, then." Nzingha squeezed her hand.

"Look," Yvonne said suddenly, pointing. "A stream. It is beautiful. Let us wade."

They removed their slippers and stepped into the cold water, pebbles pressing underfoot, laughter spilling between them. Sunlight broke through the canopy above, dancing over the surface.

"This is all so surreal," Yvonne said, voice soft with wonder. "Outside of Africa, there is an entire new world."

Both women froze at the sound of footsteps rustling through underbrush. In one smooth motion, Nzingha's hand went to her blade.

"Stay close," she whispered.

Their eyes scanned the trees until a familiar figure emerged.

"Good day to ye, Miss Yvonne, and Laird Andrew's wife," Euan called with an easy smile.

Yvonne's face lit up. She waved. "Euan. Is all well? How did you find us?"

Nzingha's frown deepened. "Why are you away from the men? Were you not given a task to hunt or carry water?"

"Aye, Mrs. Barton," he said, "but I wanted tae say hello tae Miss Yvonne. I've no' seen her all day."

"Oh, how kind of you," Yvonne said, already moving toward the bank. "I will be right out."

Nzingha caught her wrist. "Remember what I said about trusting those you do not know. Please. Have a care."

Yvonne pressed her lips together and nodded. Nzingha released her, watching as the two walked back toward the shore, talking and laughing. Euan placed a hand on the small of Yvonne's back. In turn she smiled, but the curve of her mouth was tight.

Nzingha returned to the ship with a growing knot in her chest. She did not bother to knock when she entered the captain's quarters.

Alex, Andrew, and Haemish sat around a small table, cards in hand, tankards near their elbows. Alex was halfway through a jest when he saw her face.

"Where's Yvonne?" he demanded at once.

Nzingha slipped into her husband's lap, still scowling. "She is with her friend Euan. Last I saw, she left the river with him, smiling."

Alex's expression twisted from annoyance to panic in a single breath.

"AND YE LEFT HIM WITH HER?" he roared.

"Hey!" Andrew snapped. "Dinnae shout at my wife."

Nzingha's eyes flashed. "Alex, Yvonne practically went running when she saw him. What was I to do? Order her to stay at my heel? I am not her mother."

"But ye are her princess," Alex bit out.

"And you are overreacting. I did warn her." Nzingha folded her arms. "Now it is on her to listen."

Alex shot to his feet, snatched up his sword, and strode out without another word.

By the time he reached the gangplank, Euan and Yvonne were already boarding. Euan bent to say something. Yvonne giggled, a bright, unguarded sound.

Alex stepped in out of nowhere and closed a hand around her wrist.

"I need a word with ye," he said tightly. "Euan, back tae work."

"Aye, Captain," Euan muttered, already edging away.

Alex drew Yvonne aside, lowering his voice. "I do not like ye wanderin' about with my men when they should be workin'."

She glanced over his shoulder. Several crewmen were watching, their gazes curious, their whispers obvious. Heat crept up her neck, not from affection this time, but from embarrassment. He sounded like a scolding father.

"My apologies," she whispered. "But he only came to say hello and escort me back to the ship."

"Listen to me," Alex said, fighting to keep his temper low. "Ye need tae be careful, spendin' time with strangers. I only hired him. I dinnae ken the man."

Yvonne looked past him to where Euan had already taken up work, hauling rope with apparent enthusiasm. *Why is he so determined to keep him from me? Is he… jealous?*

"Very well," she said. "I will be more careful whom I open up to."

He heard the distance in her tone and knew she did not truly grasp the danger. Frustration scraped his nerves.

"I dinnae wish tae be overbearin'," he said. "Ye're here because I want ye safe. We went tae Tafaria because we trusted a man we shouldna' have. I'll no' make that mistake again. Please, Yvonne, before ye wander off with anyone other than Nzingha, Andrew, or myself, let me know."

He pulled her into a quick hug, rocking her gently side to side. For a brief, stolen moment, the world narrowed to the strength of his arms, the steady beat of his heart under her cheek.

"I shall see ye this eve?" he asked quietly.

She nodded, eyes wide, something tender pulling at his chest. He bent and pressed a kiss to her forehead. Her eyes went round as coins.

"I'm sorry if I seemed harsh," he murmured. "I'll have Nzingha send ye books tae keep ye busy. It'll be after the evenin' meal when I come tae yer cabin."

He turned to go on, but in passing, gave Euan a look that could have cut sailcloth. "Ye have one more time to disobey me." He walked on.

Yvonne fled to her cabin, flung herself on the bed, and groaned into the pillow.

"Should I blush, or be angry? How can you tell me not to be friends with Euan? He seems kind enough." She slapped the mattress. "Ugh. You make me so upset. Always treating me as if I cannot defend myself."

The truth burned under the anger. She knew she was not strong. She hated that she was not a warrior like the women she'd known back home, like Nzingha.

A knock sounded.

"Yes?" she called.

A low voice came from the other side. "'Tis me. Euan."

Her spine stiffened. His presence at her door, after Alex's clear warning and Nzingha's caution, felt suddenly wrong.

His voice came again. "Well? Are ye goin' tae let me in?"

She hesitated, hand on the latch. "Euan… what are you doing here? It would be best if you were working. If Alex sees you…"

She opened the door mid-sentence. He cut her off by pressing something cool into her hand.

A necklace, fashioned from small shells threaded on a thin cord.

Her face lit. "Oh, Euan. It is beautiful."

"I wanted tae surprise ye earlier," he said, shrugging, "but Lord Andrew's wife looked as if she'd skewer me with her blade." He chuckled. "I thought I'd best keep a distance."

Yvonne giggled despite herself. "Nae, do not say such things. The princess has been through a great ordeal. She is simply careful."

"Careful o' me?" He laughed softly. "Och, I'm harmless."

He took her hand and lifted it, brushing his lips across her knuckles. The gesture sent a ripple of unease through her.

Without asking, he stepped behind her, drawing closer than was proper, breath warm against her neck as he fastened the necklace. He inhaled deeply, almost greedily.

She smiled automatically, but every instinct prickled. Like a snake, she thought. Pretty and slow until it strikes.

"Everyone thinks I must be careful with you," she said lightly, trying to turn the moment into jest. "Tell me, can I trust you?"

He bowed and kissed her hand again. "Of course ye can trust me. Dinnae let anyone tell ye otherwise."

Another knock rattled the door.

"Euan," a man's voice called, "the Captain's askin' for ye. Ye're needed in the crow's nest."

Euan winked. "Duty calls, my lady." He slipped out, his scent and his unease lingering behind him.

The Coax

Days blurred.

Euan paid Yvonne court in little, stolen moments, on deck, by the rail, with a jest here, a compliment there. She found herself half-looking forward to his visits, half remembering Alex's warning and Nzingha's eyes, sharp as a hawk's.

Nights belonged to someone else.

Every evening, after his duties were done, and the ship had settled into its long, groaning rhythm, Alex came to her cabin. Sometimes he arrived with the smell of salt still clinging to him, sometimes with ink-smudged fingers and a tired set to his shoulders.

They fell into a quiet routine. Yvonne would read aloud from the English books Nzingha had lent her, sounding out unfamiliar words, pausing when her tongue stumbled. Alex would listen from the desk, sketching by candlelight, lifting his gaze now and then as if committing the sound of her voice to memory.

When the candle burned low and the words blurred, he would stretch out on the narrow pallet beside her. She would turn instinctively, tucking herself into the steady warmth of his arms, her breath slowing as the ship rocked them both.

On rough nights, when the timbers groaned and sleep came poorly, he murmured nonsense stories or pressed a calming hand between her shoulders until the tension left her body.

In those hours, he was not the overbearing captain or the sharp-tongued chieftain. He was simply Alex. The man who made her laugh in whispers. Who steadied her when the deck pitched beneath her feet. Who woke her gently from nightmares, never asking what she saw there.

One afternoon, while Nzingha sketched a likeness of baby Destiny from memory, Yvonne sat across from her, twisting her fingers in her lap.

"Princess, though we have only known each other six months, may I ask… a personal question?"

Nzingha set down her charcoal at once. "Of course. You may ask me anything."

"You know of my marriage to King Oyomo," Yvonne began.

"I do," Nzingha said slowly. "Why bring him up?"

"It concerns my wedding night." Yvonne stared at her hands. "The reason I ran away was not only his age or my fear. It was… my beliefs. I hate our traditions. A man taking many wives disgusts me. I could not share a bed with someone who already had five women and countless concubines. I have always wanted what you have: a union. Just one man and one woman, devoted only to each other."

She lifted her gaze. "How does it feel? To know you are the only woman Andrew Barton will ever love and treasure? That there is no other you must compete with?"

Nzingha rose and crossed to her, taking her hands, her eyes warm.

"Being married to Andrew," she said softly, "makes me feel like a goddess. I sleep beside him every night. That is when he holds me the tightest. When I am homesick, he listens to my endless tales of war and my lioness. His body belongs to me and only me. We are not just lovers. Our souls are mated. When he travels, I can smell him before I see him, and my stomach fills with butterflies. I would not trade him for anything. Only death will part us."

Yvonne smiled, her eyes bright with unshed tears. "May I tell you something private?"

"Of course."

"When I ran from the Oyomo tribe, Femi found me hiding in a tree. I was broken. He mended my arm, hid me away, took me to your mother's lands. I grew to care for him deeply. We both admitted we were fond of each other. But when he wished to… to make love to me, I refused. I am still pure. I never lay with King Oyomo. I have never been touched. Wanting to be with Femi made no sense. And being a sixth wife to a man close to the throne would have made me miserable. I want what you have. A true union."

Nzingha's gaze softened. "My circumstances were fate. Yours can be as well."

"What do you mean?" Yvonne asked.

"You and Alex have been spending a great deal of time together," Nzingha said, mischief glinting now. "He helps you sleep. He guards you from his crew. You must feel something by now."

"Nzingha!" Yvonne sprang up, laughing in disbelief. "Alex is a lustful ass. You said so yourself. Take it as kindness. Nothing more."

"Do you wish to know something?" Nzingha asked.

Yvonne dropped her hands and nodded.

"I see a change in Alex."

"Change?" Yvonne giggled at the notion. "This is the same man that invited me to his chambers the first time we met. Then he lay with not one, but two women in front of me. He is caring, yes, but demanding and infuriating. He has made it very clear he will never marry and never fall in love. Starting something with him would be hopeless."

Nzingha patted the bench. "Come. Sit. Let me share something."

Yvonne sat, wary.

"Andrew and Alex are the same," Nzingha said with a knowing smile. "Both sailors. Both with sexual appetites. But both, underneath, are caring men. When I was stranded on that island with Andrew, I knew he wanted me. I caught him spying on my bath in the river." She smirked. "My grief, my temper, he saw all of it. And he still chose me. Alex already knows your pain. He has held it, gently, without asking for anything. All you must do is open to him. Show him all of you. I say, seduce him. Then, when he burns for you, give him the best night of his life."

Yvonne stared at her. "That makes no sense at all," she said faintly. "Why would I do that? Give my body to a man who might not hold me dear? Who has given me every reason not to trust him?"

"As I said," Nzingha replied, unbothered, "Alex is like his brother. You will see him confess his love. Trust me."

Yvonne swallowed. "I… do feel for Alex," she admitted quietly. "I can see myself falling in love with him. Some nights I… wish to be touched by him."

Nzingha's grin was triumphant. "Ah-ha! I knew it. You cannot fool me."

Yvonne's cheeks heated as Nzingha leaned in conspiratorially.

"You see that little puppy that follows you? What is his name, Euan? You being friends with him will make Alex want you more. He will come around. As I said, Alex and Andrew are the same. All Alex needs is one night."

"This sounds like a violation of everything I stand for," Yvonne said weakly.

"No, just a plan to give you the union you desire."

"And if he rejects me? If he turns cold after we… after we are together? Then I will be ruined. A defiled fool."

Nzingha only sipped her wine, her eyes glinting. "Or... You will not." She smiled.

Saltwater Bath

Night settled over the ship.

Alex was bone tired. He had spent the day directing repairs, counting barrels, watching every move Euan made. The man had a talent for disappearing at convenient times.

"Crafty bastard," Alex sat alone, grumbling to himself. "Riskin' his neck for a lass he barely kens."

He looked at the hourglass and made another mark. It was later than he'd intended. Before going to Yvonne's cabin, he decided on a quick saltwater bath. If he lay down now, he'd be asleep in his boots and never hear the end of it.

In his quarters, he sat at his desk first and logged the day's events: repairs completed, stores replenished, distance to Ireland. With the voyage nearly done, he began dividing the men's pay in his ledger. Every man was owed his share of the princess's reward from Tafaria.

The cabin was quiet. The ship's gentle sway and the distant hush of waves lulled his eyes half-closed.

He stretched.

"If I dinnae move now, I'll pass out in this chair, and she'll think I've forgotten."

He stripped and lowered himself into the tub. The water was cold, but after so many days of sweat and salt, it felt like absolution.

He leaned back, closing his eyes and inevitably thought of Yvonne.

He thought of her expressions when he made her laugh. Of the way she'd pressed her forehead to his chest that morning when another nightmare had passed.

The time she said, '*I trust you with my life*', and then kissed his cheek as if it were nothing.

His lips curved.

He did not feel himself drift.

He heard the door creak and a whisper of cloth. It pulled him back. With his eyes still closed, his hand slid automatically toward the musket resting beside the tub.

"Jesus," he muttered, blinking his eyes open. "Yvonne, what are ye doin'?"

She stood by the tub, completely bare.

His eyes widened. "Lass, why are ye naked?"

Color flared hot along her cheekbones, but she lifted her chin. This was not the reaction she had imagined.

"Did I startle you?" she asked. "My apologies. The hour is late, and I feared you had fallen asleep. When I entered, the water looked inviting, so I thought to join you."

Alex stared, throat suddenly dry.

Is she daft?

His gaze roamed, traitorous, over her curves before he snapped it back to her face.

"I must be dreamin'. Ye're sayin' ye wish tae take a bath with me?"

"Yes," she said simply. "I would like to join you."

Without waiting for permission, Yvonne climbed into the tub. Cold water sloshed over the sides and onto the floor.

"Oh my," she gasped. "It is freezing."

"I dinnae think we'll fit," he said weakly.

She shifted, then, after a heartbeat, settled behind him, thighs bracketing his hips, breast against his back. She warmed quickly in spite of the cold. His heart thundered.

"Yvonne," he said hoarsely, "what are ye doin'? Are ye tryin' tae tempt me?"

"No, I told you... I trust you with my life. We are two friends taking a bath. That is all."

"If I'm in a bath with a woman, my intentions are rarely tae get clean. It involves somethin' a bit naughtier. Just sittin' behind me like that makes my blood boil. Ye should leave. This is no' proper. What of yer honor?"

"I have held my honor this long," she said softly. "That is not your concern."

"Well aye, it is my concern, Yvonne. What has gotten intae ye?"

"You have no self-control," she teased faintly, trying to hide her nerves. Her gaze fell on his shoulders. Angry red patches marked his skin. "You are so concerned about my honor; you should pay more attention to your back. It is burned."

She lathered soap between her hands and began to gently wash the raw skin, her touch careful and soothing. When she patted him dry, he flinched, more from the tenderness than the pain.

"Very well," she said. "My turn."

She stood, stepping over him. For one dizzying instant, he saw everything before he squeezed his eyes shut.

"Yvonne," he rasped, "this is not right."

"What are you afraid of?" she asked. "I washed your back. Now you must wash mine."

She sank down between his knees, back to his chest, water lapping at her collarbones. His hands hesitated, then lifted the soap.

He washed her back in slow, circular motions, the glow of candlelight turning every droplet on her skin to gold. He tried to think of anything but the way she felt against him, the soft sounds she made when the cloth grazed a bruise.

"You know," he said, voice low, "I've traveled tae many lands. I've never seen a woman like ye. Ye're… stunnin'. Yer skin is smooth as silk. It reminds me of rich clay, warm beneath the light, slick after it rains. And yer eyes... They are slanted like a cat's. Big and brown. They remind me o' the lionesses we saw on the way tae Tafaria. And yer scent…" He dipped his head closer to her hair, inhaling. "Jasmine. I can smell ye when ye're near."

"My thanks," she said shyly. "I used to massage jasmine oil into my hair every night in Tafaria. The scent never left, no matter how often I wash it."

Nzingha's words fluttered through her mind.

When he is near, I can smell him, and my stomach fills with butterflies.

A thought processed.

Does that mean he…? She smiled.

"Alex?" she asked softly.

"Mm?"

"All this talk about my beauty… what of the two women you lay with? They must have caught your eye."

"Nae," he said. "Yer beauty outshines them all. Even Nzingha, though she's a fine-lookin' woman."

She ducked her head, fingers drifting through the water.
She hesitated. "I must compliment you in return." Then she went silent before speaking.

Finally, courage broke.

"I love your hair; it is lush and full, the color like the sun at dawn."

She turned her head and studied his eyes. "Your eyes… They are like the sea, so blue that if I look long enough, I will drown in them."

Her gaze moved to his lips. "And… your lips…"
She faltered, sliding deeper into the water. "You poke them out when you sleep. It is… cute."

Heat crept up his neck. No woman had ever described him like that. They'd praised his skill, his strength, his stamina, but not him.

"I've met many women," he said roughly. "None have spoken o' me the way ye just did."

"How do you know they found you attractive?" she asked, genuinely curious.

"They wanted tae bed me." He laughed. "Ye, on the other hand, have had no desire tae. What ye said was… innocent. It felt good."

"I only speak what is true, Captain," she said.

"My thanks, but yer compliments outnumber mine. Let me even the scales." He pretended to consider. "Yer lips," he said at last, "are plump, like fruit ready tae be tasted."

The words sent a sharp ache between her thighs. Yvonne turned, water sloshing, and faced him, her chest rising and falling. She wanted to close the distance between them. Her courage, traitorous thing, only allowed her to drown in his eyes.

Alex could not resist. He leaned in and pressed his mouth to hers.

The kiss was slow at first, unsure. Then her lips parted and his tongue brushed hers, and the world narrowed to heat and breath and the way she made a small, broken sound and surged closer, pressing her body full against his chest.

Their heads tilted and turned, mouths opening and closing in a rhythm all their own. Her fingers slid into his hair; his hand cupped the back of her head, guiding, never forcing.

Desire climbed, too quick, too bright.

She gasped into his mouth.

He broke away first, breathing hard. "Did I hurt ye?" he asked. "Was there another vision?"

"No," she whispered, cheeks flushed. "I… I grew afraid. I liked it when you kissed me. I was… on a natural high. I did not wish to stop. I would like more."

He smoothed his thumb across her bottom lip where his teeth had grazed. "Remember my promise?"

She nodded. "Yes."

"I'll no' harm ye," he said softly. "Ye're delicate, like the shell o' an egg. If ye wish tae stop, we will. If ye wish tae go on, I ken a way tae give ye passion without overwhelm."

She swallowed. "I would like that. But… how?"

"Close yer eyes," he murmured. "Envision what ye want. Tell me, and I'll make it real."

She shut her eyes.

Her dream from the night before rose up, his mouth, his hands, the balcony, that strange sense of rightness.

"I wish for you to kiss my shoulder," she said.

He obeyed, lips brushing the sensitive skin just below her ear in soft, unhurried pecks. Her breasts tightened; heat surged low.

"And… to touch my skin softly," she whispered, "and give me more kisses."

His hands drifted over her shoulders, down her arms, mapping every inch with reverent care. She turned in his arms, facing him, wrapping her arms around his neck. Their chests pressed together, slick and wet, heartbeat to heartbeat.

With one quick move, he stood with her in his arms, allowing the water to drench the floor. Alex kissed her as he walked her to the bed; both of their bodies were wet and covered in soap.

He wanted her so fiercely his chest thudded against his ribs, each beat a demand he could no longer silence. Every part of him ached for the moment to repeat itself, again and again, as if his body already knew her in a way his mind hadn't yet dared to admit.

He lay over her and paused, staring into the very eyes that had captured him from the moment he first saw her.

Alex knew this was his chance to give her tenderness, not pressure. He bent close, his breath warm in her ear. "Tell me, lass… what else would ye have me do?"

"I wish for you to give me more kisses. Place your mouth upon me."

He watched her legs drew back, allowing her feet to rest flat on the bed, spreading her thighs like the wings of a sparrow.

A hungry smile curved his mouth as he drank in the sight of her.

He rose over her, lips brushing her ear as he murmured, "Tell me… what else do ye want of me?"

The low rumble of his voice curled down her spine, warming her from the inside out. Desire tangled with nerves, swelling with the tenderness of his restraint. His gentleness, his constant asking, made her ache for him even more.

She pleaded, "Please, I need you to touch me more."

His whisper drifted over her like silk, making her breath falter.

"Where, lass? Where d'ye want me tae touch ye?"

Boldly, she grabbed his hand, placing it on the warmth between her legs.

When he touched her, his lips curved. She was moist… she was ready. He took liberties, massaging her with his thumb. She muffled soft cries.

In the moment, she thrust her hips with every moving sensation.

Sly Alex dipped his head; his whisper warmed against her skin. "I've something better in mind," he murmured. "Will ye allow me tae kiss ye here?"

She closed her eyes, a trembling sigh slipping out.

"Yes… please."

He kissed her warmth deeply and passionately.

Want roared through him, ten times, a hundred times, a thousand times stronger than he expected, but he reined in. She was tender and warm. He matched her pace, not to overwhelm her.

He tasted her sex, and his thoughts were correct. She tasted like a sweet treat of custard pie. He licked and suckled, devouring her as if she were a feast at Yule.

Gently, he placed a finger inside. She gasped.

He lifted his gaze to hers, voice low and reverent.

"God above… ye're tight as a sealed glove. An untouched maiden."

He drove his face even deeper. Yvonne held on to his head, twisting her waist in a circular motion. A powerful surge rolled through her, like stepping off the peak of a mountain and free-falling into pure, dizzying sensation.

She tried to grip the pleasure rushing through her, but it was too much, too sharp, too consuming. The release slammed into her, dragging her upright as a cry tore free.

Her cry ripped through the room. "ALEX!"

Alex wiped his mouth with the back of his hand, watching the rise and fall of her chest as she fought to steady her breath. The sight should have filled him with pride; instead, guilt crept in like a shadow.

Any man would see the invitation for what it was… an age-old plea for comfort, for escape, for release.

He stood abruptly and reached for his clothes.

Yvonne blinked in surprise, pushing herself upright.

"Alex… what are you doing? Is there not more to come?"

He did not answer.

Her voice softened, uncertain. "Alex? Why are you dressing? Did I… did I do something wrong?"

He finally turned, jaw tight. "Yvonne, we cannae continue. I… gave you what you wished for. But I will not take what is most precious to you. You fought hard to keep your purity. I'll not be the man who ruins that, not until you marry, or choose someone who can truly be yours."

"What? Alex, no." Her voice trembled. "I… I care for you."

He froze.

Those words pierced him deeper than any blade.

She went on, unaware of the storm rising in him.

"I do not know who will ever love me… or treat me gently as you do. Will you not allow me to give you the same passion? Please do not leave me."

He swallowed hard and looked away. Pulling on his shirt felt like lifting stone. Respect held him back; desire urged him forward. And somewhere in the midst of her confession, the truth hit him like a crashing wave.

She was falling in love with him.

And he… was dangerously close to doing the same.

What he meant to tell her, that he was not the man for her, lodged in his throat. How did he say it without shattering her? How did he reject the only woman who'd ever looked at him as if he were worth something more than a night?

He couldn't.

Not yet.

Not like this.

"Yvonne, I…"

She silenced him with a kiss, soft at first, then blooming into something hungry, something desperate. Her fingers curled at the back of his neck, drawing him in.

"Let us allow the night to happen," she murmured against his mouth. "We will not speak of it tomorrow. Let me show you how deeply I appreciate everything you have done for me."

"Yvonne… nae," he breathed, though his resolve wavered.

But she was already slipping beneath his defenses, tugging at his shirt, her hands moving with sudden certainty. In her ears echoed Nzingha's teasing whisper from earlier:

Alex cares for you.

The truth of that, whatever shape it took, flooded her with courage she never knew she possessed. Desire, gratitude, longing… all of it swelled until she could hardly breathe.

She pressed herself to him, lips brushing his again.

"Please, Alex," she whispered. "I cannot stop myself."

He shut his eyes, pained. "Yvonne… how did it come to this? I am not the man ye want."

But even as he said it, his hands betrayed him, sliding beneath her thighs, lifting her with ease. Her legs wrapped around his waist instinctively, her breath catching when he held her so close.

Carrying her to bed felt like stepping across a line he'd sworn not to cross. His conscience thundered. She's delicate, broken, and afraid. Yet when he looked into her eyes, he saw not fear, but trust. Trust she had given no other man.

"Alex," she whispered, voice trembling. "What is the matter? Do you not… want me?"

His throat worked.

"I do," he admitted quietly. "God help me, I do. But…"

"Then take me."

The words fell from her lips like a plea and a command all at once, shattering the last of his restraint.

Without warning, he slid into her fully, deep. She gasped at the sharp sting, her eyes flying wide in instinctive fear.

She fought the urge to squeeze them shut, because she knew what waited for her there.

If she closed her eyes, even for a heartbeat, King Oyomo's face would surge from the darkness like a specter, poisoning the moment.

She pushed at his chest, breath breaking as the pain sharpened.

"Alex… wait… No… you're hurting me."

He stilled at once, voice low and strained.

"I can stop, lass. Say the word. Do ye trust me?"

Her mind spun, reaching for something, anything, to steady herself.

Her mother's voice rose from memory, soft as a lullaby whispered over braids.

The first time is always the hardest, but trust… the pain will pass, and pleasure will come.

"I do… but it hurts."

Her voice broke, and with it came tears she could not contain. Fear trembled through her, raw and unguarded.

The sight of her crying split something inside him. Alex brushed her cheeks with his thumb, gathering her into his chest as if he could shield her from the very moment he'd created.

"Yvonne…" His voice cracked with guilt. "Maybe we should stop. I dinnae wish to hurt ye. This… tonight… feels wrong. I should never…"

But when he shifted to pull out, she caught his hand in both of hers, her grip small but desperate.

"What are you doing?" she whispered, panic rising in her throat. "No… we've already come this far."

To her, retreat meant rejection, meant she had misread everything, meant she would lose him before she ever truly had him. And worse, it meant being left ruined and alone. She could not bear that.

Her fingers tightened around him. "Please. Do not leave me in the dark."

When he inched back inside her, she whimpered.

He gave her a soft kiss. "It will get better, I promise." She relaxed her legs.

His thrust became faster. "I will take you to the height of passion. Ye shall see," he whispered in her ear.

She could not take hold of her emotions from the sensation of his invasion. She yelled aloud, "Alex, I love you."

He said nothing in return. As she moaned, the passion built. He pushed upward, and his biceps flexed as they supported the movement of his waist.

His heart hammered against his ribs as he watched her in the candlelight.

Her silhouette trembled beneath him, soft curves glowing like warm gold.

It had been years, if ever, since a woman made him feel unsteady.

Yet Yvonne… Yvonne undid him without even trying.

She humbled him.

Not with seduction, nor boldness, but with the fragile way she trusted him, the quiet way she reached for him as if he were something gentle.

As he held her, something in his chest gave way, a weakening he recognized all too well.

Alex Barton, who never lost himself to anyone, had fallen for her.

"God, Yvonne, ye're so beautiful. I cannae hold it in much longer."

She wrapped both legs around him, causing the urge to release himself to build.

She cried out, "Please, do not stop. I am falling from the highest mountain."

As she climaxed, he spilled onto her stomach. His breathing labored as he fell at her side.

The two lay there in utter silence.

Normally, Alex would have cracked a foolish jest, said something stupid just to break the tension lodged in his chest.

But after what had happened, words deserted him.

Yvonne snuggled into him, warm and trusting, her breath soft against his shoulder.

He stared at the ceiling, unmoving.

How the hell do I run from this? We're on a ship.

Dawns Aftermath

Dawn crept slowly and quiet, painting the sky outside the tiny cabin window in silvers, oranges, and pale lavender.

Alex had not slept a single wink.

He lay on his side, watching Yvonne's profile, the peaceful curve of her mouth, her lashes resting softly on her cheeks. For the first time, there were no nightmares, no trembling, no whispered pleas for help in her sleep.

Just… peace.

He exhaled a long breath.

He knew he could not hide here beside her forever.

Carefully, he slid out from beneath her, dressed without making a sound, and slipped out of the cabin.

He barely made it two steps before colliding straight into Euan.

"Apologies," Euan blurted. "Good mornin', Captain. Ye're up mighty early. Could ye no' sleep?"

"Aye," Alex muttered. "Restless half the night."

Euan, oblivious and far too bold for Alex's current mood, pressed on.

"How's Miss Yvonne? Ye didna' stay with her last eve. She must be better. No more bad dreams, aye?"

A sharp, irrational heat flared in Alex's chest.

"That is none o' yer concern." he said flatly,

Euan blinked, startled, but Alex was already brushing past him.

He strode up to the main deck and stood behind the ship's wheel, letting the cold morning breeze slap against his face. The fresh air should have cleared his thoughts. It didn't.

He gripped the wood tightly, jaw ticking as the events of the night replayed behind his eyes.

Her touch.
Her trust.
And her whispered confession.

Alex... I love you.

He squeezed his eyes shut and pinched his nose..

"Bloody hell."

She deserved a life he could never give her. Peace, a home, a future untouched by chaos and wandering seas.

And he?

He was a Barton.

Destined to roam, to fight, to live half-wild with storms in his blood.

"So how did it get to this?" he muttered, pacing a short line across the deck. "I'll have Nzingha keep her busy the remaining voyage… keep distance. 'Tis for her own good."

He faced the horizon, Scotland waiting in the distance, and squared his shoulders, the decision settling like a stone in his gut.

Whatever last night had awakened between them…

It could not be allowed to grow.

Chapter Twelve

The Favor

*A*lex's nerves weighed heavy as iron in his chest.

He paced the corridor outside Andrew's cabin twice, raking a hand through his hair, then finally knocked.

No answer.

His jaw tightened. Patience had never been his strong suit. He pushed the door open and strode inside.

"Nzingha…"

He froze.

Nzingha was atop Andrew, riding him with such focus Alex nearly choked on his own breath before fleeing back into the hall.

Alex went scarlet. "Saints above," he muttered, spun on his heel, and all but leapt back into the passage, slamming the door shut behind him.

Andrew's muffled voice came through the wood. "Christ, Alex!"

Alex cleared his throat and dragged both hands down his face. He waited, shifting from foot to foot, until the latch finally clicked and the door opened.

Andrew stood there with his hair a mess, shirt half tied.

"Well, dinnae just stand there. Come in, then," Andrew grumbled. "Since ye've already barged in once."

Alex stepped inside, keeping his eyes on a crack in the floorboards like it was suddenly fascinating.

Andrew folded his arms. "Christ, Alex. I have a wife now. Ye cannae just storm in like we're still lads sharing a pallet in the loft. What do ye want?"

"Apologies, brother," Alex said, voice strained. "It's urgent. I need a word with Nzingha."

Nzingha, adjusting her gown and smoothing her braids, arched a brow. "Me?"

"Aye." He nodded quickly, still refusing to look too far below her chin. "I need a favor. 'Tis important."

He opened the door and stepped out into the passage, waiting. Nzingha joined him, pulling the door half closed behind her.

"What is the matter, are you well?" she asked. "Is it your wounds? Your head? Has something happened on deck?"

"Nae," he said. "It's no' me. It's Yvonne."

Her expression sharpened. "What of her?"

"We've only a few days till we reach Tantallon," he said, pacing the narrow corridor. "I cannae… I can no' help her sleep any longer. I gave my word I would, but…" He broke off, jaw flexing. "Can ye keep her occupied? Stay with her at night? May-hap, teach her archery, or paintin', or anything. Just… keep her... keep her busy. Away from me."

Nzingha stared at him.

"Where is all this coming from?" she demanded. "What happened between you two?"

"I cannae say," he muttered, turning away. "Please, Nzingha. This is important."

She planted a hand on her hip. "Did you bed her?"

He bit his lower lip and said nothing.

Her eyes flashed. "Alex. She cares for you deeply. She is not some tavern whore or idle chambermaid. You cannot toss her aside as if she is nothing. You will break her."

"I know that," he snapped, then forced his tone lower. "I tried to pull away, but… she insisted. I tried to leave. She wouldnae let me. I care for her, but I do not love her."

Nzingha stared at him as if he'd spat on the deck.

"Alex, I am greatly disappointed in you," she said quietly. "You took her from one world of hurt and pain only to hand her another. You will drive her into hating me, for I was the one who told her to take a chance on you. I believed you were like your brother."

He stopped pacing and turned on her. "Oh, so this is all my fault?" he hissed. "You told her what, exactly? That I was in love with her? That I'd put a ring on her finger if she climbed into my bath?"

"I did not say that," Nzingha shot back. "She told me she cared deeply for you. I only said you shared the same good qualities as Andrew. That you could love as fiercely as he does." She shook her head, disappointed. "Clearly, I was mistaken. I had faith in you."

That stung worse than a wound.

He turned his back, shoulders tight.

"Fine," she said at last. "I will keep her occupied until we reach Scotland. But you, Alex Barton, must tell her the fate of your friendship. Do not hide behind me."

She swept away down the corridor, leaving him standing alone with the echo of his own cowardice.

The Glowing Morning

Soft light filtered through the tiny cabin window, painting thin shafts of gold across the bed.

Yvonne's eyes fluttered open.

For a moment, she lay still, floating somewhere between dream and waking. Her body felt heavy and unfamiliar. She was tender in places that had never known such a deep ache before.

She turned, reaching out instinctively for warmth.

Empty.

Her hand met only rumpled sheets, still faintly warm where his body had lain.

A sharp sting pinched between her legs as she shifted.

"Stss… ouch," she hissed under her breath, one hand flying to her midsection. She hesitated, then glanced down.

Her thighs were chafed. Between them, the linen bore a smear of dried blood.

She stared at it, breath catching.

"My courses are not for another fortnight," she thought. "So this… this is from last night."

Heat rushed up her throat, part shame, part wonder, part the echo of the pleasure that had stolen her breath in his arms.

Memories flashed over her in hot, disjointed fragments.

His hands steadying her.

His voice asking, *Do ye trust me?*

Her own voice, shaking, answering yes.

The pain. The fear. The way he had held her, whispered to her, tried to ease her through it.

The moment she had finally broken, cried out his name, told him she loved him.

Love.

She swallowed hard.

Carefully, she slid from the bed. Each step reminded her brutally of what she had given, and to whom. At the trunk, she dug through spare linens, pulled out a fresh sheet, then returned to strip the evidence from the bed.

Her fingers shook as she balled the stained linen in her hands.

"This is foolish," she whispered to herself. "We are not to be wed, lovers, nothing of the sort. I simply showed him gratitude. That is all."

But the lie collapsed the moment it left her tongue.

Tears burned at the corners of her eyes.

She carried the linen to the washstand and poured water into the basin, scrubbing at the stains with too hard, frantic motions. The more she scrubbed, the more tears slipped free, falling into the water and vanishing.

"What have I done?" she whispered. "What if he regrets it? What if I am nothing more than another conquest in his stories?"

Her chest heaved.

A knock sounded at the door.

Her heart leapt, then stuttered.

"Is that Alex?" she breathed, then answered herself in a flat whisper. "No. He would have barged in without a knock."

The knock came again.

"Yvonne?" A familiar voice followed. "'Tis me, Nzingha."

Yvonne dragged in a quick breath, swiped at her cheeks, and straightened her gown.

"Come in," she said, voice too bright.

She opened the door. Nzingha stood there with a small, careful smile.

"Good morning," Yvonne said, stepping aside. "How did you know I was here?"

"I ran into Alex this morning," Nzingha said, moving into the cabin. "He mentioned you were still in his quarters."

"Oh." Yvonne's heart stumbled again. "He did?"

There was an awkward pause. Yvonne realized she still clutched the half damp linen behind her back. She tucked it quickly into the wash basin.

"How is your husband?" she asked, grasping for normal conversation. "Is he feeling better?"

"He is much improved," Nzingha said. "Well on his way to recovery."

"That is wonderful news. He is a good man."

Silence stretched between them, tight as a pulled bowstring.

Nzingha broke it. "So," she said lightly, though her eyes were sharp, "how did it go with Alex last night? Was he a gentleman?"

Yvonne's cheeks warmed. Despite the ache, despite the gnawing fear, the memory of his tenderness rose up, bright and intoxicating.

"Oh, Nzingha," she said softly, almost glowing. "It was beautiful. My whole life, I have feared men. But Alex… he is different."

Nzingha made a small, noncommittal sound. "Mhm. Yes. He surely is."

Yvonne gestured for her to sit. Nzingha chose the chair, crossing one leg over the other, studying her carefully.

"Princess, Alex is truly a gentleman," Yvonne said, unable to keep the softness from her voice. "He did not wish to go forward. I seduced him."

Nzingha's lips pressed together. She said nothing, but inwardly she ticked off each point. Consent. Hesitation. Who pushed whom. At least Alex had not lied.

"He tried to leave," Yvonne continued, fingers twisting in her skirt. "But I do not know what came over me. My body wanted him. I could not bear the thought of him leaving me in such a state. Finally, he stayed." She paused, voice dropping. "In the height of everything, I told him I loved him."

Nzingha's brows lifted. "Really? And what did he say?"

Yvonne looked away. "Nothing. I do not know if he even heard me."

Oh, he heard you, Nzingha thought grimly. *And he fled like a coward.*

Memories of her own first night with Andrew surfaced. Different, yet painfully similar. She had not loved him then. She had still mourned another. Andrew had been the one hopelessly in love.

Here, it was reversed.

"Yvonne," Nzingha said at last, rising to pace the small cabin, "I am going to be honest with you. I need you to listen, and not let your heart run wild."

Yvonne's spine stiffened. "Alright. What is it?"

"Alex does not love you," Nzingha said bluntly. "He cares. He respects you. But he does not love you. Not yet."

The words hit like a slap.

Yvonne's throat closed. "Why would you say such a thing?"

"Because he came to me this morning, and begged me to keep you busy until you arrive home. He said he could no longer help you fall asleep. That he needs distance."

Tears filled Yvonne's eyes in an instant.

"He said that?" Her voice cracked. "He does not wish to be near me?"

"He is a lady's man," Nzingha said gently. "He tried to leave last night because he did not want to hurt you. He failed in that. But I do believe he tried."

Yvonne pressed a hand over her mouth, a small broken sound escaping.

"I gave him something sacred," she whispered. "The one thing King Oyomo never even took. I trusted him. And he wishes to assign me as a duty to someone else?"

She folded in on herself, shoulders shaking as the first sobs broke free. Nzingha crossed the small space and wrapped her arms around her.

"Hush," she murmured. "You are not foolish. You are a woman who has been hurt too often, who finally found gentleness and reached for it. There is no shame in that. After all, if you wish to blame anyone, blame me. I had faith in Alex. I thought he had changed."

"I feel ashamed," Yvonne choked out. "I feel discarded."

Nzingha stroked her hair. "Listen to me. In this game of love, you must not chase him. You must be like me." Her tone turned a little wicked. "Ignore him. Give him the coldest of shoulders. Let him feel what it is to be the one waiting, watching."

Yvonne sniffed, wiping her cheeks. "And if he does not come?"

"Then he was never meant for you," Nzingha said simply. "But I have seen the way he looks at you. He is smitten, whether he admits it or not. He saved you. He has held you through nightmares for months. That is no small thing. Let him stew in his own guilt for a while."

Yvonne managed a soft, watery laugh. "And how do I do that, exactly?"

Nzingha's eyes glinted. "You have a little puppy trailing after you already. What is his name? Euan? Be pleasant with him. Laugh with him. Let Alex see that you are not waiting at his heel like a lost pup. Let him see someone else finds you delightful."

Yvonne hesitated. "That feels cruel."

"So is what he did to your heart," Nzingha replied. "We are not talking about vengeance. Only balance." She squeezed Yvonne's hand. "Let him chase for once."

Slowly, very slowly, Yvonne nodded.

"Good," Nzingha said. "Come to my quarters for dinner. The four of us will dine together." She forced a bright smile. "We shall all see how well Alex handles his own medicine."

A Jealous Rage

Later that day, Alex climbed into the crow's nest, spyglass in hand. It was easier up here, sea and sky and the honest creak of wood. No eyes. No questions.

He swept the horizon, then let the glass drop to the deck below.

That is when he saw her.

Yvonne.

She stood near the coils of rope, sleeves rolled, head bent as she tried to mimic a figure-eight knot. Her tongue peeked at the corner of her mouth in concentration. Euan stood close behind her, guiding her hands.

"Too close," he whispered to himself.

Alex's jaw worked.

"Ye have got to be jestin'," he muttered.

Yvonne laughed at something Euan said, tipping her head back. In that moment, she caught sight of Alex high above and, very deliberately, did not look away, but also did not acknowledge him.

Instead, she shifted a fraction closer to Euan.

When he reached around her to correct the loop, his chest pressed to her back. Her breath hitched, but she did not move away. Later, when they tied it successfully, she turned to hug him in thanks.

It was a quick, friendly embrace.

But she stepped in fully, letting her breasts brush his chest, holding him a heartbeat longer than necessary.

Alex saw red.

"That clever grinnin' goat-lickin' bastard." he snarled, nearly crushing the spyglass.

From the main deck, Nzingha glanced up. She saw his thunderous face and nearly doubled over laughing.

"Just look at him," she murmured to herself. "He is burning holes through the sky, like a babe whose sweets have been taken away."

She cupped her hands around her mouth, beckoning. "Yvonne! Do you have a moment?"

Yvonne waved cheerfully, and when she jumped, her full breasts bounced with absolutely no restraint. Euan's eyes dropped before his mouth did, hanging open in hopeless awe.

That was all it took.

Alex thundered down the ladder of the crow's nest, boots hitting the deck with a heavy thud. Seeing him storming toward them, Yvonne turned and hugged Euan once more, just a little tighter and a little higher on her toes before stepping away.

"EUAN!" Alex roared, his voice booming so loudly that the entire ship turned to witness their captain's fury.

The young man jumped so hard he nearly dropped the rope he was holding.

"Ah… aye, Captain?" he stammered.

Alex closed the distance in a few long strides, eyes blazing. "What, in God's holy name, do ye think ye're doin'?"

Euan blinked. "Teaching a knot, Captain?"

"Oh, a knot?" Alex barked. "Is that what ye call hoverin' over her shoulder, breathin' down her neck like a dog in heat? Is that what ye call wrappin' yer arms round her like she's a sack of flour ye're tryin' to carry off?"

Yvonne stepped forward, bristling. "Alex, that is uncalled for. Euan has done nothing wrong."

Alex didn't even look at her. His eyes stayed fixed on Euan. "Ye'll empty every chamber pot and every shit bucket on this ship until I can see my reflection in the wood beneath 'em. Then ye'll scrub the crew quarters, fore and aft. Then ye'll climb the riggin' and check every rope and every sail by hand. Twice!"

Euan gaped. "All o' that, Captain?"

"Aye, all o' that," Alex snapped. "And when ye're done, ye'll sit in the crow's nest till yer arse fuses to the wood. That should keep ye from loiterin' round Yvonne when ye should be workin'."

Euan's mouth twisted. "With respect, sir, I dinnae see the harm in teachin' her how to tie a figure-eight. Are ye… jealous?"

Nzingha pressed a fist against her lips, shoulders shaking from laughter.

Alex stepped in so close their chests almost collided. "Jealous?" he repeated softly, dangerously.

"Lad, if ye say one more word, I'll toss ye overboard and let the fish decide if ye're worth keepin'. I'm no' payin' ye to flirt with my guests. I ken your type. You're like a snake waitin' for a warm rock. Next time I see ye lay a hand on her, ye'll be on a rowboat with no wages and no teeth. Are we clear?"

Euan swallowed. "Aye, Captain. Clear as glass."

"Good," Alex growled. "Now move."

Euan hurried off, shoulders tight.

Yvonne spun on Alex. "That was unnecessary."

He finally looked at her, and the mix of fury and fear in his eyes made her stomach flip.

"It was necessary," he said low. "Ye dinnae know him. Hell, I dinnae know him. Ye cannae trust every man that shows ye his teeth."

Yvonne lifted her chin. "At least he speaks to me. At least he does not hide after taking what is precious. Euan has been kind and respectful. So much more than I can say for you this day."

That cut deep. He exhaled through his nose, fighting for control.

"Get back below deck," he said, voice tight. "It's no place for ye up here."

She gave him a small, mocking bow. "As you wish, Captain."

She turned and walked away, hips swaying with a little more defiance than usual. Nzingha caught up to her, looping their arms together as they both fought not to laugh outright.

Behind them, Alex stalked toward his quarters, muttering curses under his breath, rage and dread tangling in his chest.

The Cost of Silence

That evening, the four of them gathered in Andrew and Nzingha's quarters for supper.
The table was laid simply, stew, bread, a jug of ale, but a heavy silence hung over everything like fog. Yvonne sat across from Alex, eyes on her plate, posture perfect. Not once did she glance his way.

Nzingha noticed. So did Andrew.

Christ, what have ye done now, arseling?

Andrew thought, watching his brother's tight jaw, Yvonne's stiff shoulders, his wife's narrowed eyes.

He cleared his throat, breaking the quiet.

"So, Yvonne," Andrew called, aiming for warmth. "Tell me, what is it like in the Oyomo lands? Are they as beautiful as Tafaria's kingdom?"

Yvonne's face softened a little at the memory.

"It is beautiful, but not as grand, I come from a smaller village where my father was chief. He never allowed me to explore much beyond our grounds."

"I see," Andrew said, smiling faintly. "I suspect I may be the same with my wee lass, Destiny. Overprotective. That is, if Nzingha does not set the boundaries first."

Nzingha's mouth curved. "Husband, I will make sure she is protected," she said pointedly, still glaring at Alex. "No man will ever have the opportunity to take advantage of her mind or her body."

Alex's hand stilled around his spoon. The words landed heavy, direct as a punch. A dark look flickered over his face.

Yvonne glanced between them, unease stirring.

"So, how long have you two been wed?"

"All of twenty moons now," Andrew said, eyes warming as they settled on his wife.

"Oh my, newlyweds still. You are fortunate. Princess Nzingha is highly spoken of in our lands. There are many stories about her skills as a warrior."

Nzingha preened just a little. "Are there?" she asked with mock modesty.

Yvonne was quiet for a time, studying the way Andrew looked at his wife, like there was no one else in the world. Then she glanced at Alex.

He ate mechanically, gaze fixed on his bowl, ignoring her as if she were part of the furniture.

Her chest tightened.

"Alex," she said suddenly.

He didn't look up. "Hm?"

"Today, Euan showed me how to tie a figure eight knot," she said, voice light. "He is so much fun to be around. When we return to your lands, he will show me how to hunt with a musket."

Alex's knife slipped from his fingers and clattered against the plate.

"Dinnae be daft. Ye'll no be goin anywhere with him." he said, finally lifting his head.

"Why not?" she asked calmly.

"Yes, Alex," Nzingha added, eyes wide with innocent malice. "Why not?"

Andrew laid a hand on her wrist under the table, a mute plea for restraint. She ignored it.

Alex set his utensils down slowly. "Because ye dinnae know him," he said. "Hell, I dinnae know him. He could be any sort of perverted fool. I told ye before, stay away from him."

Yvonne's eyes flashed. "Euan has been nothing but kind," she said. "He at least keeps me occupied by teaching me things. He respects me, which is more than I can say for you this day."

Her chair scraped as she stood. She bowed her head politely to Andrew and Nzingha, pointedly skipping Alex.

"Excuse me, I must take my leave. Andrew, Nzingha, I bid you good evening."

She walked out without a backward glance.

For a moment, only the soft creak of the ship filled the room.

Then Nzingha slammed her hand flat on the table, rattling the dishes. "Fool!" she rounded on him, "How could you just let her leave without saying a word? How can you be so selfish? Go after her, you stubborn mule."

"Nae," Alex muttered. "She's angry. It'll pass."

Andrew frowned. "Alex," he said quietly, "she has feelings. Ye cannae just shut down and hope they disappear. Go and talk to her. Tell her something truthsome so she doesnae feel like she's naught to ye."

Alex stared at his bowl for a long moment, then tossed his napkin aside and pushed to his feet.

"Fine," he muttered, and left.

He walked the now familiar corridor to her cabin. For the first time, he knocked and waited.

"Yes?" came her muffled voice.

"'Tis me, Alex."

A pause. Then, flatly, "What do you want?"

"I came to apologize. May I come in? Please."

Silence filled the small area.

Then the door opened a crack. She peeked, her brown eyes sharp on him. She stepped back, arms folded, eyes swollen from crying.

He stepped inside but remained near the door, folding his arms across his chest, gaze fixed somewhere near her shoulder.

"Listen," he said, voice rough. "I'm sorry. I shouldnae have ignored ye the whole day. Ye didnae deserve that."

"Is that all?" she asked quietly. "You do not care for me?"

He shifted. "I do care for ye."

"But are you in love with me?" she pressed.

Silence.

"Alex," she said, throat tightening, "look at me. Do you love me?"

He forced himself to meet her eyes. They were raw, shining with hurt. It clawed at him, but the words would not come.

"Yvonne," he said finally, "I cannae answer that. Do no force me to say things I'm no ready to live by. Ye ken what my life is like in Scotland. I am not ready."

Her head tipped back as if struck.

"So why would you?" she whispered. "You knew I was a virgin. You knew how hard I fought to remain so. And still, you took that from me."

His temper spiked, a shield against the guilt.

"Excuse me?" he snapped. "Nae. I tried to leave, and you all but threw yourself at me. Do no' twist this to make me the villain. Ye knew what ye were doin' when ye undressed and climbed into a tub barely big enough for one. That is the oldest trick in the bloody book, lass."

Slap.

The crack of her hand against his cheek was sharp and immediate.

"Get out!" she snapped loudly.

He touched his jaw, stunned. "Yvonne."

"I said get out." Her voice went soft with hurt.

For a heartbeat, he hovered, torn between reaching for her and obeying. Then, muttering a curse under his breath, he turned and left.

The door shut behind him with a dull thud.

Inside, Yvonne stood frozen for a moment, then crumpled forward onto the bed, sobs tearing out of her chest. She pressed her face into the pillow to muffle the sound, but they still shook her from head to toe, leaking into the hall.

Outside, Alex lingered, listening to her wails, his palm splayed flat against the wood. He closed his eyes, every instinct screaming at him to go back in, to hold her, to fix it.

Instead, he dropped his hand, squared his shoulders, and walked away, each step heavier than the last.

Gone

They reached Tantallon at first light.

"LAND HO!" a crewman shouted from above.

Alex, who had barely slept, stepped onto the deck with a heaviness in his bones. He shaded his eyes, seeing the distant, jagged outline of familiar cliffs, the promise of home.

"Drop anchor!" he called.

"Aye, Captain!"

"Cast skiffs!" Haemish bellowed.

Andrew came to his side, cloak flapping in the morning wind. "Where's Nzingha?" Alex asked.

"She went to fetch Yvonne; someone had to tell her we were leaving." Andrew replied

"What did ye expect me to do? She'll no' speak to me."

"You're a whore," Andrew said without malice. "If I were her, I'd no' speak to ye either."

Alex shot him a look. "And yet ye still do. So shut up."

Before Andrew could retort, Nzingha approached, skirts swaying, her face drawn tight. A folded parchment shook slightly in her hand.

"Yvonne is gone," she said.

The words punched the breath from Alex's lungs.

"What?" he demanded. "How the hell did she leave the ship?"

As if on cue, another sailor shouted, "Captain! Anchor's set, but one o' the skiffs is missin'!"

Alex's blood turned cold.

"No one leaves this ship," he snapped. "Haemish, guard the gold."

"Aye, Captain."

Nzingha thrust the parchment at Alex. "Brace yourself. The news is not good."

Alex unfolded the letter with numb fingers.

Alex,

You once told me to trust you, and I did. Yet now you have cast me aside. I do not wish to travel to your home. I do not wish to see your face. Each time I look at you, I am filled with resentment.

Euan has offered to escort me to Andrew and Nzingha's home. Tell them I am sorry.

Yvonne.

The words blurred.

He crushed the parchment in his fist. "After all I've done for that lass, she chooses to follow an arse in a strange land? Does she no' listen to anything I say?"

Andrew stepped closer. "Where did she go?"

Alex hurled the balled paper into the sea. "With Euan," he ground out. "That crewman who's been creepin' round her, tryin' to get under her skirts. She thinks he's takin' her to your home."

"How would he even ken where we live? He's never set foot in Leith."

"It's trickery," Alex spat. "A way to lure her off the ship. I cannae believe she's this naive."

Nzingha laid a hand on his shoulder. "She is hurt, she gave you something sacred, hoping you would return something just as precious. For months, you lay beside her in innocence. She shared her horrors with you. Perhaps she gave you more than you deserve."

A vision of Sophie slammed into him. The last night he'd seen her, the way she'd tried to speak, to confess something, and how he'd shunned her, pushed her away. She had left in tears, resulting in her death.

He swallowed hard.

"I'll no' let it happen again," he muttered.

"Andrew," he said aloud, turning to his brother, "when you and Nzingha reach the castle, send for three more skiffs and enough men to secure the gold. Pay the crew their share, lock the rest away. Make sure ye've decent security."

"Of course," Andrew said.

"I'll gather volunteers for a search party, we ride after them. I will no' sit here while she wanders Scotland with a man I dinnae trust."

"Alex," Haemish said quietly, "look at the men. They're exhausted."

Alex glanced around. He saw it now, the sagging shoulders, the hollow cheeks, the way some of them leaned on the rail as if their bones ached.

He drew in a breath, then raised his voice. "Listen up!" he called. "My friend has gone ashore with Euan. Does anyone ken him or where he's from?"

There was a murmur, then one sailor stepped forward, rubbing the back of his neck.

"I've seen him at a few brothels in port, Captain, never spoke to him much. But he's no' right in the head. Somethin's loose up there."

Alex's jaw clenched. "I will pay five men one hundred and fifty Crowns each if they ride with me to find her," he announced. "You'll have rest when we return with her safe."

For a moment, no one moved.

Then one hand went up. Another. And another, until five men stood ready.

"Good. I promise ye, your help will no' be in vain."

Into the Wilderness

Yvonne's heart hammered as the small skiff scraped against the stones of the riverbank.
Euan hopped out first, then turned and lifted her easily into his arms, carrying her to the shore. She clutched at his shoulders until her feet touched the damp moss.

"Oh my," she breathed, spinning slowly. "Everything is so rich and green."

Rolling hills stretched beneath a grey sky, dotted with trees and threaded by a glittering river. Birds called overhead. The air smelled of earth, water, and something sharp and cold she did not yet know the name for.

"We'll no' linger at the water," Euan said, pulling the skiff further ashore. "I need to fetch a horse. Leith is a fair distance."

"How far?" she asked.

"Two days' walk," he said. "Maybe less with a good beast under us. Dinnae worry. I can set snares, catch us meat."

"So many trees," she murmured. "Will we be safe from wild animals?"

He smiled. "Only wee creatures in these parts. As long as the heavens dinnae open on us, we'll be fine."

They walked for hours along a narrow path through the trees. Yvonne's feet, unaccustomed to such a journey, began to throb. Finally, she slowed.

"Euan, my feet… may we stop to rest?"

"Aye," he said at once. "We'll make camp here."

He led her to a fallen tree and shrugged off his tartan, draping it around her shoulders. She pulled it close, grateful for the extra warmth, and watched as he moved about with practiced efficiency, gathering wood, striking flint, coaxing a small fire to life.

All of it felt strangely unreal. Just yesterday, she had been on a ship surrounded by men she knew by name. Now she was here, alone with one man in a land she did not understand.

"Euan?" she asked as he worked. "Is there anything I can assist with?"

He glanced up, smiling. "Aye. Sit right there and keep lookin' bonnie."

Her cheeks warmed. She settled more firmly on the log, trying not to fidget.

"I'll be back in a bit," he said, picking up a makeshift spear. "Need to find us some supper."

She nodded. "Be careful."

When he vanished into the trees, the silence closed in. Sounds she had not noticed before rose up. The rustle of leaves, the distant rush of the river, the whisper of wind between branches.

"Did I make the right choice?" she whispered to herself. "Leaving the ship like this? Not going to Alex's castle?"

She hugged the tartan tighter.

A sudden rustle in the underbrush snapped her head up. She grabbed a nearby fallen branch and held it out like a staff, heart pounding.

"Who is there?" she called.

Euan stepped out, grinning, a limp rabbit dangling from his hand.

She dropped the stick, exhaling hard. "My, that was quick."

She looked at the animal and, without thinking, spoke in her tongue. *"Nyama ya sungura?"*

He laughed. "What did ye say?"

"In my lands," she said, smiling faintly, "we call that meat *nyama ya sungura.*"

"Oh, the rabbit?" he chuckled. "Aye. Rabbit. 'Tis delicious."

She repeated it carefully. "Rab… bit. Rabbit." She brightened a little. "I am happy to learn more English words. I learned some at home, but it was not until I traveled to Tafaria that the Prince, now King, gave me a proper teacher."

Euan said little, only listened as he skinned the rabbit, skewered it on a stick, and set it over the flames.

"Do you live with your family?" she asked after a moment.

He paused, staring into the fire. "Aye, I do."

"Oh, that must be nice," Yvonne said, a wistful note in her voice. "I miss living with my mother and sisters. Before my father signed my life away to a king."

His head turned. "You're married?"

"We never consummated the marriage," she replied quickly. "I ran away."

An odd light flickered in his eyes. "So ye've never had a man inside ye?" he asked, voice low, too curious.

She froze.

The question slithered over her skin. His gaze had changed, no longer friendly, but sharp and hungry. She pulled the tartan tighter around herself, a shiver running through her.

"That is an inappropriate question," she said, forcing her voice steady. She managed a brittle laugh. "Look at me. What man would wish for me? Before the king saw me, he cast me aside. He did not even want to consummate the marriage."

Euan bit into a fig, chewing slowly as he watched the flames. "The captain wants ye," he said at last. "He slept in yer cabin every night. Some of the crew wondered if ye were a whore he brought back from Tafaria."

Yvonne shot to her feet. "What? How dare you!"

She spun, scanning the trees wildly. "Where is the rowboat? I am not staying here with you. I will go back myself."

"Wait!" He dropped the fig and hurried after her. "Yvonne, ye dinnae ken these woods. Ye'll get lost before ye find the water again. Forgive me. I shouldnae have said such filth. The men joked vulgar things. Everyone knows the sort o' man the captain is with women. I let their talk foul my tongue. I'm sorry. Truly."

Her eyes filled with tears again, for what felt like the hundredth time that day.

"I am not a whore," she said, voice trembling. "Alex saved me from death and worse. That is all anyone needs to know."

Euan gently reached for her shoulders, pulling her into a brief embrace. "Shh," he murmured. "Ye're right. Ye're no' that. I was an idiot. Come back to the fire; the rabbit's near done. We'll eat, we'll rest, and at first light we'll keep movin'. I'll see ye safe. Ye have my word."

She stood stiff in his arms, every instinct still wary, but she was cold, exhausted, and the shadows between the trees suddenly seemed far more dangerous than staying.

After a moment, she nodded once.

"Very well," she said quietly. "But do not speak of me that way again."

"Nae, never, ye have my apologies."

They returned to the fire, the rabbit sizzling between them, the silence carrying all the unease neither dared to voice.

The Hunt Begins

Hooves thundered over damp earth as Alex rode, the wind tearing at his hair, his cloak streaming behind him.
Five men galloped at his back, their faces set. They had barely left the harbor behind before his thoughts began to spiral.

Anything could have happened to her by now, he thought grimly. *Wolves. Raiders. Slavers on the roads. Or that son of a bitch Euan, takin' what he thinks he's owed.*

His hands tightened on the reins.

"This is my fault," he muttered under his breath. "My selfishness finally caught up with me."

For a long while, the only sounds were the rhythm of hooves and the creak of leather. Then, faint behind him, another horse's gait joined theirs.

Alex glanced back.

Andrew urged his mount alongside his brother's with a snort of effort. "You men are movin' too slow," he said. "I left an hour after ye and still caught ye up."

Alex managed a humorless snort. "Thought ye were headed for Ireland."

"Nae, I sent Logan in my stead, but first, I went through the crofts and asked questions. I come with news."

Alex's gut twisted. "Well? Spit it out."

"Euan's from Dundee," Andrew said. "One o' the crofters, Mr. McGreggor, knew his father. Says Euan fled after hearin' a magistrate had near built a case against him. Rape. Traffickin' young women. Lassies as young as thirteen summers."

Alex felt the world narrow to a pinpoint.

His chest burned. If he had had Euan's throat in his hands at that moment, there would have been nothing left of the man to hang.

"Mr. McGreggor found him half-starved and filthy. He took pity on the man. Gave him work and a pallet. Euan heard talk of our voyage to rescue my wife. Thought the sea the perfect place to hide. Haemish recruited him, seein' only an able pair o' hands, no' the rot beneath."

Alex swore viciously. "We were already offerin' him gold," he snarled. "Why take Yvonne as well? Why risk everythin'?"

"There could be many reasons," Andrew said quietly. "She confided in him, hurt by you. He may be smitten and want her for himself. Or he means to keep her as his own private muse for his filth. Or…" His jaw tightened. "Or he plans to sell her to slavers."

Alex's stomach roiled.

Over the pounding of hooves, Sophie's face flashed in his mind, eyes glassy, skin grey, her hand slipping from his as they laid her in the ground. Another woman he had failed. Another soul who had reached for him and found indifference instead of shelter. Alex shook his head, heart wearing on his sleeve.

"Not again. Never again."

"So, what say ye brother?" Andrew asked, "do we ride through the night?"

"Aye," Alex answered without hesitation. "We'll reach a few villages outside the city by moonrise. We'll ask at taverns, inns, stables, any place they might have passed. A black lass and a twisted-headed fool with too much eagerness in his eyes. Someone will have seen them."

Andrew nodded. "Do no' give up hope, we will find her, Alex. And when we do…"

Alex squinted his eyes. "I'll carve that bastard a new asshole."

The two brothers spurred their horses faster, streaking across the darkening hills, the men behind them following into the deepening Scottish night, toward answers, toward reckoning, and toward the fragile hope that they were not yet too late.

Chapter Thirteen

Whispers in the Village

*E*uan held Yvonne by the waist as they walked along a trail within

the forest. She was exhausted and barely able to stand. When they arrived at a small village, everyone seemed to stare at her. Some frowned; others pointed. Was it because she had not had a bath in two days since they arrived?

She looked down at her filthy clothing, then observed the buildings and the people walking in and out. Euan turned to her.

"Wait here, lass. I've a friend who owns this place. He owes me a biddin'. He'll give us a horse and food for the rest o' our travel."

She nodded, watching him walk away. People continued to stare, making her feel terribly uncomfortable. Out of nowhere, two ladies approached her. One greeted her warmly.

"Hello, lass. My, ye're a bonnie one. I've always heard about yer kind. Fancy seein' ye in Scotland. Are ye with yer master?"

Yvonne answered softly. "Apologies, I do not understand. My what?"

"Yer master. Yer owner. Ye've a strange accent. Where do ye hail from?"

"My apologies. I have no master, and I hail from lands in Africa. I am with a friend named Euan. He is aiding me in finding Lord Andrew Barton, who resides in Leith."

"Africa? My, that must be thousands o' miles away. But did ye say ye were goin' tae Leith? With the man ye arrived with, Euan?"

"Yes."

The two women exchanged looks, lips pressed together.

"Lass… are ye in some sort o' trouble?" one asked.

"No. Euan is a good person. He is helping me."

The other woman spoke. "Well, I'm Mary, and this is Agatha. If ye need assistance, do not hesitate tae find us. But have a care with Euan, sweetheart. There've been rumors. He's a bad man."

"Euan? No. He has been honorable and has not placed a finger upon me since I arrived."

Euan stepped out of the tavern with food in hand. All three women looked at him. When he glimpsed Yvonne, her eyes held fear.

Euan forced a smile. "Good day, ladies. Yvonne, I have a horse. We should reach our destination before nightfall."

Agatha spoke. "Hello, Euan. Do ye remember me?"

"Aye. How could I forget? Ye charged me double the coin for a ten-minute hand job."

He took Yvonne by the hand and walked away without another word. As they walked to the horse, Yvonne observed him. It seemed he avoided her gaze.

She asked quietly, "Euan, who are those ladies? Do you know them?"

"Aye. They work in the brothel across the way."

He helped Yvonne climb atop the horse, then sat behind her.

She said nothing during the journey, taken aback by how beautiful the land was. The path was long and empty, with not a soul in sight.

Her weariness grew as a small wooden house appeared in the distance.

Euan slowed the horse and got off, but she pushed his hand away before he could assist her.

Her fears surged. "This cannot be Andrew and Nzingha's home. Where did you bring me?"

"This is my home, lass."

"Your home? Why are we here? You said we would reach our destination before nightfall, and it is now dusk. Euan, do not jest."

He sighed. "Listen, lass. I'm tired. My home's on the way tae theirs. Will ye spend the entire night on a horse, or come inside for a hot meal an' a bath?"

"No. Please, I do not wish to go inside. May we continue the journey?"

Euan looked away and said nothing. Then, in one swift motion, he grabbed her from atop the horse and slung her over his shoulder. Yvonne kicked and screamed in fear.

"Quit all this carryin' on!" he barked. "I only want us tae rest."

He opened the door, stepped inside, and placed her feet on the ground.

"There. Was that so bad? Wait here. I'm goin' tae fetch us some things."

Before he walked away, she shouted, "Alex and those women were right. They said you were a bad man. But I vouched for you!"

"Maybe ye should've listened tae them, then."

Euan took a skeleton key and stepped outside. The door locked from the other side. Panic overtook her, and she broke into tears.

The Trail West

They reached the tavern just beyond the city as dusk thickened the air. Alex reined in hard and swung down from his horse before it fully stopped. "Split up," he ordered the men without preamble. "Ask everywhere. Taverns, stables, streets. A black lass travelin' with a man in a green tartan. Meet back here within the hour. If we've no word by the witchin' hour, go home. Ye'll have yer wages when we return."

The men scattered at once, boots pounding in different directions.

Andrew stayed at his side.

Alex shoved open the tavern door, the sketch of Yvonne already clenched in his fist. Heat, ale, and sweat hit them full in the face. Laughter stuttered and then resumed.

He went straight to the bar.

"Have ye seen her?" he asked, laying the drawing flat. "African lass. Skin like almond seed. She was travelin' with a man named Euan."

The bartender slowed his wiping, eyes narrowing as he studied the page. "Can't say I've seen 'em myself," he said at last. "But I heard talk. Guests mentioned a woman like that passin' through."

Alex leaned in. "Where?"

The man jerked his chin toward the door. "Brothel across the way."

They were already turning.

Inside, perfume and smoke wrapped around them. Two bare chested women caught Andrew's arms at once, laughing. He pulled free, ears reddening, though his eyes betrayed him.

"I'm sorry," he muttered. "I'm no' here for that."

Alex didn't slow. He lifted the sketch again. "I'm lookin' for her. Chestnut-skinned. African. Traveled with a man in a green tartan. His name's Euan."

The women exchanged a look.

"Aye," one said slowly. "Agatha an' I saw them in the mornin'. We ken Euan well. He's a regular."

Mary leaned closer, squinting at the drawing. "That's her. Big brown eyes, slanted. White dress. I told her Euan was a bad man, but she wouldnae hear it. Said he was honorable."

Alex's pulse jumped. "Which way did they go?"

"West," Mary said. "They took a horse. Try the stables."

"Where?" Andrew pressed.

"Three corners down. Left."

They found the stable by the smell.

A man was shoveling manure, back bent, ignoring them entirely until Alex produced a small bag of coins and let it chime once.

The shovel stopped.

"A man take a horse from ye yesterday?" Alex asked.

The stable owner eyed the gold. "Aye. Distant cousin o' mine. Name's Euan. Why?"

"He's travelin' with a friend," Alex said tightly. "Do ye ken where they went?"

The man hesitated. "No' exact. But head west. There's a path that cuts right into the forest. He's got a place out there."

Alex dropped the coins into his hand. "My Thanks."

"Nae," the man said quietly, closing his fingers around them. "Thank *you.*"

Alex was already turning back toward the road.

The Truth He Couldn't Outrun

The cabin door flew open, and Euan stepped inside with a bucket of water, placing it beside the hearth.

"Are ye feelin' better, lass?"

"No. You have me here against my will. I wish to go to Nzingha."

He stood and walked back outside, returning with a roasted pig. Placing it on the table, he carved slices.

"Why should I let ye leave?"

"Because you are my friend. That is what friends do. They assist each other."

"Come sit an' eat."

She shook her head. "No. I am not hungry."

Euan stabbed the knife into the table, strode toward her, and seized her by the hair.

"When I speak, ye listen. That is how it'll be."

Thoughts of King Oyomo clouded her mind, but she held her ground.

"Ouch, let go of me! You're hurting me!" she cried, then spat in his face.

His slap whipped across her cheek, sending her crashing to the floor. She scrambled to the corner in fear.

"Look what ye made me do," he growled. "I dinnae like violence, but ye force my hand when ye disobey. Now get o'er here an' eat."

She was too frightened to move. Euan took three long strides, dragged her by the arm, and forced her into the chair. He shoved the plate at her. Her hands trembled as she took it.

"There now. Was that so hard? Ye're a stubborn lass. I dinnae wish tae harm ye, but I will if ye make me. Do as I say, an' ye'll have nae problems. When ye're done with what I prepared, yer bath will be ready."

Yvonne sniffled softly as she ate. Tears rolled down her cheeks. She wondered if her life was cursed when it came to men. Her husband had been abusive. Euan was the same. Alex and Femi, two men she loved, hurt her in different ways.

No One Hurts Her Again

Alex and Andrew rode hard through the forest, branches whipping past as dusk crept in. Alex's chest tightened with every mile.
He could not shake the image of Yvonne, alone, afraid, trusting the wrong man because he had pushed her away.

If Euan harmed her. Alex did not know if he could live with himself.

Ahead, Andrew slowed and stopped beside a narrow stream. The horses trembled, froth at their mouths.

"Alex… we must let them drink," Andrew said quietly.

Alex wanted to protest, to push forward, to ignore everything but the fear clawing inside him, but he finally slid off the saddle.

The moment his boots hit the ground, a heavy silence wrapped around the brothers.

Andrew watched him a long while before speaking.

"Ye're actin' the same way I did when Uncle Graham took Nzingha," he said gently. "A man doesnae ride himself half to death unless he loves the lass."

Alex dragged a hand through his hair, breath unsteady.

"I'm confused, Andrew. None of this should have happened. When I first saw her, I acted like the arrogant bastard everyone says I am. She wanted nothin' tae do with me, and rightfully so."

He looked toward the darkening forest, guilt weighing on his features.

"But then… I learned her pain. I saw the way she flinched at raised voices, the way she tried tae hide her fear. I wanted tae protect her, be gentle, be better."

His voice cracked.
"And instead I failed her. She trusted me, and I left her cryin' on the other side of that cabin door. I broke her trust. She must hate me."

Andrew's expression softened, his tone calm and sure.
"It sounds tae me like ye grew up, brother. Ye're no' runnin' from your feelings anymore. Ye must face it. Ye're in love with her."

Alex stared at him, stunned, shaken, and whispered,
"Love?"

"Aye," Andrew said simply, as if it were the most obvious truth in the world.

He mounted his horse and rode a few paces ahead, giving Alex space to sit with the words he had avoided for far too long.

No One Hurts Her Again

Yvonne watched Euan like a hawk as he poured hot water into the wooden tub.
His face was unreadable, too calm, too collected, and that frightened her most.

"Come, lass. Yer bath is ready," he said quietly.

"I refuse to bathe with you in the room."

He lowered his head, almost as if disappointed, though the twisting of his mouth told a more dangerous truth.

"Do ye want me tae strip ye myself? Ye'll no' like how that ends."

She froze, breath catching.
Her fingers trembled against her torn dress.

"Fine... just move away from the tub," she whispered.

He stepped aside, but not far.

His shadow loomed over the corner as she undressed slowly, painfully aware of his eyes tracking every movement.
She slipped into the warm water, but instead of comfort, the heat stung her nerves. His smirk followed her like a stain.

"When I first saw ye," he murmured, voice thick with something twisted, "I couldnae believe the beauty before my eyes. Each night the captain went tae yer quarters, it burned me inside.

I've fallen deep for ye. I've never wanted a woman before… especially yer kind."

Her stomach knotted.
She watched his hand as it moved towards his intimate area, he touched himself shamelessly, while he stared.
Her skin crawled.

"Get out o' the tub," he said suddenly.

She blinked. "What?"

"Get. Out. O' the tub."

Her breath quickened. Still shaking, she rose from the water.

He stepped close, the smell of sweat and ale clinging to him.

"Please… no…" she whispered.

Euan grabbed her breast with a greedy hand, his mouth pressing against her wet skin. She whimpered as his hardened body pushed against her.

"Let go of me! No!"

She twisted sharply, driving her knee into his groin.

He collapsed forward with a groan.

Heart racing, Yvonne darted toward the door and fumbled with the handle.

Locked.

"Help! Someone, please!" she cried, pounding the wood.

Euan lunged at her from behind, rage twisting his face. His fist struck her ribs.

A loud, sickening crack filled the room.

She collapsed, agony tearing through her chest.

She screamed.

"Please... no... you're hurting me..." she sobbed.

He kicked her once, hard, sending fresh pain spiraling through her body.

Outside, a voice thundered through the trees.

"YVONNE! IS THAT YE?!"

Her heart surged.

"ALEX! PLEASE HELP ME!" she screamed.

The door burst open, wood splintering as it tore from its hinges.

Alex hit Euan like a storm breaking loose.

He drove him backward, slamming him hard into the wall. The impact rattled the cabin, jars jumping, firelight shuddering. Euan grunted as the breath was crushed from his chest.

"You son of a bitch!"

Alex's fist crashed into Euan's face. Once. Twice. Bone gave way with a wet crack, blood spraying the wall behind him.

Euan clawed at Alex, wild and desperate, but Alex seized his shirt and drove his head into the timber again. And again.

Euan slid downward, dazed, choking, his knees buckling beneath him.

Alex drew back for another blow, vision red, hands shaking with fury, ready to finish it.

"Alex!" Andrew shouted.

He rushed in and seized his brother from behind, hauling him back with all his strength. "Enough!"

Alex fought him for a heartbeat, chest heaving, teeth bared like an animal.

"He hurt her," Alex snarled. "He touched her."

"I know," Andrew said, breathless, strained. "I know. But step back."

Euan coughed, a thin, broken laugh slipping through blood as he staggered to his feet. He wiped his mouth with the back of his hand, eyes glittering with spite.

"That's right," he sneered. "Pull him off. See? You're no—"

His hand darted for the table.

"KNIFE!" Andrew shouted.

Euan lunged, blade flashing in the firelight.

Alex tore free.

The musket was in his hands in one brutal, instinctive motion.

The shot thundered through the cabin.

Euan crumpled to the floor, lifeless

Silence fell, thick and ringing.

Andrew rushed in at once, turning Yvonne's face into his shoulder as her scream tore through the room. He covered her eyes, shielding her from the sight, and wrapped her naked body in his plaid before lifting her carefully into his arms.

"Lass…" he murmured, voice gentle and steady. "Where does it hurt?"

"Beneath my breast…" she whispered, each breath shallow and broken. "It hurts to breathe…"

Alex dropped to his knees in front of her, his face torn between fury and terror.

"Thank the heavens, Yvonne," he said hoarsely. "I searched everywhere for ye."

His gaze swept over her bruises, the torn skin, the trembling of her body. He looked away at once, jaw tightening until it shook.

"He… he did not have a chance to force himself inside me," she sobbed. "You came just in time. But my side… something is broken…"

Alex tore off his blouse and slid it beneath Andrew's plaid, padding her ribs with careful, trembling hands.

"Ouch…" she cried softly. "It hurts so badly… please… put me down…"

"Aye," Alex murmured at once. "Easy, lass."

He guided Andrew to lower her onto a patch of soft grass, then leaned close, examining the bruising along her ribs.

"Ye may have fractured a rib," he said, keeping his voice calm. "Andrew, ride tae the nearest town. Bring back a buggy."

Andrew didn't hesitate. He mounted his horse and disappeared into the night at full speed.

Left alone with her, Alex leaned down and pressed a tender kiss to her forehead.

"Ye're so brave," he whispered. "Come… I must get ye off the cold ground."

She shook her head violently, panic surging.

"No… please, no… I do not wish to go back inside. Please… not in there…"

Her entire body trembled as the scent of Euan drifted from the open doorway.

"But Yvonne," Alex said gently, "the ground will only bring ye more discomfort."

She sobbed harder.

He gathered her into his arms, slow and steady, rocking her slightly.

"Shh…" he murmured. "Ye're safe now. Not a soul will harm ye again. I swear it."

She rested her head against his chest, tears soaking into his shirt.

"Alex…" she whispered. "I am sorry. I did not listen. Euan lied. He tricked me. He planned to keep me here forever… and if I did not obey… he was going to beat me. Why are men so cruel?"

Alex's breath hitched.

"None o' this is yer fault," he said quietly. "Euan saw ye as delicate and used it tae manipulate ye. Not all men are cruel, Yvonne… ye just havenae met one worth trustin' yet."

He swallowed hard.

"When ye disappeared," he admitted, "I nearly lost my mind. I care for ye… deeply. I acted like an ass… and I'm sorry."

He lifted her hand and kissed it, his lips trembling.

"Please… forgive me."

Night settled around them as Andrew returned with the buggy.

"That was quick," Alex said, rising.

"Aye," Andrew replied. "I found a small farm nearby. They sold it tae me for one gold crown. I brought blankets for the lass as well."

"What about the body?" Andrew asked quietly.

"I'll bury him," Alex said. "Behind the cabin."

"Good," Andrew muttered. "Let him rot in his hellhole."

He knelt beside Yvonne and held out his arm.

"Can ye stand, lass?"

"Yes…" she whispered, clinging to him. "I can."

The World Unmasked

Hours later, they reached the inn where the brothers had agreed to regroup.

Alex carried Yvonne inside, her head resting weakly against his chest.

The innkeeper glanced between them, uneasy.

"How may I assist ye this eve?"

"I need a room for the lass," Alex said.

The man hesitated. "We… are out of rooms."

Alex's jaw tightened. "You cannae be serious. Ye said earlier ye had availability. Is this because I'm with her? She is injured."

The innkeeper swallowed. "We… do not offer lodging for her kind."

A heavy silence fell.

Alex's temper snapped. He kicked a chair aside, still holding Yvonne carefully in his arms.

"What?" His voice trembled with fury. "How much?"

"Five crowns," the innkeeper whispered.

Alex stepped in close, lowering his voice to something cold and controlled.

"Ye dinnae ken who I am now… but when I return, ye will, for the rest o' yer life. That, I swear."

He turned sharply and carried Yvonne outside, her soft whimpers making him hold her even more carefully.

Once clear of the door, Alex bent his head, his voice barely above a whisper.

"I know it hurts. We'll have ye home an' safe, my love."

The words slipped out before he could stop them.

He stiffened. Had she heard?

Andrew approached, glancing toward the inn.

"Come," he said quietly. "Let's leave before a mob comes complainin'."

The Long Road

The road to Leith stretched under a sky streaked with autumn grays and golds. Andrew held the reins, guiding the wagon steadily, while

Alex sat beside him, tense and silent. Behind them, Yvonne lay wrapped in Andrew's plaid, her breathing shallow and pained.

For a long time, neither brother spoke.

At last, Andrew broke the silence. "Ye ken the looks will never stop, Alex. Folks will stare. They stared at Nzingha the same way when I brought her home. They whispered, wondered if she belonged."

Alex exhaled, his voice low. "I remember. And now I feel like a damned fool for ever judging her. She was always beautiful."

"Aye, she was. Still is." Andrew kept his eyes on the road. "People fear what they dinnae understand. But Yvonne's strong, like Nzingha."

Alex's jaw tightened. "I'm still furious. That tavern keeper was vile. We should've burned the place down."

"Aye, but ye did right getting her out," Andrew said quietly.

They fell silent again.

After a moment, Alex murmured, almost to himself, "How will ye raise Destiny, Andrew? Bein' half-black and half-white… she'll face challenges the other children won't."

"There's nae doubt about that," Andrew replied. "But it's my job as her father to make sure she knows who she is. She'll learn the history of both her parents. And she'll ken that love has no boundaries."

Alex nodded slowly. "Ye know, brother, I admire how ye handle life's hardships. Da would've been proud of ye."

Andrew looked over, surprised. "Truly? Why d'ye say that?"

Alex chuckled softly. "Because ye never gave up on me, for one. Ye helped me grow past my reckless ways. Ye stood up to the clan elders. And, ye know, our grandsire was half-gypsy himself. There was a stir when he married into the clan."

Andrew blinked. "I never knew that."

"Where d'ye think ye get these dark curls from?" Alex said, a hint of humor in his voice.

They shared a brief laugh, then quieted as Yvonne groaned softly in the back. Andrew slowed the wagon, mindful of her pain.

Alex glanced back at her. "Ye've always been there for me, Andrew. I just hope I can be as strong."

Andrew smiled. "Ye will be. Even if ye still have a bit of the lad in ye."

"Shut up, Andrew," Alex said, a smile tugging at his lips.

They rode on in silence, the bond between them strengthened in the cool autumn air.

Chapter Fourteen

Beneath The Autum Skies

*T*hey stopped when the light deserted them.

Andrew guided the wagon off the road into a small hollow sheltered by bare-branched trees. The autumn wind cut sharp across the open fields, and the sky had sunk into a bruised purple by the time he pulled the horses to a halt.

"We'll camp here," he said quietly. "The beasts need rest… and so does she."

Alex climbed down first, boots crunching on scattered leaves. He moved to the back of the wagon and peered beneath the plaid where Yvonne lay curled on her side. Even in the dim light, he could see the tight line of her mouth, the sheen of sweat on her brow.

"Yvonne?" His voice gentled. "We'll no' ride further this night. Ye'll be warmer by a fire."

Her lashes fluttered. She said nothing.

He slid his arms beneath her and lifted her slowly, careful of her ribs. She gasped, pain flaring across her face.

"Easy, lass," he murmured. "I've got ye."

Andrew had already laid his plaid close to where he was kindling a fire. Alex lowered her there and tucked the wool around her shoulders. Andrew coaxed a small flame to life, feeding it with dry twigs until it caught and began to glow, warm light spilling over their faces.

The world shrank to the circle of firelight, the hush of the forest, and Yvonne's ragged breaths.

Andrew rose, dusting his hands. "I'll see tae the horses," he said. "Let them drink from the stream yonder." He left them, his figure fading into the dark.

Alex sat cross-legged at Yvonne's side. He held his hands toward the fire for a moment, then laid one gently over hers.

"Are ye warm enough?"

"Yes," she whispered. "The shaking has slowed."

He watched her for a time in silence. Her skin glowed bronze and shadow by the flames, her hair loose and wild around her face. Every wince stabbed him.

"Yvonne," he said at last, voice low, "if ye'd stayed with us, none o' this would have happened."

She turned her face away. "If you had not pushed me away, I would not have gone."

The truth stung more than any blow.

He exhaled, long and tired. "Aye. I deserve that."

For a while they listened to the fire crackle, to the quiet murmur of Andrew talking softly to the horses in the distance. The air smelled of smoke, damp earth, and the faint salt of the sea carried on the wind.

"When I was ten-and-seven," Alex said quietly, "my friends dragged me tae a brothel."

Her gaze slid back to his.

"Why are you telling me this?" she asked.

"Because if I dinnae say it now, I never will." He stared into the flames. "Most o' the women there were… hard. Life had carved them that way. But there was one lass that wasnae. She was soft-spoken. Afraid. Stuck in a life she didnae choose. I thought…" He gave a humorless laugh. "I thought I could save her."

He rubbed a hand over his jaw.

"I planned tae take her away from that place. Give her coin. A cottage. A different life. Before I could say a word, Da came stormin' in with half the clan behind him. He called her every foul name ye can imagine. She broke right in front o' me."

Yvonne's brows drew together.

"What happened to her?"

"The next night, I went back." His voice roughened. "She was with another man. Old enough tae be her grandsire. I'd been a young, foolish lad back then… thought she'd wait for me. But survival doesnae wait on promises."

He picked up a twig and snapped it clean in two.

"Years later, I saw her again. Married tae a brute. He'd beat her bloody just for speakin' tae me. I took her away that night. Provided her with food. Shelter. Safety."

His throat flexed as he swallowed.

"She cared for me in the only way she ken how. I couldnae give her what she wanted. So… she ran."

His eyes darkened.

"I went after her…"

He gave a long pause, watching the fire crack softly.

"When I found her… it was too late."

He exhaled through his nose.

"The lass was attacked by wolves. They left her barely noticeable, with nae one tae mourn her."

Yvonne shut her eyes, a tear slipping free.

"I couldnae save her, Yvonne," he whispered. "I thought if I kept my distance from ye, if I stayed cold, ye'd be safer. That ye wouldnae look tae me for what I dinnae ken how tae give. And yet ye still ended up in a monster's hands. Because I was a coward."

"You were not a coward," she said softly. "You warned me about Euan. I chose not to listen. This is my punishment."

His head snapped toward her. "Dinnae say that nonsense again. Ye've suffered enough punishment for ten lifetimes."

She stared into the fire, ash and ember mirrored in her dark eyes.

"Alex," she murmured, "after a year… maybe two… I wish to return to Tafaria. I do not belong here. Everywhere I go, I feel eyes. I hear whispers. Even if you wanted me, your people would not."

He swallowed. The words scraped something raw.

"Ye think I'd let them near ye?" he asked. "Any man who uses that tongue around ye will answer tae me."

"You cannot fight every man that looks at me wrong. That will not change their hearts," she replied. "They will bear it in silence, but it will be there. And you…" She hesitated. "You said it yourself. There are women you have angered. Women who may wish to harm me out of spite. I have run from enough danger. I do not wish to live in the middle of it."

He watched the firelight moving over the planes of her face. For once, he had no clever answer. Only a knot of fear and something deeper sitting in his chest.

"I care for ye," he said finally. "More than I have any right tae. When ye vanished, I felt as though someone had ripped my heart clean out. That is the truth, whether ye go or stay."

Her lips trembled.

"And yet," she whispered, "you still speak as if I am temporary. As if your affection has an end date."

He flinched.

"I dinnae ken how tae promise forever," he admitted. "I've never kept a woman longer than a handful o' nights. I'm a poor excuse for a man when it comes tae love. But I swear this much… while ye are under my roof, under my name, I will protect ye. I will honor ye. I willnae treat ye as a plaything."

A single tear slid down her cheek.

"I believe you," she said. "And I am still afraid."

He reached out and brushed the tear away with his thumb, fingers lingering against her skin.

"Rest now, lass," he murmured. "We'll speak o' the rest when ye're no' in agony."

She nodded, too drained to argue.

He lay down beside her, stretching his plaid over them both, his body a warm barrier between her and the night. For a long time, he stared up at the cold scatter of stars, listening to her unsteady breathing.

Behind the fire, Andrew returned and settled on the other side, saying nothing. He watched his brother's arm around the injured woman, the tenderness in his posture, and smiled to himself in the dark.

Morning would bring more trouble.

But for now, they slept.

Shadows in The Manner

By the time the stone walls of Andrew's Leith manor rose into view, the sky had paled to a washed-out blue. The chimneys smoked, and the sea wind carried the smell of coal and wet stone.

Two guards in Barton colors stepped forward as the wagon rumbled up the drive. One, broad-shouldered, with a crooked nose, lifted a hand.

"Open the gate," Andrew called.

"Aye, my laird," the first guard said. His name was Chris; Alex recognized him from Tantallon. Beside him, a younger man, Jordy, worked the heavy iron latch.

Their eyes slid to the wagon bed. When they spotted Yvonne wrapped in plaid, both men exchanged a look.

Andrew dismounted and passed the reins to a stable lad.

"See tae the horses," he said. "They've been ridden hard."

"Aye, Laird Andrew."

Alex moved to the back of the wagon.

"Yvonne," he murmured, "we're at the house. I'll carry ye in, aye?"

Her eyes fluttered open. The journey had leeched what little color remained from her face.

"I will try not to scream," she whispered.

He gathered her carefully into his arms. She bit her lip against a cry as her broken rib protested.

Chris watched openly as they passed, head tilted.

"Saints," he muttered under his breath. "Never thought I'd see the day."

Jordy gave a low whistle, "Ye mean tae tell me the Chieftain brought a dark-skinned lass home? Wait till the maids hear o' this."

Andrew shot them a warning look. "Mind yer tongues," he said sharply. "She is a guest in this house."

"Aye, Laird," they answered together, though their smirks lingered as they swung the gate wider.

Inside, the manor was quieter than the castle, its halls lined with simple tapestries and polished wood. Alex climbed the stair with Yvonne held close, his jaw tight each time she winced.

He nudged open the first guest chamber with his boot.

"This will do," he said softly. "We'll settle ye here."

He laid her gently on the bed, then set about arranging pillows to lift her slightly.

"Can ye stand at all?" he asked. "I'd like tae get ye in a bath. The warmth will help."

She shook her head. "I do not think my ribs would allow it. But I feel… unclean."

He hesitated. "If ye let me, I can help. I'll keep my eyes where ye wish them."

A faint, pained smile tugged at her lips. "My body is not a stranger to you, Alex. You have already seen every part of me. I must trust that you will not take advantage while I cannot move."

His throat worked. "I willnae harm ye," he said. "On my honor."

He stepped out to fetch hot water.

Downstairs, Chris and Jordy were hauling buckets from the kitchen hearth. When they saw Alex approach, both straightened.

"Take that water tae the east guest chamber," Alex said curtly.

"Aye, Chief," Jordy replied. "For the lass?"

"For our guest," Alex corrected.

They followed him up the stairs, each carrying a steaming bucket.

Inside the chamber, Yvonne lay very still beneath the plaid. Her eyes lifted as the men entered. Chris's gaze slid over her, too slowly to be polite.

"Set it by the tub," Alex ordered.

"Aye." Jordy thumped his bucket down, then leaned close to Chris as they stepped out. Their voices carried back down the corridor.

"Ye see her?" Jordy snickered. "Wait till this place is crawlin' with blackies. First the Chieftain's brother, now him."

Chris chuckled. "Aye. Seems the Barton lads fancy strange fruit. Ye reckon he's already bedded that one? I'd nae mind a turn myself."

Their laughter echoed.

The chamber door flew open.

Before either man could blink, Alex's fists crashed into their faces, one, two, clean and brutal. Jordy slammed into the opposite wall. Chris landed hard on the floor, clutching his jaw.

"If ye wish tae keep yer posts," Alex said, his voice shaking with barely contained rage, "ye'll never let filth like that leave yer mouths again. Speak o' my sister-by-marriage or my guest that way once more, and ye'll be pickin' yer teeth out o' the courtyard mud. Are we clear?"

Blood trickled from Jordy's nose. "Aye, Chieftain," he stammered.

"Good. Now, fetch more wood for the fires. It seems the house has grown colder than I recall."

They scrambled away, cowed, leaving a spatter of red on the floorboards.

Alex shut the door and turned back to Yvonne. She was sitting up slightly, one arm across her chest, eyes wide.

"I heard them," she whispered. "Is this what I must grow used to?"

He crossed to her in three strides and knelt by the bed.

"Ye must grow used tae nothin'," he said firmly. "They will learn. Or they'll leave Barton service." His expression softened. "Ye've come through too much for me tae let a pair o' witless fools break ye now."

He helped her from the bed, careful of her side. With one arm looped around his neck and the other braced against his shoulder, she shuffled to the tub. He kept his eyes on her face as she stepped in, then knelt to pour water over her skin with a cloth.

She flinched only once, when his hand grazed the dark bloom of bruising beneath her breast.

"Does it look terrible?" she asked.

"It looks like ye survived," he answered. "That's all that matters tae me."

He washed her shoulders, arms, and back with gentle, steady strokes. Her hair loosened in the water, coils springing free.

"I have never touched your hair like this," he said quietly. "'Tis…
different. Like soft wool."

Yvonne let out a small huff of amusement. "One of many differences
between us."

"Aye," he agreed. "An' I find I like every one o' them."

He rinsed the soap from her hair, then helped her stand and step
carefully from the tub. After patting her dry, he dressed her in a clean
shift taken from Nzingha's trunk. The fabric strained over her chest.

Yvonne struggled with the shift, breath tight from pain. Alex eyed
the strain across the fabric and muttered under his breath,

"Saint Peter's cross… yer breasts are far larger than Nzingha's.
Though God has surely blessed ye. Dinnae hurt yerself tryin' tae
force it to fit."

Before she could scold him, he stepped forward.

"Here, hold still."

He drew his dagger and made a small, neat slit down the front of the
shift, just enough to loosen the pull around her chest.

"There. Ye'll breathe easier now."

He settled her back on the bed, then took the small vial Andrew had pressed into his palm earlier.

"This will dull the pain," he said, lifting a cup of bitter-smelling tea to her lips. "Opium and willow bark. The taste is foul, but it will help."

She made a face as she swallowed. "You and your potions."

He chuckled. "My mother always said if it tastes bad, it's good for ye."

"Then your mother misled you," she murmured, but her eyes were soft.

He fed her small bites of bread and mutton until she pushed his hand away.

"Enough. I will burst."

"Ye've barely eaten in days," he protested.

"Then let my stomach remember what food is slowly," she replied. "I am tired now."

He brushed the back of his fingers over her cheek. "Rest, then. I'll be in the next chamber. One knock, and I'm here."

Her eyes closed, the drug already dragging her toward sleep.

"Alex?" she murmured.

"Aye, lass?"

"Thank you… for coming for me."

His heart clenched.

"I'd cross every sea in Christendom tae find ye," he said softly. But she was already gone.

He watched her a moment longer, then slipped into the adjoining room, leaving the door slightly ajar.

What Followed Him Home

Morning came with the sound of footsteps and hushed voices in the hall.

Yvonne stirred as someone moved about her chamber, the rustle of fabric and the creak of a trunk opening and closing.

She opened one eye to see a young woman with pale skin and light blond hair folding linen into a chest. The girl moved quickly, efficient and quiet, though her eyes kept flickering toward the bed.

Yvonne coughed, a small sound. Immediately, the girl dropped what she was doing and rushed over.

"Oh, nae, miss, dinna try tae sit up," she said. "Lord Andrew said ye've a fractured rib."

Her accent lilted like the others', but her touch was gentle as she propped pillows behind Yvonne's back.

"I am Sarah McDonald," the girl said with a quick curtsy. "Lord Andrew sent a message tae Tantallon for extra hands. The head chambermaid chose me tae come with a cook and a few guards."

Yvonne blinked, still heavy with sleep. "It is… nice to meet you. You came all this way to help?"

"Aye." Sarah smiled, though it did not quite reach her eyes. "Word spread quick that there was a lady here who needed care. I… volunteered."

She glanced over her shoulder, then back. "I brought some o' Lady Nzingha's dresses. Lord Andrew left the trunk outside yer door; I just carried it in."

"You are kind," Yvonne said. "Thank you for seeing to me. I cannot bend well enough to dress myself."

"I'll help ye when the time comes," Sarah assured her. "For now, ye should rest. The household's been in a stir, preparin' for the journey tae see King James, tendin' wee Destiny, now makin' room for ye as well."

"Destiny," Yvonne repeated softly. "Andrew's daughter?"

"Aye. Sweetest bairn ye'll ever see." Sarah's smile warmed genuinely at that. "Crawlin' everywhere, keepin' Lady Nzingha on her toes."

She moved back to the trunk, lifting out folded chemises and placing them in the small wardrobe.

"May I ask you something?" Yvonne said after a moment.

"O' course, miss."

"Have you ever seen someone like me… here? In Scotland?"

Sarah hesitated, fingers tightening on the linen.

"No," she admitted. "No' in the flesh. I heard stories, mind. Sailors' tales. But…" She turned, studying Yvonne openly now. "Ye're bonnie. Different, aye, but… bonnie. I can see why folk talk."

Yvonne flushed, unsure if it was a compliment or a warning.

Before she could reply, the side door connecting to the neighboring chamber burst open.

Alex stood there, hair mussed, shirt half-laced, eyes locking on Sarah.

"What in the seven hells are ye doin' here?" he demanded.

Sarah froze, clutching a folded shift to her chest.

"Chieftain," she stammered. "I… I came from Tantallon. The head chambermaid, she said Lord Andrew needed help. I only wished tae be of service."

"Alex!" Yvonne hissed. "You are being rude. She has done nothing but assist me."

Sarah's eyes glistened. "I am sorry," she whispered, bowing her head. "I didnae mean tae cause trouble. I'll go if…"

Alex scrubbed a hand over his face, temper cracking.

"Nae," he said sharply, then forced his tone softer. "Nae, stay. I… spoke out o' turn. Carry on."

He turned on his heel and slammed the connecting door behind him.

Chapter Fifteen

⚓

Brothers, Blades and Doubts

Sweat poured from their bare backs as they moved in the yard, blades flashing in the morning light. Alex feinted left, then swept his sword back hard to the right, forcing Andrew several steps backward over the packed earth.

Andrew's arm trembled. He lifted his free hand, laughing between breaths.

"I yield, I yield, ye cursed brute!"

He dropped his blade and bent to snatch up the leather flask. After a long drink, he wiped his mouth and handed it to Alex.

Alex took a pull, but the water did little to cool the tightness in his chest. His gaze drifted away from the yard, toward the manor, toward the distant line of the road that led back to Tantallon.

Andrew watched him a moment. "How's Yvonne? Is she comin' along with her healin'?"

"Aye," Alex said. "She looks much better. I sent word to our family physician this morn. She'll be here in a few hours to look in on her."

Andrew nodded. "Good."

Alex hesitated, then added, "Haemish and Nzingha are well? Destiny still eatin' half the stores?"

Andrew's lips curved. "Aye. Nzingha says the babe's grown since ye last saw her. Strong as an ox, that one. We're blessed she's here with us. All of us."

His tone softened. "Ye looked troubled, brother. This about Sarah still?"

Alex's jaw ticked. "Not only that." He tossed the flask back. "The two groundmen yesterday, what they said o' Yvonne. As if she were some curse upon the land. Then the tavern keeper refusin' to serve us. She did nothin' tae those men. And now Sarah says there's already gossip at the castle." His voice went low, tired. "What am I tae do when I return? How do I answer my own clan's venom? They'll talk about her. About me. They might even blame you for puttin' thoughts in my head."

Andrew let out a slow breath. "Alex… come. Sit with me a bit."

They walked to the shade of a wide old oak and sank down against the trunk, the bark rough at their backs. Andrew scrubbed a hand over his face, then looked sideways at his brother.

"Ye're lettin' fear have more say than sense," he said quietly. "Ye ken that, aye?"

Alex gave a half-hearted scoff. "Dinnae start preachin', Andrew."

"Well, I'm goin' tae anyway." Andrew's mouth quirked. "Ye mind when I first met Nzingha?"

"Aye," Alex said. "Ye act as if she is the queen of Scotland."

Andrew laughed. "It's true. I wanted her from the moment I saw her. Wanted her with every foolish part o' me. But she scared the livin' daylight out o' me. She was rough, rude, with a wicked tongue that could make any man feel like a lad."

He grinned at the memory. "We lay together, aye, but when I asked her tae come back with me, she said nae. Rejected me outright, called me an ox. I was so angry I stormed out into the night like a bairn. That's when I found Haemish half-dead at the shore."

Alex glanced over, frowning. "I still cannae believe he took his boot tae her face."

"Aye, the man was mad with pain," Andrew said, wincing. "Hot metal to flesh would make ye do it." Andrew shook his head at the memory. "The next mornin', I saw her face bruised, and, Saints forgive me, I still wanted her so badly I took her boldly as Haemish slept above us." He shook his head with a rueful smile. "Fool that I was."

Alex barked a laugh. "Ye humped the woman ye cared for while Haemish lay sleepin' above ye? Saints, Andrew. Ye truly are a madman."

"Aye, well. Passion makes idiots o' us all." Andrew sobered again. "But that's no' the important bit. Later that mornin', Haemish started runnin' his mouth about how our clan would never accept a woman like Nzingha. He didnae ken she was outside, hearin' every word."

He exhaled slowly. "It angered me so badly I stormed out o' the cabin. I went down tae the shore, where the fires in me were still burnin', flames pokin' at the sky. Nzingha found me there. I told her I'd stand with her. She told me a story instead."

He leaned his head back against the tree, eyes distant.

"She asked if I knew the difference between a lion and a sheep. I said nae. She said, 'When a lion is cast out of his pride, he learns tae make a new one. Stands alone if he must. When a sheep is cast from the flock, he's lost, bleatin' until he's eaten.'" Andrew looked at

Alex, voice lower now. "She said a lion's roar can make anythin' tremble, beast or man. In her lands, the lion is king o' the safari." His gaze sharpened. "Brother, our clan is yer pride. Ye are the lion. They answer tae you. You decide who belongs, not them."

Alex stared at the ground, jaw locked, the words cutting deep. Andrew pushed off the tree and clapped his shoulder as he rose.

"I chose tae live with my lioness," Andrew said, jerking his chin toward the manor, where Nzingha and Destiny would be inside. "Ye'd do well tae be more like one yerself."

He started back toward the house, calling over his shoulder, "Be the lion, Alex!"

Alex sat there a long moment, fingers wrapping tighter around his sword hilt. The idea of marriage, of standin' before clan and kin bindin' himself tae Yvonne, rose up fierce and wild.

"Could I marry?"

His heart thudded faster. Sweat beaded fresh at his temples. When he looked at his hand, it shook.

"Nae," he muttered under his breath. "That's no' me. I'm no' suited for wedlock. What am I even thinkin'…"

He stood abruptly and strode toward the house.

"Andrew!"

His brother turned at the foot of the stairs. "Aye?"

"I must ride tae Tantallon Castle. I'll be back afore Haemish and Nzingha need me for aught."

"Will ye tell Yvonne ye're leavin'?" Andrew asked.

Alex waved a hand, placing a finger to his lips with a half-smile he didnae quite feel. "Just ken I'll be back."

He grabbed his plaid, called for his horse, and rode out, the hooves pounding away the sound of Andrew's worried sigh.

Sarah's Bitterness

Sarah watched from the small casement window of her servant's chamber as the chieftain rode out. The sight of him, broad shoulders bare from training, plaid tucked and tied with that careless confidence, sent a familiar heat up her neck.

He never once looked back to the window where she stood.

She sat on the edge of her narrow bed, fingers knotting in her apron, mind spinning. The memory of blood-stained sheets flashed before her eyes. His sheets. The ones she'd washed with shaking hands after he'd taken her maidenhead without a promise, without a word the next day.

Now he was gathering roses for another.

Yvonne's bell rang from down the hall.

Sarah forced her shoulders straight, smoothed her dress, and went.

She opened the door to Yvonne's chamber. "Aye, miss?"

Yvonne struggled to sit, one hand pressed lightly to her side where the rib had been cracked. "Forgive me for bothering you again. Could you help me stand? I must see to… my needs."

"Of course." Sarah slipped an arm around her and eased her carefully to her feet. As they moved, Sarah studied her face, her soft expression, the way she tried to smile through the pain.

What does he see in you that he never saw in me? she thought darkly.

"Have you seen Alex today?" Yvonne asked, her voice hopeful.

"Aye, miss. He was sparrin' with his brother in the gardens."

"That sounds nice," Yvonne sighed. "I'd give anything just to stand in the sun a while. I'm tired of these four walls."

"Would ye like a bath?" Sarah offered. "We could freshen ye, and after, I might ask the chief tae carry ye tae the garden for a bit."

"I'd love a bath," Yvonne said. "But I don't wish to trouble him. I'll stay inside for now. Best to do as I'm told and rest."

Sarah kept her smile in place, even as jealousy gnawed deeper.

She bathed Yvonne gently, helping her in and out of the tub, then helped her dress. She had just finished tying the last ribbon when the door flew open.

"Yvonne!"

Alex stood there, breathless, wind-tossed, a bouquet of white roses clutched in his hand.

Both women jumped.

He stepped inside without waiting, eyes fixed on Yvonne. "These are for ye," he said, thrusting the flowers toward her. "I must ride tae Tantallon for a day or two. Some matters need seein' tae. I wanted tae tell ye myself."

"Oh," Yvonne said softly, taking the roses. "They're lovely. Must you leave so soon? I thought you'd stay until Nzingha and Haemish returned from the village."

"It was my intent," he said. "But I need tae ensure what we brought back from the voyage is secured."

Sarah's throat tightened. *Flowers. For her.*

She dipped a quick curtsy. "Ye must excuse me," she said, her voice tight. She hurried past him, leaving the chamber, her heart pounding.

Yvonne watched her go, the truth settling heavy in her chest.

Whatever had been between Alex and Sarah, it was written all over the lass's face.

The Deal at The Well

Later that day, Sarah walked out to the well behind the manor, the wooden bucket knocking against her leg. She set it down, gripped the pump, and worked it with jerky movements, watching the cold-water spill and splash.

"All I got were bloody sheets," she muttered under her breath. "He took what he wanted and left me with laundry. She gets roses."

Two guards walked past, Jordy and Chris, laughing low as they spoke.

"Aye," Jordy said, "but I ken one who'll pay double for an exotic lass. The darker, the better, he said."

"Ye're thinkin' o' sellin' one o' the ladies?" Chris snorted. "What about Lord Andrew's wife? She's foreign enough."

"Have ye seen her fight?" Jordy scoffed. "She'd have our heads. Naw. We wait till she's away. There's another one, though. That honored guest o' the chieftain. The one with the cracked rib. Easier tae take, and he's grown stupid about her."

Sarah froze. The pump handle creaked as she stopped.

For a long beat, she listened, the water overflowing the bucket at her feet.

Then she wiped her hands on her apron and walked over, keeping her expression carefully pleasant.

"Good day, tae ye," she said. "Forgive me, I couldna help overhearin' a bit o' what ye said."

Both men stiffened. Chris turned slowly. "And what did ye hear, lass?"

Sarah swallowed, feigning a timid sort of bravery. "Enough tae ken ye might be plannin' somethin' foolish. But… I think I may be able tae help ye."

Jordy stepped closer, narrowing his eyes. "Help us? And why in God's name would a lass like you do that?"

"Because," she said, and this time there was no softness in her eyes at all, "the Barton brothers have lost their minds, bringin' foreign women into our lands and settin' them above the rest o' us. She'll fill his bed. She'll carry his bairns. And the likes o' us will be left with scraps. Why should I be content with that?"

Chris and Jordy exchanged a look.

"What are ye proposin'?" Chris asked.

She bit her lip as if hesitating, then spoke low.

"From what I've heard, the lady's rib is cracked. She'll be slow tae move, careful. The chief is out at the castle now, but when he returns, he'll surely take her out, show her the lands, flaunt her on his arm. When that happens, ye can lie in wait for them on the road. Take them both if ye like. But if ye're wise, ye'll hold her for ransom. The gold that came from his brother's wife's lands was no small sum. He'd pay through the nose tae see his precious guest returned."

Jordy's eyes lit. "Gold? How'd ye ken it's that much?"

"There was talk." Sarah fidgeted with her fingers. "Five skiffs filled with gold bars."

Both men choked. "Ye must be jestin'."

Sarah shook her head slowly.

Chris studied her for a heartbeat longer. "And what do ye get from this?"

Sarah's fingers tightened at her sides. "I get tae see her gone."

A slow smile spread across Chris's face. "I think I like ye, lass."

"Aye," Jordy agreed. "We'll need someone tae carry the missive tae Lord Andrew when the time comes. Someone they'd never suspect."

Sarah smiled back, thin and sharp. "Leave that tae me."

Babies, Fears and Confessions

Weeks later, the chill in the air told that winter was approaching.

Nzingha, Andrew, and their wee lass Destiny were all safe at Leith, and Yvonne's rib had fully mended. She had grown used to the rhythm of the manor, the creak of floorboards, the sound of laughter from the yard, the crackle of fires in the hearth.

Yet no matter how settled the house felt, her heart would not follow.

Surprisingly, after that wild night back on the ship, when Alex had taken her hastily and left her feeling more confused than cherished, he had never pressed her for more. Since she had come to Scotland, he had treated her with care, as if he were afraid of breaking her, as if he were not sure what to do with what lay between them.

One evening after supper, Yvonne sat in Destiny's nursery, watching the baby kick on a soft blanket near the hearth. Nzingha rocked gently in a chair, humming an old song from her homeland.

"Nzingha," Yvonne murmured, "do you think Alex will be back soon? He's been gone a full month now. Sometimes I wonder if my being here troubles him."

Nzingha looked up, brows arching. "Where did that come from?"

"We have… a strange bond," Yvonne said, her eyes fixed on the baby. "At first he frightened me. Then he saved me. Then in Tafaria he behaved like a man I wanted no part of. I thought what happened between us that night was… a mistake." Her throat tightened. "When he brought me here, he said his own clan might not take kindly to me. He keeps a distance, as if his care for me can only stretch so far. And there's Sarah…"

"Ah." Nzingha's eyes sharpened. "Sarah."

"When Alex brought me roses, she stormed from the room," Yvonne continued softly. "She has not been unkind, but there's a coldness. A look I recognize. Nyema looked at me that way when she thought Femi cared for me more than was right."

Nzingha bounced Destiny gently on her lap. "Men and their half-finished affections," she muttered. Then she went on, more evenly, "Alex is a man pulled in many directions, by duty, by fear, by pride. But he is not cruel. If any servant makes you feel unsafe, tell me or Andrew. You are not a guest here, Yvonne. You are family."

Destiny let out a delighted shout and rolled toward Yvonne. The little lass grabbed at her sleeve. Yvonne laughed and scooped her up.

"Someday I'd like a babe of my own," Yvonne murmured, kissing the soft, warm cheek. "One that laughs like this. One that knows only love and no hate."

"She'll likely eat as much as this one does," Nzingha teased. "Saints, look at her. She has her father's appetite."

Yvonne offered the baby a bit of cheese. Destiny snatched it at once and gummed it fiercely.

"Oh, greedy," Yvonne laughed. "You'd eat the whole larder if we let you."

Destiny tried to share the cheese back, pressing it clumsily against Yvonne's mouth.

"No, that's for you, my little princess, not for me," Yvonne said, her heart warmed through.

She handed Destiny back, then rose. "The hour's late. I should get to my chamber. Thank you, Nzingha, for listening."

"Any time," Nzingha said. "Rest well, sister."

Yvonne took a candle from the table and headed down the corridor toward the guest chambers. The manor was quiet now, most fires banked low for the night, only a few sconces still lit.

Halfway down the hall, she slowed.

It felt as though someone walked just behind her. The hairs on the back of her neck prickled.

She turned abruptly. "Hello? Is someone there?"

A figure stepped from the shadows.

"It is only me," Sarah said, her hands folded. "I didna mean tae frighten ye, miss. I was just comin' tae see if ye needed anythin' before bed."

Relief warred with unease. "Oh. No, thank you. You've done enough."

Sarah smiled, but there was something too tight about it. "Ye've been most pleasant tae serve. I dinnae mind."

An awkward silence stretched.

"Well. Goodnight, then," Yvonne said at last.

Sarah lifted a hand. "Um… a moment, Miss Yvonne?"

"Yes?"

"Would ye like tae join me in the kitchens for a cup o' tea before bed?" Sarah asked. Her voice was sweet, but her eyes glittered oddly in the half-light.

Weariness washed over Yvonne, and a cautious instinct, the same one that had kept her alive back in Tafaria, stirred.

"I… I'm feeling a bit tired," she said slowly. "Not tonight, perhaps tomorrow?"

Sarah's gaze flicked, just for a heartbeat, toward Yvonne's locked door farther down the hall. Then her smile snapped back into place.

"Of course, miss. Tomorrow, then," she said, and turned away.

Yvonne walked the remaining distance to her chamber, closed the door, and slid the bolt with unsteady hands.

Someone is scheming, she thought. *And I need to ask Alex if I'm imagining it, or if he's the cause of it.*

She slid into bed, the candle burning low beside her, and sleep finally crept over her like a slow tide.

The Door Between Them

BAP.

She woke to the sound of something heavy hitting the floor.

Yvonne jolted upright, heart slamming against her ribs. The room was dim, the candle she'd left flickering low. For a moment she listened, breath held, but heard only the creak of the old beams and the distant hush of wind outside the stone walls.

"Perhaps I was dreaming," she whispered to herself.

She swung her legs over the side of the bed and crossed to the small table, taking a sip of water. As she lowered the cup, another sound came, metal against wood, this time from the other side of the shared wall.

Her eyes flicked to the small inner door that connected her chamber to the one beside it.

"Could it be…? Is he back?"

Barefoot, she padded across the rug and pressed her ear against the door. She heard a soft thud… then the faint scrape of a chair.

Gathering her courage, she eased the latch and pushed the door open.

"Alex?"

He turned at once.

He stood in the middle of the chamber, half dressed, hair still damp from a wash, his kilt slung low at his hips. The fire in the hearth painted light and shadow across his bare chest.

His expression broke into something warm and startled.

"Yvonne? Lass, what are ye doin' up at this hour?"

"I… heard noises," she admitted, cheeks warming. "It frightened me. I woke from sleep and… I thought perhaps there was an intruder."

His features softened. "My apologies, love. That'd be me. Dropped my belt like a fool." He took a step toward her, voice lowering. "My, have I missed ye."

Her breath caught. "You've been gone so long. I thought…" She hesitated. "I thought perhaps you wished to stay away."

"Na," he said firmly. "Never by choice. I've been buried in matters at Tantallon, clan business, taxes, that new bathhouse I'm buildin' after seein' Tafaria's." A faint smile tugged at his mouth. "But ye were in my mind the entire time."

She looked down at her hands. "My sleep's not been well. The terrors have come back. Some nights it's Oyomo I see. Other nights… Euan."

He stepped closer, close enough she could feel his heat. "Listen tae me, lass. There is no way Oyomo can touch ye here. And Euan is gone tae his judgment. When my own mind won't quiet, I look tae the scriptures. If ye'd like, I'll share them with ye. It helps."

"I'd like that," she said, surprised at how much the promise comforted her.

Silence stretched between them, full and heavy. The fire popped softly. Her thumb brushed the edge of the door. There was something else gnawing at her.

"Alex," she said, her voice barely above a whisper, "before you left… did you sleep with the servant girl?"

He blinked, the question clearly catching him off guard. For a moment he said nothing. Then he let out a breath and shook his head at himself, not at her.

"Sarah," he repeated quietly. "Aye… once. But that was long before Tafaria, before I ever kenned who ye were. I ended it, and I gave her no promise."

Yvonne's fingers tightened around the edge of the door. "I see…"

"Lass, did she say somethin'?"

"No. She hasn't said anything. But since you left, she's… different. Colder. She looks at me as if I've taken something that should have been hers. It reminds me of Nyema, back when she thought Femi's kindness meant he wanted me."

Alex's jaw tightened. "I can assure ye, there is nothin' between me and Sarah now. Perhaps she hoped there might be, but I gave her no promise." His eyes flashed. "If she makes ye uneasy, I'll relieve her o' her duties. I willnae have ye feelin' cornered in my own house."

Yvonne lowered her gaze, teeth catching her lower lip. "Have you… lain with anyone since you've been gone?"

He huffed a short laugh, walking toward the small table where a glass and whisky bottle waited. "Many women would happily warm my bed," he said, pouring himself a dram. "But none o' them are ye."

Heat rushed to her face. Jealousy and something sweeter tangled in her chest.

He took a slow sip, then set the glass down and crossed back to her.

"Ye ken," he said, voice softer, "it's been far too long since I last kissed ye."

She swallowed. "Friends do not kiss."

"Aye," he said. "They do. Leastways, I do."

"No, we don't…"

She never finished.

His mouth claimed hers, tentative at first, as if offering her every chance to pull away. When she didn't, when instead her fingers fisted in the skin of his shoulder and pulled him closer, the kiss deepened.

It was not the clumsy heat they'd shared that first time in his tiny cabin at sea, rushed and muddled and wrong. This was different, slower, sure, full of every word he hadn't had the courage to say aloud. Their tongues danced to a melody named desire. His hand slid up to cradle the back of her head, his thumb brushing her jaw as if she were something fragile and precious all at once.

Her knees went weak. The world shrank to the feel of his lips, the faint taste of whisky, the sound of his breath catching when she kissed him back.

After a long, breathless moment, he drew back just enough to speak, his forehead leaning against hers.

"I meant tae give ye an innocent kiss," he murmured, lips curving in a crooked smile. "But that was far better."

She laughed shakily, cheeks flushed, heart racing.

He did not take advantage of the moment. Instead, his hand lifted slowly, giving her time to stop him. When she didn't, his fingers brushed a curl from her face, knuckles grazing her cheek with deliberate care. His gaze searched hers, not hungry, not playful, but steady. Intent.

He leaned closer, close enough that their foreheads nearly touched, his breath warm against her skin. There was no rush in him now. No careless need. Only patience held tight, as if he were bracing himself to do this differently.

"Yvonne," he said softly, "I want tae make love tae ye. Not like I did that first time on the ship, no' rushed, no' half drunk and full o' shame. Slow. Real. If ye'll have me."

Her throat tightened at the difference in his voice. No swagger. No jest. Just honesty.

"I've wanted you for so long," she whispered.

It was all the permission he needed.

Confessions From a Rogue

His fingers moved to the ties of her night rail, slow enough she could stop him at any point. When she didn't, when she lifted her chin instead, her breath coming quick, he eased the fabric over her shoulders. It slid down her body in a soft whisper, pooling at her feet.

For a heartbeat he just looked at her, as if trying to fix the image in his mind forever.

"Saints," he breathed. "Ye're a dream, lass."

She reached for the edge of his kilt, fingers trembling as she loosened it and pushed it down over his hips. Her hands didn't linger long before sliding up his chest, slower now, surer, learning the planes of him by sensation.

Alex's breath hitched. The contact was light, but it carried heat, awareness, and promise. Muscle shifted beneath her palms, scar and strength both, and he felt the truth of it settle deep in his bones.

She had seen him bare before, on the shores of Tafaria, but never like this. Not with a fire burning low and close. Without restraint, his body answered hers, his eyes never dark on her. The quiet between them was thick with want, never with fear.

He tugged her close, her breast pressed firm against his chest. Skin met skin, their breaths mingling as the sound of their kissing echoed through the chamber.

This time, there was no caution in it. The warmth between them built slowly, each touch layered on the next, her hands in his hair, his mouth at the curve of her neck, the hitch of her breath when he whispered her name.

As they stood pressed to each other, he took a breast into his mouth and suckled. She pushed her hips deep against him, yearning to be filled by him.

He lifted her, cuffing her thighs to wrap around his waist. With ease, he lifted her onto the bed as their tongues continued to dance. The mattress dipped under their combined weight. He lay beside her first, not rushing, a hand trailing slowly from her shoulder to her wrist, letting her grow used to the closeness. He then cupped his hand between her legs, giving her intimate area a light massage.

She whimpered at his touch.

Each and every move was deliberate, reverent. He kissed away her nervousness, answered each uncertain sound with a murmur of reassurance.

"I've got ye," he breathed against her temple. "Ye're safe with me. Always."

He smoothed his palm along her thigh and placed an arm around her waist, holding her as if he'd never let go.

"Ye undo me," he murmured against her ear. "Every time ye breathe, every time ye smile. When ye hurt, it cuts me to the bone. That's what ye are tae me."

His words alone brought her close to shattering.

But what happened next took her to heaven.

He slowly positioned her on her back and, with the strength of his shoulders, smoothed her legs open.

He tasted her. Licked her. Suckled her.

She rocked her hips with the movement of his tongue. The tension rose swiftly, coiling deep until it snapped and thrust her into blinding euphoria. Her chest tightened, and she let out a breath she didn't know she'd been holding.

In one move, Alex flipped her atop him. She looked around, uncertain what to do. He guided her hand, slipping himself inside her. Yvonne gasped, taking the fullness of him.

He placed both hands on her hips. "Move with me," his voice rumbled low.

Yvonne followed his motion back and forth. It was a hungry dance that set his heart ablaze. The sight of her breasts moving as she bounced atop him, pulling him deeper inside her walls.

He thrust beneath her with mounting intensity. She cried out once more before feeling another release.

"Alex… I am there. I am shattering." Her cries built his urgency.

Before he could climax, he quickly shifted their position, kneeling behind her.

In one swift motion, Alex entered her again, placing his chest against her back, filling his hands with her breast as he rocked, slowly, gracefully.

His lips brushed her skin as he whispered, his voice low and trembling with want, "Ye're mine, Yvonne. Every breath, every heartbeat."

He continued the steady motion, in and out. "I feel it in every part of me. Ye. Are. Mine."

His pace went faster as her cries grew louder. "Yvonne. God help me, I cannae stop feelin' it." His voice grew louder. "I'M ABOUT TAE… JESUS CHRIST!"

A raw roar tore from his chest, her name echoing through the room. "YVONNE!"

And for the first time in his entire life, Alex filled a woman with his seed.

Not just any woman. It was Yvonne.

At some point, the world outside that chamber faded completely. No castle, no clan, no gossip, no fear.

When the storm of it had passed, they lay tangled in the sheets, limbs still intertwined. Yvonne rested her head on Alex's chest, listening to the steady beat of his heart. His hand drifted lazily up and down her back, fingers drawing patterns on her skin.

"That was…" she began, then trailed off, unable to find a word big enough.

"Aye," he said, brushing a kiss into her hair. "It was."

He whispered into the dark then, telling her the things he'd never said, how her honesty leveled him, how her laughter had brought life back to his home, how he'd thought of her every day he was gone. She told him her fears, the dreams that haunted her, the shame she still carried that was not truly hers.

He listened. She listened. The true intimacy lay more in those murmured confessions than in anything their bodies had done.

Time became soft around them; their eyes became heavy, and sleep crept between them.

Outside the Servant Hall

Outside, down the servant hall, Sarah lay awake in her narrow bed, staring at the ceiling.

At first, she thought the sounds reaching her ears were dreams. A faint cry. A broken moan. A man's low murmur. But as she listened, it became clear they were not cries of pain.

They were sounds of pleasure.

Her face went white, then red.

She sat up, trembling violently. "He… he never…" Her breath came sharp, bitter. "He never made a sound like that with me."

She couldn't bear it. She threw off her blanket, wrapped a shawl around her shoulders, and stepped out into the corridor, letting her feet carry her toward the chieftain's chamber.

The closer she drew, the clearer the noise became. A soft call of the chieftain's name. A loud roar of a name.

Yvonne's.

Her hands curled into fists.

Tomorrow, she thought, rage and hurt twining into something terrible. *Tomorrow I'll make sure he never lays a finger on her again.*

Chapter Sixteen

⚓

Breaking Fast

Morning sunlight spilled across the narrow stone corridor of the

dowager house as Alex tugged the last buckle of his belt into place. His hair was still damp from washing, yet somehow nothing could wash off the faint, well-rested glow written all over him.

And of course, Andrew saw it instantly.

He leaned against the wall with a cup of tea, watching Alex approach with the slow, judgmental lift of one eyebrow.

"Well then," Andrew murmured, taking a sip. "How is Yvonne this fine mornin'?"

Alex straightened like a guilty man. "Good," he answered quickly.

Andrew nodded with exaggerated consideration. "Aye... I imagine she is."

Alex paused mid-stride. "And what exactly is that supposed tae mean?"

Andrew did not blink.

"Oh, nothing." He waved a hand lazily. "Only that she seems fully recovered. Remarkable, truly… the level o' energy she had last night."

Alex froze.

Andrew continued, his voice smooth as silk.

"Some might even call it… vigorous."

Alex narrowed his eyes. "Andrew…"

"In fact," Andrew added, taking another slow sip, "I'd say half the bloody dowager house is also aware of her recovery."

Alex choked. "You're jestin'. Tell me you're jestin'."

Andrew clapped him on the shoulder, almost sympathetic. Almost.

"I wish I were."

And with that, Andrew strolled past him toward the dining room, whistling.

Trying to maintain some dignity, Alex stepped into the dining room.

Nzingha sat with Destiny bouncing happily on her lap, porridge smeared across one cheek. Yvonne sat beside them, offering Alex a shy, warm smile.

Across the table, Andrew and Nzingha exchanged a look, the look of people who knew entirely too much.

Destiny banged her spoon on the table in a wild rhythm.

CLANG, CLANG, CLANG.

The plates rattled. A cup nearly toppled.

Andrew and Nzingha cracked into sudden, uncontrollable laughter.

Alex glared.

"If the two of ye have somethin' tae say, just say it."

Andrew didn't hesitate.

"I dinnae need tae say anythin', brother."

He leaned back, folding his arms.

"We all heard it, last eve."

Alex dropped his fork.

Destiny flailed her spoon and shrieked joyfully,
"YA-YA! AAAAAH!"

Nzingha lifted her cup in a mock toast.

"Congratulations on your… vocal stamina."

Yvonne hung her head in shame. She could have melted.

Alex stood abruptly, grabbed Yvonne's hand, and muttered through his teeth,
"We're leavin'. Now."

"But my porridge…" Yvonne protested softly.

"Now, lass."

They fled the room hand in hand, the door swinging shut behind them as Andrew and Nzingha burst into another fit of laughter.

When the door closed, Andrew exhaled a long, amused sigh.

"You'd think the lad never had a woman before."

Nzingha smirked.

"Not one who had him shouting loud enough for the baby to repeat it." She gave a look of excitement. "Finally, husband, your brother is in love."

Destiny waved her spoon triumphantly.

"AAAAH! AAAAH!"

Riding Through the Highlands

Alex and Yvonne rode together on his black war horse, her back resting against his chest as they followed the winding road toward Tantallon. The Highlands stretched out around them, green and endless, with rolling hills that dipped into wide, sweeping valleys. Sunlight shimmered on the loch beside them, turning the surface into a silver mirror.

Yvonne looked everywhere at once, eyes wide with wonder.

"I have never seen land like this," she said softly. "With Euan… it was always deep forest. Dark and crowded."

Alex tightened his arm around her waist. "This land is home. I'm glad ye're seein' it this way."

A waterfall thundered beside the loch, tumbling down a cliff and bursting into white spray. Yvonne straightened, excitement brightening her face.

"Alex, can we stop? It's beautiful."

"Aye," he said immediately. "Of course."

He dismounted and lifted her gently from the saddle. Their fingers laced without needing to be asked. Together they walked through the purple shrubs of heather. The scent rose warm and sweet around them.

"My mother loved this smell," Alex said quietly. "Said it meant peace."

Yvonne inhaled deeply, smiling. "It's lovely."

They found a soft patch of grass. Alex set down a plaid, opened his satchel, and unwrapped bully beef, bread, and fruit.

"Eat," he said, handing her a portion. "Every bite. Ye've a long road."

She tasted the meat, and her brows shot up. "Oh, this is delicious."

"Aye." He grinned at how pleased she looked. "Road food at its finest."

For a time they ate in quiet comfort. The waterfall roared in the background, but somehow it made the moment feel more intimate, not less.

Then Yvonne's thoughts drifted, and she glanced at him, cheeks warming.

"When I first met you… I did not like you," she said honestly. "I thought you were arrogant. And after Tafaria, I lost every bit of respect I had left. I was only in your room because Nyema said if I lay with you, you might help me escape Oyomo."

Alex choked on his drink, coughing hard.

"What? That was yer plan? Why didn't ye go through with it?"

"Because I respect myself," she said simply. "And because I wanted to escape Oyomo on my own terms. But when you stood between us that night, when you protected me, I saw something different in you."

"Aye," he murmured. "And don't forget Zara. The lass ran for help the moment she saw ye were in trouble."

Yvonne nodded gratefully. "We owe her much."

Alex hesitated before speaking again. "Life has a strange way of bringin' two people together. I never thought I'd develop feelings for someone like ye."

Yvonne's smile fell.

Her hand tightened around the bread.

"What do you mean?" she asked softly. "Someone of my origin? My skin? Why should any of it matter? Why fall in love with me if it does?"

Before he could correct himself, she stood and walked away, her shoulders rigid with hurt.

"Yvonne, wait!" Alex called, scrambling up. "I never said it was about yer origin. Will ye stop for one moment?"

She kept walking, wiping at her eyes. The breeze tugged at her curls, but nothing softened the sting gathering in her chest. She didn't look back.

Alex noticed instantly.

"Yvonne?" he called, confusion roughening his voice. "Where are ye goin'?"

She didn't slow. The ache behind her ribs deepened, steady, sharp, and she hated that it hurt this much.

"Last night... You held me like I mattered. You touched me like I mattered." She drew a shaky breath. "And you said so many things to bring me over the edge, Alex. Things that felt real. But you never said you loved me."

He stopped walking.

Her steps faltered too, though she didn't turn.

"You only said I was yours," she continued, softer now. "But there is a difference between owning something and loving it."

Something in him jolted.

"Yvonne... that's no' fair..."

"Then help me understand," she said, finally facing him. Her eyes glimmered with hurt he wished he could pull into his own body. "Do you care for me only when it is convenient? Or when desire is high? Because this morning, you looked frightened. Like what happened between us was a mistake."

He dragged a hand through his hair, breath uneven. "I was no' frightened of ye."

"Then what?" she asked. "What terrifies you? Because you spilled inside me without hesitation, yet today you look as though you regret every heartbeat of it."

He flinched, hard.

"God's truth, lass, I panicked afterward," he admitted. "No' because of ye. Never because of ye. But because for the first time in my life, I didn't think. I just felt. And everythin' in me went straight tae ye."

Her breath caught.

He kept going, the words unraveling faster than he meant them to.

"I've never done that before. I've never let myself go like that. And when I realized it, I…" He swallowed, struggling. "I dinnae ken if I deserve somethin' that means that much."

She stared at him, stunned.

"Last night, you cared for me like a man who loved," she whispered. "But today you speak like a man who's already halfway out the door."

"I'm nae ready for wee ones," he snapped, too sharp, too loud. "That's no' what I want."

The moment the words left him, regret crashed over him.

Her eyes widened, wounded.

Alex's chest tightened with panic.

"Yvonne, no, listen, please. That sounded wrong. I didn't mean it like that." His voice broke. "God help me, I only fear failing ye."

She shook her head. "Failing me how?"

"By givin' ye a life that'll hurt ye," he said, his voice cracking. "Ye dinnae ken the cruelty of these lands. If ye carried my child, aye, I'm speakin' plainly now, a child of ours would face whispers, looks, judgment. And I cannae bear the thought of ye, or a bairn, sufferin' because of me."

"And what of me now?" she asked softly. "Do you think I'm not already judged? Already whispered about?"

He closed his eyes as if her words struck bone.

"I was planning to leave after Tantallon," she said, barely above a breath. "And maybe I still should."

He opened his eyes, stricken.

"Leave?" The word cracked. "Ye'd walk away after last night? After what we shared?"

She blinked, tears slipping free. "Because I don't know if you want me for a lifetime… or only for the moments when passion blinds you."

He moved to her in three long strides, catching her hand before she could pull away again. His grip trembled.

"I regret nothing about last night," he said, raw. "Not the way ye looked at me. Not the way ye touched me. Not spillin' inside ye. God's truth, lass, I've never felt anythin' like it."

She swallowed hard. "Then why can't you say what you feel? Why do you hide behind fear?"

"I'm no' hidin'," he said, though his voice betrayed him.

"You are," she whispered. "You feel something, but instead of speaking it, you avoid it. You pull back. You run."

His breath hitched at the truth of it.

"I'm no' runnin'," he insisted, though doubt flickered in his eyes.

"Then show me," she said. "Show me you want me. Not just with your hands. With your words."

Something in him finally broke, desperation fierce and wild.

"How loud must I say it?" he demanded. "Dammit all... How clear must it be for ye to believe me?"

She opened her mouth, but he didn't wait.

Alex turned toward the open glen, lifted his face to the vast Highland sky, and bellowed with everything in him:

"I LOVE YE, YVONNE!"

The words tore from him, raw and desperate, echoing off the cliffs.

He stepped forward, chest heaving, his voice breaking.

"YVONNE MEANS MORE TAE ME THAN MY OWN DAMN SENSE!"

And then, louder still, because his heart had no more room to hold it:

"I LOVE YE SO DAMN MUCH I CANNAE THINK STRAIGHT!"

His voice split across rock and water, echoing through the valley.

Her hand flew to her mouth as laughter and sobs tangled in her throat, her shoulders shaking with the impact of hearing what she had feared she might never hear.

Alex took a step toward her, one he'd never taken with any woman before.

"I love ye," he said again, rough, cracked, earnest. "I love ye with every full part of me."

She was laughing and crying at once, unable to speak, unable to move, her heart breaking open and stitching itself whole all in one breath.

But the sound died as her smile vanished.

Her eyes widened… then filled with terror.

"Alex…" she whispered.

He turned.

Two masked men sprinted toward them.

"What the…?"

BAP.

The blow struck the side of his head with brutal force. Pain flashed bright, and darkness consumed him.

"Alex!" Yvonne screamed, lunging toward him, but an arm wrapped around her waist, dragging her off her feet.

"Shut her up," a harsh voice snarled.

She kicked, clawed, fought. Another strike landed, and her world went black.

Bound In the Dark

Alex woke slowly, as though surfacing from the bottom of a dark loch.

The first thing he registered was the throbbing behind his eyes, dull at first, then sharp, pulsing in time with his heartbeat.

The second was the smell.

Damp hay.
Cold earth.
Animal shite so old it clung to the air like rot.

He drew a breath through his teeth, vision wavering as he blinked up at the faint sliver of moonlight spilling through a small, high window in the rafters. It cast thin bars of silver across the barn, illuminating dust motes drifting lazily in the cold air.

When he tried to move, pain shot through his ribs.

His wrists were bound behind him, tied cruelly tight, and his ankles were drawn forward, rope pulling them toward his hands, folding him in on himself like livestock trussed for slaughter. He could barely straighten his spine enough to lift his head.

Memory slammed into him like a hammer.

The glen.
Yvonne's laugh breaking into a cry.
Masked men.
The blow.

He sucked in breath and forced his head up, every muscle screaming, searching frantically through the dim light.

There.

Across the barn, lying on a mound of hay, a small shape curled in on itself.

"Yvonne…" he rasped.

Moonlight touched her just enough for him to see the ropes binding her wrists and ankles, the gag across her mouth, her curls spilling messily around her face.

Her chest rose and fell, shallow, frightened breaths, but she was breathing.

Relief hit him so hard it nearly knocked him senseless.

Relief, and pure, murderous fury.

"Yvonne!" he called again, louder despite the pain tearing through his skull. "Lass, can ye hear me?"

She stirred, head rolling weakly to the side. Her eyes fluttered open, unfocused at first, and then she found him in the dark.

Tears welled at once.

Her whole body shook.

"Thank God…" he whispered.

The barn door scraped open.

Alex jerked his head toward the sound, muscles straining uselessly against the ropes.

Lantern light spilled across the floor as two men stepped inside, shadows stretching long and warped behind them. They wore rough sackcloth hoods and britches instead of kilts, cowards hiding their clans and faces.

But a hood could not hide a voice.

"Good tae see ye awake, Chieftain," the first man said, his tone smug and cold.

"Thought I'd have to splash ye with cold water," the second man laughed.

Alex let out a slow, humorless laugh that tasted like blood.

"Chris," he said, voice low. "Jordy.
Ye absolute arselings."

Jordy stiffened.

Chris swore under his breath.

"Shite, I told ye he'd ken our voices," Jordy hissed.

Chris ripped the hood off in one angry jerk, eyes blazing with a bitterness Alex had clearly underestimated.

He stalked forward until he towered over Alex, lantern light throwing his expression into harsh lines.

"Two things," Chris growled. "One, ye dragged that foreign bitch into yer brother's hall, made fools o' us guardin' ye. And two, ye came back from yer last voyage richer than a bloody king, and did ye share so much as a coin? Nae. Ye strutted about like the world owed ye."

Alex spat blood at his boots.

"When I get free. I'll hang both o' ye. Slow."

Chris's face twisted.

He punched Alex once, twice, each blow snapping his head back.

Jordy kicked him hard in the ribs. Another boot went to Alex's head. They beat him until he lay nearly unconscious.

Across the barn, Yvonne sobbed into her gag, body trembling violently with every hit Alex took.

Her tears drove a knife through him deeper than any fist.

Chris turned toward her, lantern catching her tear-streaked face.

"Oh look," he sneered. "His dark-skinned lass is awake. Even prettier when she cries."

Jordy let out a vicious laugh. "Aye. And I heard him shout he loves her on the hillside. Disgustin', if ye ask me."

Chris leaned close until Alex could smell the ale on his breath.

"Say yer goodbyes," he whispered. "When we're done, she'll be sold off far from here. Maybe beyond the sea. Ye'll never see her again."

They turned, lantern swinging, and slammed the barn door behind them.

Silence settled. It was not a peaceful kind.

A trembling, fragile kind.

Yvonne immediately began dragging herself toward him, inch by inch, ropes scraping across the hay and floorboards. She winced with every movement, but she refused to stop until she reached him.

She pressed her forehead to his shoulder, her tears warm even through his shirt.

He turned his head toward her as much as the ropes allowed.

"There, there, lass," he whispered. His voice trembled, but his tone stayed gentle, steady, the anchor she needed. "Nae cry. I'm right here."

Her muffled sob broke him open inside.

"We'll get out o' this," he murmured. "I swear it. I'm sure those two arselings will send Andrew a ransom letter, demandin' coin for my release. He'll gather men from Tantallon and track us to hell itself if he must."

He swallowed hard to fight against dizziness.

"This is no' how our story ends, Yvonne."

He stared at the frame of Yvonne's face, and his world went black.

The moonlight flickered over them, two broken bodies, bound and bruised, but together, defiant even in the dark.

And for Alex Barton, the fear of death meant nothing compared to the fear of losing her.

Chapter Seventeen

⚓

Wails From a Lassie

*D*estiny had been fretful all morning.

Her tiny body felt too warm against Nzingha's chest, her cheeks flushed, her gums swollen from the cruel work of teething. The child's cries rose and fell like waves, never quite breaking into full screams, but never settling into peace either. Nzingha paced slowly in front of the nursery window, humming an old song from home under her breath, letting the familiar melody wrap around both of them. Destiny's fingers clung tightly to the fabric of her gown, kneading and clutching as if the cloth itself might somehow fix what hurt.

Outside, the winter light lay pale and thin over the Dowager House and its small grounds. A sheen of frost clung to the roof and to the low stone walls, refusing to give way even as the day edged onward. From the high nursery window, Nzingha could see a strip of yard, the packed earth of the path, and beyond that the faint line of road that curved away toward the hills.

It was not the road that caught her eye.

Movement at the side of the yard drew her. Three figures stood just beyond the main path, half in shadow where the house cast its reach. Two of them were men she knew by shape more than by face, even at that distance. Jordy's slight stoop and narrow shoulders, Chris's broader frame and the quick, impatient shift of his weight from one foot to the other. They were guards, men Andrew trusted enough to keep near, yet neither wore tartan nor kilt today. Both stood in plain, dark britches and rough shirts, like farmhands rather than posted protectors.

Between them stood Sarah.

Her apron was gathered in both hands, fingers knotted in the cloth. Her head turned once toward the house, then toward the road, as if she feared being seen and hoped for it at the same time. The three of them were close enough that Nzingha could not hear their words, but she could read the shape of them. Chris leaned in, speaking low. Jordy nodded, not with the easy agreement of a man being told what to do, but with the sharp jerk of someone making plans. Sarah did not stand with the bowed head and lowered shoulders of a servant receiving orders. Her back was straight, her chin lifted, her hands cutting the air in small, tight gestures.

It did not look like routine.

It looked like a secret.

Destiny's cry sharpened suddenly, a high, broken sound against Nzingha's collarbone. The sound dragged her focus away from the strange gathering in the yard. She pressed her lips to her baby's warm brow and rocked gently, rubbing small circles between her shoulder blades, murmuring soft comfort.

"I see you," she whispered. "I hear you. I know it hurts, little one. It will not last forever."

The nursery door opened with a soft creak behind her.

"Is my wee lassie makin' the whole house miserable again?" Andrew's voice reached them first, low and amused, edges softened by affection.

He stepped inside a heartbeat later, bringing with him the faint scent of cold air and horses. His hair was a little mussed from the wind, his jaw darkened with the first hint of stubble. For a moment, the tension in Nzingha's shoulders eased just seeing him there. His gaze went straight to Destiny, reading the flushed face and damp lashes with practiced eyes.

"She is not miserable," Nzingha said, though the tired smile tugging at her mouth betrayed her. "She is suffering. That is a very important difference."

"Aye, I ken the difference," he replied, crossing the room. "One earns my sympathy. The other earns a nap."

He held out his arms without needing to ask. After one small, stubborn pause, Nzingha allowed herself to surrender the warm, wiggling weight. Destiny fussed in protest at the change, her face scrunching as if she were about to object with all her might. Then Andrew's broad chest became her pillow, his big hand cupped the back of her head, and the cries softened into hiccups and sleepy little sighs.

"There ye go," he murmured, swaying gently. "Ye just wanted yer da, is that it? Break yer mother's heart while ye're at it."

"That is not what she wanted," Nzingha said, though laughter curled through the words. "She wanted her tooth to stop hurting. You simply arrived in time to steal my victory."

He looked toward the window as he soothed their daughter, his gaze following the thin crust of frost along the glass.

"Ye've been standin' there an age," he observed. "Watchin' for someone?"

"Not someone," she answered slowly.

She turned her head, intending to point out the three figures. The yard was empty now. No trace of Jordy's bent shoulders or Chris's broad back, no pale apron caught between them. The path lay bare and ordinary, the road beyond it quiet.

"I thought I saw something… odd," she said, frowning lightly. "But perhaps I am simply tired. Destiny's cries make the mind softer than it ought to be."

"Aye, they do," he agreed. "Come down when ye're ready. The cook's laid out a proper nooning. If the lass settles, ye might yet eat while the food is warm instead o' chasin' cold scraps."

He bent and pressed a kiss to Destiny's curls, then another to Nzingha's forehead. For a brief moment, everything narrowed down to that simple, aching normalcy: a husband, a wife, a child, ordinary worries wrapped around deeper ones.

"I will join you," she said quietly. "Once she is down."

"Dinnae be long," he replied, giving her a half-smile. "I like the meal better when ye're there tae complain about it."

She brushed her fingertips along his sleeve as he moved past her. He settled Destiny into her cradle with surprising gentleness for a man so often hard in battle, one large hand resting lightly on her chest until her breathing evened out and her lashes sank. Only when the baby slipped at last into a fretful sleep did he leave the nursery.

When the door clicked shut, Nzingha turned back to the window.

The yard looked harmless now, almost dull. Yet the picture remained in her mind with uncomfortable clarity: two men in plain clothes where tartan should have been, a maid standing upright between them as if she had forgotten her place. She tucked the unsettled feeling away, pressing it beneath the immediate need to smooth her skirts, re-pin her hair, and make herself presentable for the meal below.

It Will All Make Sense

The dining room of the Dowager House lacked the grandeur of Tantallon's great hall, but what it had instead was comfort. The fire in the hearth burned steady and low, filling the room with an even warmth. Heavy wooden chairs and a long, worn table spoke more of family meals than formal feasts.

By the time Nzingha came in, the clatter and shuffle of nooning had already begun to soften into a quieter rhythm. Destiny slept in a small basket near the hearth, her feverish flush eased for the moment, her lips parted around the soft ghost of a sigh. One of the older maids sat close with her knitting in her lap, eyes flicking up every so often to check the child.

Andrew sat at the table with a bowl of stew in front of him and a torn piece of bread beside it. He looked up as Nzingha entered, and the faint crease between his brows smoothed.

"Ye made it afore the stew turned tae stone," he said. "I'll take that as a good sign."

"I am not convinced food temperature is a reliable omen," she replied, sliding into the chair at his side. "But if it promises a quiet afternoon, I will accept it."

He pushed the bread closer to her plate. "Quiet afternoon," he echoed. "Aye. That would be a rare luxury."

Servants moved easily in and out of the room, refilling cups, setting down fresh platters of bread and roasted vegetables. Among them was Sarah, her cap neat, her apron smooth, her steps unhurried. She poured ale into Andrew's cup with a steady hand, set a small dish nearer to Nzingha, and stepped back with her head bowed just enough to be proper. To anyone glancing only once, she looked no different than she had on a hundred other days.

Only when Nzingha watched her more closely did the small cracks appear. Sarah's eyes did not move around the room as they usually did, catching stray crumbs and empty cups. They kept returning, however briefly, toward the front door, then to the head of the table where Andrew sat. When she thought no one noticed, her fingers slid over the front of her apron in a small, habitual motion, then stilled just as quickly. Her composure was good. Good enough to fool most. But Nzingha had spent too many years in courts and battle tents to miss the tension at the corners of her mouth.

"Is something the matter?" she asked her husband quietly, more to test the air than because she expected him to see what she did.

Andrew lifted the cup Sarah had just filled and took a measured sip. "Only that the ale's weaker than I remember," he muttered. "If the cook's waterin' it, I'll have words."

She allowed the comment to pass, but she did not stop watching.

The meal drifted toward its easy middle, bowls half-emptied, stomachs beginning to warm. Destiny slept on, her breathing soft and even. The fire settled into a steady crackle that underlined the soft murmur of conversation.

Then a knock sounded at the dining room door.

It was not loud, but something in its timing cut across the comfortable hum like a blade. Conversation stilled of its own accord.

"Come," Andrew called.

A young footman stepped inside, cap in hand, shoulders drawn back as if he had been given strict instructions. His gaze fixed on Andrew and did not waver.

"Beggin' yer pardon, milord," he said. "There's a letter from the road. The watcher at the gate sent it up. Said it's marked for yer eyes alone, and that it seemed… urgent."

The word sat oddly in the air, thinning the warmth around them by several degrees.

Andrew wiped his fingers carefully on a cloth, reached for the folded parchment the lad held, and felt at once the wrongness of it. There was no seal, no crest, no sign of noble origin. Just a rough fold and a weight that had nothing to do with ink.

"Who brought it?" he asked.

"Dinnae ken, sir," the lad replied. "The watcher said a woman rode up with her face covered. Handed him the letter and turned her horse before he could ask a single question."

Nzingha immediately frowned. A woman on horseback, face covered. The road. The yard. The three shapes she had seen that morning.

Sarah stood further down the wall now, hands folded neatly, gaze lowered in appropriate modesty. At the mention of a rider, her shoulders did not jerk; she did not gasp or tremble. Yet her lashes flicked up for the briefest moment toward the letter in Andrew's hand, then dropped again. If Nzingha had not already been looking, she might have missed it.

Andrew broke the fold and scanned the page once, his eyes moving quickly. Then he read it again, slower, each word seeming to carve something from his face. The color faded from his cheeks, leaving the lines of strain starker than she had seen in many months.

"Andrew," Nzingha said softly. "What news?"

He did not answer at once. His fingers tightened around the edge of the parchment until it crackled. Only when he deliberately flattened it on the table did he speak, his voice gone low and rough.

"Alex has been taken."

The room seemed to tilt. Servants looked their way.

Nzingha's breath caught, sharp and painful. "Taken," she repeated. "By whom?"

"They dinnae sign their names," he said. "But they ken mine well enough."

He lifted the letter again and read aloud, the Scots in his voice thickening as fury began to wind through it.

"To the Laird Andrew of Leith, ye've more coin than sense. Yer brother and his dark-skinned lady are in our hands. If ye wish tae see either o' them alive, ye'll bring the sum named below tae the old barn by the fork o' the Tantallon road on the next evenin', when the sun sits just above the hills. Come alone, or we'll start sendin' pieces instead o' letters. If ye tell the guard, if ye send the laird's men, ye'll never see them again.'"

The name did not appear in the ink, but it burned through Nzingha's mind all the same. Her throat tightened.

"Yvonne." she whispered. "Oh, the Gods, where is Yvonne?"

"She is not mentioned here." Andrew grew more irritated.

Destiny shifted in her basket and let out a thin, uncertain whimper.

"And here," he said tightly, "the sum they demand. An amount meant tae hurt, based on what ye brought back from Tafaria lands."

The footman lingered uneasily at the door, waiting for orders. Sarah remained in her place, her posture correct, her expression disciplined. Only the slightest sheen of sweat at her hairline betrayed strain, and even that might have been missed by any eye less sharpened than Nzingha's.

"We will pay it," Nzingha said at once, the notion of counting coins against the image of Alex and Yvonne bound and bleeding somewhere turning her stomach. "Whatever they ask, we will pay. And then we will find them."

Andrew's hand came down on the table with a sudden, controlled force.

It was not a wild blow, but a precise one. The crack sent spoons rattling. Destiny woke fully this time, her startled cry cutting through the room.

Andrew closed his eyes briefly, drawing one slow breath, then another, as if forcing the rage back into a shape he could use. When he opened them again, they were cold.

"No one leaves this house without my word," he said. "Not a servant. Not a stable hand. Not a soul steps past the yard. Do ye hear me?"

The footman straightened. "Aye, Laird Barton."

"Start at the gates," Andrew added. "Have them barred. If any rider tries tae leave, ye stop them. If they dinnae stop, ye shoot. I'll answer for the order."

The lad swallowed hard. "Aye, sir," he said, and hurried out.

Nzingha pushed back her chair, rising slowly. Her gaze drifted toward the wall where Sarah stood.

The maid was pale now, the color bled from her face, but there was no dramatic flinch, no sob or scene. She merely pressed her lips together, fingers fidgeting in front of her. When she noticed Nzingha's eyes upon her, her hands stilled.

The unease that had begun in the nursery window thickened into something sharper.

"Andrew," Nzingha said quietly, her eyes never quite leaving Sarah, "will you stay here with Destiny a while longer?"

"Aye," he answered, already turning toward the hearth. He lifted his crying daughter from the maid's arms and settled her against his shoulder, rocking slightly. "Go see tae whatever thought is crawlin' behind yer eyes. I can see ye've got one."

She did not argue.

Whatever had been tugging at the edge of Nzingha's awareness since morning now drew tight, like a rope pulled hard between two hands.

Alex's Chamber

The corridors of the Dowager House held a different sort of silence now. Not the ordinary quiet of a day unfolding, but a listening hush, drawn tight over the walls. Servants looked up as Nzingha passed, then quickly lowered their eyes again.
She walked with a steady, measured tread. A woman with purpose drew less notice than one who ran.

Nzingha kept her awareness fixed on Sarah. She did not watch openly. She noted where the maid stood, how her gaze slid toward the doors and away again.

When Nzingha left the room, she did so without urgency. She stepped into the corridor and waited.

A short time later, Sarah emerged.

The maid paused, then turned. Not toward the kitchen. Not toward the washroom. Not toward the servants' stairs or her own chamber. But down the narrow passage leading to the guest wing.

Toward Alex's chamber.

Nzingha followed without haste, fragments of unease fitting together at last.

The further she walked, the quieter the house grew. Most of the household remained downstairs. Up here, only her footsteps echoed.

She turned into the guest corridor.

Alex's door stood slightly ajar, firelight spilling across the floorboards.

Nzingha paused.

From within came the rustle of fabric, then a soft, breathy giggle. A sound that did not belong to a maid at work. A sound that did not belong here at all.

She pushed the door open.

And froze.

Sarah lay naked across Alex's bed, his plaid thrown between her open thighs, his shirt hanging off one shoulder as if she had dragged it on only moments before. Her hair spread wildly around her flushed face, her breath quick, her skin glowing with feverish excitement rather than shame.

She stroked her hand slowly down her own thigh, laughing softly to the empty room.

"My love," she whispered, voice trembling with anticipation. "Ye'll see me now. Ye will. She'll be gone, and ye'll want me, all of me."

Her hips lifted, as if reaching for an imagined lover. The plaid slipped further, baring more of her as she arched into the fantasy she had shaped in Alex's absence.

For a heartbeat, Nzingha did not move, not from shock, but at the sheer delusion of it.

Sarah did not even notice her.

She cupped her own breast, the other hand sliding lower, gripping Alex's plaid like a tether.

"Ye always belonged tae me," she murmured. "Before that foreign witch came, aye, before she stepped one dark foot inside this house. That's all she is. A dark-skinned temptation. Naught but trouble. She dinnae belong here. None o' ye do."

Nzingha's face stilled.

The air tightened.

"Sarah."

Her voice cut through the room like cold steel.

Sarah jerked violently, scrambling to cover herself, dragging the plaid over her body. Her face drained white.

"Mi-milady! I, I didnae hear ye. I was only… tidyin'!"

"Do not insult my intelligence," Nzingha said, stepping fully inside and closing the door behind her. "You are not tidying. You are not innocent. And you will tell me why you are in this room, wearing Alex's shirt, lying beneath his plaid, speaking of another woman being gone."

Sarah stood. She trembled, clutching the fabric tighter.

"I only wanted him back," she whispered. "Before she came. Before that dark-skinned woman bewitched him. He took me. He did. He kissed me. He lay with me. And now she gets his roses and his smiles and his voice in the night. She gets what should have been mine."

"That gives you no right to her life," Nzingha said, voice low and steady. "And no right to his."

Sarah's lips curled, bitter and sharp.

"She'll no' have his life long," she whispered. "Not where she's goin'. When the men are done, there'll be naught left o' her but a story. And then he'll see who belongs here. Who kent him. Who warmed his bed. Who…"

SLAP.

It cracked through the room like lightning.

Nzingha struck her so sharply Sarah dropped sideways to her knees with a stunned gasp, one hand flying to her cheek.

"You dare," Nzingha said quietly, "to speak of our origin as if it makes us lesser."

Sarah scrambled backward, breath shuddering, eyes darting toward the door.

She bolted.

She barely made two steps before Nzingha seized a fistful of her hair and yanked her back so abruptly her feet slid out from under her. Sarah crashed to her knees again, sobbing, hands clawing at Nzingha's wrist.

"Ye're hurtin' me!"

"Hurting you?" Nzingha echoed, leaning down so their faces were inches apart.

"My child cried all night from pain she could not understand. That is hurt," she said, each word deliberate.

"Yvonne cried for months over a marriage that nearly destroyed her. That is hurt. But you… you speak of selling her, of having men do foul things to her. All because you opened your legs for a man that saw you as no less than a female dog."

Her grip tightened, not cruel, but controlled, the strength of someone who knew exactly how much force to wield.

"You know my origin so well?" she continued, voice darkening. "Then know this also."

She pulled Sarah's head back, forcing her gaze upward.

"I was a warrior before I was a wife. I was a commander before I ever set foot on Scottish soil. I have killed men twice your size for less than what you've said today."

Sarah whimpered, shaking violently.

"So you will speak the truth this day," Nzingha said. "Every word. Without lies. Without trembling excuses. Because if I must ask you a second time…"

Her voice dropped into something ancient and lethal.

"Not a soul will be able to find your remains."

Sarah broke, her voice shattering.

"I'll tell ye. I'll tell ye all of it!"

And she did.

The Confession

Andrew stood bent over his desk in the drawing room. The ransom letter lay spread open before him, pinned at the corners by ink pots and the weight of his own hands. Beside it, a map of the surrounding lands was marked with faint charcoal lines, the fork in the road to Tantallon circled once, then harder, until the parchment showed the pressure.

The stillness in his body was the dangerous kind.

He traced the route from the house to the barn with the tip of a knife, calculating distances, riders, who he could trust, who might already have been bought or threatened. Each possibility played itself out in his mind: ambush, delay, trick. The rage that had burst into the drawing room had settled now into something more focused and colder.

The door slammed open, striking the stone.

Andrew's head lifted.

Nzingha strode in like a storm breaking through the walls. She did not pause. She did not speak first. With one arm, she hauled Sarah forward and flung her onto the floor at Andrew's feet like a sack of grain. The maid hit her knees hard, gasping as her palms slapped the stone.

Her hair hung half-down, her cap gone, her dress twisted from where Nzingha's fingers had seized and dragged. She looked disheveled, shaken, and very suddenly aware of the gravity of her actions.

Andrew straightened slowly.

His gaze moved once from Sarah's crouched form to Nzingha's blazing eyes, then back again.

The muscle along his jaw jumped.

"What is this?" he asked, his voice very level.

"I found her in Alex's room," Nzingha said, each word placed like a blade. "Wearing his shirt. On his bed. Speaking as if she had a claim to his life. And she has something to tell you about your letter."

Sarah trembled. Her breath came in sharp, shallow bursts. She did not try to rise.

Andrew stood slowly and folded his arms. He did not shout. He did not cross the room in a rage. He simply stood and let his presence fill the space.

"Is that so, lass?" he asked, voice quiet, controlled, chillingly calm. "Then I suggest ye start talkin', clear, full, and with nothin' left out. If ye value the breath in yer chest, ye'll no' waste it on lies."

Sarah's eyes flickered from the letter to the knife beside it, then to Andrew's steady hands, then to Nzingha's unyielding stare. What little courage she had left collapsed.

"I didnae think it would go this far," she whispered.

"Far as what?" Andrew asked calmly.

"My laird… they were angry," she said, tears spilling. "There was no coin for them. No raise. No favor. They said ye changed things. That ye listened tae yer wife more than tae the men who'd guarded this house for years."

She drew a shaking breath.

"They believed ye came back from Tafaria rich. I told them ye'd pay anything tae keep yer brother safe. And they talked… about men in the lowlands who pay silver for women who look like her."

Her voice dropped.

"And I was angry too. Alex took me into his bed once, then looked past me like I was naught. When he returned, he couldnae see anyone but her. I let their anger grow. I told them she was worth more than coin if they waited."

Andrew did not move.

"So I said…" Her voice cracked. "I said take her. Hold her. Ye would pay. And after… after they could sell her far away. I never thought of chains or blood. I only thought of her being gone."

"And the letter?" Andrew asked, the calm in his tone more frightening than any fury.

"They wrote it," she said. "Chris and Jordy. They ken their letters better than I do. I didna see every word, only that it threatened and named a sum. They needed someone tae carry it so it would look right when it reached yer hand. No one questions a maid bringin' parchment from the gate. They pressed it on me. I tucked it in my apron. I took it tae the watcher's lad and told him tae say he got it from a rider with her face covered. Then I came back inside like naught had happened."

She swallowed hard.

"I thought ye'd pay and they'd let the chief go. I didna think o' what else they might do."

The fire snapped softly in the grate. Andrew's jaw tightened, the only outward sign of the storm swelling beneath his stillness.

"Where are they holdin' them?" he asked.

"The old barn," Sarah whispered. "By the fork o' the road tae Tantallon. The one half-burnt, with the roof fallen on one side. Chris said they'd ride there in plain clothes with plain horses, wait for ye with the gold. If ye came alone, they'd make their bargain. If ye didna… they'd vanish with her and send ye pieces instead o' proof."

"And my brother?" Andrew asked, voice like sharpened steel.

"They said…" Sarah hesitated. "They said ye might pay more if ye kent he was still breathin'. But what they truly wanted was the lass. That's what the man south o' here asked them for. She's worth more to the wrong sort than any o' us."

Nzingha's fingers tightened once on Sarah's arm.

Andrew stepped closer, not quickly, but with a deliberate, measured approach that made Sarah shrink back even before he reached her. He looked down at her not as a man at a servant, but as a laird at someone who had betrayed his house.

"Ye stood under my roof," he said softly. "Ye ate my food, took my coin, seen tae my child. Ye saw the woman my brother chose after losin' near everythin' he had. And still ye thought ye could help sell another soul's life for silver. Ye thought ye could trade my brother and his heart's choice like beasts at market."

Sarah sobbed. "I was jealous," she whispered. "I was wrong."

"Aye," he said. "Jealous and wrong can be forgiven."

His eyes hardened.

"Betrayal and kidnap cannae."

He lifted his head.

"Guards."

The door opened almost instantly. Two men stepped inside, tense and ready.

"Take her," Andrew ordered. "Lock her in the small cell beneath the storehouse. No one speaks tae her but me unless I say otherwise. If she tries tae run, ye tie her tae the post until I return, then she'll ken what judgment looks like."

The guards seized Sarah under the arms. She sagged, sobbing, her feet dragging as they carried her out.

The door shut.

Silence followed.

Andrew drew a long breath, steadying the fury that trembled beneath his ribs.

Nzingha stepped to the table, bracing both hands against the map. Her voice was calm again, but the fire had not left her.

"We know where they are," she said. "We know who took them. We know when they expect you. There is still time."

"Aye," he answered, eyes locked on the charcoal circle. "There is. But not much."

Call To Arms

The yard of the Dowager House trembled with the kind of urgency that made every movement sharper, heavier, more deliberate than the simple rhythm of a normal day. Men hurried across the packed earth with saddles slung over their shoulders, reins wrapped around their palms, breath billowing in the cold air. The clang of iron and the soft thud of hooves cluttered the space with a restless energy that refused to settle.

In the center of it all stood Andrew Barton.

He was issuing instructions, firm, measured, unyielding, while his eyes swept the yard with the precision of a man who had spent half his life reading danger before it broke across a horizon. This was not panic. This was a controlled storm gathering its force.

Not every guard would ride.
Not every man could be trusted now.

So Andrew chose only those whose loyalty had never wavered, the ones shaped beside him since boyhood, the men who had stood with Alex through storms seen and unseen.

He saw Haemish first.

The Highlander crossed the yard with his usual grounded stride, broad shoulders cutting a clear line through the commotion. He did not ask what had happened. Andrew's expression alone told him enough.

"Ye'll need me," Haemish said, coming to stand beside him, his voice low but steady.

"Aye," Andrew answered, grasping his forearm. "I need men whose faith I dinnae question."

"Then ye've chosen right," Haemish replied. "Alex is my brother in arms. I'll no' stand idle while danger hunts him."

Before Andrew could speak again, Logan and Rory appeared through the open gate, riding hard. Logan dismounted first, his boots hitting the ground with the grace of a seasoned scout. He removed his gloves, sharp eyes already scanning the yard, measuring every shadow.

"Tracks lead east," Logan reported, his voice calm despite the urgency. "Two horses, maybe three. Someone was dragged for a short distance. The soil tells the tale clear enough."

Andrew's jaw tightened. "Alex or Yvonne?"

"Could be either," Logan said. "But they were movin' fast."

Rory swung down from his horse next, the youngest of the three, his usual mischief tempered now into a sober, fragile kind of resolve. He ran a hand through his hair and forced a breath into lungs that did not want to steady.

"We'll find them," he said quietly, almost to himself. Then stronger, "We'll bring them home."

Andrew nodded once, the weight of that hope settling deep in his chest.

Near the mounting block lay a heavy saddlebag, already half filled with coin. Too much. And not enough. He tied it shut himself, the full cost of what the ransom demanded carving cold lines across his face.

Nzingha stood at the foot of the stone steps, Destiny tucked against her shoulder. The baby's fever had softened her earlier cries, leaving her little body warm and tired in her mother's arms. She watched her father with wide, dark eyes, sensing the tension even if she did not understand it.

Nzingha's gaze never left Andrew.

He walked toward her with the steady stride of a man carrying the weight of two lives on his shoulders. When he reached them, he paused, not to speak first, but simply to look at his daughter, his hand lifting to touch her cheek before stopping in the air, as if the slightest contact might undo his resolve.

His eyes rose to Nzingha.

"I will bring them back," he said, quiet, certain, carved from something deeper than hope.

"Bring them both," she answered, her voice calm, strong. "Do not return with only half of what they took."

A muscle flickered in Andrew's jaw. "I ken what they meant tae us," he said. "Yvonne gave ye trust when she had none left. Alex found himself again when he chose her. I'll no' abandon either one."

"Then go," she whispered. "Every moment you stand here is a moment Yvonne could be in more danger."

For the briefest beat, he leaned his forehead to hers, grounding himself in the only peace he had left. Then he stepped back and mounted his horse with one smooth, practiced motion.

Haemish took position at his side, jaw set in grim determination.

Logan checked the straps of his gear, then rode ahead to take the forward flank.

Rory lifted his musket, checked the priming with steady hands, and settled into place behind the laird.

Andrew lifted a hand, letting his voice carry across the yard.

"Keep the house sealed," he called to Nzingha. "Trust no one who cannot meet yer eyes. If word comes late…"

She held his gaze. "I will be ready. I have survived courts, kingdoms, and storms. This house will not fall while you ride."

A ghost of a smile touched his mouth, fleeting but fierce.

Then, with a breath that steadied every man waiting behind him, Andrew lowered his hand.

"Ride out!"

The barred gates swung open.

The company surged forward.

Hooves thundered across the frozen earth, shaking the ground as the laird of Leith, flanked by Haemish, Logan, Rory, and the hardest men of his household, charged into the road that led toward the fork and the old, half burned barn where two lives hung by the hour.

Nzingha watched until the last rider vanished into the cold distance.

Only when the sound of hooves faded did she turn to the servants hovering in the doorways.

"Back to your work," she said, her tone steady. "No wandering. No gossip. We wait. We prepare. And we do not feed fear."

Part I - Fiery Barton Blood

Alex floated in and out of blackness.

Pain throbbed in his ribs with every breath, a low, sick ache that seemed to pulse with the beat of his heart. The dirt beneath his cheek smelled of old hay and damp wood. Somewhere far away, a woman was sobbing.

Thoughts ran through his head. *Oh, she's no' far away. But right over me. Yvonne?*

She muffled through her bound lips.

The barn door slid open with a hard scrape of wood on wood.

Boot steps crossed the packed earth.

Chris and Jordy walked in like men entering a tavern they owned. Chris's smile spread slow and cruel when he saw Alex struggling to lift his head.

"Well now," he drawled, "has yer handsome prince awakened?"

Jordy's chuckle was low and ugly. "The second laird kens the terms," he said to Yvonne. "He kens where tae leave the gold. Say goodbye tae yer beautiful prince while ye can."

Chris caught Yvonne's arm and yanked her away from Alex's side. She cried out, stumbling. Alex tried to twist toward them; the ropes bit into his wrists and ankles, pain tearing through his chest.

"Please," he rasped, the word scraping his throat raw. "Do not take her. I'll double yer price. Triple it. Name any sum."

Both men laughed.

"Nae," Chris said. "We've coin enough. And if it runs short, there's always a market for a lass like her. If no one wants tae buy, we'll find a port where men are no' picky."

Yvonne choked on a sob. Screams tore through her gagged lips.

The last thing Alex saw as the barn doors closed was the white flash of her skirt in the lamplight.

When silence fell, it fell hard.

His chest heaved. His eyes burned. For a long, thin stretch of time he could do nothing but lie there, feeling his pulse hammer against his bruises.

"I have failed her again," he whispered into the dark. "God help me, I have failed her again."

Pain ebbed to a dull numbness. The ropes burned at his skin. He began to move. Slow. Inch by inch. Dragging his bound wrists beneath him, rolling his shoulders, grinding his boots against the floor until he could get his knees under him.

It was clumsy, breathless work. Twice he nearly fell flat on his face again. The third time, he managed to force his back against a beam and push himself upright.

He sat in the dark, head swimming, forcing his mind to sharpen. His breath hitched. "Hh. Hh… If I could just… If I could just reach the blasted door."

Alex stilled. He heard footsteps crunch on hay.

Someone called his name. "Alex? Where are ye?"

The door swung open.

"Alex."

Andrew's voice.

"Here," Alex croaked. "Andrew, here."

His brother crossed the barn in three long strides, a torch in one hand, a knife already in the other. He knelt, the torchlight throwing his stern face into sharp planes.

"Saints," Andrew muttered, taking in the damage. "They didnae go light on ye."

"Yvonne," Alex forced out. "They took her. Chris and Jordy. They mean tae reach a ship."

Andrew gave a short, harsh laugh that had no humor in it at all.

"With what gold?" he asked. He set the torch down, drew the knife along the rope at Alex's wrists. "Nzingha saw the crack in their story before the ink dried. She squeezed the rest out o' Sarah."

Alex blinked. Even half-conscious, the name made his stomach clench.

Andrew's mouth curved into a tight, humorless line.

"I hope ye've learned yer damned lesson," he muttered. "Leave. The. Chambermaids. Alone."

He cut the last rope at Alex's ankles and tossed it aside.

"Sarah's no' right in her mind," he added, his voice dropping back to seriousness. "She's locked in the cellar till we can sort the mess. We'll deal with her once ye're no' tied up like a trussed hog waitin' for market."

The ropes fell from Alex's wrists, then his ankles. He dragged his hands free and flexed his fingers. Every joint screamed, but he could move.

"Can ye ride?" Andrew asked.

"I'll crawl if I must," Alex said through his teeth.

Part II - Fiery Barton Blood

The grove lay just off the fork in the road, where the track dipped and the trees closed in.

Chris slowed his horse first.

"Look," he breathed.

Under a lone, low-branched tree stood a neat line of sacks, tied and waiting.

"Told ye," he crowed, sliding from the saddle. "The fool paid. I told ye he would."

Yvonne lay slung across his horse like a bundle of cloth, wrists tied, blindfold tight. She heard the thud of boots, the rustle of rope, the sound of a bag being torn open.

Then Jordy's voice exploded.

"What in the seven hells is this?"

Stones. Heavy, useful only for breaking bones.

The anger in his voice shook the leaves.

"Is this some bloody jest?" Jordy snarled, hurling a handful of rocks aside.

A clear whistle cut the air.

For a heartbeat, nothing moved.

Then…

An arrow hissed.

Jordy screamed as the shaft drove clean through his calf. His leg buckled. Before he even hit the earth, a second arrow tore into his other leg. He collapsed with a howl.

Chris spun toward him. "Jordy, what's wrong?"

His answer came a heartbeat later when another arrow buried itself squarely in the fleshy curve of his backside.

Chris dropped to his knees with a strangled shriek. "Ah, my arse!"

A soft thud sounded behind them, someone dropping lightly from a branch.

Leather sandals stepped into view.

Nzingha.

She rose from her landing as if she'd simply stepped off a stair. The bow hung relaxed in her grip, another arrow already nocked and waiting. Her gaze flicked over the writhing men with only mild annoyance, then she dismissed them entirely.

Her attention went straight to Yvonne.

Without a word to the traitors, she strode to the horse, cut the rope cleanly, and eased Yvonne down with careful arms.

The blindfold fell away.

Yvonne blinked hard, vision swimming, then saw her.

Her body sagged. A sob tore free as she clutched Nzingha's shoulders and trembled. "Oh, Princess… thank you… thank you. They beat Alex. Please, we must go, now. Please."

Nzingha drew her close, holding her face between steady hands.

She whispered in their native tongue, soft as a lullaby,

"Macho mazuri ya kahawia."

Beautiful brown eyes.

Her forehead rested against Yvonne's as she breathed with her.

"Do not fret, my sister. Andrew is with him. He is not alone."

A slow inhale, a guiding exhale. "Breathe with me. You are safe now."

Behind them, Chris's voice tore through the night.

"Ye mad bitch! Ye shot me in the arse… Ye'll pay...."

Before he could finish his word, a boot slammed across his face. Alex stepped into the circle of lamplight, his face a map of swelling and bruises, one eye nearly closed, jaw tight as stone.

He looked at the arrows still lodged in Chris and Jordy, then at Yvonne clinging to Nzingha, alive, shaking but untouched.

Something in him eased. Something else sharpened.

Chris saw him and tried to sneer, but it twisted with pain. "Enjoy yer last night with her, laird," he spat. "Gold or no gold, there are men who…"

He didn't finish.

Alex's fist connected with his jaw so hard the sound cracked like a branch. Chris toppled sideways, the arrows in his leg and arse wrenching with him. His scream was hoarse and wet.

Jordy flinched. "Chief… wait…"

Alex turned on him, breathing hard, voice low and dangerous. "You put a rope on the woman I love. Do ye ken what that makes ye to me?"

Jordy swallowed. "I…"

"A dead man." Alex hit him.

Blow after blow fell, years of reckless temper and months of strain honing into something focused and savage. Jordy tried to shield his face; all he could do was curl and take it. Blood spattered the ground.

"Alex!"

Andrew's voice cut across the grove.

He caught Alex's arm mid-swing.

"That's enough," he snapped. "They're no' goin' anywhere. Let them live long enough tae hang."

Alex stood there, chest heaving, his fist still poised above Jordy's broken face. Slowly, he let it fall to his side.

He turned away from the men who'd betrayed him and went back to the one who hadn't.

Yvonne met him halfway. Her hands fluttered over his bruises as if afraid to touch him.

He cupped her cheek, careful of his swollen knuckles.

"Did they hurt ye?" he asked, searching her face, her arms, what he could see of her in the torchlight.

"Nae," she said. "They only bound and blindfolded me."

He pulled her into his arms, buried his face in her hair, and let himself breathe.

"I am so sorry," he murmured. "I thought we had torn the rot out o' this clan. First my uncle, now these two. We'll be having hard words about loyalty when we get home."

She clung to him. "How can I be happy here if every time I turn around some man wishes to take me?" she asked, voice breaking.

His grip tightened.

"Do not say such things," he said fiercely. "This was their choice. Their greed. Not the will of my people. Not mine." He drew back just enough to look into her eyes. "I swear to ye, Yvonne, I will do everything in my power to keep ye safe. I will never stand aside and let them harm ye. Not again."

Horses thundered into the clearing. Barton men poured in, dismounting, taking in the scene with grim faces, two traitors bleeding in the dirt, their laird bruised but standing, the Tafarian woman alive in his arms, Nzingha with her bow still in hand like a goddess of war.

Orders were given quietly. Ropes came out. Chris and Jordy were hauled upright with curses and limp legs, the arrows left in place until a healer could decide whether mercy or pain would serve better.

The traitors were not given horses. They were forced to walk.

Their hands were tied behind their backs, their ankles bound just enough to keep their steps short, cruel. Every uneven patch of road jarred the arrows still embedded in flesh. The horses moved at an easy pace ahead of them.

"Chieftain," Chris gasped, sweat soaking his shirt, "it hurts tae walk."

Alex reined his horse in and looked back over his shoulder.

"Oh? Does it hurt?" he said lightly, though his eyes burned. "Ye should've thought o' that before ye beat me near senseless and slung my woman over a horse like stolen treasure."

A few of the men riding nearby smothered dark chuckles.

Alex tapped the swelling on his cheek with exaggerated pity.

"Look what ye did tae my face. The portrait painter will quit. And I swear tae God, if this bruise leaves a mark, I'll carve my name across yer arses, so every healer knows who ruined ye."

Chris went silent. Jordy swallowed.

Alex clicked his horse forward.

"That's mercy, lads. Count it before I change my mind."

Chris clenched his jaw and said nothing.

Andrew's horse came up alongside Alex's.

"Chris," Andrew said, almost conversational, "if I were ye, I'd keep walkin' and hope my brother's humor holds." He tilted his head. "Ask Euan what happens when a man forgets his place."

Chris swallowed hard. "Euan's dead," he muttered.

"Aye," Andrew said softly. "He is."

Silence fell again, broken only by the labored breaths and the drag of tired boots through mud.

After a while, Jordy spoke, his voice raw.

"Chieftain," he said, looking up at Alex, "we ken what we did. We'll walk. We'll take what ye give us. Just… do nae spill our blood in the road like dogs."

Alex studied him for a long moment.

Then he faced forward again, his voice carrying clearly along the line of men.

"For drawing my blood," he said, "and for plotin' tae sell a woman from under my roof, for betrayin' the trust o' this clan…"

Every rider listened.

"…ye'll take fifty lashes each before the clan," he continued. "A year in the cells. After that, ye are exiled. If either o' ye steps so much as one foot on Barton land again, I'll hang ye from my ship's stern and let the sea finish what we began."

No one argued.

Behind the horses, bruised and bleeding and bound, Chris and Jordy kept walking.

Chapter Eighteen

⚓

Fractured at Dawn

At dawn, Haemish, Logan, and Rory met Alex's party several miles

from Tantallon Castle.

Haemish rode at the front of the garrison on his massive black

stallion. When they drew near, he swung down and clasped

Andrew's arm in a Highlander handshake.

He trotted alongside Alex and slowed his horse. The humor drained

from his face as his gaze slid to the two bound men.

Alex followed his look and nodded once. "They'll answer for it at

the courtyard."

Only then did Haemish truly see Alex's injuries. He grimaced. He

might have teased him under other circumstances, but today

sympathy won out.

"Saints above," he muttered. "Yer handsome face has taken a beating. It'll be a while before the lassies look at ye again."

Alex gave a short, humorless breath and pointed at Chris. "That one was the brains behind it. Him, and the servant girl who aided Yvonne at Leith."

Haemish's brows lifted. "Ye mean the lass ye…"

Alex cut him off with a sharp look and a shake of his head. Yvonne did not need to know his best mate knew of him having bedded her.

He then turned to Andrew. "I'll ride ahead with Yvonne. She needs settlin' before the others arrive."

He reached for her. Yvonne shifted forward as he mounted, settling in front of him and clinging to his chest as the horse surged ahead. The wind rushed past, cold and sharp. Her heart beat fast, not from the ride, but from what awaited her.

This was his world now. His castle. His people.

Fear crept in before she could stop it. She pressed her hand against his side, and he slowed at once.

"What is it?" he asked. "Do ye need a healer?"

"No," she said softly. "I am afraid. I do not wish to meet your family. I want to go back to Leith."

He closed his eyes for a brief moment, exhaustion settling deep in his bones.

"Ye cannae be serious," he said at last. "After everything we went through last eve? Why now?"

He glanced at her, his voice rough but earnest. "Ye are my woman, something I've never admitted tae my family. I've never called anyone that before. Ever. Yvonne. Please… My head's poundin', allow me tae ride home. I need a healer and rest."

"Is that supposed to make me feel better?" She crossed her arms, the cold forgotten.

"Come now." A tired breath left him, halfway between a laugh and a sigh." It'll be fine. Ye have me. Ye have Nzingha and Andrew. Ye've nothing tae fear."

She hesitated. "May I see your gloves?"

He glanced down at her hands. "Why? Are they cold?"

She slipped them on anyway, then wrapped his tartan over her nose and mouth, pulling her hood up as if she could disappear inside it.

Alex watched her, irritation stirring.

"Yvonne… are ye truly this shy? Ye look ridiculous."

She met his gaze steadily. "When we arrive, please show me directly to my chambers."

His jaw tightened. "Ye've no chambers. Ye'll stay in mine."

Her voice faltered. "Alex, all of this is so sudden. I did not realize that being with someone would place your life in danger. You heard the man at the inn. They do not accept my kind. Even your own clansmen betrayed you."

There it was again. The worry. The questions. The tightening in his chest.

His patience thinned. In his mind, she was becoming a nag. And Alex Barton had never learned how to stay once a woman reached that point. He always walked away.

"Now, my love," he said, forcing calm into his voice. "We came all this way so ye could meet my extended family. That was the reason we left Leith. I cannae turn back. It's half a day's ride. And we've punishments tae see to, along with matters of security. Word's already spread about the gold we inherited. The crofters are waitin' for audience. I've missed several."

"But Alex, I..."

 "Enough." His temper snapped. "We're goin' tae the castle, and that's final. If it eases yer mind, I'll walk ye through the servant quarters like a servant woman I'm havin' a tryst with."

The words drained what little strength she had left. Yvonne fell silent.

He urged the horse onward, his head throbbing. All he wanted was a healer and a bed, far from questions and worry.

When they reached the castle, Alex dismounted slowly, one hand gripping the saddle longer than necessary. The ground tilted beneath him, and for a moment he swayed before forcing himself upright.

Yvonne saw it at once. "Alex… is all well?"

"I'm fine," he said shortly, though his voice lacked conviction. "Come."

He lifted her down with care, then turned away, pressing his palm briefly to the saddle as the world steadied itself.

"Truly, you need a healer," she said. "Your injuries are worse than you admit."

"Aye. I'll have a servant fetch him."

They passed through the servant quarters, where curious eyes followed them and hushed whispers trailed in their wake.

"Good mornin', my laird," one servant called. "I see ye're with yer sister-in-law… Nzingha, aye?"

Yvonne nodded, too nervous to correct him.

They climbed three flights of stairs to a long corridor. Alex lit a candle, and the hall bloomed softly into view. High ceilings, rich carpets underfoot, and walls lined with paintings of horses, battlefields, and ancestral halls spoke of lineage and war.

At the far end hung a massive portrait of Alex himself, clad in formal dress, sword in hand. The artist had captured the strength in his shoulders, the confidence in his stance, the quiet authority that radiated from the canvas.

Her breath caught, warmth blooming across her cheeks. She smiled despite herself. He was undeniably ravishing.

He stopped before a heavy door. "This is my chamber."

"Are you certain this is wise?" she asked quietly. "Sleeping in the same chamber?"

He let out a breath through his teeth, one hand lifting to his temple. "Is that a problem now as well?"

"No," she said quickly. "I only did not wish to intrude. You are unwell. I feared you had grown tired of me."

Pain pulsed behind his eyes. The questions kept coming, one after another.

"Yvonne," he said sharply, "ye're becoming a bloody nag. My head's splittin', and still ye worry about sleepin' in the same room. I cannae take this."

Her voice was steady, though her eyes burned. "I only wished that you get the rest you so clearly need. But if asking questions makes me a nag… perhaps I should have stayed in Africa with my mad husband, the King."

He stared at her, anger and exhaustion colliding.

"Yvonne," he said quietly, "ye are selfish."

He turned and slammed the door behind him.

The crack echoed through her chest. Yvonne sank to the floor, breath hitching, the room suddenly too quiet.

"What am I supposed to do now…"

Andrew's Chambers

Alex staggered up one floor and burst into Andrew's chamber. He did a double take when he realized what he'd walked into. He froze mid-step, his eyes registering far too much at once.

Andrew was in the midst of riding his wife like a stallion.

"Jesus, Alex!" Andrew bellowed. "Have ye lost what little sense ye were born with?"

"I beg forgiveness," Alex turned sharply and faced the wall, "I swear I didnae ken ye were… occupied."

"Occupied?" Andrew snapped. "That's one word for it. Get Out!"

Nzingha laughed softly as she gathered her robe. "You always did have dreadful timing, Alex."

"I'll never sleep again," Alex groaned. "That image will haunt me till my grave."

Andrew shoved him toward the door. "If ye value yer eyes, leave now."

"Fine, fine," Alex said, retreating. "But I need a word with ye. It's Yvonne."

Andrew paused, then sighed. "Go to the study. I need a moment tae recover my dignity."

The Study

Alex dropped onto the sofa and covered his eyes.

Andrew entered without hurry, poured himself a whiskey, and took a long drink before speaking.

"Well," he said dryly, glass still at his lips, "ye've already ruined one part of my evenin'. Care tae explain how ye plan tae ruin the rest?"

"I cannae do this."
Alex lay sprawled on the sofa, throwing an arm over his eyes.

Andrew huffed a quiet laugh. "That bad, is it?"

"She's drivin' me mad."

"Saints preserve us." Andrew leaned back against the table. "Ye've been back on Tantallon's soil less than an hour and women are unbearable again?"

"That's no fair."

"It's entirely fair." Andrew tipped his head. "Ye've the patience of a goat."

Alex shifted, irritation tightening his jaw. "She kens how I feel about a naggin' woman."

"Aye, and yet ye brought one home." Andrew said mildly.

"That's no funny."

"It is, actually."

Alex dragged a hand down his face, the motion slow, worn. "The lass asks hundreds o' questions. Constant worries. Fears. One bloody thing after the other."

Andrew studied him for a moment before answering.
"Almost as if she's terrified."

Alex didn't respond.

"So let me guess," Andrew went on, voice calmer now. "Ye called her selfish."

Silence stretched.

"…Mayhap."

Andrew sighed, rubbing at the bridge of his nose. "Saints help us. Ye truly are daft."

Alex's arm dropped from his eyes. He stared at the ceiling, jaw tight.

"I love her," he snapped. "That's the problem."

The humor faded.

"Nae. The problem is ye love her and still expect her tae behave like the women ye used tae walk away from."

Silence stretched between them.

Andrew leaned forward. "Ye're no a lad anymore. Ye're a laird. And if every time a woman voices fear ye lash out or flee, ye'll die alone, castle full and heart empty."

Silence.

"Now go back tae yer chamber," he said. "Apologize like a man. And for God's sake, knock before enterin' my chamber next time."

"Well," Alex muttered, "if ye gave yer wife time tae breathe, I wouldnae walk in on the two of ye humpin' like it's the end of days."

Back In Alex's Cabin

A soft knock sounded at the door.

"Yvonne?" Nzingha's voice came gently through the wood. "May I come in?"

"Of course."

When Nzingha entered, her gaze went immediately to the floor. Yvonne sat there, knees drawn in, her face streaked with tears. Her expression softened at once.

"Is all well?" she asked quietly, already knowing the answer.

"I am fine," Yvonne murmured.

Nzingha crossed the room and crouched before her. "Then why are you sitting on the floor, crying? Do not lie to me."

She handed her a cloth. Yvonne took it and blew her nose, her shoulders trembling.

"If I ask you a question," Yvonne said softly, "will you promise to keep it between the two of us?"

"Of course," Nzingha replied without hesitation. "What troubles you?"

"Can you convince your husband to take me back to Africa?" Yvonne asked, the words spilling out at last. "There is nothing here for me. Unlike you, you are married. You have a child… and you carry another."

Nzingha's hand stilled. Her eyes drifted briefly to her belly, and a small smile touched her lips.

"How did you know?"

"You began to show on the ship," Yvonne said gently.

"I have not told Andrew yet," Nzingha admitted. "If he knows, he will not allow me to travel. My last pregnancy was dull and lonely. Besides, if you return home, I will not have anyone to talk to."

She rubbed Yvonne's back in comfort. "But tell me… do you not love Alex? Why do you wish to leave?"

Yvonne let out a shaky breath. "Where do I begin? He is highly irritable. When we first met, he told me women are nags, that it was why he chose not to court at all. This morning, he called me nagging. And selfish. I was only concerned he needed space."

Nzingha laughed softly. "Alex is pig-headed. Even his brother knows this. These are the actions of a man in love who still has much maturing to do." She tilted her head thoughtfully. "Tell me, have you ever been in love before?"

"Yes," Yvonne said quietly. "Your uncle, Femi. But I cannot love a man who cares for me only out of pity."

Nzingha rested her head gently against Yvonne's shoulder. "Did you know my father, King Afonso, was the greatest womanizer I ever knew?" she said frankly. "When he and my mother were matched, he did not love her. He mistreated her until she bore my brother and me. By then, my mother hated him, and he knew it."

She fell silent for a moment, her voice softening as memory took hold.

"Only after my mother died did he realize what he had lost. He never married another, making her his only queen and rightful successor. But she passed far too young. My father became cold… unapproachable. And when my older brother died, whatever bond remained between us died with him."

She drew a breath. "Most men do not realize what they have until it is gone."

Yvonne listened intently.

"When I first returned to Scotland with him, there was a servant much like Sarah. She was madly in love with Andrew. I caught her naked in his arms. I fled into the woods with no knowledge of my surroundings. Three men found me… they intended vile things."

She met Yvonne's eyes. "Do you know who saved me?"

Yvonne shook her head.

"Alex," Nzingha said. "When he first met me, his thinking was no different than the rest of the castle. But he did not allow their beliefs to shape his character or his blessing. Alex has changed greatly since then. To be truthful, I am surprised."

She smiled gently. "He has never… ever… stayed by a woman's side this long. And to hear him call you *my love*… it sealed the truth."

She took Yvonne's hands.

"Love is never easy. It is about growing together, helping one another improve. Alex has helped you trust a man again. And you, my dear, have taken Alex further than he has ever gone. Your love is new. Give it time before you decide to leave."

Yvonne's breath steadied as the ache in her chest softened.

"Thank you, Nzingha," she said quietly. "I am glad you are here with me. I am grateful to rely on you."

The two women embraced, holding one another in a sisterly hug that spoke of safety, understanding, and shared strength.

Chapter Nineteen

⚓

Where Silence Lives

*A*lex did not leave Tantallon in anger.

He did not spend the night in his chamber with Yvonne. Instead, he slept in the study, never fetching a healer.

He left before the castle fully woke.

Dawn had not yet broken. The sky hung low and colorlessly, the hills barely outlined as the night loosened its grip.
Mist clung low to the ground, rolling in quiet sheets across the land as if the earth itself still slept. From the battlements, the sea lay calm and distant, a dull silver beneath the clouds.

He stood alone in the courtyard, fastening the strap of his cloak, listening to the quiet.

By midday, the keep would be full. Crofters would arrive with grievances and expectations. Clan elders would demand his presence, his judgment, his certainty. Servants already carried lists and schedules, matters of land and defense that required a laird's attention.

Then there was Yvonne.

He stopped himself.

Andrew's words from the night before still pressed hard against his thoughts. *Apologize like a man.* Alex had wanted to. He truly had. But every time he imagined facing her, his chest tightened. He did not know whether he had wounded her beyond repair, only that he had said too much while his head still throbbed and his temper burned short.

He needed quiet.
Not because he did not care, but because he cared too much to speak recklessly again.

Before leaving, he summoned the steward in low tones.

"Postpone today's audiences," he said. "Tell the crofters they'll be heard within the fortnight."

The steward nodded, already reaching for parchment.

"My brother will sit in my stead," Alex continued. "Andrew is second laird. He'll take the chair until I return."

It was not unusual. His father had done the same when the weight of rule pressed too hard, when grief or war demanded space the castle could not give. Leadership, Alex had learned young, was not about presence alone; it was about knowing when to step back before breaking.

He penned a brief note to Andrew, sealing it with the Barton mark.

I need time. Take my place. I'll return when my head is clear.

He did not write to Yvonne.
Not because she did not matter, but because he feared he would make everything worse if he tried to speak before he understood himself.

He mounted his horse and took the eastern path, the narrow trail that wound away from Tantallon and into the Highlands beyond.

Winter was loosening its hold on the Highlands, though it had not yet released them entirely.

Alex noticed it only after he had been riding for hours. The land had changed quietly, without ceremony or announcement. Frost no longer clung as hard to the ground in the early morning, and the air carried the damp scent of thawing earth beneath the cold. Pale streaks of new grass pushed through the hillsides, tentative and thin, and the loch lay smooth and dark, reflecting a sky softened by mist.

He slowed his horse as the forest thickened, allowing the animal to pick its way along the familiar path. This route had been carved into him long before he was laird. His father had ridden it with him countless times, teaching him how to listen for movement, how to read the land, how to know when the forest welcomed you, and when it did not.

By the time the hunting lodge came into view, the sun had risen enough to warm his shoulders.

Alex dismounted and stood still for a moment, letting the quiet settle around him. No voices. No expectations. No eyes following his every step. He tied his horse, gathered what he needed, and entered the cabin.

The space was unchanged. The wooden table his father had built still stood near the hearth. The narrow bed remained tucked against the far wall. The place smelled of pine and smoke. The memory of his last visit pressed in on him. He glanced toward the spot where she had tried to make love to him and remembered how harshly he had spoken. The way she had fled afterward. Some regrets dulled with time. This one had not.

Grief did not require invitation. It arrived when it pleased.

At dawn the next morning, Alex walked to the loch.

He removed his clothes slowly, folded them, and stepped into the water. The cold was sharp enough to steal the air from his lungs, but he welcomed it. It cleared his thoughts in a way nothing else could. He waded deeper, then swam, letting the water carry him until his muscles burned and his breath came hard.

When he finally climbed out, he stood dripping on the stones, chest rising and falling, the world reduced to simple truths, breath, blood, movement.

He hunted later that morning, moving through the forest with bow and arrow the way his father had taught him. He took his time. He waited. When the moment came, it was clean.

That night, he roasted the meat over the fire and ate in silence. He chopped wood afterward, splitting log after log, stacking them neatly by the wall. The physical labor grounded him. Each swing of the axe felt purposeful, contained.

He did not drink.
The whisky flask remained untouched.

Sleep came, but reluctantly.

In his dreams, his father appeared, not as he had been at the end, but as Alex remembered him best. Strong. Solid. Standing near the loch with a fishing rod in hand, eyes kind but unyielding.

"Ye've grown into a good man," Calum said. "But being a good man doesnae excuse you from being an absent one."

Alex woke before dawn, the words lingering in his chest.

Later, Sophie appeared in his thoughts, not accusatory, not wounded. She stood quietly at the edge of the clearing, watching him with something like pride.

"Ye survived," she seemed to say. "Now ye must learn how to stay."

Days slipped into weeks without marking themselves. The routines kept him steady, meals taken alone, fires lit and left to burn low, mornings begun before thought could intrude. He told himself this was breathing space. That clarity would come if he stayed long enough.

What he did not allow himself to consider was how easily silence settles when it is fed.

And so, he stayed where nothing asked him to speak.

Where Silence Settles

Nzingha did not come to Tantallon often now.
Not without Andrew. Not without reason.

The castle felt different in Alex's absence, too large, too hollow, as though the walls themselves had been built for a man who refused to return. Sound carried strangely through its corridors. Footsteps echoed longer than they should have. Even the hearth seemed reluctant to hold warmth.

She arrived late in the afternoon, Destiny warm and heavy against her shoulder. The child's presence altered the castle at once. Servants softened, smiles coming more readily. Doors opened with less hesitation. Life moved differently when a child crossed the threshold.

Yvonne was waiting near the window.

She rose too quickly, smoothing her skirts, a smile already forming out of habit rather than joy.
It faded just as quickly when she saw that Alex was not with her.

Nzingha saw it all, the brief lift of hope, the quiet collapse that followed, and said nothing.

"You look tired," Nzingha said gently, as Destiny shifted against her shoulder.

Yvonne shook her head. "Only restless."

They moved into the sitting area of Alex's chamber, settling near the window where the light lingered longest. Destiny was set carefully between them with a small wooden cup, which she promptly brought to her mouth. Nzingha lowered herself onto the bench with care, exhaling as she did. Pregnancy had slowed her now, made her movements deliberate. The curve of her belly was unmistakable, round and full beneath her gown.

Yvonne's gaze drifted there before she could stop herself.

She did not speak at first. Her fingers twisted together in her lap, her attention fixed on that gentle rise and fall, as though it held an answer she had been circling for weeks.

Finally, she reached out, hesitant. When Nzingha did not pull away, Yvonne let her hand rest there, warm fabric, solid life beneath it.

"How did you know?" she asked quietly.

Nzingha turned toward her then, caught by the weight beneath the question.

"Well, with Destiny," she said slowly, "I did not." She smiled faintly. "I believed myself ill. I was fevered, so badly I could scarcely stand. I slept more than I woke. Andrew feared I would not recover."

The smile faded.

"And then my courses did not come. Once. Then again. By then, there was no mistaking it."

Yvonne nodded, absorbing each word.

"I have not been ill," she said. "No fever. No sickness of the stomach." She paused, her hand pressing unconsciously to her side. "Only a pain here."

She swallowed before continuing.

"I feel well," she whispered. "That is what frightens me."

Nzingha studied her carefully now, the youth in her face, the strain held in her shoulders, the way her eyes flicked to the door as though expecting someone who never arrived.

"Has he lain with you without withdrawing?" Nzingha asked gently.

Yvonne's breath caught.

"Once," she said. "Only once."

Silence settled between them, thick and heavy.

Nzingha reached for Yvonne's hand and held it firmly.

"Then we do not guess," she said. "We need to know."

Nzingha sent for the healer to arrive midday, after the household had fully stirred.

Yvonne spent the morning restlessly, unable to settle, her thoughts circling the same quiet questions. Nzingha remained with her, neither pressing nor retreating, content to sit near the hearth while Destiny slept against her breast.

It was only after the midday bell had rung that footsteps sounded in the corridor.

Yvonne stiffened at once.

Nzingha rose before she could, placing a steadying hand at her back. "I am here," she said quietly.

The healer was older than Yvonne had expected. Broad through the shoulders, his movements unhurried, as though time bent to him rather than the other way around. His hands bore the marks of years spent working bodies and beasts alike, scarred, capable, unsentimental.

He did not rush.

He asked gentle questions first. How long since her courses last came. Whether she had bled. Where the pain lived. How often it returned.

Only then did he examine her.

His touch was careful, firm where it needed to be, respectful where it mattered.

"Here," he murmured, pressing lightly inside her. "That's tenderness. No injury. No strain."

Yvonne's breath hitched.

"What does that mean?" she asked.

He answered plainly, "That'll be the womb stretchin'. Early days yet."

Her hands curled into the coverlet.

Her voice wavered. "Well... am I?"

The healer straightened slowly, meeting her eyes.

"Aye," he said. "Ye're with child."

The words did not bloom; they settled heavily and final.

Yvonne did not cry. She did not smile. She simply stared at the space between her hands, as though something invisible had been placed there.

The healer cleared his throat.

"Now listen close," he said, voice firm but not unkind. "No ridin'. No travel. No long walks. Ye rest. Ye dinnae overexert. And ye dinnae get yerself worked up."

Yvonne gave a quiet, broken laugh. "That may be difficult."

"Aye," he said dryly. "I can see that already."

He leaned closer, lowering his voice.

"Worry's no friend tae a babe. Pain, ye speak. Bleedin', ye dinnae wait. And if the man responsible for this child thinks disappearin' is acceptable, he's mistaken."

His gaze flicked to Nzingha.

"She'll need calm," he said. "Stability, and someone who stays."

When he was gone, the room felt strangely smaller.

Yvonne did not move.

Nzingha sat beside her and waited.

Minutes passed before Yvonne spoke.

"He does not want children," she said. One single tear dropped.

Nzingha did not answer at once.

Yvonne swallowed

"I thought... I thought I would feel joy. Or fear. Or something clear."
She pressed a hand to her stomach. "But I only feel… alone."

Nzingha's arm came around her shoulders.

"I am afraid to tell him," Yvonne whispered.

"Because he left?" Nzingha asked.

"Yes."

The word broke.

"Because he has not returned. Every day stretches longer than the last. Each day greets me with silence… it begins to feel like an answer." A tear slid.

She covered her face, shoulders shaking now.

"I ask. I wait. I hope. And nothing comes back to me."

Nzingha held her. There was no advice she could give, no reassurances that rang hollow. Only the presence of a friend who loved her.

She hesitated.

"Do you wish for Andrew to fetch him?"

"No." Yvonne shook her head. "He wants space."

Yvonne finally understood what frightened her most.

Not the child.
Not the uncertainty.
But the growing certainty that if Alex returned now, she no longer knew how to reach him.

X

Waiting Becomes Rejection

Time did not pass easily at Tantallon.

It pressed.

Each morning, Yvonne woke in Alex's chamber, the bed cold beside her, the air heavy with the things left unsaid. She remained there because it was the only place that still felt tethered to him. Leaving the room felt too much like admitting he was not coming back.

She opened the narrow window every dawn, just enough to let fresh air brush her face. The scents of damp earth and new grass drifted in, reminders that it was the end of winter and spring moved forward whether she did or not.

The first morning after the healer left, she needed Alex. Knowing her faith, she could not carry the news alone. Though she was afraid to say it, he needed to know.

She asked the chambermaid bright and early.

"Has the laird returned?"

The woman hesitated. "Nae, my lady. I heard he rode north."

Yvonne nodded, accepting it easily then. Men rode. Men needed space. That much she understood.

She wrote to him that afternoon, to pass the time, to keep her thoughts from turning in on themselves, though there was no location for the missive to be sent.

Day One.

Dear Alex,

I hope your time away brings you peace and that the quiet helps you breathe again; I pray you will come back to me soon.. I miss you. Nzingha visited me. Destiny is well and laughing more each day. I thought you would like to know.

She folded the letter carefully and handed it over.

"He'll be glad to hear from ye," the chambermaid said kindly.

No reply came.

By the fourth day, the question had become routine.
By the seventh, the answer never changed.

"Oh, haven't ye heard?" the chambermaid said gently one morning. "The laird's gone to the hunting lodge. God knows when he'll return."

The words struck harder than they should have.

"Did he leave word?" Yvonne asked.

"Nae. Not that I was told."

Out of nowhere, nausea took her. She ran to the chamber pot and wretched, something the chambermaid was all too familiar with.

Weeks passed. The questions were the same. So were the responses.

Another parchment was drawn.

Day Thirty.

Dear Alex,
The castle feels too large without you. I have not left your chamber. I thought perhaps you would return and find me waiting. I am trying to be patient.

She did not mention the ache in her side.
She did not mention the way sleep slipped from her.
She did not mention how the silence had begun to feel deliberate.

The chambermaid lingered longer now when she came to tidy the room. She straightened blankets that did not need straightening. She brought warm bread without being asked.

"You should walk a little, my lady," she suggested softly. "Fresh air would do ye good."

Yvonne smiled faintly. "Perhaps tomorrow."

Tomorrow came and went.

By the fifth week, Yvonne no longer waited by the window. She paced instead, slowly, carefully, counting her steps as though control might keep her steady. The fear of leaving the chamber had dulled, replaced by something heavier.

The pain in her side grew. Her appetite faded. She never asked for a healer. She just... waited.

Another letter followed weeks later.

Day Sixty.

Dear Alex,
I wonder if you think of me at all. I wonder if you meant what you said, or if it frightened you once the danger passed. I am trying not to lose myself in these thoughts.

She folded that letter and hid it in her trunk.

The chambermaid found her there later, sitting on the edge of the bed, staring at nothing.

"My lady," she said softly, "ye've barely eaten."

"I am not hungry."

"Aye," the woman replied gently. "I ken that look."

She did not press further.

By the fourteenth week, Yvonne asked out of habit rather than hope.

But this day, before the question could be voiced, the chambermaid shook her head.

"My lady. Not yet."

Yvonne stilled. Her hand hovered near the parchment, the familiar ache pressing at her side.

The woman stepped closer and took Yvonne's hand in both of hers.

"Sometimes," she said gently, "we can love a person and still lose ourselves in the loving. To love a man who has not yet learned how to stay can consume the days of yer life, one quiet hour at a time."

Yvonne's throat tightened, but she did not pull away.

"Ye are a beautiful woman," the chambermaid continued. "And I ken Laird Alex cares. But care is no' the same as presence."

She squeezed her hand.

"Some men wander. They disappear into duty and pride and grief, and forget what waits behind them."

"I've seen it before."

The words settled, not cruel, not accusing. Only true.

Yvonne looked down at the parchment, at the empty space where her questions always began.

For the first time, she understood that waiting was no longer the same as hoping.

If he wanted to return, he would have.
If he wished to speak, he would have written.

She sat at the writing table one final time.

Day One Hundred.

Dear Alex,
I will not beg to be chosen. I believed you loved me. Perhaps you once did. I cannot do this alone.

Her hand trembled only briefly before she added the truth.

I am with child.

She folded the letter and placed it with the others, all of them unanswered.

When the chambermaid entered later that day, Yvonne was already dressed.

"My lady... Ye're leavin'?" the woman asked quietly.

Yvonne nodded.

"My lady... Ye deserved better than silence." She hugged her.

"Thank you," Yvonne said.

She did not cry.
She did not look back at the bed, or the window, or the letters she left behind.

Without drama.
Without farewell.

Yvonne left.

The Moral Check Point

The morning was quiet when Yvonne reached the gates. Not peaceful, quiet in the way that felt watched. The sky was pale, the air cool, the kind of morning that carried sound too far. She stood with a small bundle at her feet, her cloak pulled tight around her shoulders, her breath steady only because she forced it to be.

The chambermaid held her tightly, tears soaking into Yvonne's cloak, weeks of helpless watching finally breaking through.

Yvonne told herself that she would be strong, because if she spoke of the pain, she would falter.

Rory was checking tack near the stables when he noticed her. He froze the moment he recognized her, his hand stilling on the strap he'd been tightening.

"Miss?" he said carefully. "Is all… is all well?"

Yvonne managed to smile a small smile. It did not reach her eyes.

"I was hoping you might help me," she said. "I wish to ride to Nzingha at Lieth."

The words landed heavier than she expected.

Rory's brow furrowed at once. "Lieth?" He glanced toward the keep, then back at her. "Has… has the laird given word?"

"No," she said simply.

That was answer enough.

Rory exhaled slowly, rubbing the back of his neck. "Miss… I dinnae ken if that's my place. If Alex finds out I took ye…"

"He will not," she said, her voice steady. "And if he does… I will answer for it."

Rory looked at her, his heart tugged. The faint shadows beneath her eyes. The way her hands trembled just slightly as she gathered her cloak.

"I cannot stay," she said quietly, before he could speak again. "Not where I am not wanted."

Something tightened in Rory's chest.

He swallowed. "Wait here," he said at last. "I'll saddle a horse."

She nodded, relief and grief crossing her face too quickly to name.

They rode out together not long after, keeping an easy pace. The road was familiar to Rory, worn paths, bends he'd traveled since boyhood, but Yvonne sat stiff in the saddle, every movement measured.

"Ye comfortable?" he asked.

"Yes," she said at once.

Too quickly.

They continued on.

After a time, Rory noticed the way she shifted, how her hand pressed briefly to her side before she dropped it again. Her breathing grew shallower, controlled.

"Miss," he said again, slower now. "Are ye sure ye're well?"

She nodded. "Just... a bit sore. It will pass."

He wasn't convinced, but he did not press her.

The path narrowed as they reached the trail that led toward Lieth. Still hours away. Still far enough that turning back felt like failure.

The pain came more sharply.

Yvonne sucked in a breath, her fingers clutching the reins. She tried to straighten, tried to ride through it, but her vision blurred, the ground tilting beneath her.

"Miss!" Rory reached for her just as she slipped.

She tumbled from the saddle awkwardly, landing hard on the dirt road, before curling inward with a cry she could not stop.

Rory dismounted at once, dropping beside her.

"Yvonne, hey, all's well, I've got ye," he said, panic creeping into his voice. "What's wrong? Tell me what hurts."

She shook her head, tears spilling freely now. Her hands pressed to her abdomen as another wave seized her, stealing the air from her lungs.

"I… I don't know," she sobbed. "It hurts. It hurts so badly."

Rory looked around wildly, as if expecting help to appear from the trees.

"Can ye stand?" he asked.

She tried.

She cried out instead, folding forward, her body betraying her.

Rory's heart pounded. He pulled his cloak from his shoulders and wrapped it around her, kneeling in the dirt beside her.

"Listen tae me," he said urgently. "I cannae leave ye. I willna. But I dinna ken what's happenin', and it is no' right."

She clutched his sleeve, breath coming in broken gasps.

"I only wanted to go where I was wanted," she whispered. "I didn't want to beg anymore."

Rory's throat burned.

He looked down the road toward Lieth.
Then back the way they had come.

He was torn clean in two.

And somewhere behind them, though neither knew it yet, the silence she had fled was finally beginning to break.

Letters from Tears

Alex had settled into the lie that time would wait for him.

The loch lay still, his fishing line slack in his hand, the world narrowed to water and breath and the fragile belief that silence could hold. He had given orders not to be disturbed while he was away. The men knew it. The castle knew it. Distance, he told himself, was a kind of control.

He heard hooves before he saw the rider.

Fast. Unmeasured. Wrong.

Alex straightened, irritation flaring for only a moment before something colder slid beneath it. For a brief, foolish heartbeat, he thought it might be Andrew. The thought vanished as the castle's messenger came into view, reining in hard, chest heaving, mud streaked up his boots.

"My laird," the runner said, breathless. "I bring word from Rory."

Alex's hand tightened around the rod. "Speak."

"Lady Yvonne has asked him tae escort her tae Leith."

The words landed, sharp but survivable. Alex turned away, already telling himself this was restlessness, grief working its way through her, nothing more. She would return. She always had.

Then the runner spoke again.

"Rory said she does no' look well. She's thin. Her eyes are dark with circles. He was worried enough tae send word before they left."

Fear shook Alexs' his chest.

Worry rose fast and decisively, leaving no room for argument. Alex nodded once. That was all the answer the runner received. He took only his sword and mounted at once, riding hard for Tantallon, the distance tearing beneath him as the lake vanished behind.

He did not announce himself on arrival.

He did not pause for guards or reports. He left the horse with the first groom he passed and took the stairs two at a time, boots striking stone, breath loud in his ears. The castle blurred around him, banners and torchlight reduced to color and motion.

Outside his chambers, he slowed.

Not from calm.
From instinct.

"Yvonne?" His voice sounded rough to his own ears, uncertain in a way he did not recognize.

Silence answered.

It pressed back at him, thick and unnatural, as though the room itself were holding its breath.

His chest tightened.

"Yvonne," he said again, sharper now, already bracing for what he would find.

He pushed the door open.

The room was wrong at once.

Too still. Too bare. The air felt emptied, stripped of warmth and habit. There was no trace of her. His chamber looked as it always did after a long voyage at sea, a space reset to order rather than lived in, the bed neatly made with clean linens, untouched.

A soft sound came behind him.

The chambermaid entered with a tray and froze when she saw him. Hurt crossed her face before she could hide it, her eyes shining despite herself.

"My laird…"

He turned slowly, dread settling heavy and undeniable.
"Where is the lady that was stayin' here?"

The maid wrung her hands.

"She was… broken-hearted." Her voice trembled. "Every day she asked for ye. Sometimes five times a day. *Has the laird returned? Has word come?*"

The words struck harder than any accusation.

Alex swallowed.

"I watched her sit by the window," the maid continued. "For hours. I watched her write letters. Every day. I dinnae ken who she meant them for."

Each word tightened something already near breaking.

"She left this mornin'," the maid said softly. "I heard Rory escorted her. Said she couldnae wait any longer."

Something inside him gave way, quietly but finally.

She crossed the room, knelt, and opened the trunk at the foot of the bed. From within she lifted a bundle of letters tied with ribbon, the edges worn thin from handling, and placed them in his hands.

Alex sat heavily at his writing desk.

He should have risen. Should have run.
Instead, he was held there, bound by the weight of what he had refused to see.

He skimmed.

The first hopeful.

The second careful.

The third restrained.

By the tenth, his chest ached.

By the ninety-fifth, his hands shook.

Then he reached the last.

Day One Hundred.

I cannot do this alone.

I am with child.

The room seemed to tilt. Alex stood so fast the chair scraped behind him. He snatched up his sword, heart hammering with a terror he had never known in battle.

"How long ago did she leave?"

"Early mornin', at dawn."

When the made turned, the door was left open and Alex was gone.

When the World went still

The beat of hooves came in like a drum, fast and uneven, tearing at the road with its urgency.

Rory stood pale and frantic, pacing in short, useless steps, his hands lifting and falling as though he could not decide whether to reach for her or pray. He knelt beside Yvonne, hovering, helpless, already afraid to touch her.

"What in God's name do ye think ye're doin'?" Alex roared as he hauled his horse to a stop.

Rory lurched to his feet. "Alex, thank Christ…"

Alex barely heard him.
From the saddle, he saw her.

Crumpled on the road, her body folded against stone and grit as though the earth itself had claimed her. Her skirts were dark with sweat and dust, her limbs drawn inward, small in a way that froze something deep in his chest.

"What's wrong with her?"

"I dinnae ken!" Rory shouted, his voice breaking under the weight of it. "She asked me tae escort her tae Leith. She complained of pain all the way. I told her we should stop, then…" He swallowed hard. "She… she tumbled from her horse. Landed hard."

Alex was already off his horse.

Yvonne lay with dirt clenched in her fist, knuckles white, her body slick with sweat, breath tearing in and out of her in ragged, broken gasps. Her other hand clawed blindly at the ground, grasping for something solid, something that would keep her anchored.

She shook her head, breath shuddering.
"It's too soon…"

Another pain ripped through her, sudden and merciless, and she screamed, raw, like an animal, stripped of dignity or restraint.

Alex caught her under the arms and hauled her upright.
Her weakened body collapsed against him.

Within a heartbeat, the truth spilled with her.
Blood surged violently from beneath her skirts, dark and sudden, striking the ground in wet, unmistakable splashes that soaked into dust and stone alike.

Rory's eyes went round as coins.

"Rory," Alex barked, panic ripping through his voice, "ride tae Leith. Tell Andrew tae send a wagon. Now!"

Rory didn't hesitate. He mounted and galloped hard, the sound of hooves tearing away down the road, fleeing the horror he could not stop.

Alex gathered Yvonne into his arms and carried her toward the edge of the woods, where the roots broke through the earth like grasping hands. He laid her there as gently as he could, his own hands shaking violently as he lifted her skirts, terror closing tight around his throat.

He barely had time to settle her before the next pain seized her.

Yvonne's body arched violently, a broken cry tearing from her throat as her fingers clawed into the soil, nails splitting, earth packing beneath them as though she might anchor herself by force alone.

"Alex!" she screamed.

The sound of his name was not a plea.

His heart slammed so hard he thought it might burst his ribs. He tried to speak, tried to steady her, to give her something solid to hold onto, but the words tangled and failed him.

"I'm here," he said hoarsely. "I'm here. Tell me what tae do. How can I help ye?"

Another contraction took her without mercy.

She sobbed, gasping, her body betraying her as she bore down again, teeth clenched so tightly he heard them grind.

She shook her head. "It's too soon."

Her scream shattered into something primal, something beyond language, beyond reason.

Alex's hands were slick with blood now, his vision blurring. He had faced battle. He had stood before death. He had never known this kind of helplessness.

"Look at me," he begged, his voice breaking apart. "Yvonne. Look at me."

Her eyes found him; they were wild, glassy, filled with pain and terror.

Her body convulsed once more.
She screamed his name again.

And then, in an instant, it was over.

Not gently.
Not mercifully.

The life she had carried now rested in Alex's hand.

He froze.

For a moment, he could not move.

Could not breathe.

Could not comprehend what he held… until the weight of it settled fully into his palm. It was far too light. Smaller than a child's apple

He shifted fast, turning away, blocking the sight of the small babe from her. His hands trembled violently as he wrapped it in a handkerchief, folding cloth over what should have been warmth and promise. Hurt came quickly to Alex, a tear sliding down his face.

Yvonne collapsed against him, her body shaking violently, sobs tearing from her chest as though they might hollow her from the inside out.

She clutched at him, her tears soaking into his shoulder, her voice breaking into something small and ruined.

"I… I waited for you," she whispered.

With one arm, he pulled her in against his chest, their lifeless child between them.

Chapter Twenty

⚓

Rowan

Alex stopped in the corridor outside the chamber where Yvonne

rested.

The Dowager's home was quieter than Tantallon, softer somehow, its stone less used to obedience and more used to endurance. He had followed the sound of voices without thinking, drawn forward by something tight beneath his ribs, and by the time his hand rose toward the latch his skin was damp, as if he had ridden hard to reach it.

Then he heard Yvonne's name spoken gently, and his stomach tightened. He set his palm against the wall and breathed through it, shallow but controlled. The corridor seemed narrower than it had a moment before, and he stayed where he was, steadying himself, because a truth spoken softly behind a door could still unseat a man who knew how to face a blade.

Inside, the voices were low and deliberate, a conversation meant to remain private, meant to be carried only by women and mercy. He should have announced himself. He should have turned away. He did neither.

"She is restin'," the healer said. "That is the best we can offer her just now."

"And the cause?" Nzingha asked, her voice composed. The restraint in it struck Alex more sharply than grief would have.

There was a pause before the healer answered, not hesitation, but care.

"The babe was never settled where it should have been. The womb felt wrong-set. Curved in a way that doesnae always show itself until it is too late."

Alex closed his eyes briefly. His hand slid along the wall until his fingers found the seam of stone, rough and cold, something solid to anchor himself to.

"This was not brought on by the fall," the man continued. "Nor by travel. Nor by fear alone. Those things strain the body, aye, but they did not cause this."

Nzingha's breath left her slowly. "So it would have happened regardless."

"Aye," the healer said. "Whether she stayed or went. Whether she waited or ran."

The words settled heavily in Alex's chest. He thought of the road. He thought of her alone. He said nothing.

"She did nothin' wrong," the healer added. "And neither did the babe."

Alex pressed his forehead briefly to the wall, then straightened.

"She will heal," the healer said, firmer now. "But not quickly. Her body will mend before her heart does. She must not be pressed."

"Pressed by what?" Nzingha asked.

"By expectation," the healer answered. "By silence. By a man who believes distance is patience."

Alex's jaw tightened.

"She waited," Nzingha said. "She waited long enough. In her waiting, there was grief from within, worry that unsettled. I believe these things contributed to the loss of her child."

The healer inclined his head. "Aye, that too can be the case. But in a time of grief, for both parents' sake, let us no' place blame."

He pressed a hand briefly to Nzingha's shoulder, then withdrew it.

"She must stay abed. No ridin'. No long journeys. And no reconciliation forced before she is ready. Loss such as this doesnae bend to apologies."

A faint sound came from within the chamber, the shift of a body in bed, and Alex stepped back instinctively. After a moment, he moved forward again. He needed to see her. To hold her. His guilt could not withstand the distance he had already created.

Just as his hand reached the door, another closed over his wrist.

Andrew stood there, his expression already set. Without a word, he guided Alex down the corridor, down the stairs, and toward the back door by the kitchens.

"I need tae see her," Alex said once they were moving.

Andrew did not answer.

Outside, Andrew turned to face him. "Ye can want what ye like. That doesnae mean ye get it."

Alex held his ground. "Brother, I need tae make it right."

Andrew gave a short, humorless breath. "Make it right," he said. "Ye think there's a sentence, a kiss, a ring, and suddenly it's right?"

Alex tried again, quieter. "Andrew."

"Aye," Andrew cut in. "Now ye've words. Now ye've urgency. Now ye've a heart. Where was it for four moons?"

Alex did not answer at once. "I had tae clear my head."

"Ye cleared it. Congratulations." Andrew's gaze was unyielding. "Meanwhile she sat alone in Tantallon, afraid tae leave yer chambers, askin' servants if ye'd returned, writin' letters until her hands ached. Ye left her in silence so long it became its own kind of cruelty."

Alex looked away.

"Dinnae," he began.

"Dinnae what?" Andrew said quietly. "Dinnae hear it? Ye're laird, Alex. Ye're meant tae carry what's hard."

Alex exhaled once. "Let me see her."

Andrew glanced toward the window above them. "Ye'll see her when she says ye may. Not when guilt drives ye. Not when grief makes ye reckless. Ye'll see her when she's strong enough tae look at ye without breakin' again."

Alex nodded once.

"And hear this," Andrew added. "Ye came back. Aye. But it was too late for what she needed then. This hurt will no' pass on yer schedule."

"I'm no askin' for comfort," Alex said.

"Good," Andrew replied. "Then stop askin' for forgiveness as if it heals. Give her what she never had. Peace. Space. Time."

Alex stood there a moment longer, then turned away.

He waited until evening before he tried again, because waiting was the only penance left that did not center him.

Nzingha met him outside the chamber, her posture upright, her face composed, and her eyes carrying the weariness of a woman who had held two kinds of grief at once.

"She's awake," Nzingha said, her English careful and regal, the way she spoke when she chose restraint over rage. "But do not press her. Do not plead. Do not attempt to win her with promises."

"I'm no here tae win," Alex said, and his voice broke slightly on the last word, humiliating and honest.

Nzingha studied him for a long moment. "Good," she said quietly. "Then go in as a man who understands that love is not possession."

When Alex entered, the room smelled of herbs, clean linens and sorrow.

Yvonne lay turned away from him, facing the window, her hair loose against the pillow. Her shoulders were still, but not relaxed. She looked like someone who had been made to endure too much and had finally learned how to survive by going quiet.

He stopped just inside the door, because even the distance between them felt like something he did not deserve to cross.

"Yvonne," he said. She jerked at the sound of his voice.

She did not answer. She did not turn.

Alex's throat tightened. He took one step forward and then stopped again, unsure where the line was now.

"I heard the healer," he said at last, voice rough. "I heard what he said tae Nzingha."

Her fingers moved against the sheet, a small sign that she was listening, but she still did not look at him.

"There is nae story I can tell that brings back what we lost. There is nae vow that undoes it. I ken that."

The silence stretched, and he felt it pressing on his lungs, on his ribs, on the weak places where he'd always hidden.

"I buried the babe, in my mother's rose garden at Tantallon. I named the babe Rowan. For protection. For… a rooted thing that stands when storms come."

Yvonne's breath hitched once, thin and quiet, and it cracked something in him.

"My love… I'm sorry for leavin'. I'm sorry for the days. I'm sorry for the silence. I'm sorry for makin' ye feel like ye had tae earn my presence."

Her voice came then, soft and controlled, and it cut clean.

"When I needed you the most, you were gone."

Alex closed his eyes, pain tightening his face.

"Four moons." she continued, still facing the window, her tone calm in a way that was worse than shouting. "For four moons, I was alone, sitting in silence, too afraid to leave the walls of your chamber, too worried to know if you still loved me, too ashamed to keep asking people who had no answer. I waited for you until waiting began to feel like I was shrinking."

Tears slid down her cheek, and she did not wipe them away.

They fell as if her body no longer cared to hide anything.

Alex moved closer then, slowly, and sank to his knees beside the bed because standing felt like arrogance. He reached for her hand, gentle, and for a moment she let him touch her, not as acceptance but as exhaustion.

"I cannae undo it," he said, voice trembling now. "But I can.... I can stay. I can be the man ye need. I swear it. I'll never leave yer side again. I want ye as my wife, Yvonne. I want tae build a future, whatever kind ye'll allow. I... I need ye."

She turned her head just enough to look at him, and her eyes were wet but clear.

"I acknowledge that you wish to try," she said quietly. "And I believe you mean it."

"But I will not leave with you."

His chest tightened.

"I cannot follow someone who disappears when I need them most. I cannot build a life around waiting to be remembered."

Alex's face went still, the hope collapsing into disbelief.

"So ye dinnae love me anymore?"

Her voice softened, and that softness broke him more than anger ever could.

"What hurts so much... is that I do."

Alex's breath shuddered.

"Then please... Please, Yvonne. This loss hurts me also. I know I've no right tae ask for anything, but I'm askin' anyway. Let me be better. Let me prove it. Let me..."

She withdrew her hand from his, not violently, not cruelly, simply as a boundary being drawn.

"You do not know how to stay," she said quietly. "You know how to come back after. And I cannot live in a love that teaches me I will always be left first."

Alex's eyes filled. He tried to speak, but his mouth could not form the words.

She turned away again, and the turn of her back felt like a door closing.

"Please, Alex," she said, her voice smaller now, tired. "Leave me alone. I wish to be left alone."

Alex stilled at her words. He knelt for a moment, and the two sat in silence. Finally, he stood with the slow care of someone carrying guilt in his bones and backed away from the bed as if he feared his presence might bruise her further.

Nzingha entered then with a tray, her expression calm, her gaze taking in Alex's wrecked face and Yvonne's turned back. She set the tray down and spoke gently, but with authority.

"Alex," she said, "I think it is time Yvonne rests."

Alex nodded once, unable to speak, and left the room like a man leaving a battlefield he did not survive.

Andrew found him near the garden wall at dusk.

Alex stood with his back to the stone, arms crossed tight over his chest, staring past the hedges as though something might appear if he waited long enough. The light had thinned to grey. Evening birds moved quietly above them.

Andrew did not soften his step.

For a long moment, he said nothing.

Then, "It's done."

Alex let out a breath that shook. "I ken."

Andrew studied him, and for once there was no anger in his eyes, only certainty.

"She doesnae need ye speakin' now," he said. "And she doesnae need ye explainin'. What she needed has already passed."

Alex's jaw tightened. "I love her."

Andrew nodded once. "Aye. That much was never in doubt."

The words landed heavier than disagreement.

"She didnae leave Tantallon because she stopped lovin' ye," Andrew went on. "She left because she learned what lovin' ye costs."

Alex closed his eyes.

Andrew stepped closer, lowering his voice, not in kindness, but in restraint.

"Ye don't get tae fix this by will. Or promises. Or guilt."

A pause.

"Ye wait now. Or ye walk away. Those are the only honorable choices left."

Alex opened his eyes, red-rimmed, searching.

"And if she never wants me back?"

Andrew held his gaze without flinching.

"Then ye carry it," he said simply. "Same as she did."

Silence stretched between them.

At last, Andrew added, quieter but final, "This is what consequences sound like."

He turned and left Alex where he stood.

Alex did not follow.

He remained by the wall as the light faded completely, the garden empty, the house behind him full of rooms he no longer had the right to enter, knowing, at last, that love offered too late does not become mercy.

EPILOGUE

Three months later, the yard at Leith carried the small sounds of life trying again. Haemish sat on a low stone near the training posts, watching little Harris play with a wooden horse, the boy's laughter bright against the chill. Alex sat beside Haemish, quieter than he used to be, his hands idle, his gaze often drifting upward as if his eyes had learned to search for someone even when his pride refused to call her name.

A missive lay in Alex's hand, the seal broken. He handed it to Haemish, "Here, this is from Annabella, the lass is devastated you willnae respond to her letters."

Haemish sighed. "Alex, ye ken I have nothing to offer her. It cannae work."

Alex gave a faint, humorless smile. "Dinnae lose what ye love because of fear," Alex said quietly. The words sounded like advice, but they were confessions.

Haemish glanced at him once, understanding more than he ever said aloud, then turned his attention back to his son.

Alex's gaze drifted upward, drawn by instinct more than intention, to the upper windows of the house. Yvonne sat there with a book in her hands, sunlight resting softly against her skin. The sight of her, whole, quiet, alive, struck him harder than any blade ever had.

For a moment, she looked down.

Their eyes met.

She did not scowl.
She did not soften.
She simply held his gaze long enough to let him know she had seen him.

Then she rose, closed her book, and walked away from the window.

Alex did not move.
He did not follow.

He remained seated beside Haemish, listening to Harris's laughter carry across the yard, letting the sound settle somewhere deep in his chest, a reminder of what had been lost, and what might still be possible.

After a long while, something inside him shifted.

Quietly, without ceremony, Alex stood and went inside.

The house was still. Too still. He paused at the foot of the stairs, then climbed them slowly, as though each step required permission. When he reached her chamber, he hesitated only a moment before pushing the door open.

Yvonne sat with her back to him, reading.

He crossed the room without a word and gently covered her eyes.

She startled, gasping as she twisted away. "What are you doing here?"

Her voice was sharp, but it wavered.

"How did you know it was me?" he asked softly.

She exhaled, a short, bitter sound. "The scent of the outdoors," she said. "And lavender."

She turned fully toward him then. "What do you want, Alex?"

He swallowed. The words he had rehearsed vanished the moment he met her eyes.

"Please," she said, quieter now. "Leave me."

Instead, he dropped to one knee.

The movement shocked her into stillness.

Alex's hands trembled as he reached into his pouch and drew out a ring, worn, simple, unmistakably old.

"This was my mother's," he said, his voice breaking despite himself. "I ken ye do not wish tae return with me. I ken ye need space. I ken I've lost the right tae ask for much of anything."

Tears slipped from his eyes freely, unashamed.

"But I need ye tae know this," he went on. "I will never stop tryin' tae earn the love ye once gave me so freely. I was selfish. I was afraid. And I left when ye needed me most."

Yvonne shook her head, tears gathering in her own eyes. "Alex…"

"Listen tae me," he pleaded. "I have not slept a full night since. I wake thinkin' God has punished me fairly. I carry it every day, what I cost us. What I cost ye."

His breath hitched. "I am a warrior reduced tae beggin' in front o' the woman I love."

She tried to pull away, but his honesty, raw and unguarded, broke through her resolve.

"I am no perfect man," he said. "But I swear tae ye, I will work every day tae be better. I want ye as my wife. I want ye as the mother of our children. And if God grants us none, then I will still choose ye, again and again."

He bowed his head. "Please."

Yvonne knelt in front of him.

Her hands cupped his face, trembling. "I love you," she whispered. "And that is what hurts the most."

Their foreheads touched. Then their lips met, softly, carefully, as though neither dared rush what had been broken.

"Alex..." she hesitated. "I am torn. I want to go back to my lands. Back to Tafaria, where life felt normal, before discovery."

She looked down.

"But my heart does not want to leave you behind. I do not understand many things. Where I fit in. Where I am needed. I do not understand love. Yet I still ache for you some nights. I miss you daily. But deep down, my inner self tells me to wait. To breathe. To live. To heal. I love you, Alex."

Hope flickered in his chest, cautious and fragile.

"But I need time," she continued. "Time to heal. Time to trust again. But I will come back."

He nodded, pressing his forehead to hers. "I'll wait, but please, I am begging ye. Before you decide that home is what ye want, let us try first."

They kissed once more, not with hunger, but with promise, and when they finally parted, it was with the understanding that love remained, but goodbye meant healing.

Alex stood and left. His intent was to try. His intent was not to shut down. His intent was to do it all over again, but this time right.

Because losing the woman he loved was not an option.

Authors Note.

RAVAGED is a story rooted in love, but not the kind that is resolved easily.

Yvonne's introduction into adulthood was not gentle. It was shaped by survival, loss, and endurance long before she ever had the freedom to choose herself. After everything she has endured, she needs time, not to punish love, but to reclaim her independence, to heal without obligation, and to discover who she is outside of fear, expectation, or attachment. Her choice to step back is not a rejection of love. It is an act of self-preservation and self-respect.

Alex's love for Yvonne is real, and costly. He is a sailor who built his life on a simple code: never promise what you cannot guarantee, never plant roots the sea will tear away, and never claim a woman if you cannot honor her fully. For years, he avoided marriage not because he lacked feeling, but because he refused to live as a hypocrite. He would not return from distant ports to a wife bound by vows he could not keep.

Yvonne is the first woman he ever called his own, and the first for whom he was willing to wait without certainty. When she asks for space, he does not chase, trap, or replace her. He stays. He learns restraint. He carries the consequence of loving her too late, understanding that love does not entitle him to her healing.

This book does not end with marriage or children because not all love stories are ready for permanence. Sometimes love must exist alongside distance. Sometimes healing requires separation. Sometimes becoming whole must come before belonging.

RAVAGED lives in that space, between devotion and readiness, between desire and accountability, between love and what it asks of us.

If you finish this story unsettled, then you have met it honestly.

Kera C. Munnings

Stay tuned for **FATE** *A Bicultural Series Book 3:*

Where blood remembers, secrets demand truth, and family can no longer look away.

This Book is a Product of SommersetyWay Novels

Copyright © 2026